THE
HOLLOW
TREE

ALSO BY THE AUTHOR

The Goldenacre

THE
HOLLOW
TREE

PHILIP MILLER

SOHO
CRIME

Published by
Soho Press, Inc.
227 W 17th Street
New York, NY 10011

Library of Congress Cataloging-in-Publication Data

Names: Miller, Philip, author.
Title: The hollow tree / Philip Miller.
Description: New York, NY : Soho Crime, 2024. | Series: A Shona Sandison
investigation ; 2
Identifiers: LCCN 2023029775

ISBN 978-1-64129-558-1
eISBN 978-1-64129-559-8

Subjects: LCSH: Journalists—Fiction. | Murder—Investigation—Fiction. |
LCGFT: Detective and mystery fiction. | Novels.
Classification: LCC PR6113.I567 H65 2024 | DDC 823/.92—dc23/
eng/20230703
LC record available at https://lccn.loc.gov/2023029775

Interior design by Janine Agro

Printed in the United States of America

10 9 8 7 6 5 4 3 2 1

For Samantha and Thomasin

In deope dalum   deora ungerim
In the deep dale   live many wild beasts
("Durham," Anglo-Saxon)

hello

Shona Sandison was going to a wedding. The day would end in death.

She stood on the deck of the ferry, leaning against the metal barrier between her and the tilting sea, which stretched grey as ash to a white horizon. The world seemed huge and unfathomable, and she felt small and damaged, and unsuited to what it offered, and challenged.

She was not alone. An old colleague and friend was beside her, shouting into the implacable Scottish wind. Shona looked down at her shoes, wet on the painted metal deck. Her stick was held tight in her left hand.

"Fact is, Shona, I think they're just bored of democracy, these people. They don't care for it," Hector Stricken bellowed. "A wee touch of fascism appeals to them. Look at them, propping up this fucking government. Seems to me, some of them prefer to be collaborators, not investigators. Cheerleaders, drunk on their access to power. They should be ashamed of themselves."

His angry monologue had begun on the train from Glasgow to the port of Gourock. Stricken, still hanging on as an undervalued and underpaid reporter at the *Edinburgh Post*, had then raged at the front pages of the national newspapers at the ferry port's newsagent. He had picked out and bought several papers, just so he could stride across the platform to a waste basket, and bin them dramatically.

"Give it a rest," Shona said. "Not all of them, and not all of us. Calm the fuck down."

Hector went on. Shona listened, or heard. She watched the neat rows of white houses on the headland drift past like a line of teeth. "They're not interested in committees, reports, policy reviews, the granular workings of a rigorous democratic system. It bores them. That's why there's no council reporters anymore. No court reporters. No specialist reporters. No local government reporters."

"Really, Hec—you sound like my dad. The old Communist digging in his allotment. I need a coffee."

"Does he still have that allotment? Good on him. Yeah, the problem is, that fear, that angry nostalgia, the appeal to a mythic past, is far more attractive and easier to package than probity, reserve, compassion, moderation, compromise, subtlety," Stricken said.

Shona nodded slowly. Not only had she heard this before, she had thought it before. Her body rocked gently as the ferry moved, slowly and massively into the cold grey waters of the Firth of Clyde.

"Nuance!" he yelled.

His bellow sunk into the air and was lost.

"Jesus Christ. Give over, man," Shona said, as firmly as she could without shouting. "It might be rotten politics but, whether you like it or not, it's good business. For those papers."

"It's a bad business," Hector mumbled. "It's the ruin of democracy."

"Och, wheesht. I know some good reporters in those papers. And the papers you binned are at least selling—more than can be said for yours."

The ferry chugged into a thick mist. It was as if they had entered an erasure. The form and volume of the hills and the sea had been rubbed out by dreary light. The distant deep hulks of mountains were smudged and edgeless. The sky was as solid as the water below—grey, lightless, unmoving.

It was cold. Winter was dying hard. It had spent its spite

and drowned the land in volumes of darkness, but spring had not yet emerged. It was as if the seasons were considering whether to continue their cycle. It was as if the seasons had paused.

"I tell you, though, it's not going to end well," Stricken said. "I think the whole country is fucked."

"Come on, Hector—wasn't it always fucked?" Shona said, turning to him. "I seem to remember everything being fucked. All the time. It's just sometimes the things that are fucked are hidden or ignored. Then we all find the hidden fucked things and are astonished—wow, isn't *this* thing fucked too? Let's add that fucking misery to the Fucked Pile. Which gets higher and higher, until it falls on fucking top of us, and then we are all well and truly fucked."

"Well, if you put it that way," Hector said, smiling.

"Contentment is about how much you are prepared to ignore," she said.

"Brief period, wasn't there," he said, quieter, "mebbe in the 1990s? When it seemed to me that things were on their way to being un-fucked. When we were all a wee bit younger. Then it was all fucked again. I think this state as a serious concern is over. No one reads the news. No one cares about anything—just shopping, sport, and celebrities."

"You're a miserable old git, Hector," she said. "I was wearing a school uniform in the 1990s. I don't remember too much light and hope and joy then."

Her fingers were freezing. Her ears were wet with sea fog. As if pushed by an invisible hand, her walking stick fell to the deck, splashing in a small puddle on the green metal. "Fuck's sake."

Stricken bent and picked it up, and handed it to her. "Anyway, enough about you, Reporter of the Year—how do I look?" he said, suddenly smiling, extending his arms.

Despite his sudden humour, he looked miserable: his long nose was red, his cheeks smarting. Under his red anorak, he was wearing a new suit: dark blue, with thin white stripes, and a vivid blue, shiny tie. A white shirt dug into his pale neck. Bobbles of cold rain gathered on his plastic shoulders.

Shona smiled. "You look like the Antichrist."

He shook his head, and turned, leaned against the barrier and looked out over the sea.

"You buy that thing?" she said, pointing at his suit.

"No, rental. From that place on George Street."

"I thought you'd go for a kilt," she said.

"I don't like my legs," he muttered. "I don't want them on display. Look, Shona—how can a man wearing a suit as fine as this look like the Antichrist?"

"You telling me Satan doesn't wear a fucking suit?" she said. He laughed.

Shona stared into the waves, which slapped against the sides of the boat.

"When you're on a ferry, do you ever look over the side and wonder what it would be like to jump?" she said. She imagined standing on the railing, her weight tipping forward, her stick spinning in the wind, her head tumbling to the sea. The sky and sea revolving about her eyes.

"What? No, Shona. I don't—do you?" he said.

"No. Never," she said. She peeked over the rail, down to the deck below. It would not be a clean fall to the water. There would be metal in the way, and breakage—rupturing, blood and splintering.

She shivered.

"Aye, it's dreich," Stricken said, noticing her quivering, raising his voice over the churning engines. The boat was rocking almost imperceptibly from side to side. Enough to unsteady them.

"Who in the name of fuck gets married in winter?" Shona said, pulling her hat over her ears.

"It's spring, actually."

"Get fucked, it's winter," she said. "I hate this time of year. Everything is dead. It's all chores, and dread. White skies and fog. Why is Viv getting married now?"

"I dunno, Shona—because people are optimistic? It's spring, it's a time of renewal, of green shoots, of . . . you know what I mean. Optimism, anyway," Stricken ventured, before blowing into his hands. His eyes were watering now, as the ferry to Dunoon picked up pace, cutting stolidly through the waves.

Shona felt the increase of the barrelling weight of the vessel beneath her feet. The sea was opening, the firth widening between the arms of grey land. The white cloud cover gently split, and the sun emerged, glowing dully. The long low waves were now gently gilded. The metal railings glistened, the deck, the flagpoles.

They were going to a wedding. Vivienne Banks and Wayne Provan were to be married in a country hotel near Dunoon. Viv was both a friend and former colleague of Shona, and of Hector, and of the gathered gaggles of former and current journalists who were huddled upon and below deck. Viv had been the editorial secretary of their paper, the *Edinburgh Post*, for many years. Wayne worked for the police. Shona had met him in a pub, many months ago. He had seemed dour, unremarkable, like an undrunk cup of cold grey tea.

Viv, bright as a needle, was from the North of England and had a way with blunt observations and crude descriptions. She could be lawless and sardonic. She was also warm, and sometimes chaotic fun. They had spent many hours and evenings together. Shona closed her eyes.

The tang and drift of the sea summoned memories. There

had been one long, hot day in July when the streets of Edinburgh shimmered and the heather on Arthur's Seat seemed to fume with the heat. The sky, untouched and fierce and blue. They had skived off work together and headed for the coast. They had waded, socks in hands, in the sea off the beach at Gullane, and lain together on the slowly sinking dunes, drinking from a cold long bottle and wondering how they could ever get back to the city, and if they cared. There were other memories, too. Shona shrugged them away. They were lost and gone. She wondered if Viv remembered them.

For the wedding, Viv had asked Shona to read a poem by the nineteenth-century Scottish magician and poet Ebenezer Mount. Shona had tried to memorise it. The folded words were in her inside pocket. She hoped she could read them without stumbling.

> *Like hands our fears do tether*
> *and once joined, disappear,*
> *like tears that run together,*
> *pool, and become our mirror.*

She thought of Viv's dullard fiancé and wondered if poetry meant anything to him.

"I'm not sure what she has seen in him," Shona muttered. A stray thought rose in her mind: she wondered if really Wayne should look a little like herself. But he looked nothing like Shona.

"Who sees what in who?" Stricken said.

"What she sees in that guy."

"You mean the handsome groom? And do you see anything in anyone?" Stricken said mildly.

"Go on then, tell me more about him," she said. "Tell me about his hidden shallows."

"Yeah, I don't know him much," Stricken said, and shrugged. "Think he's in the polis. Seen him a couple of times in the pub with Viv, seemed a pretty confident guy."

"A knob then."

"Why's that?"

"I don't trust anyone who actually wants to wear a uniform."

Stricken shook his head and looked along the deck. He saw someone he knew and waved—they nodded and waved back. "There's a lot of hacks on this wee boat."

"I know, just think if we hit a submarine and we go down. Consider the vast loss to Scotland," Shona said. "To culture."

Stricken rubbed his eyes.

"So, what's the plan? We get off this tugboat, get to the hotel, find our rooms, get pissed?" Shona said.

"That's about it," Stricken said. "Shall we go inside? I'm done in, and it's Baltic out here."

"You are hungover again."

"Yep, I drink to forget," he said, running a hand through thinning red hair.

"Forget what?"

He smiled. "I've forgotten. See? It worked. Let's keep it that way."

They moved down the slippery deck to a heavy metal white door. Hector opened it, and held it as Shona stepped unsteadily inside.

The café was busy with commuters on the short trip from Gourock to Dunoon, and packs of the wedding party, laughing and chatting in groups. Loud music played, the coffee machines screeched, and trays clacked in the canteen.

After some fussing, Hector brought hot drinks and Shona slumped onto a plastic chair fixed to the deck next to a table. He slumped beside her, almost horizontal.

"So," he said, "how is the freelance life anyway?"

Shona had been a freelancer for six months, working from home, still living with her elderly father in a small flat in the Lochend area of Edinburgh. She had taken a redundancy package from the *Edinburgh Post*. The money was running out, and her life had become solitary. It gnawed at her. She was missing the newsroom, with its easy chat, its joking and teasing, and its familiar faces. She spent most days on her bed or at her kitchen table, tapping at her laptop, with only an increasingly distracted Hugh Sandison as company—or her new rescue cat, MacDiarmid. Her dad had slowed down recently. He was often forgetful, and tired. He shuffled instead of walked. He kept losing his glasses.

"Fine," she said, smoothing the froth of her coffee with a finger. "I've got the column with the *Mercury*, and I'm on this retainer with the Buried Lede."

"How are they?" Hector peered. "It's an investigation unit, right?"

"Aye. They're not bad, actually," she said, shrugging. "They let me get on with it. Ranald is all right—the editor. He set it up. Ranald Zawadzki. He knows how to sell our stuff to the papers."

"Zawadzki?"

"Yeah—usual spelling," she said.

Hector smiled. "Ah. The old newsroom jokes are the best."

She went on: "He's a bracing guy from Shetland. We work alone or together on things and sell to the highest bidder. The Buried Lede has funding from a couple of nonprofits. Ranald directs it all. He is into looking at dark money, offshore banking, that kind of thing. I do all kinds of stuff for them. Not all of it comes with a byline. There's a clutch of us on retainer. So, I'm washing my face. But not by much."

Hector blew out heavily. "Sounds like hard graft. And uncertain. What you working on at the moment?"

Shona was working on nothing much. She'd spent weeks covering the trial of a disgraced Scottish minister. She had filed a column for the *Sunday Mercury* that morning. That was it. She was out of ideas.

"Oh, bits and pieces," she said. "Got some long-term things I am working on."

The ferry suddenly lurched to one side and Stricken swore. Then he sat up, said something about creasing, took off his coat and jacket, and slung them on a chair.

There was a burst of laughter, and Viv Banks and her parents staggered into the canteen, exaggerating, with staggered steps, the lurch of the boat. Viv waved and winked at Stricken and Shona. Her parents, looking nervous and grey, smiled thinly.

A pale man in a suit came over to their low table. He took off his jacket and laid it down on a seat. His large eyes flickered. He had a shaven head, and was holding something in one hand.

"Don't mind if I leave my stuff here, do you?" he said to Shona. He had a soft northern English accent. His face was open and mild.

Shona said not at all. His jacket was like Stricken's—blue, with thin white pinstripes.

"Thanks, pet," he said quietly, and joined Viv and her party. There was a loud cheer as the family joined the other guests. Someone hugged Viv and kissed her on the cheek. Viv beamed and wiped a tear from an eye. The pale man moved to one side, and slipped behind the crowd to the bar, where he ordered a drink.

"Who is that guy?" Shona said, nudging Stricken, who did not reply. She leant over to look at his long face, dusted with freckles and ginger stubble. He was fast asleep.

She finished her coffee, and walked to the windows overlooking the deck and the sea. The town of Dunoon was coming into view, grey and low on the coastline. The clouds had opened further. Emerald blue slashed across the sky. The drone of the ship's engines below altered their pitch as the ferry approached the harbour.

More peals of laughter rolled from the wedding party. Shona looked around, and for some reason two men were lying beside each other on the floor, flapping like beached fish. People were clapping. Viv was sat with a drink in her hand, a man with his arm around her. Her parents were looking on, smiling. The pale man was at the bar, his sleeves rolled up, looking at the joy and the laughter, and drinking with no expression. He was turning something over in his hand—a pebble or a small ball. He looked drained, barely present.

The public address system burst into life with a shudder and a squeal. The announcer said the entire crew, including the captain, wished the very best to Vivienne Banks and Wayne Provan on their imminent nuptials. People clapped and cheered. Shona grinned.

Her phone rang. It was buzzing around her inside pocket like a small animal. She took it out. The word DAD shouted at her from the screen.

"Hey," she said. "You all right?"

"Hi, darling," Hugh Sandison said. He was inside. There was no background noise. His voice was weak.

"What's up, Dad?"

"I'm not feeling too good, hen," he said. "I've called the doctor. How's the wedding?"

"It's not started yet—I'm on my way, remember?" she said. "Wait a minute."

She moved from the window, and out of the canteen, over

a bulkhead door, and into the corridor. It was quieter. The ferry moved under her feet. The sky was being pulled past a porthole. Nothing seemed to be where it should be.

"What do you mean, 'not feeling too good'—have you been sick?"

"No, not sick. Just a bit weak and woozy, and a wee bit of a pain. In my chest. In my arm. Doctor said come to the clinic, but I feel a bit too peely-wally for that. Someone's coming round."

"What, an ambulance?"

"Aye, love, the ambo. I'll be fine. You have a great time. I'll call you from the Western. Took ill at the allotment. But home now."

Shona took the phone away from her face and swore. Her heart, she noticed, was suddenly racing. She was stuck on a boat, a hundred miles from Edinburgh.

"Dad, I'll come back—I just need to get on the next ferry back to the mainland. It'll take me a while."

"No, love—Bernie will be with me. Don't worry. I'll be fine. It's probably nothing."

Bernadette Comfort was her father's friend from the allotments. A small, steely woman. Her father had insisted, when teased, that there was no hint of romance between them. Shona didn't quite believe him. She wanted to.

"Right. Is Bernie there now?"

"Aye, she is, she's packing me a bag."

The ferry shuddered, and a garbled cacophony of words over the public address system announced something. Somewhere deep in the ferry, something boomed.

"You on a boat?" he said, louder. "I'm worried about leaving MacDiarmid."

"Yes, Dad, the Gourock ferry! And don't worry about the cat," Shona found herself yelling.

"Grand—that's the taxi now, speak soon, my darling," her father yelled back.

"Taxi?" she bellowed, into silence. The call was ended.

Stricken shambled into view. His jacket and anorak were back on, a bag over his shoulder.

"Is that you calling a taxi, Shona? They've put on a minibus for the wedding party. No need to worry about—"

"Oh, for fuck's sake," Shona shouted, staring wildly at Stricken.

"Just thought I'd mention it," he said, backing off. "Dunoon has arrived. I mean, we have arrived at . . ."

"Fucking hell, Hector," she said, and shook her head. She closed her eyes, and ran her hand through her hair.

Through the windows, the port had come inexorably into view, as if dragged to them on subsea chains. A bilgy tang drifted from the porthole.

She texted her father—*Take care Dad, call me when you can*—and followed Stricken onto the main deck.

As the ferry slowed to the jetty, a text flashed back: *He's fine, I'll let you know how it goes, he doesn't want any fuss, enjoy your wedding—Bernadette.*

"It's not *my* fucking wedding," Shona said loudly as the ferry quietly slowed to a stop.

Some besuited heads turned, and Stricken whispered urgently, "You all right?"

"Fine," she said, slapping her phone into her pocket, and smiled broadly to Viv, who was peering at her from across the room. A crowd of jostling half-drunk passengers gathered by the door for foot traffic. As Shona pressed to the door, Stricken close by, the pale-faced man was still seated, alone at the bar, looking into his drink, turning the little object over and over in his hand.

Stricken turned to her as they stepped through the metal door.

"Who's this MacDiarmid you keep talking about?"

"A cat, Hector," she said.

"Oh," he said, looking flushed. "Not a fella, then."

"No—she's much better than that," she said, and pushed him in the shoulder, to encourage him to leave the ferry.

Shona had phone calls to make, and quickly.

1.

Ashley had not intended to go as far as Deepdale, the day she found the shirt.

The last guests had left her mother's bed and breakfast. She tidied and cleaned the rooms, pulled sheets from beds and replaced them, hoovered and dusted. In the en-suite bathrooms she used detergent and bleach, emptied the bins, and washed down the mirrors. Someone had left a used condom in the bin. She wrapped it in loo paper and chucked it with haste into the rubbish bag.

The Gildersleve Bed and Breakfast sat on the outskirts of Ullathorne, with green meadows on three sides, and the vicarage nearby. High trees leaned and whispered over its eaves.

As she cleaned, she could hear the rooks in the trees, and the burr of a farmer on his quad bike, humming down the fields to the wide river. The moors were silent, the woods and fields all around were silent. Ashley worked slowly and steadily. She had to: her mother had dropped any concessions for her condition years ago.

It was a bright, late winter day in Ullathorne, County Durham. Across the market town, which clutched the valley of the river Tyr, the old stones glistened, wet, in the uncommon winter sun. On a cliff overlooking the river, sharp shadows sliced through the ruined castle. The sunlight cast broad shadows on the market cross with its tiled roof and knotted pillars, on the curving cobbles on the old main street, and across the slates of the roofs as they dropped to the broad, surging river. The town seemed to gleam, as if newly washed, sluiced free of the long winter months of mud and grit and dead vegetation.

There had been snow and ice, only days before. Like a dropped cloth of lightning. The dale had been transfigured in white, with narrower roads impassable, the schools closed, the river numbed by the suddenly descended beauty.

Under the snow, the town was revealed, became fully itself—a stone town in the stony hills, an old settlement for humans to stay warm and fed in the old mountains. By the river, waterfall, tree and standing stone. It had been alive before England. In some form it would endure beyond it.

Jess needed walking, but Ashley was tired. The dog was bouncing around the stone-flagged hallway, hairily emitting tiny yelps, her paws skittering.

"We need a few pints of milk," Ashley's mother, Peg, called from the hot kitchen.

"All right, Mam," Ashley called back. She briefly looked in the mirror in the hall. Her long hair was bedraggled. She pushed it into her woollen hat and pulled on her wellies with one hand, sitting on the bottom step of the wooden stairs. Jess put her two short brown paws on Ashley's knees, and licked the air and what parts of her face she could.

"Give over," Ashley said, and soon they were out of the old lodge's door, across its gravel drive, and onto the narrow path beside the road that led into Ullathorne town.

The land was still, and the town was quiet. It was a Saturday morning—the market was silent, the children lying in bed, the bottle factory running its shifts as if the weekend didn't exist. Ullathorne days were the same as Ashley had always remembered them: quiet, the trees speaking as much as the streets, the river speaking more than the people. Flags snapping on the church roof, heritage flags snapping on the ruined castle. Trucks rumbling over cobbles, cars grinding along the main road to Darlington. The river glinted over the old ford. The morning breeze moved rattling twigs in the churchyard, but didn't reach the unmoving silence of the trees in the deep woods.

Ashley walked quickly up the wide county street. Jess, off her lead, trotted beside her—along the path, which ran past the shuttered Masonic Hall, past the old garage, past the solicitors where Ashley and her mother had been read her father's will, past the circular market cross, and down the Bank—the steep street of old stone buildings that led down to the river and the woods.

Ashley was in a dwam, her thoughts screened behind her waking eyes. As if dreaming, she walked, sure-footed, to Deepdale. She had not thought of going there, but moving smoothly as if on rails, they crossed the river at the metal pedestrian bridge—painted green-blue and creaking slightly in the wind, its Victorian rivets large like plates, its tubular towers like great funnels—crossed a narrow road, and finally stepped over a low stile to Deepdale. Tyrdale was joined in its fold in the hills by other valleys, valleys that broke off from the main course of the river, and Deepdale was one, a deep cutting that moved west into the Pennine hills.

It was a tight valley of ancient trees, unfelled since a time beyond remembrance. A beck ran through its heart, but as Ashley trudged into the trees and Jess ran about her, she realised—even though she was born and raised and had only briefly left Ullathorne—she did not know the stream's name. It chuckled and spat over low stones, and she headed into the woods that quickly closed in all around her.

The path was thick, tacky mud mixed with Durham County Council gravel, and they quickly reached a fork in the way. Onwards lay the depths of the woods, to the right a shallower basin of lighter trees and undergrowth, and a clearer path to the road across the moors. The late winter light glittered through the canopy of leafless trees. Snowdrops nodded in sprays of white life. The scent of the wild garlic drifted, heavy and green, in the air.

At the junction, Ashley leant on a tree stump.

"I didn't mean to come this far," she said. Jess briefly lifted her shaggy head, her nose a black drip of wet, and then ducked down, and snuffled on.

Ashley was tired. She had been walking too fast. She needed to catch her breath. She was tired, and knew more fatigue was to come. What was there for her in the days ahead? The weeks and months? More guests to sweep up after, more breakfasts to prepare, rooms to clean. Small talk with guests, and the dog to walk. An emptiness sat in her stomach. A tingling anxiety in her mind. The woods and the trees and the beck and the rocks: they were here when she was a bairn, when she was a teenager, when she went to university, and they were here, unchanged, unmarked by any passing of time, when she came back home with her degree unfinished and her heart sore.

Jess jumped up at her, her pink tongue lolling like ham. Her eyes reflected the clear cold sky in sparkling crescents. She smelled of dog and damp and mulch and mud.

"Howay, then," Ashley said, and they marched on, deeper into the dale. She whipped the spare undergrowth with a thin stick held in her good hand, her weak right hand clenched to a fist and plunged deep in her pocket, as her boots trod harder and faster into the woods.

The valley narrowed, and deepened, and soon Ashley, stomping through mud, was squelching alongside the water of the stream, splashing in its shallows, as the woods closed in, black and spare, all about.

Jess was up ahead, a quiver of movement in the tangled distance. The beck was swollen from the later snow melt of the moors above, leaking into the bracken and thorn, fast moving through coiled roots, and swamping the thin path.

Ashley moved further into the trees, away from the uncertain depths of water. On a slide of mud and stones she almost lost her balance, but her hand quickly found the rough trunk of a silver birch, its skin peeling, and she did not fall. She looked at her hand—there was a roll of birch skin, tightly coiled like a home-rolled cigarette. She blew on it, and it drifted into the undergrowth.

She felt like turning around now. She had to trudge home, via the Co-Op, and load up on milk. A desire clutched in her heart—to hide in her room and write her book. She was thirty-four thousand words in now. She thought about her manuscript as she marched on into the trees, which thickened and crowded about her. She wondered how to describe the next scene she planned to write—it was a party scene, with alcohol and scrapes and kissing and drama. She had been struggling with a passage about the beauty of the land, and how hostile that beauty was. How hostile any kind of beauty sometimes seemed. She would return to it later.

As she pushed on through the trees, she knew this was the only way forward—she just had to keep writing. She had to keep living this temporary, quiet, cheap life in this town, and finish the book, and keep typing, revising, correcting, and getting it right, before she sent it to someone, saw what could happen next, if anything might come of it. She wanted to be published. She wanted her story—the story of a young woman just like her—to be out there, in the world. So she could feel real.

An unfamiliar concrete wall appeared in her path. Ashley stopped. It was as if it had just been dropped in front of her. She had not been this far into Deepdale before—or, at least, not within her memory—and did not think there were any buildings here. It was a ruin, a roofless concrete block, with one side missing, stained green and brown, throttled with ivy.

She called for Jess and her mongrel head poked out of a low window, which had lost its frame and glass many years before. Ashley walked around the wall and saw the insides of the building had been retaken by the valley. There were tall, high weeds, and the ivy, all about, a flung sheet of tangled gleaming-green slung over the ruins. The concrete walls smelled damp, and empty, of loss and abandonment. She could not imagine that the building had ever had plumbing or electricity—it was a shell, its purpose lost to time.

There was a growling noise. A whiskery snarl—Jess was now in the corner, pulling at something, her back legs taut and straining.

"Jess, give over," Ashley said sharply. She did not want Jess pulling at a dead animal, getting guts and muck on her jaw and mouth.

She looked closer. In the corner of the ruin was a hole, as if newly dug, and around it were small stones—clean, as if recently polished or washed. Gleaming black, and grey, and brown. It was as if they had been lifted out from the earth. Maybe the snowmelt had raised them, she thought.

The dog kept on pulling—she was growling louder now, growling at the thing in her teeth, and the weight or knot of something had stopped her from ripping it free and whole from the ground.

"Jess!" Ashley said. Her voice fell and sank into the overgrowth, into the stands of silent watching trees.

Ashley moved to the dog, and peered at the straining clump of saliva, mess and grot in her mouth. Her white teeth were grappling with something murky and black, something made of material that was half buried in the ground, in the black sludge of time.

"What you got?" she said to the dog, who suddenly let go, and whimpered, and ran around in a jerky circle, the weeds moving and parting about her.

"What you got?" Ashley repeated. The clump of material and grime was half in and half out of the muddy hole. With a wince, she reached with her hand and pulled on it, and after something snagged, under the surface, it came free.

But she was unbalanced with the force of the pull—she fell and landed on her backside in the mud with a soft squelching thud. Jess, all legs and nose and teeth and tail, wiggled over to her and licked her forehead, and then licked at the thing in her hand.

"For God's sake, Jess," Ashley said, finding a way of pulling herself up with the aid of ivy and stone. The dog jumped up to snuffle the material, but then stood stock still, tail up, and bounded away out of the ruin and into the woods.

Ashley realised she was holding a drenched piece of clothing, folded up, coated with years of groundwater and mud, of the work of worms, and the nameless slime of the forest soil. She took her right hand from her pocket and grabbed hard at an edge of the clothing, between thumb and finger—the rest of her fingers hanging, almost unfelt, in the air. With her other hand, she pulled the folds and creases of the clothing free.

Inside, its concertinaed folds were almost clear of mud. Black and white stripes were revealed, and an elaborate yellow crest—it was a Newcastle United football jersey, torn and ragged. It was old, with the sponsor GREENALL's written across its chest. In the area where a belly would be, there was a large rip. She turned it over, and on the back the name JET was spelled out in large white letters.

Some small, pale things fell to the mud—three or four white plastic beads, with holes for hanging on a string. They lay on the mud like seeds.

In the quiet forest she held it for some time. She went back to the corner of the building, where Jess had pulled it from, and the hole had filled with mud and water, as if it had never been there at all. The earth had hidden it, the earth had now given it up, and the earth had closed again. The stones lay around the hole, as if on guard. She picked one up—heavy, solid—and dropped it in the hole. It sunk into the meltwater with a splashy thud.

The shirt hanging in her hands was old and heavy, dripping black water. The dale around her was quiet, save the running stream, the wind picking up, creaking the high boughs, the fingers of the trees snickering together.

Ashley peered around the ruin, but there was no sign of anything save plant growth and a cloud of loss. The sky had turned: from blue to grey, and a spot of rain fell on her forehead.

She yelled for the dog, and Jess appeared in a hurry and a flash, her legs up to her waist, thick and wet with new mud.

"Come on, Jess, let's gan yam," Ashley said, and trudged back to the path, and the town, clutching the folded-up shirt in her filthy hands, her legs wet from the fall.

The skies opened. It was raining as she emerged from Deepdale, the sky adding tumult to the stream. The rain fell onto the old, tattered shirt, which began to smell of something heavier than just mud.

2.

The hotel bar was roaring with pissed journalists. The noise was calamitous. The jukebox was blaring, and a hundred drunken journalists and former journalists—and their girlfriends, boyfriends, partners, second wives and first husbands—were all drinking, hollering, laughing and shouting. The hard hotel light smashed in glint from glasses and eyeglasses, from optics and beer pumps.

At the bar, Shona's former news editor, Colm, was telling a story about how he had once chased a noted footballer at a hundred miles per hour down the M8. And, in the scrum of bodies around Shona's table, Stricken was telling the outlandish tale of how he and another journalist who may or may not have been a spy had chased a story about drugs and diamond smuggling between Amsterdam and Glasgow.

Shona had only had a couple of drinks and was sitting in the bay window. She looked out the whorled window glass to the sea, a mile away, churning black, lights moving upon it. The mountains, across the water, were dark and impenetrable, their bulk cutting into the star-spattered night sky.

"And anyway," Stricken was yelling, several drams down, to a gaggle of old hacks who had heard this tale, or a version of it, all before, "when we got the tale, my contact, old Ken, didn't want to be paid at all, not in cash anyway. He just asked a blind eye to be turned to a weapon he had half-inched from the dope-dealer over the border in Haarlem—an AK-47! He kept it under his bed. Hundreds of rounds he had for it."

People exclaimed and Stricken took a large swig of his

deep brown whisky, but Shona was staring at her phone, her stomach tightening, her knees gripping her stick.

"Anyway, after we got the job done and I'd filed the story, we went out, dodgy Ken and me, in Brussels," Stricken shouted.

"I thought you were in Amsterdam?" someone said.

"Och, we'd moved on," Stricken said. "Anyway we were well gone—mortally drunk. And we were chucked out of this bar we were in. The big fat barman was like, 'Get tae fuck, you chancers.' And Ken was staggering drunk, absolutely blootered, and he yelled for a cab, and he threw himself into the car and I fell in after him. Literally fell in. My face to the floor. Ken was shouting at the taxi driver— 'Take us to the Hotel Metropole!' And the driver was like, 'Are you sure?' and Ken was yelling—'Take us to the feckin' Hotel Metropole! Tout-suite! I have many euros, fuck the cost! Vamos! Tout-suite! Schnell! Just take us there!' And I was like, on the floor, saying to Ken: 'Are you sure the Hotel Metropole is not in fucking Holland, Ken? In Amsterdam? Are we driving all the way back to Amsterdam?' And he was yelling at me: 'No, it's not. It's our hotel in Brussels, you idiot.' And I'm like: 'Whatever, Ken, I just want my bed. Drive through the night for all I care.' And the driver was shouting back: 'Minimum charge in this cab, twenty euros, there's a minimum charge!' And Ken was furious, he was raging, all up in his face. And the driver, cool as the proverbial, he just shrugged. Ken sat down and shouted 'Victory!' and I was lying on the floor. So off we go on our grand trip to the Hotel Metropole!"

Stricken paused for breath. The table were smiling and giggling. Shona had witnessed the retelling of this story at least four times before. She stopped herself from rolling her eyes.

"Anyway! So, we set off on our epic journey to the Hotel

Metropole. Ken had collapsed by now, he was done and dusted, eyes rolled back in his head. Goodbye to his SAS training. I was on the floor, breathing in the carpet. A week of hard work and a lot of grass and a day's worth of drinking. I was in a bit of a state, it must be said. And the taxi driver pulls into the road, does a neat little turn, crosses the road, and stops outside the hotel opposite—the Hotel fucking Metropole! Which was on the other side of the street!"

The table groaned. Shona smiled. Stricken, red in the face, stuck up two thumbs and grinned.

"Classic," he said. "Those were the days."

Shona looked at her text messages. No update from her father. The last text remained: *At Western General, all good so far—B.* She had received it hours ago, after she had left the ferry, and after some cajoling from Stricken and Colm, and a small hug from Viv, had continued her journey to this hotel. But she had wanted to turn around and go home.

The wedding would be in the morning in the hotel's main ballroom, and by the state of the party, would be a sombre and hungover affair. Viv, who was now wearing a pink cowboy hat and a string of Christmas baubles around her neck, was standing by the fire, surrounded by her close friends and family. Firelight glowed in their glasses and faces. Viv was laughing, her head back, her eyes closed.

Shona closed her own eyes and could only see her father's bearded face, lying in a pale hospital bed. He had been tired for a few weeks now. He had slept in until midday recently—the first time she could remember. He had been annoyed—stomping around, slamming his coffee cup down. The old journalist, the old Glasgow communist, hated being late, or feeling as if he was being lazy. He had not been up to gardening at his allotment for weeks and weeks, and it had weighed on him. She could tell he had been frustrated, angry with himself. Irritated by his own torpor, but with no energy to break out of it. There had been signs of something going wrong. But she had missed them, or ignored them.

As she looked around this room, though, with its press of happy human bodies, the heavy laughter and the drinking, the music and the firelight—she knew he would love it here, this ugly, rambling old country hotel in the Argyll countryside. He would have loved, too, the scent of the roiling sea, and the creaking lonely trees, the emptiness of the surrounding land, and the cold majesty of the night sky. She knew he would love it that she was there, too.

"Anyway," Stricken yelled, "it's my round." To loud cries of "at last!" he collected the orders from their table. Red-faced and red-haired, he turned to Shona with a grin.

"JD and Coke, Ms. Sandison?" he said.

"I'm all right, thanks," she said.

"You sure?"

"Aye, I'm off for some fresh air," she said, standing up, gripping her stick tightly.

Shona moved unsteadily through surging bodies to the double doors of the saloon. A soft hand appeared on her shoulder. She turned her head, and it was Viv.

"Hey there, my love," she said. "You all right, doll? Where you off to, need some air? By Christ, I think we all need a bit of that."

Then Viv burst out laughing. Shona smiled.

"Aye, I've had a lot in a hurry, but I'm not the only one," Shona said. "Nice party."

"Oh, it's lovely to see everyone in one place, isn't it? It's like the old days," Viv said. "I'm not sure Wayne has seen so many old hacks in one spot—he doesn't know what's hit him."

Viv laughed, the baubles around her neck gently dunting and tapping, the lights on her cowboy hat blinking on and off. She looked over to the groom, who was propped, or being held, against the bar by his friends—large men in bright suits.

"Here," she said, her mouth coming closer to Shona's ear. She smelled of perfume and wine. Her eyes were wide and almost wild. She spoke in a breathless slew. "I hope your old man is okay, pet, but I am sure he is, and as you say he has someone to look after him, and to be honest, Shona, you need a break from looking after him, and if he's texting you, he's fine, isn't he? And I am sure it's just a wee scare, and look, tomorrow, after the do, you can run back, get the ferry and you'll be home for tea, so don't fret, pet, and it'll all be fine. I am so chuffed you are here. You need to be here, with me. I love it that you are here."

Shona nodded, smiling. Viv's eyes were glinting.

"And you have a good time tonight—is your room all right? You're across the hall from my old pal Dan, from back home. Oh! There's Stuart and Donald!"

Viv spun on her heels and collapsed into a large pink embrace with two old journalists, one with a black and silver beard and the other about seven foot tall, who were the only journalists dancing, slowly and drunkenly frugging to their own unheard music.

Shona slipped from the room and the chaos and clamour and into the dimly lit hall of the hotel. The Poet's, the hotel was called. When they had arrived there, she had noticed a large garden, illuminated with a circlet of white glass globes. She headed there.

The noise of the party slowly faded. Beats became thumps, voices became meaningless, laughter untethered, and sudden shouts alarming and unbidden. In the reception area, brochures for excursions flopped out of plastic pots. A sleepy woman was clicking through something on her computer screen. Golden light fuzzed on wooden panels and brass handles. There were portraits of famous poets on the wall—old men, framed. No women, she noticed.

She made her way outside, into the darkness, and crunched on the gravel track through the hotel gardens—it led around the side of the hotel, past the bay windows, and into a small parkland. The gardens were lit by small balls of light, set in glass. Beyond was open country, the vast sky, bedazzled with stars, banks of clouds moving slowly over the three-quarter moon.

She walked between high hedges and reached a stone fountain, set in a large pond. The fountain was turned off. In the still water, the moon was rippled, shredded and pulled. She sat on the cold stone lip of the pond, and tried to call her father. It rang out. "Hugh Sandison here. Leave a message—if you like," his voice said, breathily. She remembered the day she had finally convinced her father to put a proper voicemail message on the phone: a lot of fuss and huffing, and, several takes later, this brusque, whiskery message.

She didn't leave a message. She closed the call, and found on the internet a number for the hospital. She called the number, but it rang out, too, and came to an answering message with various options, and she realised she could not face pacing her way through the bureaucracy, the waiting music, all the numbered options, and closed the call. Bernadette would call her if there was an emergency. And it was late now, and her father should be asleep, and Bernie had probably been sent home.

The night was cold. She looked up to the black and purple vault, the immensity scattered with stars—so many more than at home in Edinburgh. So many more out there, unseen, even from this almost lightless garden.

The hotel building loomed above her—three stories of piled red stone, heaped in the Scots Baronial style, with four turrets, battlements, and flags: a Saltire, a lion rampant, a forlorn EU circlet of stars. They hung limp in the windless night.

She sat there, under the height of the building, for a while, listening to the party swinging, the music pulsing.

A familiar despair spread through her stomach, her chest. It crawled up her neck, like a cold pool of water, slowly enveloping her frail injured body. She put her hand to her head. These parties, these get-togethers, they were few and far between now. The old newspaper office—her home, her comfort, her life—was gone now. Newspapers were contracting, shrivelling. Many reporters worked from home now. The old *Post* newsroom on Rose Street was shutting. Stricken worked from his dingy flat in Leith. Colm bossed around the news desk from his new build in Barnton. Fuck knows where the editor, a shaven headed idiot from Glasgow called Ingleton, lived or worked; probably a cupboard full of skulls somewhere, she thought.

The old newspaper industry, as she had known and loved it—the loud and humming newsroom, the daily deadlines, the jokes, the swearing, the smokers' gallery, the presses, the pubs—had been destroyed. That life—that lifestyle—was dead. This party would be the last gathering. Viv's wedding was a funeral for their lives in newspaper journalism.

So, no wonder everyone was mortally drunk. The future, as she saw it in her mind, was an uncertain road. An unbeaten path into darkness. As dark as the vault above. The image of a full bottle of Jack Daniel's felt very appealing. So did the deep, endless sea. Her mind reached a sheer, black wall, and retreated.

She started as feet in smart shoes snapped on the gravel. By its stuttering step, she wondered if it was Stricken. He came loping into view, holding a suit jacket in his hands.

"Dame Shona Sandison, as I live and breathe," he shouted.

She smiled, even though she had not wanted to.

"If I am not mistaken, is that Impatience on a Monument?" he bellowed. He moved towards her and then stopped. "Viv's going to do a wee speech," he said, quieter.

Shona nodded. Stricken held up his jacket.

"And this is not my jacket," he said, smiling in the night dark. "I've managed to mix mine up with someone else's. Bit of a bugger. My cash card is in my own blessed jacket. So—alas and alack—I couldn't pay for my round."

"How awful for you, Hector," she said. "You must be devastated."

He moved closer, holding the jacket out as if it was a fish on a line, lifted from water.

She put her hand to the dark suit jacket, with its pale lines barely visible in the dark. "Have you looked in the pockets?" she said.

"Why would I do that?"

"To find out whose it is, genius."

She took the jacket from him. It was light and silky in her hand. Shona looked to see if it had a name tag. It did not. No markings at all. She put her hand in the inside pocket; in it was a book of some kind. And something small and hard.

She fished out the book—a small black Moleskine diary. She then pulled out the hard object—it was a stone, a polished pebble. It was smooth as an eye, with a stripe of paler rock within it. She put it in her pocket, moved closer to one of the lamps, and, leaning her stick on the hedge, knelt, so the light fell on the diary.

"What does it say?" Stricken said. "Whose is it?"

She flipped the pages, but there was no name written in it, and none of the diary pages had any marks on them either.

She put her nose close to the spine—it smelled new. The pages were stiff in their spine. Something was tucked into the envelope slot at the back.

She pulled it out: a folded piece of paper. She opened it up. On it were four lines of text, written in small, neat black ink:

$$abdargninetytwo$$
$$sorleysays—taketherightpath—$$
$$sayyestono-$$
$$—thereisnotime—odeadaheado$$

She peered at it for a while. She could not make sense of it—it was a poem of some kind or notes for a kind of creative writing? Maybe, she thought, it was song titles. *Odeadaheado?* A nonsense word.

She put the diary in her pocket, alongside the pebble, and folded the jacket over her arm.

"Shona, the speech, come on," Stricken urged.

When they reached the bar again, Viv was already addressing the party. People were gathered around the bar, in the blazing yellow electric light. The music had been turned off, and Viv was standing on top of the bar. She was tall, and her head seemed perilously close to the ceiling and the lights. A round of applause was just coming to an end, accompanied by some whoops and cheers, as Stricken and Shona slipped through the door to the bar.

". . . and it is also lovely to have the two special people without whom I would literally not be here, my lovely, beautiful parents, here with me in Scotland . . ."

There was more clapping and whooping, and by the fireplace, Wayne put a practiced hand to her father's shoulder, and her mother dabbed an eye and chuckled. The pale-faced man was there too, his shirt sleeves rolled up, his tie askew. His eyes were half open, but he was smiling.

Viv waited for the applause to die down and passed a hand over her face. She rubbed an eye, and fiddled with her bracelet.

". . . of course, maybe not many people know this. There is one very special person, one wee boy, who cannot be here tonight, and won't be here tomorrow . . ."

There was silence, but someone shouted, "Wayne's escaped!" and there was laughter. But the laughter was short. Viv wiped an eye and held her drink in the air. She was towering over them all, her hair so close to the lights it looked as if her hair was on fire.

". . . so here's to Andrew, taken from us all so soon, so early. I do so wish my brother was here with me, here with us all. He is gone, and lost, but not forgotten."

"Hear, hear," someone from her family said, and everyone clapped. There were no cheers, but murmurs of support, a low, rising tide of sympathetic words and nodding heads.

". . . I would love for him to be here. I really would. He would be amazed! His little sister finally getting hitched! Maybe he would be embarrassed. Anyway, we miss you, Andy. I love you, wherever you are."

There was more quiet clapping.

"I didn't know she had a brother," Stricken whispered to Shona, his breath drenched with whisky.

"Me neither," she whispered back, gripping her stick tight, the suit jacket soft in her hand.

"He must be dead," Stricken said, earnestly.

"Ya think?" she said.

Stricken looked at her eyes; his own were unfocused. "Well, that's a turn up," he said, and shook his head, and looked back to Viv. Then he turned back to Shona, a drunken light in his wide eyes. "Hey, Shona, now. D'ya think you'll ever be up on there, on the bar, everyone happy for you, at a wee wedding of your own?"

Shona blinked.

"I'm more likely to hammer nails into my head," she said.

Stricken shook his head. He tilted his head to one side, as if in sympathy. "You know, Shona, when did you last even *have* . . ."

She stared at him. He didn't need to finish the sentence.

"Get to fuck, Hector," she said.

Hector blanched, and looked away out of the window, into the night.

Shona heard the rest of the speech but did not listen. Someone pushed past her to the lobby, and she lost sight of Hector, who moved away. There were several rounds of applause, and some jokes. They drifted past her. There was some loud hilarity at its end, with Viv trying to get down from the bar top, her skirt caught momentarily on a long beer tap, a high-heeled shoe came off, a glass knocked to the floor. Wayne bundled over to try and help her, and there was laughter and shouting. The music resumed, and the party continued.

Shona checked her phone—no messages, and it was late. Somewhere in Edinburgh there were machines blinking, measuring the pulse of her father's heart behind frail curtains drawn against the darkness.

It felt like it was time for her to sleep. She stood alone in the doorway, the light before her, the dark of the closed hotel behind. The fire glowed red in the hearth. The music crashed into the crowd's shouts and hollers. She needed quiet.

She draped the mislaid suit jacket on an empty chair, then headed up the two flights of stairs to her room. Her legs strained on the steps. There must be a lift, she thought. She stopped halfway up the stairs—there were red walls, and worn red carpet. The pebble had moved in her pocket. She took it out. In the glare of the hotel light, it was green—green as a bean, streaked with a kind of silver. It was impermeable, complete, and smooth, like a tiny planet, plucked from deep space. She decided to keep it.

She reached a long, dimly lit corridor that smelled of lemon carpet cleaner and bleach. The noise of the party faded into distance and night. There was just her feet and the stick on the carpet, tap tapping down the long hall.

Some doors had names painted on them: HUGHES, ELIOT, WORDSWORTH, TENNYSON, PATERSON, BERRYMAN, MORGAN. Her bedroom for the night was untitled. It was just room 27; she had dropped her bag in there earlier. She slumped to her door, fishing out her key card.

But she did not open the door to her room. She was suddenly distracted. There was a stream of air against her face. A sharp chill, and a breeze. She looked to the end of the corridor; a large blank fire door was slightly open, and beyond, metal steps led upwards. To the roof, she thought. What was up there? The battlements, the flags and the towers. The view across the darkness of Argyll, and the world.

Pale light fell on her door—it came from across the hall. A bedroom door was open. She thought she heard something: a clumping noise, footsteps, a kind of moaning. She could not tell where it was coming from—from above or the room.

She stood still.

"Hello?" she called, too quietly. Her voice barely moved beyond her mouth. She looked left and right but there was no one around. The beat of a song pulsed distantly from the bar.

Shona moved a step forward into the open bedroom. The door was ajar. Ahead, she saw a bed, a dim light from the bathroom thrown across the small bedroom like a spray of glittering dust.

"Hi?" she said.

The door, she noticed, had a name printed on it: SORLEY MACLEAN.

She peered into the room. She thought she heard another moan, and a deep, long sigh. Music pulsed down below. Laughter rang out.

She took another step into the room. The bed was made, a backpack on the floor beside it. There was a book open on the dressing table. It had been ripped; half a page hung loose and jagged like torn flesh.

With a kind of mental flinch, Shona realised something lay on the bedroom floor. She moved closer, and could see, spelled out in pebbles and stones:

THE RIGHT PATH

The stones glimmered with liquid. They were wet—she touched a pebble with a fingertip, which was suddenly darkened. It was blood.

She heard a clanging noise from the hall—the brash rasp of metal on metal. She moved out to the hall as quickly as she could. Through the frame of the door that led to the roof, something like a ribbon fell into view. It pooled on the floor in a puddle of shadow. She moved hesitantly to the stairs, as if in liquid, as if in a dream.

There were smears of blood on the wallpaper, lit by a skelf of light. The air seemed to move, like the shimmering around a bonfire. On a step lay a pair of silky suit trousers, empty and collapsed. On the next step up, a single sock. Shona moved up the steps, and the night air was suddenly upon her face, a breeze pulling at her hair, and above in the vast vault of night a drift of stars and the yellow disc of the moon.

She reached the tower top, the battlements low, the crenelations no higher than her waist.

"There is no time," a flat voice said.

She looked to her right, and a naked man stood at the edge of the tower.

His white skin glimmered in the light thrown from the garden, from the hotel, from the moon. He was looking out into the night, to the dark mountains and the invisible sea.

Shona found herself unable to move—one hand was on her stick, the other was outstretched, as if she needed to hold the air. She saw her fingers, her hand open, clutching nothing.

The man turned around. His hands were dark with blood.

On his pale chest was a dark tattoo that dropped down from his shoulder blades to his waist: a circle of the letters of the alphabet in deep black, and the numbers 0 to 9. *Yes* on his left shoulder, *No* on his right.

"Say yes to no," he said, his arms outstretched.

"No," she said weakly.

He nodded. His eyes closed.

He cannot fall. She felt a deep surge towards him.

"Hey, pal, come on, why don't you come to me. Come down, come inside," she said, in a warm voice, in the friend-liest voice she could muster.

His lean naked body, his long white body, stood between two low stone battlements. His face was blank, his eyes closed. She realised it was the pale man who had been drinking alone at the bar. It was Viv's friend.

"It's Dan, isn't it?" she said.

"Ask Sorley," he said. He opened his eyes. They looked past her. Then he stepped back, into space. Into the night.

He dropped from view.

Shona hurried to the edge, and saw the end of his fall, the tumbling over, the hurtling into darkness.

There was a loud, wet noise—of solidity meeting softness,

of a sudden human breakage. There was a brief silence, as deep as a sea. And then—shouting, and a single yelping scream.

His pale body lay tangled and broken on hard stone. The head was facing the cold earth, the line of the neck was dislodged. Legs and arms askew, like the broken branches of a leafless tree.

The music played on, for a while, as doors opened and people gathered. Then the music stopped. And then there were human voices, and the sounds of the deep night, and the murmuring of a small group gathered around the body of Daniel Merrygill.

3.

The banquet hall was full of flowers. The morning light glimmered on bunches of pale roses and on the white tablecloths that shrouded the long tables. The room smelled of blooms and clean linen. The light speared on unused cutlery.

Shona sat at the empty top table, where Viv would have sat, looking out through long elegant French windows to the rugged landscape beyond.

In the dawn light the Argyll hills and mountains emerged in a frieze of deep blues and bruise violets. A straggle of sheep lolled in a scratty brown field beyond the fence. They were huge in their winter coats, dull-eyed and mad. A rag of black plastic bag shook on the fence like a deflated bird.

The hotel's cook, in jeans and a T-shirt, had made Shona a roll and bacon, which sat uneaten beside a large mug of black coffee. He had spoken kindly to her. She had almost broken down.

The police had been at the Poet's Hotel all through the night—bustling around the hotel, sealing off the room, the corridor, speaking to staff, interviewing Shona, interviewing Viv. Blue lights had swum around the car park, but after a time they were turned off, and the night had flooded back.

Outside, more sheep had now gathered, as if for discussion. One grey-faced lump raised its stricken face and bayed.

A man in a long overcoat walked slowly across the room to Shona. His polished brogues tapped on the wooden floor. He brushed past an untethered pale balloon, which dunted under a table.

"Ms. Sandison," he said.

She shivered suddenly, as if walking through a cobweb. It was the same officer with a lean face and kind eyes she had spoken to in the middle of the night. He had interviewed her and taken a statement.

Lorimer, he was called. He was tall, dark, and she may have even said, on a better day, handsome. He had a supple Glasgow accent and grey-blue eyes.

"Thank you for your help, Ms. Sandison—we need not detain you any further," he said. "Much appreciated, your clarity and candour. You are free to go, although of course we may be back in touch depending on how the case proceeds. There may be further formalities. Right now, I think we have what we need."

Shona nodded.

The detective stood for a while, hands in his pockets, looking out at the fields, the sheep, the distant mountains. "Ms. Banks has informed us that the wedding has been called off," he said, in a low voice.

"No shit," Shona said eventually.

"Well," the man said, "indeed."

No one would be dancing in this banquet hall today. No cake would be cut. No speeches made. No poetry.

"How is she?" she asked.

The detective turned to her, his face calm and unchanging, and then turned back to the window. "She was very distressed. But she seems okay now. I believe she is planning to travel back to Edinburgh with her fiancé today."

Shona nodded. She would see Viv on the boat.

"What was his name again? Dan, wasn't it?" Lorimer asked. He should know the answer, Shona thought. Maybe it was a test.

"Yes," she said, and poked the soft white dough of her roll.

"Mr. Merrygill. Daniel John Merrygill," he said. "He was

an old friend of Ms. Banks. I understand they grew up in the same town in the north of England."

Shona nodded. She still had Merrygill's book and pebble in her pocket. "Poor man," she said flatly. "It might have been a slip, but still . . ."

The detective turned to her. "Ms. Sandison, you said he turned and fell."

"I did. You're right. That's what he did. He knew what he was doing."

Lorimer looked at her, levelly, for a moment. "Nothing's been confirmed," he said, "but I think you can probably guess we are not looking for any further evidence. Your account seems to match what we know, and he was full of drink, by the looks of it. Postmortem to follow, but . . ."

"But what?"

"We found a lot of drugs in his room. Uppers, downers. He seems to have taken a few and . . . intentionally injured his hands with something."

He opened his hands, as if that concluded the sentence.

"Do you think he felt any pain?"

"The medics say he was dead on impact. Broken neck."

"Naked," she said.

"As a baby," he said.

"He had a strange tattoo," she said. "On his chest."

Lorimer nodded. He moved a step closer and looked at her with clear eyes. "Shona—you have the number we gave you if you need any help dealing with this. If you want someone to talk to."

She nodded. The steam rose from the black coffee, and she reached for the cup.

"Take your time," he said, softly.

She sipped the coffee, and he stared at his watch, as if it was going to tell him something.

"What was the book?" she said. "In the room?"

"It's bagged up now," Lorimer said. "I don't have that information. If I remember rightly, it was a book about geology."

"Geology? Weird," she said, quietly.

Lorimer sighed, and rubbed his face.

"Yes. And all this, on the night before a wedding," he said. "But I've seen weirder. You're a pal of Detective Reculver, are you not?"

He peered at her.

"I know him, aye," she said.

Reculver was her best contact in the force. A large, gruff, veteran detective. He usually wore makeup—mascara, foundation, and blusher. Sometimes beauty spots would appear on his face. He had a large head, rugged as a stump. He dressed immaculately and was often angry as a badger. Like his many pairs of handmade leather shoes, he was both tough and elegant.

"Well, you will have seen weirder too, then. Now—I will be going," Lorimer said. "We have your details. Keep your phone on." He smiled briefly, and padded out of the room.

The day became bleary and formless—a mess of organisation, of brief exhausted hungover chats in the lobby and the bar, of looking up timetables, of phone calls, and hurried texts and emails pressed into mobile phones. Stricken had emerged, green with drink, sucking black coffee and talking in a traumatised murmur. People sat around whispering and mumbling, their faces pale and sick. Viv bundled down the stairs with her silent parents, waved and mouthed a "goodbye" to the remnants of the wedding party, and ducked into a private hire cab, which whisked her to Dunoon. Wayne had gone already, Stricken muttered, holding his coffee in two hands.

The blue lights had gone. One police van was outside, and

a uniformed officer was still at the reception, rumbling in a low voice to the receptionist. The hotel manager was there, too, in his shirtsleeves, wringing his hands, his eyes wide as the moon.

Eventually a small fleet of minivans and taxis took guests to the port, and they shambled onto the ferry back to Gourock. White gulls circled over the still, salty quay. The sea was a slowly rumpling mass of porridge-grey expanse.

Shona had called her father, and texted, but there had been no reply. In the silent canteen Stricken was slumped, his head in his hands.

"Hey, anything from your dad?" he said, his voice muffled by his palms.

"Nah," she said, shaking her head.

"Have you called that Bernie woman? His friend," he said, raising his face. His eyes were bloodshot.

"No, I haven't," she said. "I don't have her bloody number, do I?"

"Chill, Shona—Jesus. I just thought you might?"

"Why the fuck would I, Hector? Some random woman from the allotment? No. Go back to your sleep."

The ferry was loud, grinding its way through the short strait. Shona stood up and walked slowly to the metal steps to the deck. There was no cheering and laughing now in the wedding party. Just huddled groups staring out at the slumping waves. Shona's head was heavy now, her body exhausted.

The cold air slapped her skin. On the bleak deck she saw Viv, alone, a heavy jacket on, her hood up, staring at her phone. A sudden wind whipped about the boat, the waves began to move, to slash white. Seabirds hung in the air, unmoving, as if dangling from unseen strings.

Shona walked slowly to Viv, her stick clipping the deck, and Viv looked up and smiled.

"Hey, sweetheart," she said softly. She stood as Shona came closer, and put her arms around her. They hugged. Shona could smell day-old perfume and shower gel, stale alcohol and tears. They sat, embracing, for a while, Viv wiping tears from her eyes and cheeks with the back of her hand, a soggy tissue in her fingers.

She started talking.

"He was a good friend at school, Dan," Viv said. "Back in Ully, back in them days. Even though he was a couple of years older than me. Poor Dan. Poor, poor Dan. What's he done that for? What's he gone and done that for?"

Viv shook her head, and wiped her eyes again. The ferry plowed on, the sky white, the sea grey, the mountains looming like a congregation.

"But I guess this has saved you having to read that daft poem?" Viv said, with a smile.

"It can wait," Shona said.

"Ach, doubt it will ever be needed," Viv said.

"Poor fella," Shona said.

Viv nodded, sniffed, pulled herself up.

"He used to knock around with our Andrew," she went on. "He got back in touch about ten years ago. Lovely man . . . kind, quiet, funny. He led a bit of a lonely life. Looked after his mam till it got too much."

She shook her head. Something was being intoned over the tannoy, but Shona could not quite hear—it was a garble of words, metallic and meaningless. Viv blew her nose on the scratty ball of tissue. She sighed deeply.

"Fuck the wedding, it doesn't matter," she said, suddenly. "Fuck all that shit. That can happen anytime. But what a thing to happen. For fuck's sake. Maybe we'll skip the wedding altogether now—who cares? I don't care."

Shona nodded, and held her friend's hand.

"I didn't know you had a brother, Viv. You never said before," Shona said, quietly.

Viv blew her nose again, shrugged, raised her eyebrows.

"He would have been fifty this year, you know," she said. "A middle-aged man. But no. He is always eighteen."

"You never said," Shona repeated. "I was surprised."

She had been more than surprised. She could not imagine Vivienne with a brother. She wondered if he looked like her.

"Maybe I didn't," Viv said. "Dan and Andy were good friends. Were tight. Now both are gone. Both gone. No, I probably never said. I don't. Andrew would be a big bald man probably, like his dad. Like my dad."

She pulled her head to one side, as if tearing it away from something.

"How are you, Shona—are you all right?" she said, her voice shaking, looking off, out over the sea.

Shona looked at her for a while and shook her head gently. "I'm fine."

"I guess you've seen worse," Viv said, turning back with a crooked smile.

"Don't you worry about me," Shona said.

Viv rubbed her face and spoke quietly and quickly as Shona studied her intensely.

"I don't even know who to tell. Dan was an only child. Where his folks are now, I don't know. I seem to remember his dad was long gone. His mam might be in an Ully care home, but she could be gone, too. Just like Andrew. Like all of us one day. We'll drop into the sea, won't we? We all go down, one day."

Viv added, rapidly: "We don't know where our Andy is. I used to walk with Jet, our dog, in the woods, trying to find him. After the police had gone. But nothing. They had looked. It was on the telly. Nothing. It was like he'd melted into the trees. Vanished into the stones."

Shona opened her mouth to ask more. She winced at herself, felt a pang, both of shame and irritation at herself. Instead, she moved her head and looked out to the sullen grey sea.

"I bet you're dying to know more about my brother now," Viv said, with a brief smile.

"Maybe another time," Shona said.

"I guess you think it's odd that I've kept it a secret."

"No. And I don't mind secrets. I have some myself. And at least secrets are true."

Viv smiled, then put her head on Shona's shoulder. "It was Mam and Dad who suffered the most, not me. He was their baby. It's the not knowing. The waiting. And then the waiting turns into silence. And people forget. Or don't want to remember. They're waiting for an answer and it never comes, so they switch off, switch out. And then, for us, those who remember, it's just weeks and months and years of nothing. No news. You start to think it never happened."

Viv wiped her eyes. The sonorous rumble of the ferry engines was rhythmic, and lulling. It quietened them. Viv's head was heavy on Shona's shoulder, as if she was asleep.

"Where's your Wayne?" Shona asked, eventually. "Why are you alone?"

"I'm not alone, you're here. Fuck knows about Wayne. He was being annoying. Talking about money. I told him to go and boil his head. But shush. Let me rest on you awhile, pet," Viv said. "You're nice and warm."

"Aye, that's me," Shona said, "I'm exothermic. That's what Dad says. High metabolism."

Viv murmured something that Shona could not hear.

"You what?" she said softly.

"Remember that lovely time we went down to Yorkshire," Viv said, barely audible above the grind of the boat's engine.

"I remember," Shona said, brightly, happy to move into a good memory. "Fish and chips in Robin Hood's Bay. Then we went to see where the Brontës lived."

"We drank too much, didn't we? You felt sorry for the donkeys in Scarborough and tried to buy one. We got lost for a bit on the Yorkshire moors."

"I'd rather be lost on the moors with you than most other things," Shona said, remembering those days—the flat hit of the hammering sun on the bare brown moorland, Viv laughing at their disintegrated map, which had come apart in a mad drenching summer rain the day before. Drinking cider from a brown plastic bottle at the jagged ruins of Fountains Abbey. Falling asleep together at a cheap B&B in Helmsley, both drunk, both stoned, both sunburnt and delirious. Clapping along to old soul tunes. Yelling, hysterical, to Beyoncé.

"Me too, love, me too," Viv said softly. "I'd rather be lost on the moors than sitting here on this fucking ferry boat right now, that's for sure." She moaned and held her head. "My folks, Shona, they are distraught. The money they have spent . . ."

"I know, love, I know," Shona said.

"You never even saw my dress," Viv said.

"I'm sure you would have been a sight to behold."

Viv laughed a short, sharp laugh, and shook her head. Her fingers were soft on Shona's soft hands. As the Gourock port came into view, and houses and roads glided past on the headland, a text buzzed on Shona's phone.

Hugh still in hospital. Give me a call when you can thanks Bernie x

Viv stood up and composed herself, flattening her coat, wiping her eyes. She gave Shona a farewell hug. Her parents, pale as sand, had appeared on the deck, and she went to join them. Shona nodded, and her friend half-staggered away across the tilting deck.

The ferry rolled into the dock, roiling white foam behind its massive weight. Shona's phone buzzed again—a call. She looked at the screen. It was Ranald, the editor of the Buried Lede: her boss.

She answered. She felt a presence nearby on the deck—Stricken was nearby, leaning on the handrail.

"Ranald," she said.

"So, Shona," he said warmly in his Shetland accent, sweet and curled as caramel.

"At your service."

"So, you said you were at a wedding this weekend?"

"Aye."

"In Argyll?"

"What you getting at?"

"Was it the DEATH SHOCK HORROR AT HOTEL WEDDING wedding?"

"Jesus fuck. Where is that?"

"In the *Record*. Says someone was found dead at the Poet's Hotel, near Holy Loch. A suicide? Reading between the lines."

"Aye. I saw it happen."

"Jeez, Shona. You all right?"

"Aye. Fine. Seen worse."

"You sure?"

"I refer you to my previous answer, Ranald."

"So."

"So, what?"

The ferry clunked hugely into the terminal. Stricken was waving at her as he turned to leave. Viv had gone down into the decks below with her family, with what was left of the wedding party.

"I was wondering if you'd like to write a piece on it. There must be more to it," Ranald said.

Shona rolled her eyes. But she had the notebook in her pocket, with the strange writing on it, the lines of eldritch text.

"Let me think on it, Ranald. Let me have a think."

"This report, Shona—it says the man left a message on his body? Is that right?"

"No, no. That's not right. Not sure where that has come from. I saw him."

"You saw him?"

"I said, Ranald, I would think about it. Hold your horses."

"Okay, Shona, do that. Give me a call."

"I will, I will," she said. She blew out a blast of breath. "I am amazed the story is in the paper today. Already."

"You shouldn't be amazed. Someone at the hotel has blabbed. There's all kinds of detail."

"Some fucker. Someone wanted a bit of cash and got the tip-off fee. Look, Ranald, I'll be in touch."

The call ended. The boat came to a halt, and the train to Glasgow was waiting. A journey had begun.

4.

Hugh Sandison was recovering, and sleeping. Shona held her father's frail, pale hand in hers. His steady breath gently shook the long white hairs around his dry lips. His chest hair, curled and grey, rambled from his bed shirt. Her thumb moved over the frail skin of his hand. Blue veins still pulsed, for now. He was pink, and tender, vulnerable. Suddenly small.

Bernie had been there. When Shona arrived, she had moved away to another part of the hospital.

"Can you check on the allotment, love?" he had said. At some point past, she thought, he had been weeping. His remaining hair was a little wild, and one of his eyes was swollen and tender.

"Of course, of course," she said. "But you can't go digging around there again for a while. You'll need to take it easy. You can't . . ."

"It's winter. But it's spring soon," he said. "And I've been neglecting it. It's a bit of a mess. I didn't want to say. It's a fair mess, you know."

"It's okay, Dad. The allotment isn't going anywhere."

"There's snowbells on the verges, by the bicycle path. Lovely, they are."

"They are."

"You don't need to worry about me, love."

"Of course I am worrying about you."

"I'm fine. I'm better off in here. How was the wedding? I do like Viv, she is one of your nicer friends . . . she's a bonny lass."

"It was fine," Shona lied. "Look, you were lucky, Dad, and I am glad Bernie was with you . . ."

"Och, she's a doll. Did they tell you, they're talking about having something put in my artery, some kind of clip or something? Amazing stuff. Shame my old man never had one. He would still be alive now. Tough as old boots was Da. A fisherman, like his dad. Fifer fisherman: tough men. Not much give in them. Out on the cruel sea. He didn't want me out on the boats, like him. Didn't want me out there. Oh, no. He was clear about that. He'd lost his brother, out there. Terrible business. Tough men. Not like me. He had a dram for his brother every twenty-third February, for Tam. Every year. Said nothing. Tam: his brother. Tough men, out on the boats."

He had looked out of the window then, quivering, a little bit tipsy with drugs.

Shona had tried to return to the point. "A stent, yes, the doctor told me. But this was a warning, Dad, a warning to . . ."

"*A warning from history*, isn't that what someone once wrote?" he had said, smiling. "Ain't that the case?"

"Is that bloomin' Marx again, Dad?"

He had shaken his head, frowning.

"No, no. Maybe. Shona—my love—I'm tired now. I will sleep. Can you bring my book in for me? There's nothing to read in here."

"Is it by your bed? What is it?"

"Oh, it's old Terence. The Eagleton. It's by the bed, love, yes, that's right. If you could. Thank you. How is wee MacDiarmid?"

"She's been fed, Dad, she's fine."

"Shona—see your pal Vivienne?"

Shona had nodded.

"Keep her close. Friends are worth their weight in gold.

It's not like family, like me. You can't choose your family. Unfortunately for you. That's what makes friends special. You have found them and loved them. If you do love them. Love your friends, hen. It's important."

She nodded. She could not think of what to say.

"Good, good. I need to sleep now. Takes it out of you, the heart stopping. For a wee moment there." He had smiled at her, then closed his eyes and fallen into a deep fissure of exhausted sleep.

He was still sleeping, his chest moving slowly up and down. A thread of cotton was caught in the hair of his ear. Shona reached for it carefully, to pull it away.

The nurses were closing the curtains. Shona watched, unmoving as the fabric swished along the rails. The machines still beeping. The beds, metal and heavy. A tiny ring of rust around a dial. A scar by her father's ear she had not noticed before.

He slept on, deeply. His eyes were moving behind his lids, like an old dog by the fire, remembering old chases in the high grass.

A nurse smiled and pointed to her watch. It was time to go.

Shona stood up and kissed her father on his forehead. It was warm and solid. She kissed him again, with a hand to his balding head, fugitive mad hairs between her fingers.

He had nearly left her. Taken the final step into the place where she could not reach him. But he was there. Still there, for her, for himself.

She walked to the corridor, and through the hospital, passing doctors and nurses murmuring in corridors. She took a lift to the foyer, and the café was busy, but she could not see Bernie. She must have left.

In a bathroom, she put her hands to her face. Her stick dropped with a clunk to the floor. She felt the tingle of tears in the corners of her eyes, but they did not come. She rubbed her face. She needed, she felt with an urge overwhelming, to work. She needed this story—any story—to follow, to find, to write. A story to put her name beside. A story to tell to the dark.

The bus home across dark and wet Edinburgh was long and slow, grinding between wheezy stops. In her satchel she had the notebook from Dan Merrygill's jacket. She took it out again.

s a y y e s t o n o

What could that mean? Be positive to a negative? Agree to something that is not happening? Maybe it was, like she first thought, a song title. Maybe Daniel had been in a band.

She began an internet search on her phone, as the bus moved down the long straight Ferry Road, past the handsome houses of Trinity and Goldenacre, and into the closer tenements of Leith.

a b d a r g n i n e t y t w o
s o r l e y s a y s—t a k e t h e r i g h t p a t
h—s a y y e s t o n o -
—t h e r e i s n o t i m e—o d e a d a h e a d o

If they were song titles, they were not by any band or composer that had been recorded on the internet. If they had existed, they were gone. The emptiness of a hollow internet search lay awkwardly in her mind—a fidgety, annoyed sense of something being mislaid, being missed, being lost.

The word *Abdarg*. She wondered if it was Gaelic, or the name of a place or person. Again, she searched for it. She could not find anything. It was an ugly word. The *b* and the *d* like eyes with horns.

She realised, as if for the first time, and with a mild leap in her heart, that she had effectively stolen from a man who would then kill himself. But what did it matter now? No one knew it existed, apart from Stricken—and he had been so drunk, so it was doubtful he remembered.

The handwriting was neat. The ink was thick, and flowing. It may even have been written with a fountain pen. She closed it again, and slipped it into an inside pocket of her bag.

The bus slowed to her stop, and she quickly bundled her stick and her bag together and left, shouting a quick thank-you to the driver.

From one window of the flat, the bare bulk of the city's extinct volcano, Arthur's Seat, loomed, and from another, above the brown roofs of housing, the green metal of the Hibernian Football Club's stadium gleamed. Her father's room was dark, the curtains drawn. Someone had made the bed; it was neat and had clean sheets. His old blanket had been folded and put at the foot of the bed. His writing table and bookshelves were cleaned, too. His slippers neatly paired.

As she dumped her bag and coat on the sofa, she realised someone had cleaned and tidied the entire flat. The narrow kitchen was spick and span. The living room had been hoovered. Only her bedroom, which doubled as her study, had been left as it was. Bernie must have been given a key, she thought.

There was a note on the dining table in the living room. Folded, propped up like a tent: *WEE DINNER IN THE OVEN. B X* it said. Shona found herself shaking her head. She screwed up the note and threw it in the general direction of a bin, newly emptied, by the television.

MacDiarmid, a length of warm coiled fluff, raised a tawny

head. The cat was female but for some reason her father insisted on her being named after the poet, so she was Mac-Diarmid. The cat was on the soft blue chair—Hugh's chair. She raised her head and yawned, her pink tongue curling, her teeth white. She stood up and arched her back, her tail straight in the air like an antenna. Shona scratched her behind the ear and trailed a finger down to her soft cheek.

"How is the wee refugee," Shona whispered to the rescue cat.

MacDiarmid purred and rubbed her head against Shona's hand. A tiny white skull beneath the warm hair.

"Glad someone is happy," Shona said, and moved to the table and flipped open her laptop. She sat down and searched for Daniel Merrygill.

A few stories came up: the lurid tabloid account of his death, and other, more sober, descriptions of a death at a hotel in Argyll. There were errors, and a lack of detail. One description from a news agency was carried in multiple media outlets. It read:

> *Mr. Daniel Merrygill, 49, of Darlington, County Durham, a civil servant, was found dead in his room at the Poet's Hotel, near Dunoon, the night before he was due to attend a wedding. Police have said there are no suspicious circumstances. The wedding which he had been planning to attend has been cancelled, it is understood. A spokesman for the hotel declined to comment.*

She searched for him, in Darlington. She knew the northern English town for its railway station and its position on the main east coast line to London, but that was about it. She remembered rows of red brick houses, a wrought-iron Victorian station, maybe a distant tower.

There was one old link to Merrygill on an employment search company. She clicked on it.

Daniel John Merrygill
Senior Policy Outcomes Officer, UK Government
(Darlington: Dept. of Administrative Affairs) (21 years)

There was a CV and a small photo. The CV said he had attended Ullathorne Comprehensive, then Manchester University in 1992. Entry-level civil service, a few years in various departments in London, then on to one of the satellite civil service departments based in the north. No other details, and no personal information at all. She searched on social media, but there was not a mark of him. Nothing on any of the major channels. She looked back at the photo. There was a vacancy there. Vulnerability, perhaps, in the open stare, the boyish short-cropped hair.

She sighed and sat back, and rubbed her eyes. She could see the scene again: his body adrift in the air, then dislocated on the flagstones. Black blood, pooling about his head like a hideous halo. The letters on his chest, the numbers, the sun and the moon.

She looked out the window. A light was flashing on the tip of Arthur's Seat—the sun had caught someone's glasses, or a camera, or binoculars.

Her computer screen had gone to sleep. She slapped her hand on the table, to wake herself up.

Shona knew she needed to speak to Viv. But she could not face it. There was a call she could make first. But before that, she needed a cup of tea. She flicked on the BBC News channel before she walked through to the kitchen. It was a politics show. White men in suits were sitting in a semicircle in a studio. As if prompted by her movement, MacDiarmid slid down from the soft chair to lie in a bar of light.

One of the politicians was dominating the conversation. He had colourless hair, clipped short. He wore a tight grey suit and a blue tie. His face was almost featureless, as if drawn by a child. His voice was flat and persistent.

"Fact is, Suzanne," he said, nodding to the presenter, "and let's be perfectly blunt about it, this kind of growth-restricting practice belongs to the past. To the failed policies of another era. Unions are by their nature divisive—we are all one nation, one people—are we not? Unions are just clubs to fix wages. Personally, I'd like to look at the idea of a National Labour Force organisation. But that's for another time. Now, free of ridiculous interference, free of unwanted migration cutting off the legs of the proud English worker, we can free our workforces of the globalist obligation to organise in these restrictive ways, work with employers to grow profits, and increase growth, target growth, maximise growth. We have to take the right path. There is no time."

"Mr. Watson," someone interjected.

"Fact is," he said, waving away the interruption, "let's take a broader look, a common sense look at this situation. Common sense, like the way it used to be. Look: we have to reject certain ideas. In a sense, we have to say yes to saying no to the alien ideas that have somehow taken root in this nation. Because the answers, let's be frank here, lie around us—we should look at the lessons of history. A thousand years ago, this land was part of the Roman Empire. Greatest empire the world has ever seen. There's a bloody great wall built right across the north of England to remind us of their greatness, their industry, their civilisation." His eyes were flashing, and he had turned to the audience.

"But what brought down the Roman Empire? Now let

me tell you, because I'm a bit of a history buff. It wasn't a land battle, they never had their Waterloo. It wasn't a naval disaster, there was no Trafalgar for them. No, the Roman Empire was brought down because of migration. Swarming into the empire from outside. Uncontrolled immigration did for the greatest empire the world has ever seen—until the British Empire of course—and now, if we are not vigilant and staunch in our vigilance, it will do the same to us. It cannot continue as it has. Common sense just says otherwise . . ."

"We have slightly gone off topic, Mr. Watson . . ." the presenter said, weakly.

People in the TV audience were clapping loudly, some shouting their approval. Shona left the room. She put the kettle on, and her phone buzzed in her pocket.

It was Detective Benedict Reculver. She flicked off the angry kettle. She opened the call.

"I wondered how long it would take for you to call," she said.

"Good day to you too, Ms. Sandison," he burred in his rumbling voice.

"What's the fucking problem this time?"

"Shona, step down from your well-accustomed sweary pulpit for a moment," he said.

It sounded as if he was walking down a street. She could hear his footsteps on cobbles. She imagined his polished brown brogues on some street in Edinburgh's Old Town, his large frame gliding past stones, spires and archways like a lolling ocean liner.

"I have something to exchange with you," he growled.

"Not sure I want anything you've got," she said, pouring the hot water into her old mug with GLASGOW MERCURY printed on its side.

"Hear me out. You might be surprised. Meet me in the Café Royal in forty minutes," he said.

"Fine," she said. "I guess."

"And before you run for the bus . . ."

"What?"

"How's your old man?"

"See you in half an hour," she snapped, and hung up.

She left her steaming kettle and nearly tripped over a stretching MacDiarmid as she grabbed her jacket and bag and stick and made for the door. Her stick rapped hard on the doorframe as she left the flat in a hurry.

The cat watched her go, blinked heavily, and proceeded to lick a paw languorously, as if there was no yesterday, today or tomorrow.

5.

Shona was on the bus when Viv called her. Shona answered. Edinburgh was slowly moving past the windows—elegant, cold and silent beyond the humming bus.

"Eighty thousand pounds!" Viv shouted.

"Hi, Viv, what?"

"Someone has tried to put a load of cash in my bank account." Viv was speaking loudly. She sounded out of breath. "Eighty grand!" she shouted.

"Viv: are you okay?"

"No, I'm not okay, Shona! What's going on? Fuck's sake!"

"Where are you?"

"I'm having to go into the bank, aren't I? I'm storming down George Street. The bank called me. Suspicious activity! I know nowt about it. It's the last thing I need right now."

"Surely they know who tried to deposit it? Is it an error?"

"It's not an error, Shona, someone's tried to put eighty grand in my bank account! Now I have to go in and prove it's not money laundering or something."

"Is it a wedding gift?"

"Shona! Who would do that? No one I know has that kind of cash lying about."

Shona waited a few moments.

The bus wheezed its way to the top of Leith Walk, where it haphazardly made its way around a messy roundabout. Lights blinked in cafés and restaurants as it turned tentatively.

"Fuck's sake!" Viv shouted again. "This is the last thing I need. Where are you anyway?"

"I'm on the way to meet someone. This bus is slow. Milk

turns faster. Look—I'll be done in a bit, do you think you'll still be in town in an hour?"

"Probably! Give me a text and let's meet."

"Okay—take care—I'm sure it's not . . ."

"Eighty thousand pounds!"

The line went dead.

Shona got off the bus outside the Scottish National Portrait Gallery, a beautiful red stone building that sat poised on the edge of the New Town. She looked up at the statues that adorned its blocky exterior. Their eyes empty in their languid faces. Their swords sleeping in carved hands. The statues blindly looked down at her: what couldn't they see? A small woman with a black puffer jacket, leaning on a stick, a laptop bag over one shoulder, a copper streak in her hassled hair.

As she walked on, a cold wind was whipping across St. Andrew Square, a large open space between her bus stop and the Café Royal, and it was getting dark. The sky was cloudless, but its light was fading to a violet blue. She thought of her father, receiving his supper in hospital, safe in those white sheets.

The Café Royal stood resplendent in a narrow lane between elegant public buildings. She pushed her way through a heavy door, and her eyes adjusted to pub light—the diffuse air, glinting with brass and glass, purring with the low murmur of early evening drinkers. The elaborate ceiling was green and gold. Old soul music was cooing through speakers.

Detective Reculver sat in a padded booth under a glimmering tiled mural. The large man was dressed in a three-piece suit, a red shirt, a big tie, a large overcoat, and polished brown brogues. Today his adornments were limited, it appeared, to mascara and a temporary beauty spot on one cheek.

He sat with an amber pint, his clenched hands, as big as

babies, on the table. Shona slumped in front of him. She tipped sideways a little as she slapped down her stick on the seat.

"Shona Sandison, I presume," he said.

"You getting me a drink or what?" she said, unzipping her coat.

"As ever, it is fairly easy to distinguish you from a ray of sunshine. Some of that awful American bourbon you drink?"

"Yep. With Coke and ice. Ta."

Reculver stood up, his frame moving slowly but solidly to the bar, where he leaned forward to order, as if he were exchanging a secret.

"I don't know how you drink that stuff," he said when he returned, sliding the brown glass across to Shona.

"I open my mouth and tip it in," she said. "So—what's cracking?"

"I pity your clearly inexpensive education," he said, and sipped his beer. The low light was falling in pale beams through the stencilled windowpanes. "Anyway—I was sorry to hear you are involved in this nastiness in Argyll. Are you bearing up?"

She shrugged. "I've seen blood before," she said. "I've seen bodies before. The real shame was for Viv, whose wedding it was meant to be. That's all fucked now."

He nodded. His eyes were dark. His lips seemed to be briefly iridescent. The pub murmured and glowed. Men and women in suits gathered around wineglasses and pints.

"She is a friend of yours?"

Shona sighed and flicked her glass.

"No, I was invited to a wedding in the middle of nowhere by a total stranger. Yes—she's an old friend. What does it matter?"

"I assume it was not you, then, that tipped off the papers?"

Shona glared. "I don't need thirty quid for a lame tip-off to the red tops. I'm not that skint—yet."

Reculver smiled. "Thought as much. So. I am guessing you might now be writing about the whole terrible business?"

His voice rumbled like coal being poured from a sack.

"I don't think so," she lied. "Why would I do that?"

"You're freelance now, and it's good material. No doubt some media platform would take a feature on the poor man, and the wedding he ruined."

Shona said nothing and drank more. They sat silent for a time. Shona noticed a small brown bandage on Reculver's wrist.

"Even if I was going to do that," she said, eventually, "what could you tell me? The poor guy did himself in for some reason. He chose a bad time to do it. Not that there's a good time."

"No," Reculver said, shaking his head. "Although of course there may have been a method in his . . ."

"So, what is it, this information you are talking about?" she asked again.

Reculver blinked heavily and traced a circle around the lip of his pint glass. "First, I was wondering if you might tell me something," he said.

"Fire away."

"The wedding guests—were they mainly journalists and so on?"

Shona peered at him. "Why don't you ask Lorimer? He'll have a rundown of everyone in the building. Won't he?"

He smiled. "The brave and handsome Lorimer is many things, but he is not as sharp or as reliable as you."

Shona shrugged. "There were a lot of journalists," she said. "Of course. A lot of old hacks from the *Post* and the *Glasgow Mercury*. Viv has worked in papers for twenty-five years. Some of her fiancé's friends were there, I think. They would not have been journalists. Then there was her mum and dad. Then this Merrygill, who she knew from school."

"Were there any politicians?"

"Who like? MSPs and whatever?"

He took a large swig of beer and nodded. A rime of foam was briefly on his large upper lip. He smeared it away, and a gentle pink tone was moved in a line across his bulky cheek.

"No," she said, "I don't think so. I think we would have spotted them. Hector certainly would have, the tedious sod that he is. Nope. I don't think Viv knows any politicians, to be honest. Not her type. Not our circle. So, no."

The drink had warmed her. The buzz of alcohol was flickering in her brain like a low guttering candle.

"Who, in particular, are you thinking of?" she asked.

"An MP called Watson," he said, with emphasis.

"Who's he?"

"Member of Parliament for Tyrdale. In the north of England—Durham. Part of the new breed. Got in at the last election, talks loudly about immigration, historic traditions, sinking migrant boats. Wealthy. Widower. His young wife died in a car accident, way back."

"Car accident?" she said.

"Single-driver crash in Kent. She drove on the wrong side of the road for some reason. He almost immediately and efficiently threw himself into politics. Likes to stir it up with a bit of the culture war—he is loud about all kinds of things. In his maiden speech he talked a lot about civilisation. He has talked in fringe events about 'Anglo-Saxon values'—whatever they are. Not a big fan of the exceptions to his rules. I suspect he and I would have the odd disagreement, should we meet."

"Sounds like someone to absolutely not invite to a fucking wedding, then," she said. "No, he wasn't there. What does he look like? Wait a second."

She looked for the MP on her phone. Many pictures

popped up—it was the politician she had seen on television. Hueless hair clipped short. Tight grey suits, a taut gym body, and red ties. A constituency photo showed Watson standing in front of a Union Jack.

"Nope, he wasn't there. Not sure why some English MP would be at my pal's wedding? At all."

"He went to the same school as her—in Ullathorne, Tyrdale."

"She's never mentioned him. So what?"

Reculver nodded and turned his head slightly, as if registering the sound of a voice from somewhere else.

Shona drained her short glass and grinned. "I know you. You and your friends are watching this guy—what's he into?"

He raised a finger.

"You were with the security services before you joined the force, I believe?" she said, smiling, raising a finger of her own.

They realised they were pointing at each other, and both dropped their hands.

"As I always say, Shona, you are indeed the impossible pencil—both sharp and blunt. I cannot say. But I—we—they—are beginning to be interested in him. A wee bit."

"Surely a wee bit out of your jurisdiction, Reculver? He's a Westminster MP. Nothing to do with Scotland."

"Well—I can't say any more. We do, in general, like to keep an eye on any cream that's about to curdle. However, if you do come across him, in your scurrilous business, I would be most obliged if you could let me know. Here—read this, an interview with the fellow," he said.

He reached into his jacket and pulled out a piece of folded paper.

"He has his own posse, and they are smart," he added, in a low voice. "He has a very good, experienced election agent, and a personal bodyguard, they say."

She took the piece of paper and slipped it into a pocket. "Why?"

Reculver shook his large, solid head. "As I say—if you bump into anything to do with him on your travels—do let me know. He still runs a company or two in Ullathorne, I believe."

"Come on, you're not going to tell me anything else?"

"No, darling Shona," he said, and took an extravagant glug of beer.

Shona huffed and crossed her arms.

Her mobile phone lit up and buzzed. It was a text from Viv: *Ready for coffee in 15? Wellington?*

"I've got to go soon," she said.

Reculver pulled out another piece of A4 paper, folded lengthways, from the darkness of his voluminous coat.

Over the other side of the bar, someone dropped a glass with a brief shattering noise.

"Whoops," Reculver said, glancing over. "A slip betwixt cup and lip." He then put the paper on the table. "Our poor suicide," he said. "We ran some checks. Lovely Lorimer over there was a wee bit out of his depth. So: this Merrygill. No partner, no history of ever having a partner, no kids. One parent, still in Tyrdale. Seems he left his job in the civil service recently. Gave no reason and worked out his notice. He also sold his house in Darlington. A terraced red brick house, two beds—got two hundred thousand for it. Moved a month ago to a caravan on a farm."

Shona took the paper.

"Looks like he was downsizing," Reculver said. "Maybe preparing."

"Simplifying," she said.

Reculver leaned forward. His dark-lined eyes glittered in his massive head. "Three nights ago, his caravan went up in smoke. Farmer found it burning in the field. Totally wiped out. Daniel Merrygill was nowhere to be seen. The farmer's finally reported it to the Durham force. Marton's Farm, isolated place on the moor, halfway between Ullathorne and Appleby."

Shona opened the paper, and squinted. There was an image of a small house in a road of red-bricked terrace houses. A photo of a burned-out caravan in a lonely field, a twisted tree the only feature on a bleak horizon.

Reculver abruptly stood up. "So, there you go—something for you to ponder. No doubt there's a wee tale for you, Shona."

"I'm suspicious," she said.

"You should be," he said.

"No—of you. Why give me all this stuff? What do you want?"

He shook his head. "I'm sure you will be able to think of something," he said. "This is our relationship, is it not? I give you things, you give me things. We are but dealers in the underworld of facts, Miss Sandison."

Shona shook her head, and stood up, and grabbed her stick and bag. There was a glinting crescent of bourbon and Coke left in the bottom of the glass, which she reached for and quickly drank.

Reculver rose slowly. He plopped a large fedora on his head. It was beautifully made, sleek, with a purple ribbon around its crown. He looked like a psychedelic gangster from an alternative 1950s. He nodded to Shona, and smiled, and then departed largely, and deliberately, like a tanker exiting a tight strait.

Shona waited, checking her phone for anything from her father—nothing.

She knew she would have to travel to Ullathorne. As

she exchanged texts with Viv, arranging where to meet, she wondered whether her friend knew about Merrygill's fiery caravan on a shattered moor. She walked quickly through the gathering dusk, across the now dark square, along the elegant, wide George Street, to a basement café on the corner of Hanover Street. "Hangover Street," they used to call it, when the *Post* was in an office around the corner—no more.

Viv was sitting on a high stool, by the window of the café. She already had the drinks ready—a large latte for herself, an Americano for Shona. She slipped off her stool and came towards her, and they hugged. They held each other, and asked each other if they were okay. They both said they were, and, grinning, shrugged.

"You been drinking?" Viv said, sniffing exaggeratingly.

"Just a wee one. With a contact," Shona said.

"You and your contacts. Total mystery, half your sources."

"Well, they wouldn't be sources if I told everyone who they were."

"You're a big secret an' all."

Shona thanked her for the coffee and swigged it. Her blood was buzzing.

"So," Viv said, stirring her drink vigorously.

"So?" Shona said.

Viv dropped her spoon. It landed in a puddle of bubbles and cream. "The money!" she said. "Don't you want to know?"

"Yes, yes, of course," Shona said. "Tell me more . . ."

"What's up with you?"

"Dinnae fash. Carry on."

"The bank, well, they say it was an attempted deposit from a bank in the Isle of Man. Proper bank account."

Viv produced a slip of paper from her wide red purse. The blue and white paper bore the legend of her bank, and below it were details of the attempted money transfer.

"Wow," Shona said. "It's a lot of money, Vivienne."

"Tell me about it," Viv said. She threw up her hands. "The bank was asking questions. Whoever was trying to give me the money didn't have the right account number. Just my name, the sort code. So, I have to wait, or something."

Shona shivered. "Do you know who it could be?" she said, eventually.

"No, not at all," Viv said. She was gulping down her coffee like it was water. "I have no idea what it means or what is going on. I rang Mam and Dad, they have no idea either. Can't think of who it might be."

Shona shook her head, and put her hand on Viv's hand. "Jeez Louise, you've had a time," she said, softly.

It was dark outside now. Shona wanted to get home, and pack. Call Bernie, and Ranald, and make plans. But she needed to ask a question.

"Viv."

"Yes, pet."

"At the hotel the other night. You made that lovely speech."

"Thanks, love. Probably the highlight of the whole shambles. Did I tell you they're holding Dan's body, they can't contact a next of kin? For fuck's sake. I think his mam is in Ullathorne. She might not have a phone, mind you."

"That speech—your brother."

"Aye," she said, and looked out the window.

"What . . ."

"No, Shona," Viv said, an edge to her voice. Her eyes widened. "I don't want to talk about that now. Thirty years and it's still too much."

"All I mean is—as I said on the ferry back: I didn't even know you had a brother," Shona said, retracing her steps.

"He's been gone a long time," Viv said. "I thought I'd

mention him because . . . me mam was there. She doesn't travel and poor Dad . . . he . . ."

Viv's face crumpled. She began crying, and reached for a paper napkin. Shona, after a moment of hesitation, put an arm around her.

Viv sobbed for a few moments. Then she recovered. She wiped her eyes with the back of her hand. She went to the bathroom, and adjusted herself, and they talked of smaller things. Of irrelevancies, of tiny items. Viv said she was going to spend the new money on a long holiday if it ever cleared. Shona said she should buy a house. Viv shook her head—it all seemed too much, too odd, too sudden. She said Wayne was being a bit distant, and Shona bit her tongue.

On the bus home, Shona listened to a stream of electronic music, and gripped her stick as if it might float away. Immersed in the mesh of rippling arpeggios, she tried to temporarily forget what she was now determined to do.

6.

L ondon, its unending roar, the immensity of it, filled Alison's ears, parched her mouth, and drowned her heart.

The children needed to be picked up from school, and in her car the radio was full of noise about the government calling a snap general election. The prime minister was hoping to expand his majority, building on gains in the areas of England previously unknown to his party.

Alison was alone again. And stuck, again, in traffic. White buildings with fluted pillars outside their doors stood silently in the blocked street. All else was movement: the glint of a far plane indented a furrow of vapour overhead. A train thundered past, a blur of velocity, on the tatty railway bridge. There was a man on a bicycle, and a delivery man on a motorbike. The scene reminded her of an educational transport poster from her youth: all laid out in bright colours on the wall of Ullathorne Primary School—a blue sky, a clean town, all manners of transport illustrated and brightly painted. Happy people, in happy places. Two dimensional and free of pain.

Up ahead the lights turned to green, she moved forward five yards, and then the lights were red again. She thumped the steering wheel with an open hand.

She had to get to the school by 3:35 P.M. and she was running late. Her throat was thick and her eyes were itching. Her hands were wet with sweat.

Sitting in the hum of the air-conditioning in the armoured box of the car, Alison Harmire closed her eyes and thought of home. Not the house she lived in now, with two loud children and her soon to be ex-husband. Not that. But her real home, where the deep wide river ran from the fells to the dales, through the meadows and the woods, and on to the steel dark sea.

More and more, as she faced the end of her forties, with one career in business over and another career yet to be made, she dreamt of Ullathorne. Not just as a landscape for the inscrutable and absurd night adventures of the mind, but in daydreams, daydreams amid the crash and rush and battle of the city. Memories of her childhood and youth in the old stone town, by the old cold river. But then, her mind would race to her teens, and that night in the old mill, and she would be snapped back into the real. Of her loved but insatiable children, and her looming divorce and London, a centrifuge with a gravity inescapable. London made her tired of life.

Even though, and as ever and always, in the wet hills of the north the rain dripped on old rocks and old graves, and moss grew like skin on the old stone walls, and shivers of fish slept in the round bends of the old brown river.

In that moment of recollection, the lights had changed to green, and then back to red. It was 3:25 P.M. and she wasn't going to make it on time. "Fuck it," she said, and pulled the car into a space beside the road gripped by a double yellow line. She needed water.

She parked the car she hated and locked it with a flick, and walked quickly down the street. At the junction there was a newspaper shop. Her mouth was tacky and thick. The door flashed as she approached, and she caught her reflection—her body misshapen as if in water. Her hair was cut short. She wondered if she was invisible. If anyone could see her. Her dark glasses, with wide white frames, distorted her face. Her eyes were outsize, globular, as if she were some kind of sea creature. She swam into the dark store. She picked up a green glass bottle of water. There was a man at the till, buying wine, chatting to the shopkeeper.

Her phone beeped. A text from Nigel.

When I'm back we need to talk.

Nigel, in between allegedly consulting at various financial institutions she had not heard of, had been taking a lot of time off. And as well as shouting at the children, buying new trousers and taking flying lessons, he had been attempting to write a business book, with a ghost writer called Phaedra.

She shook her head involuntarily and moved forward, closer to the gossiping men. She looked at her phone. She was so late now, but she was desperate for water. She felt her temperature rising. She considered opening the bottle.

Alison was waiting by the newsstand. The UK newspaper front pages were on display, their headlines blaring like red drunk men shouting in the sun. There were European papers too. There was a tabloid paper she had not read before, with a large photo, half covered by another paper. One eye, half a nose, a closed mouth. The mouth was familiar: thin, turned down at the corners. But the eyes had it—so pale and sere.

She reached for the paper, her hands suddenly shaking.

DEATH SHOCK AT HOTEL WEDDING

On the front page was a picture of her old school friend Daniel. His face was fuzzed by the cheap paper and unkind magnification. Grey at the temples, and thinner than she remembered. But it was him. She had not seen him for years. Not since her wedding. Not long after university, before children, before the stalling of her career. Before she had said yes to Nigel Osbourne.

She held the paper, staring at it. The words swam and then stilled.

EXCLUSIVE BY JON INNES

A STUNNING BRIDE was shocked last night to have her perfect day DESTROYED by the bloody suicide of a deranged guest.

Blood

The glitzy bash at the Poet's Hotel near Dunoon in Scotland was rocked by the discovery of the body of WEIRDO Daniel Merrygill, 48, who killed himself by HURLING himself from the window of his £300-a-night luxury bedroom. TRAGIC Dan is said to have SMEARED the room with his own blood and left a shocking message before his bloody death.

Naked

STUNNED guests were horrified to find his NAKED body in the early hours, covered in tattoos of SATANIC symbols. GORGEOUS media secretary Vivien Banks, 44, was forced to cancel the wedding to handsome COPPER boyfriend Wayne Provan after the discovery of TWISTED Daniel in the early hours of the morning by shocked guests at the deluxe hotel in Scotland's romantic Highlands.

Alison put her hand to her mouth.

Glass moved in her hand. She dropped the bottle, and it hit the floor, but did not smash. It rolled under the newsstand and lay glinting in the shadows cast by the papers, the water inside glaring like an eye staring from the past.

7.

I t was the morning after the orgy.

Gary Watson MP was woken by his phone buzzing on the floor. It vibrated and moved on a bed of silvery ripped condom wrappers glinting in the morning light.

He was naked. Alyce, beside him, was also stirring, the light gleaming on her bare legs and feet, the rest of her body covered in a pale silk sheet. On the side table, there were empty plastic baggies, caked with white powder, their edges gleaming. Other powders and small sprays of crystals lay, scratched and in mounds, on surfaces across the room. Empty bottles had been stacked by the door by someone. A large tube of lubricant lay on the floor, squeezed into two like a fat link sausage.

Watson pushed himself up. He had a message from his private secretary, Knott:

PM TO CALL GE BE READY

He raised his plucked eyebrows, scratched his tingling shaved balls, and wiped his scorched nose.

"Well, well," he mumbled.

He was only gently surprised. A general election had been on the cards for a while. The Whips had warned him of it, and his constituency team had plans well advanced. It had been the talk of the back benches, of course. Some of his fellow northern MPs, sitting precariously on thin majorities, were nervous. But those with safe seats, like him, were looking forward to the six-week holiday until the day of the poll. He scrolled through his phone. There were similar messages from some fellow MPs. Three more from Knott, with links to emails on some mundane practical matters, now that Parliament would shortly be dissolved.

He felt the cocaine burn twinge in his nose, and sneezed. His phone buzzed again.

GET UP. PM ON WAY TO THE PALACE TO DISSOLVE PARLY

Alyce, beautiful and severe, turned over under the sheets. She did not stir. He contemplated the days and weeks ahead. The dissolution of Parliament. A month in the open air, tramping around Tyrdale, being fed lines by the special advisors, shaking hands with farmers and police, meeting small businesses, making speeches at the Party Club, a long arm around the local party chairman, repeating his well-beaten lines, being chummily interviewed by regional television and the local paper.

Watson, a mind full of jackhammers, stood up and stretched and looked about, pulling at his itchy dick. He peered down at it. There were dried clumps of blood around the stubble of his lower stomach. With a slight but passing tremble in his heart, he looked to a door to an adjoining suite. He padded slowly across to it.

He looked in. He remembered, in dim slides of memory, the exertions of the night before. The single bed had been stripped, and everything removed. A large blue bag of trash was full, tied off, ready to be disposed of. An arc of black blood sprayed across the mirrored cupboard. Watson saw flickering tessellated clouds of blue and yellow lights at the corners of his eyes—the drugs were wearing off. He walked unsteadily back, back across the master bedroom, to the bathroom.

It was all marble and silver, and a painful, icy clear light. There was a woman sloshing in a full warm bath. She was lying with her head back, in the bubbling water. The tidal plane of water tipped as she moved. Her eyes widened as he shuffled in. She was middle-aged, her hair cut short. He didn't remember her. She had a collar around her neck.

He stood before a large mirror, shrouded by condensation. He wiped his hand over it—behind the mist was his face, pale and open. His eyes were dark. He had encrusted dark powder or something else around his upper lip, which he wiped off.

Under his left breast there was a black, neat tattoo, with depictions of the sun and the moon, letters, and numbers. The sun, with a circlet of flames. The moon, radiating dotted lines of glow.

"How do," he said to the woman, who was now washing herself with a large orange sponge. He ambled to the loo and unfurled from a distance a lengthy arc of orange piss.

"Bonjour," she said woozily.

He smiled as he drained himself.

People were stirring—the remnants, those who had been overwhelmed by drink, pills, or otherwise. Men from business and politics, the media and security services, were pulling on clothes, drinking water, checking their phones. An editor of a national newspaper was being unclipped from his restraining gear. Among the paid participants, and those drafted in, there had been some enthusiastic swingers from the Newcastle suburbs, happily filming themselves stolidly rutting in various lubricated combinations.

Watson wandered back into the bedroom. He put a hand on Alyce's side—still warm, still breathing. He touched her side, and pulled back her shroud, and she opened her eyes suddenly. They were violet.

It was not Alyce at all. It was another woman. He did not remember seeing her before.

"Hi," she said.

Watson looked surprised for a fleeting moment. Then his face aligned. "Here, you from Bulgaria?"

"What?"

"You the lass from Bulgaria?"

"No, Spennymoor."

"Spennymoor? What—down the road?"

"Is there another one? What time is it?"

"What time is it? Time for you to toddle off, pet."

"Oh, fuck off, will ya," she said. She rolled over with a sigh. She made a clicking noise with her lips. "You fucking people," she muttered, and pulled the sheet over her head.

Watson pulled on a bathrobe and moved to the window. The cold morning light was clear on the fields outside, and on the stone balustrade above the gardens, the carved lips of the fountain. Mist was rising from the stands of trees. The Palladian villa, secluded in the west Durham hills, belonged to one of his wealthiest funders. It was hidden by a half mile of woods from the moving eyes of the A66, and squatted like a stone toad at the end of a long, winding drive.

He knew he had to leave, to go back to his constituency house near Ullathorne, to begin his campaign. "To take the right path," he said. The windowpane was cold against his warm fingers.

The woman in the bed was now getting up, and pulling her hair away from her eyes. She looked at him impassively, and then walked slowly into the bathroom.

He reached for his phone and called a restricted number. Raymond's number. Waiting for the phone to be picked up, Watson looked around the room. Damp towels lay in a pile by the fireplace.

The phone was picked up.

"Gary," an elderly man's voice said.

Watson's heart picked up its beat. Raymond's voice was a blade of black ice. They had never met. Watson did not want to meet him—he was outmatched.

Raymond ran the project to see certain MPs chosen, elected, and protected. Watson took him seriously.

"Morning," Watson said. "That's the starting pistol sounded. Kickoff."

"I know," Raymond said, cold as a wall.

"So, the fat man has sung and wants to increase his majority. So off we go. It'll be a doddle."

"He wants Sally to run, too," Raymond said, with no emotion.

Watson winced.

"Sally . . . ?"

"His wife, Gary. The prime minister's wife. He wants her to run. In a safe seat."

"Nice," he said. "What a pretty picture that will be."

"He wants her to succeed him."

"To suck his seed? I think she has done that already," Watson said.

There was silence.

"Excuse my humour," Watson murmured.

"Are you all set in Tyrdale?"

He blew out a sigh.

"Yes, all ready to go. Been on it for months, haven't we. Knott has his plans. A consultant . . . you know Alyce . . . has been working on the social media campaign with her team. But you know the drill. I will be present and available in Ullathorne for six weeks. Meet the Women's Institute, the business group, the Young Farmers. Pose pretty. Certain things will have to be done. I'm there now, actually, funny you called—just getting the house out of mothballs."

"Knott there?"

"Yep, present and correct."

"I might visit."

Watson closed his eyes, as if in pain.

"Is Alyce with you?" Raymond asked.

"No, she's not."

"Gary?"

"Yes?"

"Remember our chat out in Bayreuth?"

"How could I forget."

"If there's any more mess . . . or potential mess . . ."

"There won't be."

"We don't want another Margate, do we? Another shambles. We can't do another Kent. These events strain our capacity."

The phone line became very quiet. Watson heard Raymond's breath.

"Raymond—come on now," Watson said, chuckling as much as he could. "That was a different kettle of . . . and that's my wife you are talking about now."

Raymond snorted. "We monitor your interests. But fuck it up again, and we'll have to think on it," he said, and the line went dead.

There was a sudden thump and crash somewhere else in the house. A tinkling noise of settling broken glass. Watson dressed quickly—shirt, suit, jacket—and left the room. The doors on the landing were open, and a trickle of people were leaving. A naked man with a leather jacket over his shoulder exited a room. Watson passed a room with the door slightly open and a slapping noise within. He looked in.

Three naked people were entwined, steadily fucking on a distressed bed. One of them was filming it all on his mobile phone. Glaring above its tiny fierce spotlight, the tall, bald man, another MP from his party, looked demented.

Watson nodded to him with a smile. On the stairwell, he stepped over a sleeping big man, his shoulders as hairy as a badger.

He called Knott on his phone, but there was no answer.

The main room of the house was being cleaned. Two women were tipping trash into large black bin liners. Empty bottles were being put into some large plastic cartons. A heap of clothes was gathered by the ripped sofa. A rotating platform was being dismantled. A pair of ripped boxer shorts were hanging like a skinned face from the black glass chandelier.

A stocky figure rolled into view, emerging from the door to the kitchen. It was Knott.

"Knott—fuck's sake. Answer me when I call," Watson said.

"I've just arrived," Knott said, unmoved. He held up his phone.

"Did you get my message?"

"Yes," Watson said. "Have you seen Alyce?"

"Alyce? She left last night," Knott said, wiping his hands.

"Did she?"

"Yes. Around one A.M., when I did. You said goodbye to her."

Watson didn't remember. "Oh, yes, of course," he said.

"I will follow, I need to make some calls," Knott said.

"No—I need a driver," Watson said, and clicked his fingers.

Knott stared for a moment, and then nodded.

Watson walked away, his footsteps silent like a cat on the thick white carpet. In the long mirrored hallway, a cleaner was swabbing the tiled floor. A young woman in a large puffer jacket, red tights and high heels was weeping on the shoulder of another.

He paced quickly through the austere beauty of the surrounding parkland. Knott crunched behind, murmuring into his phone.

The world was asleep. The fields were flat and empty. A diffuse scramble of birds rose suddenly from the high, leafless trees.

Watson checked the news on his phone: stories about hospitals and Brexit, football, and some celebrity or other. He looked at the news in Wales: nothing. He flipped to the Scottish section, and stopped.

DEATH AT WEDDING IN ARGYLL
PA Reporter

Police have said there are no suspicious circumstances around the death of a guest at a wedding at a hotel near Dunoon.

The naked body of Daniel Merrygill, 49, was found on the hotel grounds in the early hours.

It is believed he had taken his own life.

A guest at the wedding said that Merrygill, a civil servant, had written a message in his own blood on the hotel wall.

The 48-year-old was found naked, eyewitnesses say, his body found in the early hours of this morning.

"It was a horrible thing to have at what would have been a beautiful wedding," the source said. "We were all partying and then the body landed in the garden. I recognised him, he was part of the wedding party. He was naked and covered in tattoos, all letters, and numbers, like a Ouija board. It's clear he was dead from the fall. I pity the bride, that's her big day ruined. How can you get over that?"

A spokesman for the Poet's Hotel, Argyll and Bute, declined to comment.

The wedding, of a Ms. Vivienne Banks and Mr. Wayne Provan, has been cancelled and police have ruled out any further investigations in the case.

People walked past him as he stared at his phone. A woman giggled as she carried her shoes. A man spoke in Russian.

Watson was frozen. He shook his head.

"Sir?" Knott said, stopping beside Watson. His breath was silver in the air.

"Where is Bax?" Watson said, eventually.

"At Scar Top. I assume."

Scar Top was the Watson home in the Tyrdale valley.

"You know, we should start thinking about Bax's responsibilities. His capacity," Knott said. "He takes on a lot for you. For us. How much do you pay him?"

"I don't. But he's a soldier, he can take it. He's loyal. But where the fuck is he? I need to speak to him."

"I'll give him a call," Knott said. "Now the big game is afoot."

"Can you let him know I need a word, urgently?"

Knott sighed and checked his watch.

"I will," Knott said. "What is this urgency?"

Watson shook his head.

"Let's get out of here."

In the car park, hidden behind frosted topiary, they found Knott's large dark car.

Watson slumped in the back. The car hummed to life.

He looked out the windows as the woods began to move past.

"Did Raymond call?" Knott said, impassively.

Watson nodded, and closed his eyes. The glass moved in his mind. Gliding over words, over combinations and paths, tracing its own occult parabola.

Words could not be unsaid, and sights could not be unseen. But he had to take the right path, as Sorley said. As Sorley always said. Right, and right, and right again. And the right path led to Ullathorne.

As Knott hit the main road, Watson opened his eyes, and phoned Alyce.

The phone made a strange beeping noise. He took it from his ear and looked at it. The beeping continued.

"I'm sorry. This number is no longer available," a metallic voice said, as cold as the dead.

8.

It was three in the morning, and again Shona could not sleep. The streetlamp's corona glimmered around the edges of her window. A faint glow on the wall, cast by a tiny light on her charging laptop, pulsed weakly. Dim lights, small lights, all faint in the dark.

She could check on her father, who was being released from hospital in the morning. But she could not constantly check on him.

She sat up, her long black T-shirt draped over her knees. She felt alone. She felt alone because she was alone. The world outside was vast and hostile, and here, this place of safety, was changing. It was drifting, untethered. The walls about her suddenly seemed to be cardboard, paper— temporary. Her father, probably safe now, and warm and dreaming of gardens and skies—temporarily. One day, he would be gone. And then—what?

"Fuck's sake," she said.

She stood up and rubbed her face and felt her side. Moving to the window, she pulled aside a blind. Nothing out there amid the parked cars. A stilled ice cream van. The short strip of shops was closed and shuttered. The sick yellow light of the sleeping city tainted the sad heavy clouds, like cotton wool soaked in piss.

There was a sudden loping movement. A fox, russet and sleek, snuffled in the street. Lit dimly by the electric lights, it was alert and driven. It bobbed and slinked between two hedges, and was gone.

Shona thought of her mother. Long gone, now. Dead in her youth. Her father weeping, and a dark church, filled with more weeping. What could she remember of her? Just an uncertain smile, and reddened eyes looking down from a metal hospital bed. No grave. Her ashes, cast by her father, somewhere in the hills. Shona pushed it all away, as she had always done. She turned around. There was another movement in her room.

MacDiarmid leapt onto her bed, and yawned, and then in a sleek instant formed a neat furry circle in the heat of the sheet. Shona sat beside her and ruffled with a finger the short hair around her cheek. MacDiarmid leaned into her, rubbing Shona's fingers with a heavy head, her eyes half closed. She began to purr, the tip of her tail twitching.

"Dopey cat," Shona whispered.

She lay beside the humming feline, and looked to her side table—there were two folded papers from Reculver. One was an interview with Gary Watson MP. She reached for it and flicked on the side lamp, which flung sudden shadows across her room. The corners retreated. The furniture gained edges, surfaces, weight, and mass.

"What's this fucking nonsense, then," she said, to herself, unfolding the paper.

It was a printout of a short online interview with the *Northern Recorder*, a mass-market tabloid in northeastern England. There was a large picture of Watson. He had shaved the sides of his hair, and his longer hair on top had been swept into a kind of quiff.

He beamed from the page, teeth white and straight, his tie knotted tight, his neck and shoulders gym-toned, his skin unmarked by age or illness. His clothes were new and immaculate. His eyes gleamed.

Westminster Focus: Question Time with Tyrdale MP Gary Watson

The outspoken MP talks to Northern Recorder's political editor Paul Tankard.

How you doing, Gary?

Never been better, Paul. You call me in my office in Westminster; been a busy day doing the people's work. A few key votes, but as I said to the PM from the stage of the Tyrdale vote—you'll never need the Whips to speak to me. I'm fully on board with the project. Blood, sweat, and tears: that's what I am prepared to give. But today's been a good day, we won the votes handily—so it always feels that way when you know you have taken the right path. But as I always say, any day spent outside Tyrdale is not a perfect day— looking forward to racing back up for constituency work in the recess. Can't get home soon enough.

What are the key priorities for the year ahead, Gary?

There's many—fulfilling our manifesto must be the main commitment: we put in that document many promises, many pledges, which we have to see through. We must honour those. So, there's migration reform—hopefully we'll see the back of that. There's the Safe Seas Charter for protecting the south coast from refugees—very close to my head and my heart, as you know. There's the Constitution Act to protect the Union, unravel the error of devolution, and bring back some measure of sensible control back to the centre. The major free trade deal with the nuclear powers. And, of course, I'll be fighting for the Tyrdale people: especially traditional families: protecting them from others who may do them harm, restoring their faith in nation and honour, and ensuring their healthy, decent numbers grow. But there is no time. We have to work for it—to strive, to fight and to win.

You're a Tyrdale lad—is your voice heard in Westminster?

I am indeed, and proud of it. I've always said my vision for the nation starts on the banks of the Tyr and the generations my own family have spent in and around the dale. It's in your blood, that soil. My childhood in those vales was idyllic.

From the Pennines you can see for miles—and I've always said you can see the future of Great Britain from there. As you know there's a cadre of northern MPs now, and we have the Say Yes to North group at Westminster. Some say I am their leader, which is very kind. I am the chair of the group in Parliament. I wouldn't say we are acknowledged as a major force as yet, but the PM knows we are there, and to be fair to him, he spends time with us and knows what we're all about. He is sound that way. I think he's smashing it, despite the doubters and the weaklings.

You're a back bench MP right now—what are your ambitions for higher office?

We all have ambitions, Paul: didn't you always strive to be at the top of your game? I'm no different—I am ready to serve King and Country in any way that the PM sees fit. If a role of duty was to be offered to

me, I would put my all into it. But first and fore-
most, my ambitions are for this country—to be a
lean, mean machine of a modern country with
an empire of opportunity behind it and ahead of
it. A great, strong, unashamed nation—tough as
teak with both feet set in the glories of our past
and our blue eyes set fearlessly on the time when
tomorrow comes.

How do you relax, Gary?
To be brutally honest, Paul, I try not to. Since my
wife, Sarah, passed, I mash the sixteen-hour work
days, wherever I am. That's how I was brought
up and that's what I expect of myself. I expect
and demand rigour and discipline within myself,
and thus, Paul, those around me. I do like to read
when I can—mainly the Romans, the Greeks. Big
fan of the Stoics. Look them up. Top advice. And
I like to listen to audiobooks on my train journey
north—innovative business theory, mainly, and a
spot of modern hard rock when I need a lift. I slap
on some of the heavy stuff when I'm cracking on
with the irons. I like gyms. But you would know
that if you've seen me!

Thanks, Gary.
Over and out. Got to crack on. See you round the
'dale.

"Fuck's sake," Shona said, shaking her head.

The cat opened her eyes and mewed. Tiny teeth gleamed in a pink mouth. She trilled. It seemed as loud as a roar in the night.

"Shut up, fatty," Shona whispered, and dropped the paper onto the floor, flicked off the lamp and closed her eyes again in the restored darkness.

She needed to sleep, even if, at its end, she would have to endure waking up again.

9.

There was a lot to do and a train to catch. Shona needed to pack.

Her father was now home, watching TV, slumped in his corduroys. Bernie was there, too, bashing pots in the kitchen and loudly singing an old folk song. Shona, holding her half-empty travel bag, raised a theatrical eyebrow to her father as Bernie ululated.

Hugh Sandison had shaved off his beard. It made him look older, his jowls pink and tender, and he had a small white scar on his chin she had not noticed before. He acknowledged his daughter's mild display of sass with open hands.

"She has a fine voice, Shona," he said. "What can I say?"

Shona was kneeling on the carpet in their living room, trying to extract her laptop charger from a complicated mass of cables that coiled in and around a table leg.

"Well, she has *a* voice," she said. "You're right there."

"Aye, well, young lady," he huffed. "As I see it, you're buggering off to that England chasing some story. Ms. Comfort, on the other hand, is volunteering to look after this old man while he ails in his dotage, so I think I can bear an old folk song now and again."

Bernie bashed pots and sang "Hares on the Mountain." Shona pulled angrily at a white cable, which only made a loose tangle into a fast knot. There was a large pair of grey headphones attached to a plug socket, charging.

"Are these Bernie's?" she said, pointing to them.

"No, she bought them for me, to listen to my music," he said. "Grand, aren't they?"

Shona nodded briefly, and yanked forlornly at her charger cable.

"For fuck's sake," she muttered. "This is a fucking snake's wedding."

"Your language, my love, is still abominable," her father said, smiling. "You wouldn't catch me using rough words in that manner."

"Dad, you called that Henry at the allotment an 'arrogant cunt' a wee while ago, so," she said.

"That was a factual observation. I've heard enough about his onions. He was saying my patch is getting too messy, out of control. The cheek of it."

"Is it?"

He shook his head. Then, reluctantly, he nodded. "But maybe there's some benefit to having the bugs and insects in the long weeds. I hope."

"Didn't you say there's a load of junk equipment to get rid of?"

"There is, but it's none of Henry's beeswax. Snob. You should see the nick of his shed: solar panels! Cunt."

Bernie was trilling away in the kitchen. She sounded happy.

Shona looked to her father. His eyes were watery. His ears seemed larger. "Well, maybe you were slowing down with the gardening because you weren't feeling too good, and—"

"Mind yourself," he interrupted. "I haven't been slowing down. My allotment just needs a wee tidy-up. A bit of moving things about. Bernie will help me."

Shona took a deep breath, and finally freed the offending cable, which swung heavily in her hand. "Thank fuck," she said.

"Anyway—when's your train, and when you back again?" her father said, sounding tired, looking to the TV.

"There's one every hour," she said, pushing away a stray

lock of hair. "And I'll be back in a few days. Got a place to stay in the town. Ranald wants a news feature—if there's a story there."

"Ah—so you've been commissioned?" he said, with a sudden burst of informed interest. Hugh had been a journalist in his day. Decades at the *Herald*, including a decade as night editor, and a few before that in local press in Fife. He often said he had printer's ink under his fingernails. He knew the trade, inside and out.

"Yep. Ranald wants it sooner rather than later," Shona said, noticing the change in his mood.

"Can you rustle up the tale in a week?"

"I'll bloody have to, won't I?" she said, jamming a pair of drying black and silver socks into her bag. "And let's face it, Dad," she added, rolling a top and sliding it down the side of her belongings, "we're bloody skint."

"Need the cash," he said, nodding. "That's no lie."

Shona was running late. She bent over and stroked MacDiarmid, who was lying regally on a bill from the council, which had been dropped on the carpet. MacDiarmid evidently thought it was her new bed. The cat slowly blinked, unimpressed.

"So, it will be one of those human-interest tales? Because in my experience, love," her father went on, "the story behind a suicide is not often dramatic or of interest to other people. Sad, tragic, devastating to the family, but not of interest to readers of the papers. We used to avoid them, back in the day. Not in the public interest. The public might be interested, but that's different, you know."

Shona knew this—which irritated her—but knew there was more to this story. The messages, the stones, the burning caravan, the money appearing in Viv's bank account. There was something else. Beyond her ken. But not for long.

"So, what's your plan?" her dad asked. His eyes were back on the snooker. Perfect coloured globes clinked politely on an enclosed jade lawn.

"I'm meeting one of Ranald's freelance snappers at Darlington station," she said, "and going to the caravan place, then he's dropping me at Ullathorne. So, I'll be on my phone the whole time. If I need to turn around and come back, I can do—okay?"

She zipped her bag, and rested it on the table, and knelt beside her father.

His eyes moved from the screen to hers. His eyes were pink at the edges, watery. His newly revealed skin was tender. He put a slow hand to her face. His fingers trembled on her skin. "Best of luck, my love," he said, softly. "I'm fine. Don't you worry about me. Get the story. But come back soon now."

"I will, Da," she said, and kissed him on his forehead. He smelled of soap and coffee. His skin moved under her lips.

He raised a hand, and with a tender finger moved a lock of hair from her eye and placed it behind her ear.

"I'm in need of a haircut badly," she said, smiling.

"Looks like someone has already done it badly," he said.

"Dad."

"Off you go. Get the story," he said, winking, "and haste ye back."

She stood, and kissed him again, but could not say goodbye.

"Bernie!" she called to the kitchen, as she rushed to her room to grab her mobile phone.

Bernie stopped singing for a moment. "Yes, my dear?" she yelled.

"Don't let Dad cook," Shona shouted. "And don't let him on that allotment."

"Shona?" Bernie called back, and Shona heard footsteps, and her father loudly complaining.

Bernie appeared in the frame of her bedroom door. At the end of her short arms were pink rubber gloves. "Are you in charge of the shopping around here, Shona?" she said, quietly.

"Yeah, why?" Shona said, grabbing her phone from the side table of her bed.

"It's just I've been going through the cupboard and there's a lot of out-of-date food there. There's some tins well past their sell-by date," Bernie said.

She had an oval face and deep brown eyes. Her long grey hair was held back by a tortoiseshell clasp. She looked as if she held something profound, maybe ecumenical, in her small busy body.

"Well, you'd know about being past sell-by dates," Shona said, rapidly opening her bag again and throwing in her phone charger.

Bernie blinked heavily and carried on.

"I mean there's a tin of tuna there that will shortly be expecting a telegram from the king," she said.

"Laldy!" Shona said, looking for her tiny white earphones, which she found under a half-read book.

"And Shona, my dear," Bernie said, producing a wooden bowl of fruit from behind her back, "you don't rotate your fruit. The fruit at the bottom was rotten. You should make sure the older fruit is at the top. The new fruit is put at the bottom. So that everything is eaten in its right time. You need to rotate your limes."

"Rotate my limes," Shona said, struggling with a zip.

"Yes. I don't think Hugh has the energy to rotate the limes. I hope you don't mind, but I will do a wee stock take, a little bit of an update on your larder essentials," Bernie said.

Shona zipped the bag again, looked up and smiled as broadly as she could manage. "Sure. Knock yourself out. See you later—oh, and Bernie?"

"Yes?"

"Don't eat that tuna."

Within the hour Shona was on the train south from Edinburgh. She was on the King's Cross train. It would pass through Newcastle and Durham before stopping at Darlington. It was a weekday afternoon and the carriages were not busy. No one else sat at her table, and she watched with a surprising sense of alarm as Waverley station and then the outskirts of Edinburgh slipped away. She texted Bernie, and said for her to call if anything changed.

A message—*Don't worry he is fine fast asleep after big brunch*—came back immediately.

She plugged in her laptop and watched the landscape pass by for a while. There were fields and low hills, and then suddenly on the left, the grey sea, a plain of steel to the horizon. The waves were engraved, barely moving, with light on them in fine lines, like tiny wires.

After a time, Shona texted the photographer who was to pick her up at Darlington. Shona did not drive anymore. She just could not face the stress of being behind the wheel of a car again. Her left side ached just to ponder it. The photographer set up by Ranald was called Terry Green. She texted him a message to check everything was okay—but there was no response. She opened her laptop and logged on to the internet via a hotspot on her phone.

She had put it off, but she began to search for what she could find on Andrew Banks, Viv's brother. There were some businessmen of that name. But she could not find an Andrew Banks related to Ullathorne. Screeds of useless web pages scrolled before her. A sinking sea of digital sand.

Tyrdale's local newspaper, the *Tyrdale Times*, came out every Wednesday. It had an old gothic masthead, and still carried news from cattle marts and animal auctions. It had a clear and frequently updated website. For an independent local newspaper, she thought, it wasn't all that bad. A former colleague of hers, John Fallon, had worked on it, many years ago. He had been features editor at the *Glasgow Mercury* when she had been a junior reporter. That had been the first broadsheet she had worked on—now it was nothing but a website. A ghost. Fallon was long gone, his whisky-poisoned body found on a bleak scrag of island in Loch Lomond. Another body, another face, another needle of pain pricking from the past.

As the train neared Newcastle, she looked at the *Tyrdale Times* archive online. There was nothing for Andrew Banks. There were many pictures of Ullathorne. It was unchanging: two wide main streets, a market cross marked by a conical roof, large stone houses with square windows. Cobbles and lanes. A ruined castle on a cliff, and below, the river Tyr. In the background of every photo in the paper—be it a story from the market or a football match, a factory opening or random rural vandalism—there were the dark stands of trees, and the distant moors.

The online archive only went back to 1999, for some reason. She shook her head and slapped the laptop shut. Newcastle went by, its broad river and bridge-spanned quayside reminding her of Glasgow, and next the train passed Durham, with its castle and cathedral on their hill. The old strongholds stood still, the modern world swimming about them. Shona remembered reading how Scottish prisoners had been held in Durham Cathedral, back in some pointless bloody war, many years ago.

She was in England now. Scotland and its concerns were another country. She was a stranger now—people would notice her Glasgow accent. She wondered what it might conjure for them.

The accents of the other passengers on the train changed with each stop. Looking for their seats, they spoke in flat vowels, the arrested roll and clipped restraint of the north of England. Outside, there were streets of red brick, lifeless business parks, large fields brown and dull green, glimpses of motorways. And in the distance, to the east, the distant dark hills—the spine of England, the Pennines. Vast clouds moved across the bare moors in drifting inky shadows.

Somewhere in those eye-blue folds, the river Tyr ran from its source as a stream over cold moorland rocks, down through a green rich dale and then disappeared, ancient and deep and slow, into the swallowing sea.

Somewhere in that crease of country, there were old rules, and old secrets, and maybe old reasons why people now were doing strange and violent things—why a man might throw himself to his death from the roof of a hotel. Why he might suddenly destroy his life, and carry messages, rhymes, and legends on his body.

Out of a red plastic wallet she took a front page, ripped from the *Record,* with Merrygill's wide white face over the story of his death. His eyes like dried-up puddles on a sunless day. Lips as thin as hair. His face was a mask over something awful—or nothing, nothing at all. Just emptiness, a life wasted, and at the end, a short burst of needless pain, and hot, pooling blood.

Darlington arrived. A steeple rose above a grey town huddled on dreary flat land, and as Shona wearily descended from the train, her stick smacking on the receding door, cold air slapped her face, and the platform stank of piss.

10.

Preparations were being made for the coming election. But Watson had slipped out, into the wild.

He had taken his sleek silver motor, and driven quickly to the rendezvous. He had to be back in time for an online meeting with the Say Yes to North group of MPs. They would be talking about strategy, joint hustings during the run-up to the election, and discussing the latest press lines from the special advisors in central office. Watson wanted to reemphasise the grip of his leadership. The PM knew he led the cadre. And after election day, he would impress on the Whips how influential he now was: twice elected, he would be. In the media, and in the Commons, he would be the voice of the wall of northern MPs who held seats from Wallsend to Carlisle. He would be a Carl himself. A king, or at least, a kingmaker. He already was vice-chair of the Intelligence and Security Committee; more power would follow.

He drove quickly through the gathering gloom of the wintry afternoon. Silver flashed in the still puddles beside the quiet country road. Shadows grew in the tangled hedges. His stomach was tight, his shoulders were hunched.

Up ahead, on the low glacial hills of the lower dale, stood the standing stones. Out of sight, high above the river, clear above the tree line. He had never received messages from Sorley here, but he thought he should, one day. The signal would be strong, a granite receiver—stone circles being, he had read, the primeval Ouija boards of the rock-inhabiting dead.

The darkening, rising fields blurred past: first the low

winter grass, streaked with brown and lush ochre mushrooms, then the dead stubble, then the trampled mud, then thistles, peat and rocks. He reached the empty car park, switched off the engine, and slid out from his seat. The lights of his car drifted into nothing. He pulled up his collar, pulled on a black beanie, and walked quickly past the information sign.

Shoes crunching, he made his way up the steep gravel path, the smell of pine and mud around him. Tall conifers ringed the bare hill like a tonsure. No one knew how old these stones were. They stood jagged like the torn nails of an embedded giant's hand.

He stopped halfway up. A figure was moving in the vacancies of the stone circle. Above the sky had become soaked in the shadows of the void. Blue turned to black. Cold stars glittering. The sun would set, soon. He looked back, to the west—the sky was a sick yellow.

Bax could wait. He reached inside his jacket. There was a gramme of cocaine in an old camera film case. He chalked a line out onto his shaking hand and snorted it violently. Stars and a shiver, like the thinning tines of a splintered orgasm, surged around his face and eyes.

He shook his head, and leapt up the remaining steps, to the head of the hill.

Bax appeared from behind a standing stone, as if stepping out of it. A former soldier, bearded and all in black, he was all ligaments, quick twitch and clenched bodily potential. He had been with Watson for the last few years, appointed to him by Raymond as an aide, a bodyguard when needed. A fetcher, a carrier, a booker, an office clerk, a cleaner.

"Sir," Bax said, nodding.

Nine stones stood in the wide circle. They stood straight, wider at their crests than their roots. Three more stood athwart, uneven, spattered with lichen. In the centre, like the pupil of an eye, a low stone was slumped. It was on a tipped plane, like a table chopped of half its legs.

The river's valley was wide below them. The path of the Tyr was wide here, and slow. Trees hugged its edges. The bruise-blue distant high hills had already become one with the falling night, and disappeared.

"Election," Bax said.

"Yes, all ready to kick off. PM's going to the country. You ready?" Watson said, sniffing. The inside of his nose was aflame with chemical embers.

"Of course," Bax said, nodding.

"Where've you been?" Watson asked. He moved to the central stone, and sat on it. He ushered Bax close to him, with a swift undulation of his fingers.

"Brussels," Bax said, and shrugged.

"For Raymond?"

Bax walked slowly towards him, and nodded. "I'm back now," he said, smiling his lopsided grin. His beard was neatly trimmed about his neck and lips. His teeth were even, gleaming.

Watson plunged his hands into the pockets of his thick black jacket. "Well, Bax, we have some urgent business."

"Always do, boss," Bax said.

"I read somewhere—a good operator like you is like a good poisoner: anonymous. A bad one becomes famous. Look—I have something a little different to your normal kind of job, Bax. It's a bit of a tricky one. A delicate matter."

Watson took out his phone, and brought up a note on its screen. He tapped the screen, and the note was sent to Bax. Watson deleted it.

Bax's phone buzzed, and he peered at it. Its blue light was gentle on his hard face. "What's this?"

"Last weekend, that fellow at the top of the list—he

fucking died," Watson said, quietly and evenly. But no one else could hear. Only a hawk spiralling above in the last thermals of the short day. A breeze rose and fell. The short grass ruffled and settled.

Bax nodded.

"Topped himself, like a twat. Those other people, they knew him—and knew me," Watson said.

"Knew?"

"Know," Watson said, tilting his head.

Bax waited.

"This is the thing. This is the urgent thing, Bax. They cannot be troublesome to me now. Not in the coming weeks."

Watson sniffed and rubbed his hands together. From the stone circle, he could see the whole valley. He had read, somewhere, that you could trace a straight line between the waterfall at the top of the dale, through the old Coine Tree, to this hill. An eldritch geometry. He shook his head. No. A swell of black anxiety and anger rose through his chest, like acid, like ichor.

"Look, this loser has gone and done it around people who might know me. And he's gone and done it with my fucking tattoo on his chest. Mine. He's gone and stolen it from me. And Sorley. From me and Sorley."

Bax looked to him, lines between his eyes. "Does Knott know?"

"No. Forget fucking Knott. Fucking outrageous, right? To do that, to me, the selfish prick," Watson said. "So, that sad little dick is one thing. That's one thing. The other is the location: the wedding. A gathering of half-wits. Someone, somewhere—they might not but we cannot risk it—might make the connection between him and me. I don't want that. We can't fucking have that."

"Right."

"Not now, not before I am elected."

"Raymond . . ."

"Raymond doesn't know about this. It's way below his pay grade. And I don't want his pals at MI6 tapping on his sarcophagus about it. All right?"

"Raymond isn't MI6 no more," Bax said, smiling his half-raised smile, with slow blinks of his grey eyes, like a resting cat.

"You don't need to tell me that," Watson said. "That list—learn it and lose it. You've got their details, right there."

"Who are they? Politicians?"

"No, worse than that. They're amateurs. They probably think they have a clue. Worthless people, Bax. Empty people. Pitiful. Losers. They're all still lying around the dale like unflushed turds, apart from Ali—apart from Alison—she's in London. I just want them to be out of my mind. For me, for us. For the future of this nation—do you understand? I need rid of this."

Watson had been slapping the stone with his hands, he realised. They were now smarting. The clean conifer air was sharp and painful in his swollen nostrils.

Bax looked at him impassively. He was now all shadow in the gloom.

"Am I important to you, Bax?" Watson said, in a low voice.

"Of course."

"How important am I?"

"Very important."

"Where we are going, you know—few Britons have been before, Bax. A new land, burnt free from the old. A cleansed slate, a revived and deloused population. We are going slowly because no one will want to see the destination right now. They won't be able to stomach it, will they? No. We inch there. The cities could burn. Redundant towns might wither away. But places like my Ullathorne—ancient, hard, safe—will prosper and survive. Thing is, we have the guts for it, and they don't. So: we win. We win."

"Yes, sir." Bax nodded, chewing his lower lip.

"But, Bax, before all that . . . I need these people to be quiet. To stop what they are doing. To not meddle. Okay?"

"Okay. Got it. Do you know what they are planning? *Are* they planning?"

Watson shook his head. His mind was full of fierce light. It was as if the acid of his stomach had risen past his throat and into his brain. His mind was now alight, ablaze. "I just can't have them all gathering together," he said, rapidly. "I can't have them laughing and giggling, laughing at me. Giggling little girls in their little lives, their tiny pathetic landfill lives—do you understand Bax, do you know what I mean here? I can't have it."

The moon was up and clear now, its scars threaded and interlinked. It seemed the only light in the sky. It was a circular doorway. It could have been an entrance into a galaxy of bone.

Watson went on. He was pointing at the air. The air between the listening stones. "Obviously that prick was trying to get at me, do you see? He was trying to put me off. To make me nervous. To put me off my game, Bax. That's my tattoo he has. It's pathetic. Outrageous, really. If I'd known I would have got you to stave his head in. But no, he goes and makes his fucking *death statement* in Scotland. But the others. We can't have the others jabbering on, blabbing to the press, now he's done this. About what they know or don't know. Understand?"

"Yes, boss. You want rid."

"Yes! I want rid." Watson gasped. "I need them to be

silent." His chest hurt—a solid, throbbing pain, like something was trying to get out of his rib cage.

"I can sort it," Bax said. He crossed his arms.

"You sure?"

"They won't get near you. They won't say owt. Is there a danger, though?"

"What danger?" Watson hissed.

"By . . . making them quiet, we make them loud. If you know what I mean."

"People go silent all the time, Bax," Watson said. "People fall by the wayside. That's just the way it is."

He clapped his hands together. Beyond the bend in the valley, the streetlights of Ullathorne were glowing. They tipped light up to the fell, to the gathering clouds.

"And you know, Bax, that Sorley has been with me from the beginning. From the very start. And he has always got it right. And he's telling me that this is what we need to do. This is the right path. And Raymond has backed me, even after . . . other things. Bumps in the road. So."

Watson reached into his jacket. There were pills in a foil twist. He took one out, and sank it. Bax looked away.

A light rain began to fall. The stones were slowly blushing black. The grass gently bent, and a freshness rose from the earth. Across the dale, sightlines shortened, distant peaks receded into grey.

Watson rubbed his thorax. The acid dipped away. Oxy-Contin breathed warm kisses.

"You can do wrong things, for the right reason, Bax," Watson said. "Wrong things for the right reasons. That's us. That's me."

"Yeah."

"We're just plain Englishmen, putting the country first."

"Yes, sir."

The stones about them seemed to move in the descended night. Swaying—their edges smearing. Watson's eyesight began to frazzle. The moon repeated, was doubled, like two owl eyes.

Watson was shaking. He needed to get back.

"I need a lift," Watson said. "I can't take the Tesla."

Bax nodded.

As he left the hill of stones, Watson looked towards the deep forest in the valley.

For one suspended moment, caught in a flare of starlight, he could see the upper branches of the great Hollow Tree, and caught in their mass and tangle, the plunging tumult of the Great Fosse. White water, hammering down in fury, held by black unyielding branches, encircled by living stones.

But no: that could not be. It was not possible. The geography, the geometry, the distance was all wrong. You could not see the Coine Tree from here. You could not see the great waterfall.

He blinked hard, and perspective and depth returned. The real world. All there was in the dale was darkness, and the drive of the valley delving into the earth. Its sides, like huge, cupped hands: a trough of hard flesh, gulping blood.

11.

Terry was driving, her eyes fixed on the road. They had left Darlington, and were heading west, into a land of small villages and whitewashed farms, and, as the hills rose, the deepening valley of Tyrdale.

Terry had turned out to be a woman. She was slim and tall, and had closely cropped white-blond hair. She had greeted Shona with a wide smile and a heavy handshake.

Her car was a mess—the back seat was home to a large black battered camera bag with multiple torn pockets and worn compartments, various items of camera equipment, a large tripod, a light, several umbrellas, discarded take-away coffee cups, fast-food wrappers, a distraught map, a pair of dirty green trainers, a couple of anoraks, and an open plastic supermarket bag which seemed to contain old clothes, and boots thick with unusual clumps of wet sand.

For a while they drove in silence, as Shona tried to find Marton's Farm on the map on her phone.

"So, star reporter, you worked for Ranald for long?" Terry said cheerily, as the road bit deeper into the hills. A broad river ran to the left of the road. The river Tyr, Shona's map said. They were sixteen miles from Ullathorne. Terry's voice was lightly accented. Shona could not place it.

"About six months," Shona said. "Can't find this farm on this bloody map."

"It's up on the moor, past Stainton, I found it earlier," Terry said. "I did a recce. No one was about. Saw the big burnt-out thing."

Shona glared at her and then looked out the window. "Did the farmer see you?"

"No one was about."

"Right."

"You from Glasgow?" Terry said, speeding up as the road straightened. The hills were higher and more wooded now. The fields were held by dry stone walls. Barns stood darkly. Feeding pens slumped in sumps of mud. In a distant field, sheep moved as one towards a gate, harried by a black dog, its mouth agape. The moors loomed like the return of a bad memory.

Shona felt the landscape briefly overwhelm her—the emptiness, the scale, the far horizons. There were no streets here to shorten perspective, no junctions and paths to cut the earth into journeys and neighbourhoods. Just a silence, and space, and hidden life behind and within the folds of the earth itself. She was far from the wrecked and gorgeous Glasgow of her youth. Far from the neat parks and languid crescents of Edinburgh.

Terry's question had been left unanswered, and Shona remembered. "Aye, Glasgow," she said at last. She gave up looking for the farm and thumped her phone back into her pocket.

"My old man is from Glasgow. Bearsden, you know it?" Terry said.

"Yeah. Dump," Shona said.

Terry burst into a short laugh. "That's not what he says."

"Yeah, I have been six months with the Buried Lede. Ranald pays my invoices on time," Shona said, attempting to change the subject.

"He does, aye," Terry said.

"He never said you were a lass, though," Shona said.

"Why should he?" Terry shrugged, and switched on the radio, which blasted out a liquid silver rope of electronic music. She flicked a look at Shona. "How long you had the stick?"

"Since I was a kid," Shona lied.

Terry raised her eyebrows. It seemed she had heard a different story. But she let it go.

They came to a roundabout near a country pub with a large black sign of a Victorian prize bull.

"Aye, it's a right here, I think," Terry said, and took the turn. The road narrowed to a B-road and headed steeply through high hedges and thorns through the foothills of the Pennines.

Shona looked into the back of the car. "Your car's a midden."

"Hah—that's what my ex always said," Terry said, and grinned. "Well, I'm a snapper. That's how it is. I need all this shit."

Shona smiled. "Right enough. Wait a second . . ."

"What?"

"So, you're Terry."

"Yeah," Terry said.

"Short for—Theresa?"

"Right. Theresa."

"So, your name is Theresa Green?"

Theresa looked to Shona, unsmiling, and then quickly nodded. "Trees are green. Funny, right? My parents are idiots."

Shona laughed. She felt something hard and tight leave her chest as she did. She felt her cheeks blush. "I'm sorry for your troubles."

"I bet."

"You know, there was a girl at my school called Iona Carr," Shona said.

"Really?"

"Nah," Shona said, smiling, looking the other way.

Terry glanced across to Shona. "Listen, Ranald said you

were stabbed back in the day. In the line of duty. Is that the reason for the stick?"

"Jesus fuck, what's with all the medical queries? Wee Ranald should keep his neb out," Shona said, irritated, tapping the top of her stick.

"Right. Of course. Look—sorry," Terry said. She held up a hand.

Shona sighed. "Aye, I was stabbed by . . . I was on a job," she murmured.

"Well, that's shite."

"Wasn't the best night of my life, but."

"But what?"

"Got the story, didn't I?"

They looked at each other briefly, and then turned their eyes to the road.

"So, you live in Darlington?" Shona said.

"Nah, not in Darlo," Terry said. "I'm in a village, Newsham. Not far from here. Do stuff for Ranald now and then, but mainly it's *Yorkshire Post, Northern Echo, Guardian*. Do some commercial stuff as well—pays the bills. No weddings, funerals or bar-mitzvahs."

"Ever been to Scotland?"

"Aye. Went to Edinburgh College of Art, didn't I? Did I not say that?"

"Ah, right. Nice."

"It was. A degree in fine art," Terry said, shaking her head. "A lot of good that did me."

The fields weren't fields now, but wide rolling acres of unfarmable land—dull marsh, hard grass, gorse and rocky hills. The sky was vast. Cold becks ran in rocky runs. There were abandoned stone buildings—houses or barns. Large buildings, holding volumes of darkness and stench. The desolate heath ran to the arc of a white horizon.

They came to a halt beside a hard, rocky, high cambered track, which bent raggedly off the main road.

"It's here," said Terry, and they turned into it, and the car bumped along the track. They rumbled over a low rise, and down, and they saw a large farm half a mile away—a central stone house, outbuildings, a concrete yard, parked tractors. But before the farm, there was a field, with a black mess near its edge amid twisted trees tortured by the moor gales.

As they slowed, the black mess became clearer—it was the burnt-out caravan. It was listing on burst, melted wheels, its sides folded in and black, and charred metal parts lay sunk in the mud and ashes and mess. It was black and ruined, and open to the sky, like a gutted metallic animal, gralloched and charred.

Terry pulled the car around so that it faced the main road. "You gonna speak to the farmer?"

Shona nodded. She left her bag on the seat and, holding her notebook out and with her Dictaphone app on her phone turned on, started to walk down the lonely road to the farm. She had taken a few steps before she felt the cold air on her skin, and the breeze across the moorland, ruffling her hair. Her feet, in trainers, walked unevenly on the road. Her stick banged on myriad tiny hard surfaces, dunting edges with worn rubber.

The farm seemed to be empty of life. There was no one in the yard. Nothing was moving. She looked back, and Terry was doing her work—photographing the remains of the caravan. She was crouching, her elbows out, the lens an extension of her hands, her eyes.

Shona reached the farm. Something flickered in her vision, and she looked up. A bird of prey swung around in circles, looking for a tiny life to kill in the land below. The moors were a dry purgatory of emptiness. A watchful desert.

"What's all this?" a deep voice said.

A man in blue overalls had appeared. He was in his late teens, fresh faced, with a large grey bucket in one of his pink hands.

"Hi, maybe you can help me—is Mr. Marton about?" Shona asked.

The youth rubbed his hair and looked behind him. The large sheds were silent. The stone house was in good order—it looked solid and clean. "Nah, he's away in town," he said. He pointed to Terry. "What's all this?"

"We're from the papers, just doing a piece on the fire," Shona said.

"*Tyrdale Times*?" the boy said, pulling at an ear. He looked down at her stick and furrowed his brow.

"No . . . we're freelance," she said. "When is Mr. Marton back?"

"He'll be a bit," he said. "I don't think he wants any of this business. I'd come back another time." He stood looking at Terry and shook his head. "Aye, I'll tell him you've been, like. Come back another time." He sucked his lower lip. He looked concerned, his cheeks blotching.

"Were you here when the fire happened?" Shona asked.

He studied his heavy fingernails.

"Did you help put it out?"

"Nah, it was all out by the time I shipped up," he said. "All out. You could see it, like. Marton had called in the engine, but he had got the foam on it from the house. Near put it out. The fella had removed the gas tank. Or it would have gone up."

"It did go up," Shona said, with a smile.

The boy kept staring at Terry.

"The fella—I hear he's died. Something like that," he said, quietly.

"That's right—what was he like?"

"Quiet."

"Would you say he kept himself to himself?" Shona said, wincing at the cliché. Hector would have laughed at her.

"Aye." He gestured to Terry. "Is she done?"

"Think so," she said. "How long was the man living here for?"

"Oh, couple of weeks. Maybe three. Mebbe a month. He went away for a bit—down south I think—then he was back. Then we heard he was in Scotland. He was no bother. Never saw him. And then the news. Marton was happy he wasn't in there when it went up, mind. Are you off now?"

"I'll be giving Mr. Marton a call," she said.

"Right, well," he said, peering again at Terry.

"Did the man have a car?" Shona asked.

"Aye—police took it. But it was scrap, even when it were working. He had a bike, too. That was probably in the fire, like."

She nodded. "What kind of bike?"

He shrugged. "Red one."

"And what's your name—so I can tell Mr. Marton you told us to piss off?" she said, lightly.

A flicker of a smile briefly played across his mouth and eyes. Then it was gone. "Tell him you spoke to Mark and I told you both to get lost," he said.

"Fine," she said.

"Mebbe . . ." he said. He scratched his nose.

"Mebbe what?"

"Mebbe you should speak to Old John," he said. "He was friendly with the fella."

"Who is Old John?"

"Old guy lives down there, on the fellside. They were always talking, like. That's him," he said—pointing past Shona with a thick finger.

She turned around. Past the burnt-out caravan, and across the lonely moor road, there was a track leading further down into the valley. Amidst a small stand of firs huddled a cottage, with dim smoke rising from it.

"Well, that's me," he said, and without a change of expression, stomped off across the concrete yard. He did not look back, and disappeared through a large door into one of the barns.

Shona walked up the track again. The sky was changing colour—high white clouds were smeared across the sky, and it felt colder. She noticed remnants of snow on the high moors, white lines across the long banks of rock.

Terry was taking general views of the area with a different lens. She was standing on a large flat rock, blotched with lichen, wincing with her spare eye. She pulled down her camera as Shona approached.

"That's me done," Terry said. "Farmer about?"

"No. I think he'd probably tell us to get fucked anyway. I'm just going to look at that house over there. There's some old dude who apparently used to speak to Merrygill."

"Oh yeah? I'm going to take some more GVs. Call me if you need me over there. Caravan was well and truly torched, wasn't it?" Terry said, tilting her camera in the direction of the pyre.

"I like it when snappers state the bloody obvious once in a while," Shona said.

"Ya what?"

"It's kind of comforting," Shona said.

"Give over," Terry said, and resumed her work.

Shona walked down the track and crossed the main road, her stick skittering on the gravel. As she neared the cottage, in a copse of twisted firs, she could see a raked slate roof, tiny windows, and a tatty fence around an overgrown garden. Outside, lopsided on the uneven track, was an old green bicycle, spattered with mud, with rust around its wheels. It had a basket attached, and inside was an open canvass bag of sooty potatoes. Out the back she saw a glimpse a pile of clapped-out machinery and white goods, a shattered caravan, and a gross peeling oil sump amid knots of high grass.

Beyond it, the watching moors rose and fell. This could be the first house of the moor, or the last.

The front door was peeling and green. There was a foggy window set in it, a diamond of blur. A glare of light suddenly fell on the house. She looked up—the sun had emerged from the high clouds. Light glittered on the door knocker: a bearded man, cast in brass. She looked closer: the beard was vines and leaves, and the eyes acorns. The knocker between his teeth was a tongue, bowed. On a board attached to the door were painted the words: THE GROVE.

She knocked on the door and, to her surprise, it boomed, hollow and deep. Her hand jumped from the metal. She looked up to the main road—but the lie of the land meant Terry, the burnt-out caravan, and the farm were all out of view. They may as well have not been there.

Shona banged the knocker again. Again, it boomed as if behind the shabby door there was a tunnel dug deep into the guts of the earth. Then she turned it, and it rotated clockwise. The door opened. A long hall was now ahead, shadowy with dim shapes of bulk and weight. The marble eyes of a dead rabbit stared at her, chilly teeth in its open dead mouth. Its body was laid, with other mounds of fur, on the top of a sideboard.

Shona moved into the hall, her feet and stick tapping on bare floorboards. There was a thick smell, a sweet soup of mould and spores. Her eyes adjusted to the gloom and began to tingle with itch. There was heavy furniture everywhere— a large wooden wardrobe, several chests of drawers, a stand filled with walking sticks, some topped with smooth brass heads of dogs and deer. Heavy coats hung from hooks, and beneath them, a glossy slop pile of waterproofs, slung on top of filthy wellies, rank with mud and slime.

"Hello?" she called. No answer. Just the ticking of a large clock, somewhere, and a wheezing noise. There were paintings on the wall: hunting scenes of men in red on horses chasing invisible foxes. There were blotchy scenes of rural disarray. There was one large portrait of a woman, pale and severe, in a high-backed chair. She was in black, with a large ruff about her throat. Her head looked decapitated, as if presented on a plate. The eyes had been scored out with a knife. There were circles of bare wall where the pupils should have been.

She looked up; the rough ceiling was stained with smoke and grime, and a flowering field of mould in dark patches, tiny black spots, scattered like acne.

Halfway down the hall, an open door exposed a room with wooden floors. She peeked in. It was an empty room, lit by a large window. But it was not quite empty. On the floorboards, in a circle, were various stones.

Shona looked at the strange arrangement. The stones had been cleaned or polished, and seemed to gleam. The circle was carefully arranged and exact. The pebbles were pale and brown, orange and grey. At the centre there was a candle, a wooden cup, and a small pile of gravel and pebbles. Leant against a plain white wall was a large mirror.

The mirror distracted her. Something was written on it in white paint, or a correction fluid. Shona looked closer. There were two shapes in the shape of empty eyes. Inches apart, five feet up the glass. Two white dots where a nose might be. Where the mouth might be, someone had written: **s o r l e y**

She heard a loud snort, or snore, and jumped.

"Hello?" she called again, less sure. She moved back into the hall. The wheezing was still there. She listened closely.

It was breathing. There was a solid propulsion to it, a pneumatic certainty.

She reached forward and pushed at the door at the end of the hall, and it moved inwards with a creak. She put her head around the edges, smile fixed, ready for human contact. She saw a small, busy, dark room. It was warm. Low flames moved slowly behind the sooty window of a stove, and heat throbbed from the squat iron.

On a small couch by the fire, covered in a woollen blanket, a large old man slept soundly. The brown couch was burst, the stuffing hanging in shags from its green seams. Across multiple deep brown wooden surfaces there was a sea of rumpled, rolled papers and open books. On either side of the stove, recessed shelves were jammed with antiquarian volumes and yet more papers, rolled and tied, folded and open.

The chaotically bearded man was bundled. He had a shock of white grey hair with tawny streaks. His lined brown face was at rest, his lower lip hanging, his mouth slightly ajar. His eyes were screwed tight, like two walnuts pushed into a warm dough. He was wearing heavy overalls and several pairs of stringy woollen socks. His hairy hands were clasped on his chest over a rifle with a wooden stock. Its metal gleamed dully.

On the floor beside him was a glass of brown liquid and a dropped book. There was a heap of chopped wood by the fire, and the contents of a box of firelighters was trailed across the floor. On a circular table, bottles of alcohol stood, many without corks or lids: wine and vodka, whisky and rum. Some had no labels and were fastened with stoppers.

The smell of damp was sweet and thick. Shona looked to the unshelved walls; there were stains rising from the floor, and down from the corners. The paint was blistered and popped, and behind the flaking paint, the exposed skin of the wall was black as a wine-stained tongue.

"John?" Shona whispered, looking intently at the dull grey gun. The man slept on, and a log gently broke and slid in the fire.

She stepped fully into the room, and her leg glanced against a pile of newspapers, which slithered to the floor and spread in a fan. The old sleeping man did not stir. She bent down to look closer at the papers: they were all old from the 1980s. She could now see the title of the book that had been dropped: *The Occult Roots of Nazism*.

Old John carried on sleeping with his gun. Shona now stood in the middle of the cramped room and wondered what to do.

She moved as quietly as she could to the bookshelves; there were many volumes in old covers, and rows in German and French. The covers were dull green and grey, heavily creased, their spines askew; some were ripped and torn, with tiny binding strings sticking out like fish bones.

One slim volume had been set, open, on the shelf, as if it was a lectern. Shona reached for it. It was titled *The Thanosophy of Stone: On the Allotment of Souls in Clay, Granite, Marble, and Sedimentary Rocks*, by a Dr. J. Kinninvie. She flicked through it. It had been published in 1989 by Kinninvie Publishing, in one edition.

The frontispiece said:

> *This Thesis and Thanosophy is both my contribution to the Study of Afterlives and the Spiritual Realms and represents a Life Work.*
>
> *It contends, supported by objective evidence and Representations from the Incarcerated Dead, that there are no human souls in any Heaven or Heavens or any Hell. It proves that, after Death, mankind's eternal Lights migrate to the Stones, Shelfs, Rocks,*

and Mantle of the Earth As It Is. In the following chapters I shall prove . . .

The man wheezed on in his deep sleep. She flicked through the book—there were depictions of rock formations, of the layers of the earth, and diagrams showing the souls of humans—depicted as small almond flames—flattening, reducing, and moving as if in flight to illustrations of various stones, rock types, and formations.

At the back of the book was a list of further books on the subject by Kinninvie: *The Distribution of Immortal Light in Igneous Rock*; *A Study Upon the Settlements of Animal and Human Child Souls in Pebbles, Gravel, and Sand*; and *Dinosaur Souls, Primal Souls, and the Movement of Continental Plates*.

By the fire, she noticed, there was a chart of some kind, tacked to board: photographs of stones, with strange markings beside each, and writing in another language. On the mantelpiece were more stones, arranged neatly in a regular line. Cold grey and deep black. Red stone and marble. Sandstone and igneous rock.

Old John wheezed on. She moved closer to him. His toes wriggled. He smelled of sweat, of unwashed flesh, of mud and alcohol. A thick, earthy, acrid scent.

She did not want to touch him, to wake him. She certainly did not want to shake him. Not with that gun in his arms. Not with his size and drunken slumber. So she moved to the windows instead, and pulled back a blind, to let the cold light fall on his face.

But Old John did not stir. The light settled in a pale line along the gun barrel. His chest rose and fell steadily. His hands remained over the gun, as if holding a pet dog. Shona thought of her father, lying somewhere. Hopefully warm and dry. In their flat in Edinburgh, clean and sane and cared for. Not alone like this, lying alone in a filthy shack on the top of a bleak moor. She wondered if Old John had anyone to care for him. She wondered how old he was. He could have been in his fifties, he could be over a hundred. He could be a body stolen from time by faeries, and left here to wheeze forever.

She suddenly decided to leave. She took her notebook from her bag, and on a page wrote down her name and contact details in capital letters, and that she wanted to talk to him about Daniel Merrygill. She gently tore it off, and slipped the paper under his drink, then stepped gingerly over the books and paper on the floor to the door. The hall was cold again.

She pushed the back door, and she was outside again. The fresh air cut away the fug of mould. There was a field of dereliction before her. A window frame and several mirrors, stacked against a wall, reflected the garden back upon itself, shimmering with shreds of displaced sky. A heap of full black bin bags slumped by the door, soft and yielding like wrapped bodies. There was a stench of mulch and bin juice and rot. The mess unnerved her. A caught plastic bag was high on a twisted tree. It flapped and snapped like a flag.

She looked once more around the back yard, before turning to go. Something was glinting in the tall weeds—a red bicycle, dropped in the mud, and surrounded by boot marks. Shona put her stick down to the earth and moved to it. Immediately her feet sunk into a patch of mud with a queasy softness. She pulled her feet with a suck out of the mud and tramped to the bicycle.

The bicycle was broken—its greasy black chain was ragged and loose, and one of its pedals was missing. There was a rime of rust around its joints. But it was red. There was a heavy black pannier attached to the back.

Shona reached down, and pulled at it. It refused to open.

"Anything in it?"

Shona jumped. Terry had appeared. She stood close to Shona, and was peering at the bag.

"What the absolute fuck?" Shona gasped.

"Hello to you too. I just followed you," Terry said, and stuck a thumb back over her shoulder. "Anything inside that shambles?"

"There's a man asleep by a fire. It must be the old man the farmer mentioned. He's surrounded by a load of weirdness."

"Shall I wake the old codger then?"

"No, he has a gun."

"A fucking gun!" Terry said, loudly.

"Shh! Jesus wept," Shona hissed. "I'm not risking it. I left a message for him. And then I found this."

"Okay, Sherlock. Well, let's not hang around. Not sure I want to surprise some old fucker with his own artillery waking up to two intruders. Especially someone radge like you."

"What?" Shona whispered fiercely.

"Let me look inside this thing," Terry said, looking around. "I wanna get out of this place."

"I think I can manage," Shona said, and tried to detach the bag from the bike. It was fastened tightly by a flap and a plastic lock.

Terry was already on her knees beside her, and her hair and warm head brushed Shona. There was a sweet scent from her, a nip of limey shower gel. They were both kneeling on the soggy grass now before the bicycle, as if praying at a shrine.

"Ach, I can't move it. It's stuck tight," Shona said.

"Not for long," Terry whispered. She reached inside her small camera bag, and pulled out a pen knife. With a fingernail she flicked out a blade.

"What you doing?" Shona said, looking about.

"I'm about to murder you," Terry said, lightly, and started cutting.

"Hurry up, then," Shona said. She looked behind her. The back door remained open. There was darkness within.

Terry sliced through the material around the lock, and pulled the bag away. "Go on, have a look."

Shona reached for the bag. "Something's inside this."

"Now who is stating the fucking obvious?" Terry said, flicking her knife shut.

It began to spot with rain—the white sky had darkened to cloud. It lay like a grey sheet over the landscape. A wind rose. They needed to move.

They both stood up, and looked back at the house. Smoke still rose from the chimney. The windows were dark. Nothing seemed to move.

"Let's get out of here," Terry said quickly, standing up.

Shona held the bag tightly.

The back fence was bent low, pushed almost horizontal by years of gales and snow. They struggled over it, and tramped over springy moor grass and heather, their trousers wet, their heads wet in the slew of light rain, back to the main road, and the car.

Shona kept looking back over her shoulder, but nothing moved in the house, or its grounds.

In the car, as they drove on the tarmac main road again, the small car filled with the smell of earth and mud and grass.

"What's in it?" Terry said. The swish of the windscreen wipers moved shadows across her face.

Shona opened the bag. It was a brand-new pannier, and, apart from its torn fastener, was intact. She opened it wide. Inside there was what looked like a lens from a pair of spectacles: a circular, convex sliver of glass. The glass was held within a plastic ring, as if it were a monocle.

There was also a large brown envelope, bloated by bubble wrap, with several new stamps on it. There was something hard inside.

"Interesting," Shona said.

"Open it then," Terry said. She had now lit a menthol cigarette, and was blowing smoke out of a slightly opened window.

"Mind the road, not my business," Shona said.

Inside the package was a small, green, boxy disposable camera.

"An instant . . . haven't seen one of those for ages," Terry said.

Shona held it, turned it over in her hand. "It hasn't been developed."

"Nope," Terry said. "Or it wouldn't be around. You turn in the whole thing to the chemist's. Or that's how it used to be."

"Can you develop these things?"

"No, it's a machine that does it. Take it to Boots," Terry said. "What condition is it in?"

"It's old," Shona said, peering at the fading packaging, the dated font and design. "But it's dry, it's not deformed."

"Old, dry, but not deformed. Sounds like Ranald," Terry said.

Shona smiled, and put the instant camera in her satchel.

Soon the car was climbing a steep slope at the edge of an old country town. There were stone buildings, old and weathered, with small windows and slate roofs. There were church spires, a blocky business park, and the drab bricks of a large modern school. The ruin of a medieval castle, with a shattered cylinder of a main tower and the remains of a craggy sheet wall, sat on a cliff over the brown slow river.

The sign on the edge of the town, as Terry slowed at a bridge, was painted clear in black on metal: ULLATHORNE.

12.

Ashley was ready to go out.

Her mother was downstairs, welcoming a new guest. She had arrived in someone else's car, and had a stick. She spoke with a strong Scottish accent and seemed to be fed up about something. The woman had asked if they had Wi-Fi, as if Ullathorne was still in the Dark Ages. Yes, we have broadband, her mother had said, far too kindly. We also have electricity and indoor toilets, Ashley thought.

Now it was six o'clock and she was meeting Amy in the Lion for a drink in twenty minutes. She had spent the afternoon reading and writing. Halfway through writing, she remembered the old football shirt she had found that morning. On the way out, she had stuffed it in the black bin liner lying on the kitchen floor—tomorrow was the day the bins would be taken away. She slinked out the house, and walked into town.

It was Folk Night at the Lion pub. Ashley liked folk music now—she had barely known it growing up. There was no folk music on her mother's radio, and none was taught or even mentioned at Ullathorne Comprehensive. It was only at university that she had heard folk-rock from the 1960s, and she had realised that "Matty Groves" had probably first been sung in Tyrdale. She had listened to a lot of the old records now, and loved Sandy Denny's voice.

There was a loss and knowledge in the old songs, she thought. The songs were both from the past, and alive in the present, and they would endure into the future, too. The old songs did not age, or rise and fail, even if societies did. They rang true, singing from a world of wounding, and loss, of those who thought themselves superior, and those who were deemed inferior, and the cruelty that flowed from such a reckoning. Much the same as now, she thought—much the same as ever.

So, it was no discomfort to sit in the cosy Lion and drink with Amy—her old friend from school, now a hairdresser who still lived and worked in the town—and listen to someone sing the old songs.

There was a sign tacked to the door to the bar: TONIGHT: FOLK NIGHT—BUNDLE OF TWINE.

Amy was already seated in a booth by the window, with drinks ready for both of them. They hugged and sat down. Amy's mam was babysitter for the night, she said excitedly.

On a low stage, at the far end of the pub, a PA hummed to life. Bundle of Twine were a small band—a singer, a guitarist, a drummer. The singer was a woman with a long dress, many bangles, and dangling earrings. Her long hair was streaked with grey. Ashley knew she had been at school with her mother—Beverley, she was called. Beverley Moore. Which was apt, as she lived on the moor.

The band began to play. The barman—shaven headed, with a large black beard, a jerkin covered in patches—pretended to put his fingers in his ears. The pub was half full; some sullen teenagers sat at a long table and a clutch of old men leaned at the bar, nodding to the rap of the drums.

Ashley was nodding to the beat and the sway of the melody and she turned to Amy, who was doing the same. They had a quick catch up between songs. Ashley was "fine, but bored," Amy was the same. The snow had been madly deep and fierce, but spring would soon come. The music stopped, and the large, heavily bearded guitarist held up his hand in apology, as he retuned. People went to the bar for more drinks.

"'Little Musgrave,'" the singer whispered into the microphone eventually, and the audience clapped. The singer wiped her wet eyes. She fanned her hands down the front of her dress.

"I'm sorry, we've had some bad news today," she said. "But it's good to sing. This one's for Dan. A little bit of 'Little Musgrave' for him. He liked this old tale."

Ashley and Amy turned to each other and shrugged. They opened a packet of crisps and listened to the old, long, sad song. After a time, the guitar ended its rhapsodic echoing chime and the singer stood away from the microphone, and the song, leaving its tragedy to stand, like a dagger in the soil. The music ended. There was a silence. Then people clapped and hollered, and the band nodded their heads, and the singer called to the bar for a pint of cider.

"That's Bundle of Twine, ladies and gentlemen," the barman whispered over a microphone, and people clapped again. "Appearing at the Dentdale Folk Festival in June! And regular here at the Lion. Now, lads and lasses, a break."

The pub was full of a hum of chat and drink. Quiet music played over speakers. A TV came on over the bar—the prime minister, talking about a new general election. It was muted, and no one was watching. Ashley and Amy began talking in earnest.

Ashley liked Amy. She was warm and didn't ask her about what happened at uni, or what her plans were, or what she was thinking about her future. Now they were laughing. Amy had said her little boy's first words had been "Dada." Amy laughed how she said to him, "Dada! What about bloody Mama! Don't you know your dada is a fucking dick? Who's feeding you, eh?"

"Classic," said Ashley.

"He never sees his bloody dada. And that's his first word?" Amy said, eyes wide, shaking her head.

The singer from Bundle of Twine stalked over from the bar and sat down at the girls' table with a loud sigh and grunt. She smiled at them both. Her eye makeup was smudged but she was smiling, a light sweat on her forehead, her hair now tied up, swept back from her face. Even sitting down, she loomed over them. She was a tall woman, big in frame and bone.

"Hi, Ashley," she said, her deep voice rolling.

"It's Beverley, isn't it? Loved the music," Ashley said.

"Aye, it were right good," Amy said.

"Thanks, loves. We're getting there. Karl is a great guitarist, isn't he? The great lummox. Anyways, look at you, what a pair of darlings," she said, and sipped from a fizzing pint of coppery cider.

"Give over," Amy said.

"Oh, to be beautiful and young again," the singer said.

Ashley laughed.

"You cracking on to us or what?" Amy said.

"Amy!" Ashley said, gasping.

"You'd be so lucky, madame!" Beverley said, and poked Amy's hand with long painted fingernails. She turned to Ashley. "Sorry to disturb, but I was wondering if you might pass a message to your mam," she said, looking to her with wide eyes.

"Sure," Ashley said.

"Just tell Peg that Beverley asks if she has heard the news about Dan. Daniel Merrygill—he's passed away. Your mam knew him, back in the day. Could you do that for me?"

"Dan Merrygill. I will do, Beverley," Ashley said. Beverley's eyes filled with tears. "I'm sorry to hear that," Ashley added.

"Just let her know. It's been a long time, and there's not many of our year left in Tyrdale now. Class of ninety-two! That's what they would say in America. God's sake," she said, looking into her pint. Bubbles flew vertically to the surface, popped, and disappeared.

"I will," Ashley said. "What happened?"

"He was an old soul, was Dan," Beverley said. "He was sensitive. To all kinds of things. So, it's no surprise, in some ways. I didn't know he was still friends with Viv and her family. He died when he was with her. But it figures. I guess they leant on each other. Supported each other. So that makes sense. I know he was only living in Darlington but he may as well have been on the moon—I hadn't seen him for years. Doubt your mother had either."

Amy had left the table. She was walking to the bar, talking on her phone.

"Who's Viv?" Ashley asked.

"Oh, sister of a friend of ours. Viv Banks. She's up in Scotland now. Her brother Andrew—you might have been told about him."

Beverley was running her finger around the pint glass now, her eyes focussed on something else, far away. Someone had lit the fire in the long grate, and flames were glittering on her jewellery, on her eyes.

"No, I don't think so," Ashley said. "That was a lovely song, earlier."

"Ach, that is a bad old song. Just like all the folk songs," Beverley said. "You know they never teach folk songs in school do they? You know why. Because they sing about the same things that are happening now. The poor people hooded and blinded. Look at that arsehole. He pretends to be on the side of the people, an' all." She was pointing now, to the prime minister on the silent TV. "Nowt's changed."

"You're right enough," Ashley said. She was nervous now, her back prickling.

"You know that song we sing? *Buck and doe, believe it*

so, a pheasant and a hare/ Were set on earth for everyone/ quite equal for to share.' There's truth in the old songs. That's why we have to keep singing them."

Amy had returned with two more drinks.

Beverley suddenly looked surprised that she was sitting where she was. She looked about her as if awakening from sleep. "I'd better get back, pet," she said. She reached across to pat Ashley's hand. "Tell yer mother about Dan, won't you, love."

She stood up and wandered off, walking solidly to the bar, her jewellery gently clanking. The huge guitarist at the bar bent gently and kissed her on the forehead.

Amy raised her eyebrows and said, "Looks like you've got yerself a new friend."

"Give over," Ashley said. "She seemed a bit upset."

"Pissed and randy, more like," Amy said. "What was she on about?"

"Have you heard of Viv Banks—Andrew Banks?"

Amy nodded. "Oh, aye," she said, and drank from her tall glass.

"What's that all about, then?" Ashley said.

"Oh, it was ages ago," Amy said. "Some local lad—he went missing. Disappeared. Big search for him up and down the dale, but no sign. It was in the papers for a bit. It was on *Crimewatch* or something like that. Anyway—he probably ran away. Joined the navy."

"Disappeared?"

"Aye," Amy said. "Without a trace. Sad. But that was the old days. People go missing all the time. All the time. After a while, everyone stops looking. Everyone except for the family. It's too much bother, isn't it?"

Ashley looked over, and saw Beverley at the bar, who was staring at her.

13.

Shona had slept fitfully.

Now she was hissing at her slow laptop in the breakfast room of the Gildersleve Bed and Breakfast as it tried to connect to the Wi-Fi. A hot coffee was steaming by her elbow and she had picked at some tawny bacon and slippery eggs. She'd texted her father. Bernie had replied on his phone. She said he was still sleeping.

The woman who had met her and given her breakfast said her name was Peg. She wore a T-shirt and jeans. Her hair was scraped back in a bun. There was a younger girl, too, who had slipped out last night as Shona was arriving. She had a blue streak in her unruly hair, and, like Shona, walked with a slight limp. Shona wondered why.

The late spring light flooded the breakfast room of the old lodge, glowing on the stone walls, on the wooden tables, the crockery on the shelves. There were pictures of old Ullathorne, framed on the walls—the old mill, now a ruin, the castle. Men in flat caps gathered beside a prize white bull, its vast sides like a canvas. Outside, a murder of crows cawed in high branches. Someone, somewhere, slammed a car door. But all else was quiet. The stones settled in their mortar.

There was a sudden shout from the kitchen next door and Shona, startled, knocked her coffee over with her elbow.

"Fuck's sake!" she said. The coffee spread like blood across the white tablecloth. She stood up her coffee cup and covered the spillage with a napkin.

Her phone buzzed. It was a text from Terry.

How's the digs? You going to the paper archives? Let me know if you need pix ta T.

That was Shona's plan for the day. She was going to visit the *Tyrdale Times* to look for the cuttings on the death of Andrew Banks. Where she would go from there, she did not quite know. She texted Terry back. *Thanks. Yep, that's the plan. Will do. Might need your help. You free today?*

Never free, Terry texted back immediately. *Can do snaps for cash.*

Shona smiled. There were more raised voices in the kitchen. Shona tried to listen. Peg was arguing with the young girl.

"I was going to show it to you later," the girl said.

"Were you heck-as-like," Peg said, sharply.

"I just forgot. Anyway, it's straight for the bin. An old football shirt, so what? The dog found it."

"In Deepdale?" Peg said. "Where in Deepdale?"

"I dunno," the girl said, whining a little, "deep in the dale. There's an old building there."

"There's no old building there," Peg said. "In Deepdale? What you on about?"

"Aye, in Deepdale. You follow the beck instead of the path and then there's this old building. It's all ruined."

Peg's voice softened. "What, like a water maintenance building or something?"

"I dunno. Yeah, maybe. Anyway, Jess was digging away in the corner, pulled out this. What's the big deal? It's ancient."

There was silence for a time. Shona heard a rustling sound.

"It's not ancient. I remember the Newcastle shirts with that design. Here, what's this on the back?"

"Just a name," the girl said.

"Was it buried?"

"Nature claims things, doesn't it? It's all overgrown there."

"Jet," Peg said. "*Jet.*"

"What about it, Mam?"

Shona heard a sigh, and the sound of a woman sitting heavily.

There was a long silence. Shona listened intently. There was a shuffling of feet.

"Where was it again, Ashley-love?"

"Told you. It was half buried, in the corner of the old building. Jess smelled it, she was pulling at it. Maybe she ripped it."

There was silence again.

"There's been floods in Deepdale, has there not?" Peg said.

"It's always wet there."

"Floods disturbing the ground."

"Floods from the snow melting."

Shona picked up her plate of half-eaten food and went to the kitchen door. She stepped through.

Peg was standing by an Aga cooker, looking at a dirty old football shirt which she had lain out on the stovetop. The shirt had once been striped black and white, but was now almost entirely green and brown, with a series of dark blotches around a deep rip. The young girl, holding one hand in another, was by the sink, and looked surprised when Shona entered.

"Oh. Hi there," Peg said. "You can just leave that, I'll get it—did you have enough?"

She spoke with a flat northern English accent. Brief and plain, as if the language's corners had been rounded off. An old, tempered sound, like something hardy and weathered, that had survived.

"Lovely, thank you," Shona said.

She put the plate down on the side. The kitchen was large and stone walled. As well as the Aga, there was an electric oven, and two large fridges. The walls were hung with cooking implements and lined with shelves of plates and pots. There was a magnetic strip laden with large knives.

"That needs a bit of a clean," Shona said, nodding to the shirt.

Peg looked at her, as if waiting for something, and then answered. "Aye, it does that."

"Dog found it," the girl said.

The three stood, unmoving. Peg ran a hand through her hair. Somewhere in the fields, a dog barked.

"I was wondering if you might help me?" Shona said.

Peg answered with a smile, as if relieved to change the subject. Shona asked where the office for the *Tyrdale Times* was, and Peg said she could not miss it, as it was on the high street, it was next to the Lion pub.

"Meanwhile," Peg said, sighing, turning back to the shirt, "I think I have some calls to make."

"About a lost football shirt?" Shona said.

Peg flicked her a look. "You've got to be going, I guess?"

In a short while, after a rapid shower and tidy up, Shona headed into the town. As she left the bed and breakfast, she heard crunching on the gravel behind her—she turned her head, and it was the girl.

"Hiya," she said to Shona. "I need to get some supplies for Mam. I'll walk you in. Not that you'd get lost, there's only three roads here anyway."

"Thanks," Shona said. She looked at her phone—nothing from her father, and a missed call from Hector Stricken. That night in Argyll already felt a long time ago.

"I'm Ashley," the girl said.

"And I'm Shona."

They walked on the broad silent streets. The road was broad and cobbled in stretches. Elms grew along its length.

Ashley walked alongside her, staring at her phone, making little movements on its screen with a cramped right hand. She was dressed all in baggy black.

Shona's stick clipped on the pavement as the centre of the town neared—there were church spires, and snapping flags. Between the buildings, the distance could be seen—ranks of trees, the dip of the river channel, the blue moors, watching.

Ashley looked sideways at Shona and her stick. "You down from Scotland then?" she said.

"Aye. Here for a job—I'm a journalist."

"To work at the *Times*?"

"No, but I do need their help with something."

"Man, I don't think there's much to report in this town," Ashley said, smiling. "Nowt happens here."

"Why you here, then?"

"Wondering meself. I left uni. Taking some time to think on what happens next. Did you go to uni?"

"Yeah. Back in the day. Glasgow Uni, then Strathclyde for the journalism course. Fun times—what I remember of them."

"I want to write," Ashley said. "Not sure journalism is for me, though."

"You should check it out," Shona said. "It beats working for a living."

The road they had walked along had gradually become lined with shops and offices, and now they were in the centre of Ullathorne: a wide cobbled market square. It was old, and watchful. People walked the streets, but no one was talking. A car was waiting by a pelican crossing, as two riders on gleaming chestnut horses slowly clopped along. Their hoofs cracked and lolloped, their eyes like polished stones.

"Horses," Shona said, surprised. She found herself pointing at them.

"That's right," Ashley said, amused. "That's what they are."

Shona laughed. "I don't see them often. Look, before I go to work—want a coffee or something? I could do with a low-down on Ullathorne. Can you fill me in?"

Ashley peered at her briefly. "Aye, all right—let's go to the Market Caff."

As they crossed the road, Shona saw the main street disappear down a steep hill to the river. At the bottom of the Bank, amid flats and housing, was a large ruin, a shambles of roofless stone and brick.

"What's that big ruin down there?" Shona said.

"Old Ullathorne Mill. Been a wreck as long as I remember it. Used to have a big water wheel. There's been plans over the years. Someone wanted to turn it into flats. There was talk of a bookshop or something. There was a fire there a while back. Mainly, the sixth formers go in there and get pissed."

The café was small, with five small tables and nothing on its plain walls. A pale teenager covered in freckles shouted at them from the till, asking what they wanted whilst dangling a large phone from one hand. They ordered two coffees.

"Fine," the teenager bellowed back, slamming down her phone, and got to work thumping at an array of beverage equipment.

"Latte, eh? Fancy," Shona said.

"I know right? That's what Hull Uni does for you. Forgetting my place," Ashley said, in a singsong tone.

"Hull? Jesus wept."

Ashley laughed. "Give over! Larkin was there. It's all right. I quite liked it. City of Culture."

"Don't come with all that. So was Glasgow, so I know what a load of fuck-all that means," Shona said.

The drinks were thumped down by the teenager, who retreated into her inchoate rage behind the counter.

"Can I ask you something?" Ashley said, dropping sugar into her coffee. Fugitive brown sugar granules clung desperately to the white coffee foam before falling through tiny, bubbled tunnels to their melting end.

"Fire away," Shona said.

"Your stick—do you have hemiplegia? CP?"

"No. What's that?"

Ashley held up her right hand. One of her fingers sloped across the others. It was half-closed. "One side of your body is weaker than the other. I have it on the right side. It's cerebral palsy really. I have it mildly. That's what they say."

"So, you had a stroke?"

"In the womb. They called it an 'insult to the brain.' Which it is really."

Shona nodded. "You type one-handed? Fair play to you. I can barely type with two."

"I use my right thumb and forefinger for the mouse— slowly."

Shona smiled. "Well, Ashley, you're doing all right. You've been through school, to uni, and you want to be a writer. If you need any advice on journalism, ignore my cynicism and ask away."

"Thanks. I saw your stick and wondered if you had the same. If you were the same. Sorry." Ashley shook her head and looked out the window, suddenly shy. She winced, as if remembering something painful.

"No, I just had an accident," Shona said. "And don't say sorry."

"An accident? That sucks."

"It does." Shona nodded. "As you get on in the world you'll realise most things suck. To be honest. But you'll be fine."

Ashley nodded and sipped her drink.

"That football shirt," Shona said. "Where did you find it?"

"I was walking Jess down Deepdale. It was in this old building. Dunno why me mam is so mad about it. She gets crazy now and then."

"What's Deepdale? Is it near here?"

"Aye," Ashley said. "It's over the river, a beck, it goes right up to the moors. Jess loves walking there, all the smells, I guess—there's wild garlic."

"Near here?"

"Aye, just over the county bridge. You'd be there in ten minutes from here. But Deepdale goes on and on. You could walk for twenty miles, then suddenly you're on the moor top. Old trees there. Gets a bit spooky at night. I like it."

"Are there signs for it?"

"I dunno, maybe—you don't need one. You just go down to the river, cross the bridge and road. There's a stile, and you can see the path, and the trees. Walk into them."

Shona nodded. She cleared her throat and said, "I was wondering if you might help me. Have you heard of someone called Dan Merrygill?"

Ashley's mouth opened and then she put her left hand to her face. "Fuck!" she said loudly, loud enough to make the teenager at the till look up from her phone.

"What's up?" Shona asked.

"I was meant to tell me mam something and I never. Argh," she said. "I have heard that name—just last night. Bev told me to tell my mother that—wait, why do you ask?"

"I am doing a story which involves him," Shona said.

"What kind of story?"

Shona lifted her cup and sipped the hot coffee. She peered over its steaming lip. "I'm not sure yet."

"Bev said he was dead," Ashley said. "I'd never heard of him. He was at school with me mam."

"Right."

"Was he dodgy?"

"He's certainly dead."

"I haven't told Mam yet, so could you wait before you mention it to her? How long you in Ully for?"

"I'm not sure. Yes, of course. I'll wait. I might want to ask her what she remembers of him."

"Right, well," Ashley said, and suddenly stood up. "Good luck. I better get going. We can gan down to Deepdale later?"

They said goodbye, but as Ashley stood, Shona asked, "Who is Bev?"

"Beverley Moore—she was at the pub last night. In the band. I'd better go."

Ashley pulled up her hood. Shona watched her walk away. She ordered another coffee from the angry teen, listened to her clattering about for a moment, and then called Hector Stricken.

Outside, a large green tractor rolled past. Shona was surprised by its bulk, and the hugeness of its tyres. It rolled past like a tank.

"Shona!" Hector yelled.

Shona held the phone away from her ear briefly. "Fuck's sake, Hector. You know I hold the phone right next to my ear like any normal person. You trying to deafen me? I missed your call."

"Sorry. I need a bit of help. Thought you might oblige."

"I'm fucking doubtful," Shona said.

"Right."

"But carry on."

"Your pal, Detective Reculver—do you know how I can get hold of him? He's changed his number."

Shona tapped the side of her mug, annoyed. "You've asked me this before. As I said last time, and the time before that—no. You can go through the police press office like any other hack. He has changed his number—for a reason."

"Ah, Shona! I just really need a word with him for this story."

"What story?"

"Och, just this story I am trying to work on."

"On what?"

Hector's voice dropped into quiet. "Human trafficking."

"Ah, right, nasty."

"Yeah," Hector said.

Another coffee appeared before Shona, crashed down before her with a jolt and a slop.

"So?" Hector said.

"No," Shona said. "Look, sorry, Hector. But I can't give you his number. In any case, if I did, and you called him, he wouldn't help you, and worse, he probably wouldn't help me anymore. I'm not burning my contacts book for you."

A loud exhalation of breath blushed over the receiver, somewhere in Edinburgh. "Jeezo, Shona. Oh, well, I tried. I'll get him some other way. Man, I'm knackered."

"From thinking too hard?"

"Ha ha. It's this new digital-first regime that this prick editor has brought in. Did I not tell you at the wedding? We're all on digital shifts, they call them. Seven A.M. to seven P.M. Regurgitating wire copy, nicking stuff from the BBC, putting up our own headlines and pictures—there's no picture desk anymore, there's no subs checking anything. We are just constantly shovelling copy up onto the website, slapping a clickbait headline on it, and moving on. I've been working on these proper stories in between all that nonsense. In my own time, at night, at weekends. I'm exhausted."

"That's shite."

"It's not journalism, Shona."

"It's churnalism. And no, back to the point you made—you won't get Reculver another way. He is a secretive fella."

Hector sighed and swore at the same time. "That poor fella at the wedding—I saw he was from Ullathorne in County Durham. Isn't that where old John Fallon was from, back in the day? You know, the features editor?"

"Aye, Fallon's old stomping ground. But he's long gone now, isn't he. He might have been some help."

"Help? For who?"

Shona's heart quickened a little. "For Viv, maybe."

"Okay, I guess so. Well—better go. Shall we go for a drink soon?"

"Nope."

"Well, okay then . . ."

"Wait," Shona suddenly said. All the bubbles had popped in her coffee. The prolate lip of her cup had a pleasing smoothness.

"What?"

"Do you know what *Odeadaheado* means? Ever heard of it?"

Stricken made a whistling noise and asked her to spell it. She did.

"No, means nothing to me. Is it some kind of fantasy thing? Science fiction? Like a character from a film or something?"

"I've looked—it means nothing."

"Well, you've answered your own question, then. It means nothing. Why do you ask?"

"None of your beeswax, Hector—bye."

Shona paid for the coffees, left the café, and walked to the *Tyrdale Times*, only yards down the quiet main street.

As she walked, she felt a creeping, tensing chill in her shoulders. She was alone again. By herself, again. The stone buildings leaned in on her. The white sky was smaller.

She opened the door to the newspaper office.

A tiny bell sounded as she entered, tolling tinnily in the forest of quiet, glimmering alone, like the chimes of Mass at the Eucharist in an empty church.

14.

She had been prepared to find it difficult to access the newspaper's archives. But the woman behind the high counter, flipping through a celebrity magazine, had expressed a surprised delight in her interest, and offered to help. The newspaper office itself was upstairs. At street level, it ran a shop which sold that week's edition of the paper, as well as Tyrdale calendars, postcards, maps, and sweets.

"Do you want me to get Colin?" the woman said. She was wearing thick glasses and smelled of lavender. A small white badge on her orange blouse said WATSON WINS.

"Er . . . no," Shona said. She did not know who Colin was.

"Oh, I thought you might want to speak to the editor? Colin Mickle?"

"No, no, thanks. Just some family history to look up."

"Oh, lovely. Are your family from round these parts?"

"That's what I am trying to find out."

Nodding, the woman introduced herself as Angela and ushered Shona to a large, carpeted, whitewashed room behind the shop where a dozen or more filing cabinets stood under a sloping ceiling. A single microfiche reader—with a boxy screen and a large plastic hood like an ancient computer—was on a table in the corner. A magnifying glass on a poseable metal stand was placed in one corner of a long desk.

Angela, her hands moving like fish in a stream, said that the *Times'* archive was only digitised from 1999 because of the strict and random stipulations of a millennium project grant. Before that, the microfiche and paper records of the newspaper went back to 1914. And before then, single printed editions of the paper were stored at Durham University. Shona explained that she wanted to look at newspapers from the 1990s.

Angela opened one of the cabinets. Fifty-five editions a year, she said, were stored in here. "They are all filed by week and month and year. I'll leave you to it," she said. "Now, would you like a cup of tea? Where did you say you were from?"

"Stirling in Scotland," Shona said. "A cup of tea, milk and two, would be lovely, thank you."

"Stirling, how lovely, and what do you do there?"

"I design luxury yachts," Shona said.

"How lovely," Angela said and padded away.

Shona looked for 1992 in the files. The room was silent. A high, small square window looked into a white sky. The room hummed with low-wattage electricity. She put her gear down, and laid her stick against the microfiche table. A shiver of something moved through her—she smiled: this was journalism, real work, with paper and pen and the potential for discovery.

The papers for 1992 took up a quarter of one filing cabinet drawer. She looked to the middle of the year, when classes were breaking up for the summer, grabbed the first half of the year in two tranches, and put them on the table. The papers were held together with neat strings with metal tips, like laces. The newspaper looked old-fashioned—a gothic title, and many stories crammed on each broadsheet page.

As Shona flipped over the pages, the paper rolling and whispering, and saw the stories pass by—the commonplace and the trivial, the serious and the comedic, births, deaths and marriages—her mind drifted . . . She wondered if she should jettison her anxious freelance life . . . work for a local paper in Fife or the Western Isles or maybe even Northumberland . . . move to the sticks, edit a weekly . . . make friends with a flinty but twinkling local policeman . . . report on fishing and farming, mild crime and milder entertainments . . . put the paper to bed on an early Thursday night and watch the birds wheeling over the mercury sea . . . sip coffee with someone on a tawny cliff . . . interview the local MP over whisky in the distillery . . . sleep at night lulled by wind and sea . . . the cities far distant, a fire burning beyond the horizon . . . her father, happy somewhere, smiling as he pulled potatoes from the ground . . . and maybe there would be a strong old river, too, in this new life . . . implacable, relentless, like the Tyr, here in this old dale, an intractable old God, ever present and ever moving, a constant unblinking murmuring living deity . . .

Angela broke the reverie, planting Shona's tea, brown as a kidney, in a large mug beside her.

Shona thanked her and continued to flick through the papers. She was looking for a photo of the sixth form at the Ullathorne Comprehensive. There were none in May, June, or July, 1992. Just prize winners with awkward smiles and little trophies. Then Shona realised—the class photos would be from the beginning of the year, in 1991.

She hauled the papers back to the cabinet, and looked for papers from the late summer and autumn of the year before. She looked through August—nothing. September: there they were, a page of class photos: first year, second year, third year, fourth, fifth. The images were all in black and white. Rows of faces, pale as petals, young and open. All the children stood on the parquet floor of a school gymnasium. Some were smiling, others were blank, some were serious. Some stood out. A boy with a manic grin, a girl with a hand over one eye, a boy looking hard to the left, a girl in the front row looking down at her feet, the top of her head showing her fiercely parted hair. All in the school uniform: V-neck sweaters, a stripy tie, dark skirts, and trousers. They were all stilled in time. Beside each group of children was a teacher: there were smart suits and floppy suits, long skirts, perms and large jewellery. Smiles and scowls. Big hair.

There were plenty of photos—but none of the sixth form. She opened the paper for the first week in October. The headline on the front page was something about a local company escaping charges for dumping sewage in the river.

And there, at the back, before the classified ads for cars and furniture, puppies and flower arranging—was a small photo of that year's upper sixth class.

The teacher was an old man with long grey hair, tall and lanky, half sitting on the table before which the pupils stood. It seemed there were only seven students in the year—all going into their A-levels, all soon to leave school. They were arranged in two rows.

Shona pulled over a magnifying glass on a heavy stand, and placed it over the picture.

Underneath the photo there was a caption in splodgy old type, ink sunk into the cheap newsprint:

This Year's Upper Sixth at Ullathorne Comprehensive, led by U6 Head Mr. Norloch. From L to R (back row) Daniel Merrygill, Beverley Moore, Alison Harmire, Andrew Banks, (front row) Gary Watson, Margaret Gildersleve, Robert Stang. Ms. Harmire is the Sixth Form Captain for 1991/2 and Head Girl.

Shona realised she was holding her breath. She leant in, looking closely. At the back and on the left stood Dan. His clothes were neat, and he did not wear a tie. His face was softer, plumper, and he had more hair, but there he was—pale, poised, taut. Beverley, next to him, was a tall girl with long hair and a long face. Alison was a shorter girl, pretty with her hair pulled neatly up, smiling in a smart uniform. She had a Nike swoosh on her sweater. There was a sense of ease and optimism about her, and a neat, almost withheld, smile. Then, the lost boy—Andrew—with neat, wavy hair and large dark eyes. He was handsome. He looked like Viv. She looked closer. His eyes sparkled, or maybe he had just been crying. There, in the front row, was the MP: unmistakably a young Gary Watson. His eyes like chisel dunts in stone. He wore an ironed shirt and a straight tie and an air of impatience. Next to him, looking nervous, was a youthful Peg, from the B&B, with a frizz of red hair. Then there was a large boy Robert, with thick thighs and arms, staring out, defiant. He seemed to have the smudge of a moustache at the corners of his mouth. He looked ready to run out of the picture and thump someone.

Andrew, Dan, Gary, Peg . . . the others. All together for one captured moment. And something still held them all together. Something from thirty years ago, or maybe longer. Something from the past, living inside the present.

She pulled the newspaper out of its loose string binding, folded it over, and put it to one side.

She was closing the folder of papers when her eye caught something in the rippling pages. There was the same picture, the same photograph—but enlarged. The splash of the paper, from July 1992:

SEARCH FOR MISSING ULLATHORNE TEEN
Family call for information on search for Andy Banks, 18

THE FAMILY of missing Tyrdale boy Andy Banks, 18, have appealed for more witnesses as the search continues.

Andrew did not return home after spending a night out with friends on Friday.

The popular Tyrdale student had recently completed his A-levels and was looking forward to his summer holiday before his planned attendance at the University of Kent at Canterbury to study History.

Friends and family have been left distraught by his disappearance.

Last week police confirmed they had searched the river and the ruined Ullathorne mill—popular with local teenagers.

Andrew's father Ken said: "Caroline and I, and Vivienne, his sister, are beside ourselves. We would like to appeal to anyone who saw Andrew that Friday to come forward with any information. Even a small detail could help us find Andrew again.

"He is a friendly lad but no fool and we don't believe he would have got in someone's car. We hope he has just been having an adventure but we want him home now."

A spokesman for the police added: "Anyone with further information on Andrew can call police operations here in Ullathorne. We have

spoken to his friends and they all believe this is
out of character. If anyone has any further details,
please get in touch."

Shona pulled out the edition, and the other, and walked
quickly back to the shop, where Angela was hovering by a
large photocopier.

"Found something?" she said.

Shona looked down at the papers. "Aye, some interesting
things. I need to make copies."

"Sorry, love, the machine's broken at the moment," Angela
said.

"Oh—is it? Its lights are on," Shona said, pointing.

"It's broken. I'm getting a man in. Why don't I take those
and photocopy what you want, and you can pop back in later
and pick them up?"

Shona eyed Angela, who stood as innocuous as a glass of milk.
Shona said that would be fine, and noted down the images she
wanted copying, spelling out the pages, and the dates.

Angela nodded and smiled, and slowly folded Shona's note
and put it on the countertop. "Ta-ra, then," she said.

Shona said her thanks, gathered her belongings, and made
her way to the Lion to find more information about Beverley
Moore.

As she walked, her thoughts moved over the faces in the
picture, from side to side, and up and down, and again over
the words in the caption, as if her mind was an eyeglass
empowered by something beyond its time. Moving over the
faces. Moving over their names and words. Spelling out messages that she did not understand.

15.

It was a bright, cold day in Tyrdale. The snow had long melted away, and the world was wide and empty, the valley brown and enfolded upon itself, clutching its trees and river.

Robert Stang had woken from another slow nightmare. The sweat of it was wet in the small of his back. His mouth was heavy and thick.

He had seen bodies, limp, heavy as rocks, being tipped into pits. Heavy boots, kicking them in. The dull roll of the body onto other bodies. The clunk of dead heads. A dark forest of silent pines, and a row of holes, pale with the infilled dead. And then, a single quavering candle which glittered in a circle of frightened eyes. A wheel of fingers resting on a glass as it moved over letters and words.

Moving, and no one could deny it. Moving, but no one knew how, or why. Just movement, with no explanation. Moving, like the earth around the sun, or vast rotations of the galaxies in flight—with silent movement and unseen, implacable force. Mass, and speed, and gravity.

Bobby rubbed his eyes. In the small, neat living room, his daughter Becky was watching a cartoon, loudly. He had a day off work, between shifts at the bottle factory, but she still needed to go to school.

He made a coffee in the pin-clean kitchen. Becky, still in her PJs, ate a bowl of cereal on her knee and laughed at the TV, as, after a jolt of caffeine, he laid out her ironed school clothes and made her snacks. Her mother, Karen, would pick Becky up today. He just needed to see her to school, down in the dale.

His house was in a small cul-de-sac of former council houses, pebble dashed, squat and pale brown, halfway up the valley. Behind them, a barren hill led up a thistly bristle of land, to the moors. Below, the tree line fell in a sheer fall to the Tyr.

"Teeth," he rumbled to his daughter, and she moaned and reluctantly padded out the living room to the bathroom.

He looked at the news again, on his phone. He had read it late the night before. He reckoned it led to the nightmare. Little Dan Merrygill, dead. Dead in some place in Scotland. He recognised Viv's name as well. They must have kept in touch. It made sense they were friends. He had not seen Dan since that night, all those years ago. After it all went dark. He had not seen Viv either, not since her brother went missing. He wondered what she was up to, and how she got to Scotland.

Dan: dead, by his own hand. In the army, he had seen it. A body in a shed, deep in a Balkan ravine, a man with his head missing, a gun between his knees. An open neck, and the roof blown open.

He was curious about one detail—Dan's body was reported to be heavily tattooed. He did not think Dan had it in him to get a tattoo. Not his kind of thing. Not something he could imagine Dan enduring.

Bobby rubbed his arm over his own regimental tattoo, as he was wont to. Deep blue, it was now. Deeper in his skin than all those years.

Bobby's phone blinked—out of battery. He swore and plugged it in. He wouldn't need it for the school run. He'd just leave it.

Becky danced through to the kitchen, immaculate and small, and he picked her up in a swoop. She giggled, and he looked at her face—clean apart from toothpaste at the corners of her mouth. He pressed it off with a finger and she winced and smiled. He kissed her small forehead.

"Okay, Little Miss Freckle," he said, "school for you."

In the car, she played with her hair as the cold dale rolled by. Stone walls black with moss. The sky was huge above, clouds of white and dark grey together, a soft, slow paving of vapour and weight.

A large black car joined the empty road at a junction and stayed close behind them. It was large, a 4x4, and had dark windows. It was too close.

"Get out of my backside, tosser," Bobby said.

"Language, Dad," the girl said.

"There's a right halfwit behind me in that big car," he said.

"Who is it?"

"Someone looking for a clip around the ear."

They came to a crossroads. Ahead, the roofs and spires of Ullathorne nestled in the valley. Bobby looked across the fields to the business park where the factory where he worked lay, and slowed the car to a halt.

"At holiday are we going to Scarborough again, Daddy?" Becky piped up.

"We can do, love. I've been saving up."

"I like it there a lot," she said.

"Me too, pet, me too," he muttered, peering into his rearview mirror.

"Do you like it there?" she said, searching for something.

"I like it there when I'm with you."

"We can get a caravan," she said.

"We can get a caravan," he said quietly.

The black car stopped behind them. A foot from his rear bumper.

A line of bright blue had emerged in the southern sky. It would be brighter, later. The trees rustled in a new breeze.

Bobby waited for a car and horse box—a long brown head lolled dark eyed in the window—to turn at the crossing, and then he followed, putting on speed. The black car kept close.

"God's sake," Bobby said.

He slowed down, and, rolling down his window, waved the dark car on.

"Go on then, soft lad, overtake," he said.

The black car just slowed down and stayed behind them.

"Are we going to be late for school?" Becky said.

"No, pet, we're fine," he said, and sped up.

He drove quickly down the long straight road to the town, then dropped his daughter off outside the primary school, indicators clicking. She skipped out, grinned, and waved to him in the car park before joining her friends.

"Remember, yer mam is picking you up," he yelled after her, and his deep brown voice made a few small heads turn.

She looked around with furrowed brows, mouthed "I know" to him, and disappeared into the school.

Bobby knew the large black car was waiting on the main road. The drive to the school was a dead end, and there was no way out without driving past it again.

The school car park was for teachers only. "Fuck it," he said. He parked up. There was a narrow footpath between stone houses, away from the school grounds. Bobby walked down it, hood up, hands deep in his pockets.

As he left the footpath and entered the main street of the town, he could not hear any footsteps behind him. He looked over his shoulder as he turned. No one there. He had nowhere to go in particular, but he pounded down the main street, coming in a blur to the market cross. The Lion was open but he could not drink. He had given that up.

He stomped down the Bank. He was shaking his head. "Being daft," he told himself. "Paranoid."

But he carried on. Down past the old toy shop where, as a child, he had begged his grandpa for soldiers. Past the crooked old shop where, legend had it, before the tarmac was laid and electricity threaded through the town's stones, Oliver Cromwell had slept overnight. Past a boarded-up shop, and down to the road that ran alongside the river Tyr. The ruined mill was ahead, its empty windows gaping, its smashed portal a door into the dark. There, where something in him changed, where his path to uniform and service and death was laid. He had not been in there since.

He turned right, past another pub, its whorled windows swollen like an old drunk's eyes, and walked along the river. He stopped for a while, leaning his large body against the wall. The south bank of the river was all trees and bungalows, windows glinting like teeth between bare branches.

The black car came down the bank and turned onto the road along the river. It slowed steadily as it reached him. Grinding on the tarmac. A dark shadow behind the wheel.

Bobby set off again, walking faster along the side of the churning river. Over the old county bridge, and onto the other bank. He crossed the road which led to the moors.

The car was slowly moving over the bridge. Bobby was being hunted. He saw the stile, leading into the darkness of the Deepdale woods. He jumped over it and moved quickly into the trees. He walked quickly along the beck, into the tree line, and was gone, into the night of the daylight forest.

The black car mounted the grassy verge, and a tall bearded man stepped out. He locked the 4x4, and followed Bobby into the trees.

As he entered the trees, crunching on the undergrowth, stepping on a rotten branch, splintering it underfoot, hearing the cold beck run over black stones, he drew a short blade from a long sheath.

16.

Bobby looked behind, briefly, and saw the tall, lithe, bearded man walking slowly into the woods, something lethal glinting in his hand.

He began to run, deeper into the woods, into the thickest stands of trees of Deepdale. He knew it well, and his hunter did not. Bobby was heavy, but he was fit, and he could move. He heard snap and whip of the man crashing through the undergrowth. Bobby knew he had the advantage. He was a soldier, and he knew this ground. His heart was beating fast, but he was thinking clearly.

Bobby veered hard, off the main path, and scrambled and dove into the trees. He half-crouched in a thick stand of trees and bush. He could see the man, now only twenty yards away, standing still on the track, knees bent, holding a sharp blade. His body was still. He was looking from side to side.

Bobby could not move now. The man would see him. His nose was close to the earth of Deepdale—it smelled wet from rain, deep and old.

The bearded man moved slowly forward, keeping his shoulders low. Bobby's legs were exposed, but his body and head were hidden in the tall weeds and thorns. If he stayed still, the man might not see him. But if he did, he was vulnerable.

A tiny green insect settled on his broad wrist. He noticed, in his dive from the path, he had ripped the back of his hand. There was a ribbon of skin, tremulous and half ripped, and new blood flooding the tear.

Who was this killer on his trail? Bobby was momentarily angry. Angry because he had panicked, and run. He should have stood his ground. Angry, too, for his daughter. Angry at the violence, which like an animal, was entering his life again. He had moved back home to be free of it. Now it was here, dressed in black, bearded, ready—for some reason—to harm him.

Bobby looked closer at the man's blade. It was more like a stiletto blade than a machete. If it pierced him, it could breach the walls of his heart, or slice a new mouth into his guts. Bobby sized him up. The man was tall, but not that big. Bobby could overpower him.

Images flitted in his skittering mind—the rapid click clack of machine gun fire in the fir trees of Bosnia. Splinters about his helmeted head. The thump of mortars. And later, much later, the thunder of strikes in the desert. The vicious sucking of air. Mangled bodies, humans wrenched inside out. A basement full of choked bodies in T-shirts and sports clothes. A man, at a distance, decapitated by rifle fire.

Then, he was here. In the woods of his hometown. His ripped hand closed on something hard; he looked to it, a strange, sickle-shaped rock. Hard and curved, it jutted from the moss and the bracken. He grabbed it.

The bearded man at last moved. He walked forward, tentatively, and then quicker, crouching along the path. Then he stopped, and turned, and faced the thicket where Bobby lay. Then he turned again, all black clothes and lethal poise, to face the way he had come.

Bobby gripped the rock, and rose to his feet.

The bearded man swung around, but the rock had already left Bobby's hand, flung hard. It flew lower than he wanted, and thumped into the man's chest. The man grunted with the sharp pain and staggered back.

Bobby charged him, his head down, his shoulders square, pushing his weight forward to crush the bearded man. But his foot snagged and he tumbled. Some hard loop in the undergrowth had tripped him. The bearded man stepped aside neatly, and, as Bobby fell past him, plunged his blade down.

Bobby felt force, not pain. The bearded man raised the blade again in a clear arc again, and Bobby prone, kicked at him, hit something solid, and pulled himself up.

For a moment, they stood, both crouched, one armed, one wounded, and looked at each other. The bearded man, his face pale like dough, his eyes fetid as pond water. Bobby was tattered and huge and wild—and bleeding.

"What are you doing?" he found himself saying. It came from him, came from somewhere near or above him.

The sword moved again, on a deadly arc—and it missed Bobby.

He turned and ran. Deep into the deep of the Deepdale, as hard as he could. He ran, knees high, through bushes and undergrowth. Thin branches whipped and snapped. The ground rolled and jutted beneath his feet. Up ahead was another path, coming down from the edge of the dale to this wooded valley. He turned around. He could see a figure flitting through the trees. There was no time. He needed to arc a U-turn, and find his way back to the town.

For speed, he followed the beaten path. It pressed uphill, a steep slope. The man would reach it soon, also. Bobby reached for his phone as he pelted along the track—jumping over rocks and boulders—but he had left it behind, charging in his house.

On his right was a barbed wire fence, and over it, there were thinning trees and flat fields. To his left, the dark of the dale, and the heavy woods. He did not want to try and leap the fence. And open fields were a killing ground. He came to a thin, muddy stream, a trickle of water leaking brown from the field. He shuddered left, and took off, helter-skelter, down into the trees again.

But the hill was too steep and treacherous underfoot. And Bobby was weakening. He shot forward, fell, and came to a battering halt at the base of a thick tree.

He was still and blank with pain. Before he could move, the man was at him. There was a moment of violence and confusion. The bearded man's breath was in his face. His elbow chopping back and forward. Pain ripped through Bobby's side, in his guts, and with a fiery heat spread fast over his belly and his thighs.

The bearded man stood up, unsmiling, and nodded. His glove was red with blood, and the blade in it, sharp as a razor, thin like a spine. His arm dripped death. And then he was gone, like a blown shadow, disappearing into the trees.

Bobby pulled himself up. He felt his side. He moved his hand away and it was shockingly wet with hot dark blood. Dark and red. He looked to his jacket, and in it there were savage rips, its stuffing hanging out in a wisp of white. He pulled up his ripped sweatshirt. His body had been changed—there were swellings and tears and undulations. New ragged apertures in his flesh. He was suddenly exhausted. He was punctured, leaking. His side suddenly shrieked with pain and he bellowed.

In slow motion, as if caught in mud, or water, or a living dream, he crawled down the thickly wooded slope, his eyesight blurring. He was deep in the woods, the sky only flashes of ice-blue in the canopy.

He slipped again, and fell further, and then rested on his side. He lay in the mud and green for a short while, pain thrashing across his body. He saw, clearly, the blood on his fingers, red as a berries, red as a postbox sending messages.

He knew that if he lay down and slept, he would bleed out. He had to refuse the sudden warm offer of the long night. That would come, anyway. He refused, right now. Until it could not be refused.

Staggering to his feet, crouching, he lurched forward to a concrete wall that emerged out of the thick green branches and trunks. He had been to Deepdale many times before and not seen this building, this abandoned place. In his slipping mind, he wondered why it was here, so far from the town, from roads and people and civilisation. Maybe the woods themselves had built this ruin. Or it had grown out of the mud, out of the stone.

Bobby knew he could not stop moving. He had to get back to the town. He lurched left again and headed the way he thought Ullathorne lay. It would be easier if he found the beck—the beck would lead him home.

Trees ghosted past him. Thorns tore at him. Weeds gripped his legs. He held his side, held his sides inside, held his blood in his wounds, and suddenly found himself, after another brief fall, facedown in the water. He looked down into the clear stream. His blood had flowed into it—it swirled and misted. A nebula of blood, slowly blooming.

Momentarily, his mind stilled. He felt warm and calm. His mind shrank and focussed. Past his eyes he saw something move.

He saw feet—bare muddy feet, feet in sandals. Feet also marching, on legs matted and filthy. Claws, glinting with resinous death. He smelled old skin, and new leather.

Prone, unmoving, he looked wildly into the trees. Dark eyes moved between bare branches. The trees had thickened. The beck was now a river, and was thick as dye. On the far shore, there was a silent procession. People moving, carrying a long stretcher. On it was a dead king, with coins for eyes, clean shaven, with a circlet beside his cold and wounded head. Metal was glinting in the glimmering tree dark. Many hands held him. The dead king seemed to lie in suit trousers, a white shirt, his arms enfolded, hands holding branches of vine and ash, elm and yew.

Women in green, their hair braided and long, sang a low, lowing melody, and children walked silently, their faces hidden in painted masks. Men strode, low and loping—bronze glimmered, iron was held fast. As silent as dreams the figures moved through the bars of trees.

The sky in the cracks of the canopy was blue, but the stars shone. More stars than he had seen before—a beach of stars, shoals of shattered light. He looked across the entire arc of the sky, his eyes glittering with the revealed sky. He did not blink, he did not sigh. Bobby lay bleeding, run through in the running river.

Then, after a while, there was movement, soft feet on moss and pebble, and through the nettles and gleaming wild garlic, a short man in brown and black came near. Clad in soft garments, in treated skins.

His face was a crumple of creased leather, his eyes dark as wet stone, his voice slick like sap and the slither of white root. The man sat beside the stream, his black hair long and braided. He had brown eyes—deep brown eyes, like the forgotten peaty pools in the heart of the hills. He reached out, across time and into the still and always flowing stream, and touched Bobby between his eyes. Blood swirled, and spiraled out of the nebula, back into the body. Out of the earth, and into the living.

Then he was gone.

Bobby was in the stream. He lay, his face half under the cold water of the Deepdale beck, hidden miles into the occluded valley, the branches low about him. His body was drenched in chill moor waters, and his blood had washed away. His fingers were white and gently wrinkling, his boots cleaned of the mud and dust of life.

He thought only in shreds and fractals. But in those fluttering shreds was his daughter at her school, working her way through lessons, laughing with her friends. Her day advanced beyond the moment of her father's death. Like love, he was now outside time.

Robert Stang, lying in the cold stream, opened his mouth to call his daughter's name, and then his mind stilled, his eyes closed, and he dropped into the sea of everlasting dark.

The Hollow Tree

The sun had still not crested the hilltops, and in the clearing of the hollow tree, there was darkness and silence. Dew was forming like eye gleams on the still leaves of the spare undergrowth. Without the sun, the giant tree cast no shadow. It was sunk deep into the enclosing dark, like a bone inside a body. Buds on its healthy branches were minute, waxy, and unready. No birds were singing in the dawn. The fading moon was caught in sinews of moving cloud. Stars were still in the darkest blue sky but the trees do not count or name the patterns. Their business was with the earth.

The hollow tree stood, as it had, age after age. Its roots held the earth and rock, it drew water, and drank it, and breathed it, and fed it to the sky.

Everything was inside it, and it was inside everything. Dumb, but not numb, it was as alive as the world, but still and silent. It was dead and alive, motionless, and always moving. It was a bridge—a home—a tower—a vast flower.

There was movement in the glade about it: something, unafraid, was slowly pacing beyond the borders of the undergrowth. The rabbit's fur, as it moved, was pricked and puffed, as, black-eyed, it shuffled onto the ring of bare earth around the hollow tree. It moved to the spine of a submerging root that spanned from the central black trunk. The rabbit sniffed and blinked. A ripple ran through its brown-grey pelt. Ears up, it looked left, right, and up, to the city of branches above. There was the breath of a flutter in the undergrowth. Another flutter, and a crack. In a bound, the rabbit returned to the weeds and was gone.

The hollow tree had stood for countless unremembered

dawns like this. The world had moved and the sun's light had come again. It was blushing the eastern skin of the Pennines; a sheet of light laid over the plunging fells and the tumbling white-teethed ghylls. Shadows seemed to seep from the hill-sides, drawing pools of darkness from the trunks, as if they had absorbed in their night of submergence the sunless dark, and now could be tapped of it, like sap.

Dew now lay in tiny pools on bark and limb. A rime of moisture shivered on cold branches and many-knotted twigs.

A single brown bird emerged from a feathery hold. It opened its mouth and croaked. A gentle wind had risen, and was bringing on its gusts the smell of the river, its mulch and jetsam, and a metallic, thin scent—iron, and the murky residue of foulage and farm-spill.

The bird was not alone. Across the waking forest, the hunters, the mothers, rose or peeked from their nests.

A drifting owl, exhausted, cooed a pale hoot to its home. Its silver wings skimmed through the upper canopy of naked branches. It drifted on a rising heat, and looked down upon the giant tree, black and alone in its own clearing, the surrounding woods standing back, giving the old ogre space, heat, light, water.

The rising sun and the fading moon glimmered in the owl's round eyes—it saw all as it flitted on the opening air. On the far bank of the ancient river, a shudder of a fox headed to the warm town for scraps. It saw a tiny mouse exiting at pace away from the field's open killing floor. As the owl dipped to its home. It sensed, higher up, a swifter killer.

There, the hawk, high above, lolling on the heat of the exhaling earth, gently tipped its weight below the cloud line. The river below was a running ribbon being pulled into the sea, and the fields about, all slick with soil sleep and the condensation of vegetation, glistened. A sudden gleam caught its deadly eye.

It dipped, its body as light as a knife, and below, in the old woods it scanned the clearing of the hollow tree. Human-sweat was there, and footprints. The hawk remembered the glade: it had snapped a shrew there, several turns of the sun ago—a whiskery visitor to the glade, who stopped fatally to stare up at the falling hawk, until it was too late.

Inside the tree there was dark, and an iron hardness, and things the hawk did not want to disturb. But the gleam had gone. He saw nothing below in the grove of the giant—only the coal-glint of a black armoured beetle tending to its morning chores, free of dread—and it rose again, scanning the lightening fields, the mist now gathering like frost in the hollows of the valley.

The hawk had a home, and it turned in a tight arc towards it, barrelled down in wide circles, the world tilted as if turning on a hip socket.

It spiralled on, a ranging dot above the morning glade of the hollow tree, where tiny insects were stirred and hovered over the hard fern and thorns, flitting in fizzing flight between beech and red oak, between old acid firs and sweet chestnut.

A tawny squirrel, skittering about in its quick twitch business, clung to an old fir near the hollow tree. Its head trembled and scanned, its pebble eyes gleaming. Vertical, it moved in its own dream, up the bark.

It had run on the hollow tree's bark, once, several moon-tides ago. A memory clung to the silver innards of its bubble skull. On the hard bark, smooth and unrelenting as stone, it had crept up the holy tree.

In the moonlight, the tree was not flora—it was a building, a castle—vast and wide, and the squirrel's eyes could not always sense the end of it. It was a tipped plane of wood, a monster clinging to the bedrock with its earth-arms, rising to the rain with its air-tails.

It had reached a rent in the tree skin, and it had crept, trembling to the lip of the crevasse. A low wind rose from inside the tree and the fine hairs around its bead eyes had fluttered.

No food was there, in the dark inside. Down into the sunless, moonless dark, the swift rodent had stared into the wreckage of bark, of wood-death, of fungus rot and mange. The gleaming eyes saw the circlet of yellow bone, a hanging human jaw, a tumble of teeth. Finger bones dislocated and adrift in the enclosed soil. Deep below, deep to be never found, was a human body in a rotted bag, a sacred gift long faded and frayed. A stomach of barley, flax, glass beads, and pig. A curled corpse, clean shaven, one arm missing, long since given to the hollow tree.

The sun was quarter high now, and the squirrel and its memory were long gone. The river ran loud, and the cars of humans began to grind on the nearby road. The giant tree cast a shadow aslant the glade.

Rodents scattered, and birds crouched. A man walked into the shadow. He walked slowly, and was dressed all in black. Insects moved on, unmoved by the bulk and the weight. The birds flustered and flew.

The man looked around, he looked up. His cheek was red with blood, a line scored out by a sharp twig, dragged across the soft flesh. He shook his head. He said something loud, and paced. He walked back and forth, and was saying something, cursing to himself.

Hung on the side of a nearby oak, the squirrel watched, unmoving, as the human walked back and forth, back and forth. It smelled him: sweat, sweat from his armpits, from his thighs, deep sweat from his black trousers. The metallic ions of sprayed deodorant. And mixed with that the scent of wild garlic, of crushed bracken, of mud from another vale. And blood: the iron tang of it, this man's, and another's. The squirrel's nose twitched, and it ascended the oak noiselessly.

The man took off his bloody gloves. He folded them together. He looked around and above. He saw the apertures in the sides of the hollow tree, and pushed them in, and pushed them down.

The gloves, balled, tacky with drying blood, fell into the gloom of the inner tree. In its fall it gathered dusty murk and fungal spores, clogged moss hairs and thicker cobwebs. The gloves tumbled down to a knoll within, a damp cave brown with wet flopped mushrooms, stained with seeping brown and the rot of inner wood. The gloves lay now in the darkness, and would, in weeks, be covered and shielded by fallings, by droppings, by sheets of webs and spots of mould. They would not be found.

The man still paced, and suddenly clapped his hands. The clap shook through the undergrowth, and up into the trees, but nothing stirred. The world was silent, and waiting. He turned on a heel, digging a sudden semicircle into the mud, and left the glade.

The day began to pass again, in and around the hollow tree.

The fingers of the furthest branches arced towards the sun, still growing, still breathing, still reaching for the light.

17.

Terry pulled up her car on the kerb outside the entrance to the ruined castle in the middle of the town.

Shona stuck her head into the open passenger window.

"You're late," she said.

"Thanks for coming all the way from Richmond to pick me up, Theresa, thanks very much," Terry said, putting on a ridiculous Scottish accent. "Thanks for coming thirty miles out of your way for me."

Shona clambered into the car, dropped her stick, and shook her head. "Oh, bolt ya rocket," she said.

Terry burst out laughing.

"Right," Shona said. "This woman, she lives further away, into the hills."

"Up the dale?"

"I guess so."

"Fine. Up the dale."

"Where?"

Shona squinted at her notes. She had told the barman at the Lion that she wanted to speak to the singer of Bundle of Twine for a newspaper article. She had flashed her National Union of Journalists card, and he had given her Beverley Moore's number. She had spoken to Beverley, told her she wanted to talk about her band, for a feature for the paper. After a pause, in her deep, flat voice, Beverley had given her an address.

"So, it's in a place called Thorsgill?" Shona said.

"Oh, aye, halfway up. Be there in forty-five minutes, longer if we are caught behind a tractor," Terry said. She turned the car around, and guided it through the streets of Ullathorne.

Shona rang her father.

"Good morning, Shona," Bernie replied.

Shona snorted. "Can you please stop answering Dad's bloody phone for him?"

"But he's asleep, darling." Bernie said.

"It's just annoying," Shona said. "Is he all right?"

"There's no need to be so rude," Bernie said. "I am not at all rude to you, am I? Yes, he is fine. He was very tired. MacDiarmid is asleep on top of him. It is so sweet, you should see them together. Mac is purring away, the wee thing."

"Fine. Can you say I called, please?"

"Shall I tell that to the cat or your father?"

Shona drew her breath sharply and shook her head. "Both. And can you not call the cat Mac, please? That's not her fucking name."

"Shona!" Bernie exhaled. "I mean—honestly?"

"Bye." Shona hung up.

Terry smiled and put a luminescent yellow cough drop in her mouth. "Someone taking your cat's name in vain, eh? Something to rage about. Good use of your body's finite resources of energy."

Shona looked out at the deepening valley. "My dad is poorly, and that was meant to be his nurse. Instead, she's wibbling on about the cat."

"I'm sorry to hear that—how old?"

"About a year. Just settling in."

"Your dad."

"Nearly seventy-five, going on sixteen. Him and his *girl-friend*."

Terry let the silence settle for a moment.

"I've got a cat," Terry said, as stands of trees rushed past her head.

"Amazing. How nice for you."

"He's old now, he's getting thin, losing his teeth."

"Fascinating."

Terry shook her head and flicked on the radio.

They drove on, following the course of the river.

"Not far now to Thorsgill," Terry said. "Has this woman agreed to have her photo taken?"

"About that—I've said we are shipping up there for an article on her folk band," Shona said.

"It's not, is it?"

"No, course not. Who gives a fuck about her sodding folk band? But she went to school with Dan Merrygill. She can tell us more."

"You going to be angry all day?"

"Shut up," Shona said, softly.

Terry suddenly pulled over into a passing place. Then she turned off the engine, and the radio fell from a burble to nothing. "Can you hear that?"

Shona listened and couldn't hear anything unusual. Birds were singing in the roadside bushes, hawthorn and black-thorn, and a brave pioneer bee was doodling between thistles in the pasture beyond the wall. Then she realised what to her was the usual roar of life in the city was now somehow present here. Coming from somewhere beyond the high trees in the crease of the valley above.

"That's the big waterfall, the Great Fosse, up there in the trees," Terry said. "It's where the Tyr falls 'bout eighty feet. It's pretty bloody loud when you get near it. I've had some nice jobs there over the years. There's a big hotel there, the Fosse and Rainbow."

"Nice," Shona said. She could hear the distant rumble,

but without seeing it, she could not imagine the waterfall, its relentless power, its constant cloud of spray and foam. "Can we get going?"

"Aye," Terry said, "Green Northern Tours continues, after the break."

"It's grim up north," Shona said, quietly.

The car moved on.

"You have to remember, this is south for me," Shona said, tapping the top of her stick.

"How you finding it?"

"Nice landscape, shame about the people."

Terry grinned. "Fair enough. I blame William the Conqueror."

"Oh, aye, what did he do then?"

"Tried to kill everyone north of the Trent, I do believe. The Scourging of the North."

"I'm sure he had his reasons."

"It's all right for you rebellious Scots," Terry said. "We're stuck with those fuckers, still lording over all of us today."

Thick stands of bare budding trees pulled in around them.

"Down that way is the Coine Tree." Terry pointed to a gravel track that led into the woods. There was a green sign which Shona could not read. They sped past.

"The—what?"

"The oldest, biggest tree in England, they say," Terry said.

Shona sighed heavily.

"What now?" Terry said.

"Well, it's probably good colour for the article," Shona said. "For my feature. Can we go back and see it?"

Terry smiled, and they sat momentarily in a still, humming car in the depth of the woods at the valley floor. Then they reversed and turned on the tight road.

They returned to the gravel path, and Shona could see the sign now: THE COINE TREE: THE OLDEST TREE IN ALL ANGLE-LAND.

They parked up on a kidney-shaped area of small stones beside the road. Shona stepped out and her stick felt slick and heavy in her hand, as if the valley had its own gravity, or by some unsaid kinship the wood in her hand was drawn to the trees around her. She waited while Terry pulled equipment from the car: a black bag of cameras and lenses. A tripod, folded like a gun.

They set off down the path. The world closed in on either side. Roots straggled over banks of rock. Green moss as bright as jewels glimmered wetly. Fronds of ferns unfurled.

"It's a yew tree," Terry said, lumbering a little with her gear. Shona was crunching along the track, her stick skipping and tapping.

"Would yew believe it!" Shona said, and looked to Terry for a smile, which was not forthcoming.

"It's massive, must be, what—eight metres around," Terry said.

They tramped in silence and arrived at a large clearing. In the centre was a silent monster—a huge, wide tree, which looked like a tight clutch of smooth wooden towers. The grim growth of its trunk over hundreds of years had split it into multiple bodies: it was a stand of trees, or several trunks all clustered together. Like a petrified family of giants, back-to-back, facing out to the world.

There was a large slit in its side, dark and wet, and Shona could see that its largest trunk had a cavity within. The trees in the woods looked like children around it. Feeble and scared.

Shona moved closer. The Coine Tree towered above her. It looked like it had grown in the wrong world. It was too big. She looked up to its canopy, shorn of leaves in the long winter. It was a maze of twisting black branches, crisp and clear and black against the sky.

"Jeez Louise," Shona said. "That is a big tree. My dad would love it."

"The druids worshipped it, they say," Terry murmured, staring at the back of her camera.

"I'm not surprised. I feel quite close to uttering a prayer myself," Shona said.

They stood for a while before the hollow tree. Shona wondered if there was something missing in her—she felt as if this vast entity should have been telling her something. Offering an insight. But all she could sense was its sheer scale.

She shook her head. There was something else there—but she could not immediately fathom it. She did not have the means to measure and understand it. It seemed to be timeless. She, on the other hand, was stuck with time. It was passing even as she considered it. She was rootless, and tender. This thing was gripping the earth, and it was as hard as stone or iron—as hard as death.

Terry started taking photographs.

"This light is murder," she muttered.

Shona walked to the tree, its trunk like a grey wall. She put her hand to it. It was cold. She noticed there were other doors into the hollow trunk, apertures into the night inside. Its bark was smooth, rippling like a frozen waterwall.

"Why is it called the Coine Tree?" Shona said, peering through a hole into its depths.

"Go around the other side, Sherlock," Terry said, without looking up from her camera.

Shona slowly walked around the vast tree. The tree wall glittered, studded with curved edges of metal. Coins had been forced into its skin.

She moved closer, and could see gleaming coppers, and wincing silvers, the odd pound coin, and a galaxy of thin old coins pressed into the bark many years ago. Some were now green like algae, some were bent, some were almost submerged in the growing bark.

"People push the coins in and make wishes," Terry said. She was standing with camera in hand, cocked like a gun.

"People," Shona said quietly, running her hand over the coins. They were like scales, like rusted old armour on a sleeping old giant in the woods.

"People, yeah," Terry said, and looked at her watch. "The coins are killing it. They had a sign up a few years back, asking people not to stick the coins in, but people ignored it, and so it just carries on. The coins are poisoning it."

"People are idiots," Shona said, and turned back to the path. She found herself glancing back at the tree, as if it may have moved, or disappeared. Terry followed, and they walked in silence again.

At the car, they slung their bodies back into the seats.

"Nice tree, eh?" Terry said.

"It's not bad," Shona said. "How old is it?"

"Thousands of years."

"Poisoned or not, it will probably be here when we are long gone."

"It already is," Terry said, as the car pulled away.

They drove on and the weather brightened and the valley widened as they moved higher. The fells on either side were wide and gentle. They passed more farms, and isolated houses, and at last came to Thorsgill.

They pulled over at its small village green, which had a roofed well at its centre and neat old stone buildings clustered around. A small road led up the side of the fell to a group of new houses. Beverley Moore lived in one of them.

As they prepared to walk across the main road—Shona gripping her notebook, Terry lumbered with her bag—a large black car sped into the village, spurting dust and grit from its thick wheels. It slowed momentarily, with the driver hidden behind tinted glass and then, with a grind of massive wheels, sped on, down the dale.

Terry shook her head.

"Dick," Shona said, watching it disappear down the valley.

"He'll be dead in a ditch soon, going at that speed," Terry said.

Like the hunters who once lived under the same sky, they hobbled and heaved their kit up a path up steep fellside to the high homes. A breeze rose in the lane, carrying the scents of sheep from the high fields, wet earth, and damp vegetation.

They walked to the last house in the row. The pebble-dashed semi had a large garden, with a low fence about it. Dream catchers swung on low branches, chimes dangled from two gnarled cherry trees, and a wicker lantern in the shape of a dog hung from an apple tree, swinging in the light breeze. Around the sides of the two-storey house, vegetables had been grown—all harvested months ago. A stone badger stood by the front door, and several figures made from concrete and wire—bearded, in robes—huddled in the long grass. They stared with open blank eyes to the north of the dale.

The low gate, painted yellow and red, opened with a creak like a cry and they walked up the path to the door, which had been painted purple and had a yin-yang painting above the knocker.

"So, what gives here?" Terry said lightly.

"I'll knock and see what happens," Shona said. "Don't get your camera out."

"I've done door knocks before."

Shona knocked on the door. The rap sunk into the landscape, and there was no answer. Shona tried again.

A deep voice sounded from within. "Wait a minute!"

There was the sound of soft padding feet and the door suddenly opened. A tall woman with long hair and a yellow smock stood in a colourful hallway decorated with many small mirrors. She wore long earrings and had a hand-rolled cigarette in her hand.

"Oh hello," she said, her voice low and sonorous.

"Hi, Beverley?" Shona said. "I was wondering if you would like to talk to me. I'm a friend of Viv Banks. We worked together. I was at her wedding. I was there when Dan died."

"Oh," Beverley said, raising her thick eyebrows. "So, you're the lass that called."

"That's me."

"So, you're not really here to talk about my band, then?" Beverley said, her voice hardening.

"We can talk about that too," Shona said, with a generous shrug.

Beverley took a short drag of her cigarette, which was actually a joint. Sweet marijuana smoke drifted in a whiskery trail.

"Who's this young lady?" she said, nodding to Terry.

"Terry's a photographer. I'd just like a word. I'm trying to find out about Daniel. About what happened."

"Well, if you were there, what more is there to know? It's already been in the papers," Beverley said, folding her arms across her body.

There was a silence, and the three stood, waiting.

Shona decided to grin at her. Beverley seemed to take in the grin, like a gift. Her body moved back, as if receiving something unwanted but painless.

"*About what happened,*" she said, slowly. She took another drag.

"To Daniel," Shona said.

"Who do you work for?"

"Myself. I'm freelance."

"So, for nobody—or anybody," Beverley said.

"Well, exactly," Shona said.

Beverley smiled. "And this pretty one an' all?" she said, nodding to Terry.

"I'm just happy to be here, miss." Terry beamed.

Shona found herself grinning again, amused by Terry's sudden perkiness. "Beverley," she said. "I'm just looking for background—for information. I'm not here to interview you on the record, or quote you. I'm just trying to find out what might have led to Daniel's death."

"It was at his own hand, love," Beverley said. "I'm not sure I can really help you."

"I know. But I'm thinking there must have been reasons. Maybe going back a long way. Going back to his school days, maybe."

"Maybe," Beverley said.

There was silence again. A bird was singing overhead. Terry peered at her camera lens, as if it had something to say.

Shona pressed on. "I am just looking for background," she said. "You were there, back when he was a lad. You might provide some context for me, some accuracy, some facts."

"No quotes, no interview—just the gen," Beverley said, seemingly to herself.

Like a cloud, a large and bearded man suddenly appeared behind her in the hallway. His face was ruddy, and almost entirely covered in a grey, curling beard. He had tattoos on his neck, and his arms. Fine hairs stuck out of his ears, and his large eyebrows. He looked like a bear, or an outsized owl.

"Everything all right, love?" he said. His deep voice burred like timpani.

"Aye, Karl, love," she said. "Put the kettle on."

He disappeared again after a stiff nod.

"That's my Karl," Beverley said, to Shona. Then she seemed to peer into the distance and make a decision.

"Come in, then."

Shona felt a rush of relief. She crossed the threshold, with Terry not far behind.

They passed a large metal Buddha in one corner of the hall, and then walked into a sun-filled living room. There were windows on three sides. Leaning in the corner of the room was a large decorative axe, with a leather handle and blades etched with runes. Orchids stood stiff in decorated pots, and a knitted rug had been draped over a small television in the corner, by heavy wooden shelves filled with vinyl records and CDs. There was smooth wooden furniture, bare floorboards, and a large, geometric rug from India or Pakistan. A scented candle, black and huge, stood on a metal holder, expelling wisps of a thick perfume. Music was burbling from a small radio, next to a large statue of the Virgin Mary near the stone fireplace. The Virgin, in blue, looked sorrowfully down, her face cracked, her robes flaked and stained with smoke. Leant against the fireplace were two large acoustic guitars. The light glimmered on their tigerish red and orange varnish.

"They say never let the devil cross your threshold," Beverley said brightly. "But here we are."

She asked Shona to sit, and she did, on a wooden chair beside the coffee table. Both looked homemade, and the table was slightly higher at one end than the other. Terry peeked around the room and squinted. She mumbled something about the light, and that she would wait outside, and quietly left. Shona watched her leave with a frown.

Karl arrived, bristling massive hands like shovels, holding

a wooden tray of tea. Beverley asked Shona to call her Bev. There was small talk about the weather, the slow spring, and Bev asked Karl to make something more substantial for an early lunch. He rumbled that he would and returned to the kitchen. They spoke of Shona's journey south, and how she knew Viv. Bev asked how Viv was, kindly.

Shona looked around. There was a large painting of astrological signs. There was a framed poster from the 1980s which said: *Before Margaret Thatcher came to power the UK stood on the edge of a precipice—since then we've taken a step forward.*

"We're old socialists. Old Labour," Bev said, catching Shona's eye. "Sorry about that. You feel the need to apologise these days."

"Not many of you left, is there? You and my Dad," Shona said.

"Problem with fascists," Bev said, mildly, "is you'd have to beat them all. It's too tiring. So, we give up."

Shona raised her eyebrows. Karl put the mugs on the coffee table. The mugs slid a little.

"Unusual table," Shona said, getting out her pad and pen.

Karl moved back to the kitchen.

"No need to buy expensive furniture when you can make it yourself," Bev said. "All that traipsing to the shops, to those fucking awful IKEA places. What a rip-off. My soul dies a little in those places and what a scam it all is—you have to put them together yourself."

"Thieves," Karl called through from the kitchen. He had put some folk music on. A beautiful woman's voice was lilting over electric guitars, and Karl was humming along.

"So, Karl makes our furniture. Makes sense to us." Bev put out her joint with a solid fizzle in a clay ashtray and sipped her tea.

She peered at Shona.

"So, you saw poor Dan?" Bev said, eventually.

Shona nodded.

Bev pushed her hair behind her ear and pulled a new neatly prepared joint, white as a finger, from behind it. She lit it with a plastic lighter, its flame tall and orange, quivering like a bird.

"Poor Dan," she said. "Poor sod."

"Had you seen him recently?"

"No, love," she said, inhaling and exhaling. The dope smelled sweet and strong.

"That smells good," Shona said, smiling.

"We grow it ourselves," Bev said.

"Don't tell the cops," Karl shouted through.

"Karl, can you get on with lunch and leave us be?" Bev shouted.

Shona asked again—had she seen Daniel Merrygill recently?

Bev shook her head. "No sight nor sign of him, not recently. Maybe a year ago, saw him in Ully, he was visiting his mum in the care home, maybe. He was never for talking much and he didn't then either. I never knew he was still friends with Viv. I had no idea."

"He was in sixth form with you, though—had you not seen him since then?"

"Not really. Not since Andrew's funeral. The one with no body in the coffin. It was more of memorial, really—not a funeral. In 1998, or was it 1999. Years after he went missing. Years."

"What about Dan after school? You were in a small sixth form with him—Viv told me."

Bev blew out more smoke, tilting her head up into the air.

"Shona, pet, this is ancient history, really. But yeah, sixth form was daft. Looking back on it. It was so small. After the GCSEs, everyone left. There were all these people, loads of friends, and then they left. Off to trades or apprenticeships, off to sixth form in Darlington maybe. Some just left, to who knows where. So suddenly in Lower Sixth, there was just a handful of us. A couple left after that year, and then that final year, there were even fewer of us. Bobby and Andy, Dan, meself, Alison and Peg, Watson. That was it."

"All doing the same subjects?"

"No. Let me remember now. There was me, Andy, and Alison all doing English. Can't remember what Gary Watson did—maybe some business or sciences. Maths. Bobby was just doing General Studies and something else by upper sixth. Andy did History, I remember that, so did Dan, I think. We'd spend most of our time in the library, or the sixth form common room, lolling about. It was all baggy clothes in those days. Paisley shirts."

She sipped her tea, and so did Shona—it was hot and brown and sweet.

"No mobiles or laptops then, remember, love. This was '91 or '92. So, we'd listen to Stone Roses and Happy Mondays on a small cassette radio we had. Gary Watson would put 808 State on and some crappy rave tunes. Andy would put old music on—the Beatles and the Stones. We'd nip off to the Old Well sometimes at lunchtimes, or after school—have a pint and a game of pool. I snogged Dan in the fields once. I think I gave him a fright."

"How did the exams go for you all in the end?"

"Oh, I did all right. Seemed so important then, I don't know how important it was. All that has drifted away. It was going to be the last summer before real life began, but then it happened. Andy disappeared. We all never really spoke again. We went our separate ways. You have to remember there was no emails, no texting, no internet, no social media, in them days: we lost touch. It was easy to, back then. Seems nuts now."

"But you came back, to Tyrdale."

"Yeah, I came back eventually. I got sick in Liverpool. Then I got homesick. Got a job in the council, been here ever since. Planning, of course. Got married to a prick, got divorced, all in eighteen months. Then I met Karl at Glastonbury. He moved here to be with me, didn't you, Karl? Daft apeth."

Karl rumbled something inaudible from the kitchen.

"I was in two bands by then," Bev said, with a chuckle. "Not that we had any success, of course. But we had fun."

Shona nodded, smiling, and then tapped on her notepad with a finger. "Your ex-husband, what was his name?"

Bev shook her head. "He's irrelevant. I intend to keep him that way."

"Right. So—what about the others? Do you know what they got up to?"

"Bobby went off to war, didn't he? Can't remember seeing much of him. Was he in Bosnia? Might have been in Iraq or Afghanistan. I know he was in Germany mainly. Saw him in the Lion once with a crew cut, looking massive."

"Always was a big lad," Karl boomed from the kitchen.

"Yep, always a big lad. He lives over the way now. Works at the bottle factory, got a wee lass. Quiet. Then Alison—I don't think we saw her again, after that night. She went down to London and stayed there. She was always a smart cookie. Bright. I saw on Facebook she is married, but don't think the wedding was up here. Her dad, he had some bad times. Think it knocked the family."

"What about Daniel?"

Bev peered at her for a moment, but carried on.

"Not sure what was going on with him. He just vanished. Maybe something to do with his mum. His dad had buggered off years before. Peg—Peg had a kid. She went off to catering college, I remember. She runs a B and B now in the town. Nice, is Peg. I like her. Had some problems with her girl, but what's new. She's got palsy. Nice girl, though. Bright, like Peg. Poor Peg's husband died—cancer."

"And Gary went into politics after business—an MP now," Shona said.

"Yeah—suits him," Beverley said, and flicked away some ash. A curl of silver drifted and was gone.

"Tosspot!" Karl shouted from the kitchen. "All that nonsense he talks and what-have-yer."

"Karl!"

"That cunt needs fucked up," Karl said, in a low but audible tone.

"Anyway," Beverley went on, shaking her head sadly. "We could see that all coming. Watson had a briefcase in third year. Always talking about his mam and dad buying shares in British Telecom and British Gas. Had a Filofax. Silly, really. He was one of the more well-off kids. Didn't have much time for anyone else. Not for me anyway. Ambitious."

"What did his parents do?"

"They owned the abattoirs first," Bev said. "And some other businesses, by the end of the 1980s. They bought the bottle factory. Video stores, too. Watson's Videos—chain across the northeast."

"So, Watson was as ambitious as his folks?"

Bev tapped her finger on the sloping table, and her voice quietened. "Yes—but. I do remember one night that was a bit different with him . . . there was what we kind of called a rave. We all piled into someone's car. Gary came. Tunes all the way over in the car. We ended up in some old quarry over by Appleby. It were mad. Gary was out of it. We all were. It was pretty great—we were only seventeen, eighteen. Seemed like the world was changing. Of course it wasn't. But the music, and I guess we must say, the drugs . . ."

"Ecstasy," Karl hollered.

"Yeah, all that. It felt, at the time, optimistic. You know? Probably for the last time. Anyway, Gary that night was weird. He was odd, he was quite emotional. I remember. Maybe it was the music! Anyway. He was crying there, in the corner of the tent. Weeping. I think his dad was a right arse-hole, to be honest. He liked dressing up in army uniforms in his spare time. He's dead now—the old twat. His mum was a scared little thing. Anyway, Gary was upset that one time. He maybe had a rough one. Especially around A-levels. Maybe felt the pressure. So, I remember that one night. Never saw that side of him again."

"Loaded," Karl shouted.

"Yeah, they were loaded," Bev said, shrugging. "Didn't seem to make them very happy, mind. Think they sold the whole chain of video stores for a sackload. Helped Gary set himself up as what he is now. He still owns a load of busi-nesses—the bottle factory. Not the abattoir, though, they closed that down for whatever reason."

"Wanker," Karl shouted.

"An MP," Bev said. "He's quite a big deal, I guess. Not my kind of deal, though. I think he got married, but she died in a car crash."

"Rum do, that," Karl shouted.

"So," Shona said, "you said 'that night' there—what night?"

"Did I?"

"Yes. You said you didn't see Alison again after 'that night.'"

"Oh, that night. The night Andy went missing."

"What happened that night?"

Bev looked out the window. Her eyes reflected the sun outside. She pulled at an earring, and sucked her joint. Karl came into the room and put a plate of thick sandwiches down on the table. The plate slid a little on the slanting surface and then came to a halt.

Karl pulled a large conical joint from behind an ear. "I'll be outside, love," he said, and opened the back door and disappeared into the garden. Shona could hear him greeting Terry, and their voices rising in laughter.

"Have a sarnie," Bev said. "We make our own hummus. Cheaper than the supermarket. Tomatoes from the greenhouse. Karl makes the bread, it's delicious. I don't tell him that, though. It's the only dough he makes around here."

"Thanks," Shona said, but ignored the food. "So Karl is out of work?"

"He's always worked in the garment industry." Bev shrugged. "Good with his hands. But that's all gone to buggery now, hasn't it? Out of Europe, and now the business is cost-cutting. Corner-cutting. He lost his job a year ago. Like everything else: he was lied to."

There was a silence.

"Have you spoken to Viv about her brother?" Bev asked.

"You know, I didn't even know she had one," Shona said.

"She had a brother. Maybe everyone has forgotten about how he disappeared. Certainly no one in Ully speaks of it now. Viv's away in Scotland. The police have forgotten. Those that worked on the case, they have all retired or died. Alison's dad—he was a copper here. He led the search. It was all in the papers back then, but the police downgraded it all after a while, stopped looking. It all seemed half-hearted at the time an' all. No internet, of course. No social media. It was on *Crimewatch* on the telly, I remember that. Then it was gone and forgotten. As if everyone wanted to forget."

Shona was taking notes in her pad. Little ticks, swoops, and flicks of shorthand.

Bev added: "He was a nice lad, Andy. Lovely, big lad. We all liked him. He was going to be an engineer, he said. Had something lined up, some kind of summer job. Handsome, like Viv is pretty. He had the most beautiful eyes, you know. Long eyelashes."

"When was the last time you saw him? What were you up to?"

Bev blew out a gust of blue, sweet smoke. "We were all bored with town. Bored with Ullathorne and school. Bored with living in the sticks. Bored with modern life. It's a terrible feeling, boredom, when you're young. But, you know, we were maybe scared as well—scared of leaving the town, of leaving Tyrdale. Even though we knew we had to—or at least some of us. Look at Bobby joining the army—he was desperate to get out. Mind you, his parents were hard work. Alison and me, too. But also . . . it's a hard place to leave. We'd get drunk to try and avoid all the choices, all the inevitable things we were going to have to do. The exams. Uni. Jobs. Money worries. All them. Some hormones too! I was fancying everyone at the time. I even fancied Peg for a bit. Don't tell her."

"So—you were getting drunk a lot?"

"Aye, of course. Like you Scots. English people can't bloody live without alcohol. Stops us all jumping off a cliff, I think."

Shona winced.

Bev held up a hand. "Sorry—must have been a bad scene for you," she said, tilting her head.

Shona pressed on. "What else was there—you had parties? Those raves you mentioned?"

"Well, of course there was the drink, as I said." Bev shook her head. "We were minced at the weekends. Cider and black. We used to drink this mix—Castaway and Diamond White. We called it Blastaway. In pints! Jesus! And Aftershock—we would get trays of them at the Lion. Gary was always on the lager. I remember Dan liked rum and Coke. Andy couldn't hold his drink—it was funny at the time."

"So, there was a final party? Like some kind of going-away do?" Shona asked.

Bev rubbed her hand through her hair. She looked outside. Shona could hear Karl and Terry laughing.

"Has anyone told you about the *sessions*?" Bev said, with emphasis.

"Drinking sessions?"

"No, not that kind of session." Bev paused, and crunched the joint into the clay ashtray. The light dimmed. The sun was occluded. A shadow fell across the room.

"Ouija boards," Shona said, quietly.

Bev blinked hard. "Was that a guess?"

"Not entirely," Shona said. She remembered Daniel's tattoo.

Bev stood up and nodded to Karl through the window. Then she slumped back down again. "It was all daft. We shouldn't have. But we did. We should have said no, should have said yes to no. But we carried on because it was scary, and a secret, and it's exciting. When the glass moves! When you think you're speaking to the dead. Or something. Or someone."

"Who was doing this?"

"All of us, even Gary. I used to think he was messing with us, but he was well into it."

"What, in the evenings?"

"No. You won't believe it, but we started doing it in the

sixth form common room, during the day. We had these empty periods—study periods. Hours long. There was this round table we had—the top would come off the metal legs. Shoddy Durham County Council furniture. So, we took it off, and flipped it over. Got some chalk from the classroom, and drew out the board. The letters and the numbers."

"Hello, goodbye, yes, no," Shona said.

"Yes. The sun and the moon. And we'd do little sessions in these break times. And then flip it back over when the teachers or other kids came around. Sometimes we sneaked into the backstage area in the main hall. Behind the curtains. It was pretty dark back there. Sometimes the glass would move. Sometimes it didn't. But then it did. But it was stopped."

"Stopped?"

"Yeah, someone found out. Not sure what happened. But the head teacher found out—got us into his office, gave us all a fucking telling off, I tell you. Gary probably crapped himself. Alison was embarrassed, didn't want her parents to know. Her dad. Anyway, we were all told we had to stop doing it at school. Peg got scared. She kind of drifted away from the rest of us a wee bit. She got into The Cure! I remember her big hair and T-shirts."

"What would happen in these sessions?"

"You ever done it?"

"No," Shona said, truthfully. "Were you not moving the glass? Was not someone moving the glass? Is it not just suggestible . . . a kind of game?"

Bev took a long swig of tea. Her eyes moved, swiftly. She was thinking on something. She shook her head, as if that was the end of it, then murmured, "The glass moved. Of course, there was a lot of mucking about—Bobby mainly." She seemed to shiver. "Actually, it's freaking me out thinking about it now."

"What did the Ouija board say?"

"Nothing," Bev said, firmly.

"Nothing?"

"No. Just jumbles of letters. All gibberish."

"Really?" Shona said. "So why keep doing it?"

"We were desperate to get something, some message or other. But we never did. It was mad, really. We were just this little hysterical, mad club there, for a bit."

Bev stood up. She was momentarily unsteady, and rested her hand on another wooden chair which rocked slightly on uneven feet. She tottered out of the living room, and into the kitchen.

Shona reached for her stick and stood, too. She moved to a window, and looked outside. She could see the rest of the garden, separated from the hillside by a low wooden fence. There were more vegetable patches, a glassy plastic bubble with plants of some kind inside, and the sheds. There were several long benches, and on one of them Terry was sitting with Karl, getting stoned and talking. Her cameras lay untouched in a large bag beside her.

Something moved into Shona's head—a notion. It formed fully and clearly. The names of the six students: Alison—A, Bev—B, Dan—D, Andrew—A, Robert or Bobby—R, Gary Watson—G. *Abdarg.*

Shona looked into the kitchen. There were wooden cupboards and shelves. A large poster of a hare pounding a tabor. Pans and skillets hanging from hooks—an electric oven, two microwaves. Knives were glinting on a magnetic strip near the toaster. Shona heard footsteps.

Bev was behind her, in a coat that looked half leather, half knitted.

"Shall we have a little walk?" she said. "I need fresh air."

"Sure," Shona said.

Bev opened another door, which led outside, and shouted to Karl and Terry that she and Shona would be back in twenty minutes.

"Let's gan up the hill," Bev said.

Shona looked to Terry, who gave a brief thumbs-up. Karl was now bent over in the garden, his large hands among the wintering plants, his beard tickling the soil.

Shona and Bev tramped over the soft ground of the garden, and then climbed over a stile and clumped into a barren, steep field. Thistles sprouted in patches. In the far corner, a knot of shy grey sheep slumped.

Shona silently cursed her shoes—trainers, which were sinking into the soft turf and mud. Her stick sinking by inches. Tiny brown balls of sheep shit lay scattered like seeds.

They walked quietly for a while up the steepening field. The width and depth of the valley opened as they rose. Cars flashed on the road. All above, the sky. A vastness, and silence.

In the next field there was an abandoned barn. Its doorless entry was black, its windowless windows were black. It was built of grey stone, streaked with yellow lichen. Propped against the outer wall was a long bench.

"Let's have a sit here, save your legs," Bev said.

Shona slumped down. She could feel her toes were damp. Her shoulder was sore. They sat beside each other, a metre apart, their backs to the barn, looking out over the dale. Below, Bev's house was small, like a toy house dropped from above.

"It's strange talking about all this now," Bev said.

"I'm sure it is," Shona said. "I'd like to say thanks for all this. All your help."

"That last night," Bev said, and shook her head.

"The night Andrew went missing."

"I wish I could remember more. But I was so drunk. I

was rat-arsed. I told the police the same at the time. Alison's dad. He didn't take many notes, I remember. And the years . . . they have not been good on my memory. It's funny, I remember it like pictures."

"Like pictures?"

"Some are lost, some are faded, some are framed and some are treasured. Some are torn up and thrown away."

A vast shadow moved across the fell. Shona looked up: a cloud like a dirigible swiftly scudding on an invisible current.

Bev began to speak again. She seemed to be picking her words carefully. "We'd all been in the Lion. Drinking at the end of the week. Me and Alison and Peg. Andy with Dan. Bobby. Gary with his numbskull pals. But somehow we all came together. It were warm. We walked down to the mill in pairs, or in separate groups. I remember telling the cops—it was me with Ali. Peg went home. Bobby on his tod. Dan and Andy. Gary came down later. There was not a cloud in the sky. Warm night, as I said. I was drunk, we all were. Nervous about the summer, about the A-level results, about going to uni. Bobby was all signed up, ready to ship himself off to Catterick garrison. To the army."

She reached inside her jacket and fished out a packet of cigarettes. She offered one to Shona, who shook her head. Bev lit up, sucked a drag, and blew smoke up into the windless air.

She smoked her cigarette for a while more, and Shona waited. She had learned, long ago now, that silence was often worth waiting through. It was best to not interrupt, or second guess what might be said next.

"It's hazy now, it really is," Bev said. "Or more like shadowy. We were in the basement of the mill, sitting on our seats—deckchairs, collapsing chairs from school. Gary had a little stool. It were late by that point. Did a little session with the board—nothing doing. Then we all left. Andy left on his own. I remember him climbing those stone stairs, and his silhouette against the blue night sky—it were nearly July—and then he was gone. No one saw him again. I remember him waving goodbye—a thumbs-up, and a smile. I remember. He was wearing his Newcastle top, as per usual. Loved his football."

"Did the police ask what you were up to? Down there in the mill?"

"Yeah, course. We said we were drinking. Which we were—cider, beer. Ali was petrified, I think. Gary—I dunno what he said. It's not like we were ever interviewed as a group. We were never asked to go to the station to make statements. It didn't seem to matter to them."

"What do you think happened to Andrew?"

Bev ground her cigarette stub into the wet grass with her boot. "I think he went in the river. I don't know why. But I think he went in the water. Out at sea, now."

"Why's that?"

"Well, he was mangled with drink. Like we all were. He might have gone down by the river there, for some reason, and fallen in. I don't know. He wasn't picked up by someone—he only had a ten-minute walk home. He just needed to go up the Bank, into the town centre, and up to his estate. I mean, maybe a twenty-minute walk. So, he wouldn't have accepted a lift from some nutcase. Why would he do that?"

"What was Dan doing?"

"I never really saw him," Bev said, slurring her words a little. "He left the mill after Andy, but he went straight home, back to his mam's. He was seen in the chip shop, buying a supper. Chips and gravy. Then it was Gary—he drove home, I think—pissed. Shame he didn't crash. Ali left, too. Then I walked into town for a bit. I think Ali said she was sick before she got back to her folks."

Shona was taking notes. The light was uneven across her notepad. Bev did not seem to care.

"They never found Andy's body," Bev said, almost whispering now. "And there were no sightings. He just vanished. There was a search, there was the telly stuff—and then nothing. There was nowhere for the thing to go, so it died. And then the family held the memorial, a few years later. It seemed to end it all. Andy's parents sold up, moved on, Viv went to uni in Glasgow I think? Yeah, Glasgow. She's not been back here for a good while. Why would she? Nowt here for her."

"No?"

"No. What is there anywhere? There's nothing holding anything together. It's just families trying to get by, isn't it? The dream is over. You got kids?" Bev looked to Shona.

"No."

"Well, probably for the best—that's what I tell meself an' all." Bev sighed, long and hard. She rubbed her face. "And that's me, Shona. That's all there is. I am sorry—I don't know more."

Shona nodded. "Thank you. I know you weren't expecting to talk about this today."

"You never know what a day might bring," Bev said quietly.

They walked without words down the hill, through the scraggy field. The sheep were now gathered around a large metal feeder, yelling and crying.

Shona remembered something. "Bev, I was wondering, why did Dan have a tattoo of a Ouija board?"

Bev glanced at her. "Did he?"

"Yeah, on his chest. I saw it."

They stood before the stile into the back garden. Bev's eyes flickered for a moment, and she looked away. "I don't know about any tattoos, love."

"Do you know why Dan might have spelled out a phrase in his . . . in a suicide note?" Shona asked.

"What phrase?"

"'Take the Right Path'?" Shona said, raising her voice. "He also wrote 'Say Yes to No,' and 'There Is No Time,' and a name, 'Sorley.' Was he a friend? Sorley?"

Bev moved suddenly, and climbed over the stile. Karl was poking at something in the garden with a shovel—he looked up as she climbed over.

"No, love, sorry," she said. "I've no idea. And your friend there seems nice, but I'm not posing for any pictures for you or your papers."

Shona followed her silently to the house.

Shona and Terry gathered their belongings and Bev waited by the front door.

"Nowt in the papers, now," Bev said. Her face had hardened and her eyes were glassy. She wanted them to leave.

"There won't be," Shona said. "Not of you. Not about you." She nodded at the ornamental axe. It looked heavy, deadly, and ridiculous. "What's with the exotic weaponry?"

"That's Karl—his fantasy stuff," Bev said, shaking her head. She added: "The band's playing at the Lion again this week—you're welcome to come."

"If I'm still here," Shona said.

"Time for them to go, love," Karl called, kindly.

Bev opened the front door. "Aye, off you trot."

Shona and Terry left the house. Bev stood for a while, watching them, and then suddenly nodded, turned, and closed the front door, which shut with a heavy clunk.

Terry and Shona walked silently back to the car. Terry slung her gear into the boot. Shona leaned against the bodywork and tapped her muddy stick on the tarmac.

"Did you get what you needed?" Terry said.

"I don't know."

"I got the feeling she wouldn't play for pics."

"You felt right."

Shona chewed a fingernail. Something was wrong—and something was missing.

"Where to now, boss?" Terry said.

"I need to get back to the town," Shona said. "I need to visit someone."

18.

Gary Watson MP was watching himself fucking.

It was one of his many recordings. He watched his toned hairless back thrusting, gleaming in hard bright hotel light, a pair of nodding ankles high around his ears. He watched, his eyes unblinking, his mouth hanging open, a hand down his black silken pants.

He was suddenly startled by a bleep from his other phone. He moved his hand. His mouth snapped shut. He shut down the video. He peered out over the valley from his glassy, clean, stone-and-steel kitchen at Scar Top. Shirtless, he spat on the slate floor and closed his phone.

Scar Top was the old Watson mansion on the outskirts of Ullathorne, set back along a long drive and in trees, standing on its own hill overlooking the town. In recent years, it had been refurbished, redeveloped, built upon. Now its interior was all white concrete, polished stone and glass. Clean surfaces. Wipe-down steel and long planes of blue glass. It had gates and grounds, but it retained the old cellars and hiding places.

He moved closer to the window. A notification bleeped again on the phone lying on the long glass tabletop. Shadows murmured in the glass like depths of water.

He hoped it was a message from Alyce.

But no. It was an encrypted text:

<call>

It was Raymond. Watson read it, and it was instantly deleted.

He made a strong drink, and moved through to the living room area, divided from the kitchen by a change in flooring. It was all grey, soft furnishings and black stone. The large television was silent. There was a large dark stain on the white rug. Knott would sort it.

There was a slim laptop, silver like a shield, on the stone mantelpiece, and he took it down. He sat and opened it and the light cast a glow on his smooth face. He looked over the election plans. Posters and flyers. Social media messages. Five proactive news releases. Reactive lines already cleared with his agent and the Whips. A question-and-answer document, already written, running to ten pages. Top lines in bold and underlined, key facts in boxes, statistics in italics. All ready.

Watson had access to the Party communications grid, and it was full, and had been for months. There was a map of his constituency, broken down into smaller areas, each with a campaigning target. The section on social media was long and colourful: dozens of messages for microblogs, for Facebook, for other sites. Short videos. Blip-ads. Targeted scare messaging for older voters. Wheedling, anxious lines for middle-income households. Smart short ads with big lies for the undecideds and the ignorant. He smiled, and shut his laptop with a hard tap.

He was ready for his win. He looked at the list of forth-coming events—a speech outside one of his family's factories in Ullathorne for the cameras. A launch speech to small businesses and supporters at the Great Fosse. A chat to the Territorial Army at the old drill hall named after his dead father. He considered his win a formality. A ministry awaited and then—the new dominions.

The front door opened and closed. He moved back through to the gleaming kitchen. He expected to see Knott, but, manifesting like a ripple of dropped shadow, it was Bax.

"Fuck's sake, man," Watson said, his heart skipping in his chest.

"Reporting in," Bax said.

"You shouldn't be here."

Bax barely moved. He shrugged.

"Yet here you are. Get yourself a drink," Watson said to his man.

Bax nodded and reached for a long bottle of clear liquid near the stone sink. He poured some into a long glass, and scrunched into it some ice from a nozzle in the freezer. It squealed and popped.

Bax's shoes were covered in mud and there were thick smears on his trousers. He leaned against a marble counter. He opened his mouth to say something, but didn't. He carried on drinking. He wiped blood away from a vivid unhealed scratch on his cheek.

"Shall I get your robe? You'll catch your death," Bax said, nodding at Watson's naked torso.

"Not me," Watson said, and stretched. His shoulders popped. He stretched his fingers. Under his fingernails was a grotty line of scum. He stared at it for a while. His nail looked like a tiny painting of a dirty horizon on a grey day.

"Is Knott here?" Bax said.

"Briefing the leaflet team," Watson said.

"So . . ."

Watson waved a hand. "Don't need to know."

Bax shrugged and sucked his drink. He looked at his hand, as if there was an answer.

"Remember, Bax: Sorley agreed with all this," Watson said, quietly but firmly.

"Aye?"

"He said: '*Mute*.' I know what he means. He's led me this

far. I'm not going to start ignoring him now. Not now. He's not been wrong about owt."

Bax shrugged, minutely. He was tapping the kitchen island's top. "He has been . . . vague about stuff."

"Not to me, that's the important thing," Watson said.

Bax put his drink down, empty, and nodded. He blinked heavily and rubbed his face.

"You look worried," Watson said.

"I'm not worried."

"Sure?"

"Sure."

"Any word from Alyce?" Watson asked.

Bax shook his head.

Watson looked closely at Bax, to see if he could divine more. His eyes were two small dark marbles. "What has Raymond been saying?"

"Nothing," Bax said. "Much."

"Much?"

"He was saying you are on the cabinet list. But you know that."

"Ah, Bax, my friend. You know as well as I do: they need a northern MP in there. They're thinking long-term on localities, on regions. Waiting for Scotland to go its own way. Matter of time. And then you have a northern border, all of a sudden. We'll need a watch on the Rhine. A tower on the Tweed."

Bax nodded. He looked outside, into the forest. His hands were entwined, fretting.

"I had Chief Whip on at me yesterday," Watson said, sweat still glimmering on his bare chest. "Prodding around on my 'interests.'"

"And you said . . ."

"You know the drill. Kept it vague. Anyway, fuck that old twat—my voting record for this lot is immaculate. On the NHS I'm more hawkish than they'd like right now. You know how I stuck my head above the parapet on abortion. But I kept the pot simmering. Ready to boil. And Raymond has my back. We know that."

Bax, fidgeting, moved closer. Watson could see mud and dirt in the pores of his face. The slash of blood was still tacky, red. Watson wiped his lips with the back of his manicured hand.

"I'm making progress," Bax said.

"Good, good," Watson said, raising a hand. "I just don't want to hear . . . I just want to reiterate the importance of it, to me."

"I understand," Bax said, and looked down at his hands.

Watson smiled. He looked at Bax in admiration. "Look at that beautiful skull of yours."

"What?"

"Your lovely long skull. It's ideal, isn't it? Your long nose, your blue eyes. You must know you can admire it. Your ideal form. How it should be. How it will be. You're a handsome lad. You remind me of someone . . . it's the eyes, the cheekbones. You know, you should have a bit of fun with my friends sometime." He burst out laughing. He traced his fingers over his own hairless chest. "You'd be very popular."

"No, no. Not for me," Bax said, almost whispering, smiling.

"Let's be honest: you're a picture, my lad," Watson said. "A picture of the ideal. One day, one day—we'll be masters again. We'll be masters, and that lot—they'll be servants. Just as it was, it will be. Where did you say your old man was from? Bristol?"

"Cirencester."

"Lovely town, lovely town," Watson said. "Full of the right

kind of people. Stout villains and maidens. My late wife was from near there."

"Was she?"

"You'll know about the incident in Kent," Watson said. "Adds to my CV. Everyone these days loves a bit of personal tragedy. An obstacle to overcome. Some kind of emotional redemption storyline. It's all a load of fucking shite. But I'm happy to milk it. They all lap it up."

Watson sipped his drink, and stared into the black marble top for a time. Bax waited.

"The thing we always have to remember," Watson said, "is that we are winning. The other side can't get out of their own way, and they lost the will to fight many years ago. We're winning and they don't even fucking realise it."

"Yes, sir."

"We're going to fuck them all to death," Watson said, swilling his drink, staring into the marble, as if faces could be seen in its swirls and clouds. "You know how we are going to win this thing? Not with policies. Not with fucking details, who cares about the fucking details? With a war of anger. That's how we win. All emotion. All reaction."

Bax nodded. His eyes blank as stone.

"Right. Get one of the glasses," Watson said. "Let's do this. See what he is saying."

"Sir." Bax reached for a small pink shot glass on a high, empty shelf.

Watson lay down on a long black leather sofa. Outside, the sun was beginning to slowly drop behind the Pennines. Liquid copper light gleamed wetly on bark and rock and twig.

Bax walked over, and took off his heavy jacket. He stepped around a pool of thick vomit which sunk stinking near the sofa.

"Man," Bax said, shaking his head.

He sat down beside Watson, and pulled up his shirt cuffs. The room was now in dusk. A night had fallen.

Bax put the glass on Watson's chest on the tattoo of the Ouija board. He placed it carefully on *HELLO*. Watson did not flinch. His head lay back on the leather, his eyes were closed. His arms lay limp and flat. His fingers soft and relaxed and open on his chest.

"Okay, let's talk," Watson said.

"Do you ever think someone will find out?" Bax said, softly.

"About what?" Watson was lying back, as if entering sleep.

"About all this," Bax said.

"How would they? And I trust you, Bax. To make sure no one else does."

Bax and Watson each placed a finger on the upturned glass, which rose and fell with his slow, shallow breathing.

After a time, the glass appeared to move across his hairless flesh. The message came:

hellogary

19.

Shona and Terry were driving back to Ullathorne on the tight and winding dale roads lined with stone walls. On the uncut verges, pink foxgloves were nodding, and sprays of cow parsley stood in clouds of held seed.

Terry was changing radio channels with one hand, looking for music. Shona was on her phone and exasperated. She was sighing. Bernie had called, and was upset.

Bernie's voice had risen by an octave.

"The committee says in this letter that we have two weeks to sort it, Shona, or they're going to think about taking your father's rights away," she said. "Hugh opened the letter before I could get to it. He was awfully upset and he's gone to bed."

"How is he feeling? Is he all right?"

"No, he's not, Shona. As I said, he's very upset," Bernie said. Her voice was quavering a little.

Shona sighed and bit her lip. She looked out the window, the dale flashing by. She felt a great emptiness in her stomach. "What does the letter say *exactly*?"

"I'll go and fetch it," Bernie said, and there was a clunk as the phone was put down.

"Fuck this! No radio reception," Terry said.

"What music you got?" Shona said shortly.

Terry scrabbled in the shelf inside her door: there was a scramble of CDs, in and out of their covers. Light suddenly strobed rainbows on the plastic discs.

A large truck, full of catatonic sheep, was stationary at the tight crossroads in front of them. Terry pulled up. Pale heads stuck their snouts out of the truck, which was caked in moulded mud.

Terry picked one CD out. Shona held her phone close to her ear, and could hear Bernie thumping around her flat.

"Rolling Stones?" Terry said, putting a glinting disc into the CD player.

"No chance," Shona said, scowling.

"Why not?"

"Hate those old fuckers," Shona said.

"Jeezo," Terry said. She ejected the CD and looked at the other options.

Ahead the sheep bleated in the truck, which still wasn't moving.

"I can't see what the holdup is," Terry murmured, and tried to peer around the truck.

"Your music is shite—that's the fucking holdup," Shona said.

"Here: what about The Smiths?"

"I think not," Shona said, abruptly.

Terry smiled and cast Shona a bemused look with glittering eyes. When she smiled, dimples popped in her cheeks, and her ears rose slightly, as if on strings.

A sheep turned its trapped brown head and stared at Shona. Its eyes were jet black, and it had black patches around its mouth. It looked Satanic.

"Have you any electronic music?" Shona.

Terry scrambled further, and threw some cases onto the back seat.

"Not really—how about Kate Bush?"

"*Hounds of Love?*"

"Yeah."

"Fine."

Terry put the CD in and picked a track. A second

passed—a second of the truck engine grinding, of a baffled sheep bleating, of a shoal of birds chattering over the high hedges, of a distant cow moaning. Then a beautiful song began, and Shona closed her eyes. It reminded her, instantly, of her mother.

Bernie huffed back to the phone. "Found it."

"I thought you'd gone off and died somewhere," Shona said.

"Shona Sandison!" Bernie said, aghast.

"Go on, then. I'm stuck behind some sheep. What does the letter say?"

Bernie started reading in a singsong voice: "*The council considered that your allotment garden, plot seventeen, is in a poor state and condition, being untidy with an accumulation of items behind and to the side of your shed, and two large buddleias on two sides of the allotment garden which require cutting back substantially and are a nuisance to neighbouring tenants.*"

"Is that true?" Shona said. She did not know what a buddleia was, but assumed it was a weed.

"It's very overgrown," Bernie said, "but they're going to come and take it off Hugh if it's not tidied. '*A nuisance to neighbouring tenants!*' My foot!"

"Take it away—does it actually say that?"

"They say they are going to inspect his patch next week— Monday or Tuesday. It's signed by a Mr. Colin McCall, Allotment Officer. He says they're going to '*engage a contractor to undertake the remaining tasks and claim the full cost of this in damages from you.*' I don't think Hugh has the money or wherewithal for that. Damages!"

"Has he read this?"

"Yes, it was addressed to him."

The sheep truck finally moved. With a shudder it inched

forward, a solid weight slowly advancing, and then sped up, and passed through the narrow crossroads. A foam of black eyes inside the truck blinked.

"Thank the Lord," Terry whispered, and they moved.

"What a bunch of fascists," Shona said. "Do they know Dad's been sick?"

"I don't think they care. I haven't known how to respond. I bet it was that man with his solar panels who reported him. I am furious. Hugh is furious, too, but hasn't replied either. He can't lose his allotment, Shona. It will be a disaster for him. He will be absolutely scunnered—he loves that place . . ."

"I know, I know," Shona said, irritated.

". . . and in his condition . . ." Bernie went on.

"Yes, I know."

". . . it's cruelty . . . that's what it is . . ."

"Bernie! I know!" Shona said loudly. "Look, can you use email?"

"Yes, of course I can, I'm not demented," Bernie said. "I email my son all the time."

Shona suddenly laughed. "Newsflash! I didn't know you had a son!"

"There's a lot about me you don't know," Bernie said primly. "I bet you didn't know I used to be a nun either."

"Ya what?" Shona said, after a moment. "How did you have a son, then?"

"That's another long story. Oh—I hear Hugh rising. I'll take a picture and send to you. Can you ring the council? I'd love it if . . ."

"I'll sort it, Sister Bernadette," Shona said.

There was a silence.

"You and I need to talk," Bernie said, and the call ended.

"Who was that you were barking and laughing at?" Terry said, as the road fell down a hill. Rising ahead were the grey, black, and brown buildings of Ullathorne, and the ruined castle staring on its bare cliff.

"A nun," Shona said, "a nun who had a son."

"Sounds like the beginning of a song."

"Or the end of one," Shona said.

"So—Beverley wasn't that interesting?" Terry said, as the town moved around them. Cars were parked on cobbles, and shoppers drifted on wide pavements. There was a queue outside the butcher's—men checking notes on paper, a young woman shouting into a mobile phone.

"I wouldn't say that," Shona said. "There was something about her . . ."

"That you didn't trust?"

"Yeah. On the one hand, she volunteered a lot. But how much was true, I don't know. There was something she wasn't saying. But then, I was asking about things she probably didn't want to talk about that much. Did you get any pics at all?"

"Aye, on the down-low, when you were talking and I was smoking weed with the big fella. Some clear ones of her. I could crop you out."

"Great. I need to meet someone now," Shona said. "But I'll need some general views of the town—and the ruined mill at the bottom of the Bank. Can you find time to do that?"

"Could do, could do," Terry said. "I'll let you know how I get on."

"Fine. Well, drop me off here," Shona said, and Terry nodded. They parked at an angle on the cobbles, and Shona grabbed her things and almost rolled out of the car.

"Thanks, see you later," she mumbled, and Terry drove off. Shona watched her drive away for a while, her blond head disappearing, and then walked into the tangle of stone buildings, following the map on her phone.

St. Mary's Care Home was in the centre of the old town: a

large low building with tidily pitched roofs, set back in neat gardens. It looked like it had been built in the 1970s. The glass on the large windows shimmered in orange and brown. There were low flat gardens about it. The sun glimmered on enclosing railings, and the main door gleamed black.

Shona pushed a nagging irritation out of her mind. She had missed a phone call while she was talking to Bernie—it had been Vivienne. Her heart had leapt a little. She would call Viv later.

Shona refocused on the task in hand. She pulled her clothes together tightly and walked down the path to the main doors of St. Mary's. She pressed on the button for the intercom, but before she could speak, she was buzzed inside.

Down an adjoining long corridor, Shona could see pictures of flowers hanging in white frames, and a trolley with rows of white cups on it. The dull floors of the corridors were uncarpeted. A woman in a blue uniform emerged from a side door, rubbing her hands together. She glanced at Shona and stepped away.

Shona walked to the desk. She looked down at her clothes—a buttoned jacket, black jeans, black shoes. Her stick. It would do.

"Can I help you?" a woman behind the desk said at last, putting down the brown plastic phone.

"I hope I have the right place," Shona said, changing her voice slightly. She sometimes put on what she called her "posh Scots" accent when she felt it was useful. In her mind's ear she now sounded like a confident second-year law student at St. Andrew's University.

The woman nodded, smiling. She was wearing a small white watch, upside down on her chest. Her hair was tight and orange.

"I think you have my email—my name is Eliza . . . Field. I am a friend of Dan Merrygill. I would like to speak to his mother. I saw him last week before he . . . before the incident. I'd love to speak to her, even if for a short while."

"Martha Merrygill's boy?" the woman said, quietly.

"That's right, Daniel. I've come down from Scotland . . . I was at the wedding where he . . ."

"Yes, of course," the woman said. She put a hand on the phone again, and said she needed to speak to someone. "Eliza what, love?"

"Field. I won't bother her for long, I just need to tell her something that Daniel said."

"Okay."

"Something he wanted his mother to know."

"Okay, pet," the woman said, and waited for someone to pick up an internal line.

Shona looked about, her stomach turning, and sweat gathering on her shoulders. There was a small table in this foyer, with a truculent stack of old magazines lolling on it, waiting to be thrown away. There was flock wallpaper, and sturdy chairs.

"No," the woman said, to someone else. "Well, she's here right now. She's come all the way from Scotland."

Shona moved to one of the wide wood-and-metal seats and sat down. She placed her bag on her lap. The woman had been speaking for a few minutes now. Shona eyed the door. She could leave and no one would know her, or what she was doing. A clean, swift exit.

"A young woman," the woman said, louder, looking at Shona. "Yes, she was at the wedding when . . . yes."

Shona smiled back, as sweetly as she could manage.

"Okay," the woman said and stood. She flattened down her blue tunic and walked around the desk. "If you could come with me?"

"Thank you," Shona said. Her stick pecked the carpet silently and then tapped as they made their way down a brightly lit corridor. A door was open as they passed—she looked into a large room, with windows looking on into an internal courtyard. Several pensioners sat slumped in massive chairs pointed towards a lit television.

The orange-haired nurse stopped at an office door, rapped lightly with her long fingers, and they walked in.

In a bright small office, a large woman in a suit was sitting behind a desk. Shona was ushered in, and then the door closed behind her.

She sat down and smiled. Her left leg shook a little.

"I'm Fiona Cox, assistant manager," the woman said. "And you want to see Ms. Merrygill?"

"Yes," Shona said. "Following the terrible news about her son. I am—I was—a friend of Dan's. I came to speak to his mother. To talk about him."

Ms. Cox nodded slowly. "Terrible news indeed. It is not often the children of residents die before them. So, you were at the wedding where he . . ."

"That's right."

Ms. Cox looked at her steadily. Shona smelled flowers and cleaning fluid. The room was square and airless. The carpet was clean, the surfaces were clean.

"Terrible thing," Shona said, quietly.

"Of course," the woman said. "What is it you want to tell Ms. Merrygill? You could leave a note. Send a card, send flowers."

"I'd rather not . . . share. It's something Dan wanted her to know. He told me to tell her."

"And you've come down from Scotland especially?"

"Yes, from Leven."

"You could have emailed, or called."

"I very much felt the need to be here in person," Shona

said, as sadly as she could. "Some things are too important. I had to come."

"Well, as I am sure Daniel told you," Ms. Cox said, lowering her voice, "his mother is not very well and can get confused. Daniel valued the care and support we give her here. He used to visit every week. I never would have guessed . . ."

"No," Shona said, and put a hand to her eye, as if to wipe a nascent tear.

"But who knows these things?" Ms. Cox said. "People can be in trouble, in deep pain and . . ."

"Not show a thing," Shona said.

"Not give a glimpse of it to the outside world—to their friends or partners. I think it was that way with Daniel. You'd never know what was going in that head of his. And he was so pale. So pale. Pale and quiet. Like his mother."

"He mentioned how much comfort he got, knowing she was here, being looked after," Shona lied. "Still in his hometown."

Ms. Cox smiled. "Well, I am not sure he thought much of Ullathorne, but he did visit. Is it true he sold his house in Darlo and moved into a caravan? I read somewhere."

"I don't know about his caravan," Shona said, suddenly nervous. "I didn't know that."

"I'm sure I saw that in the piece about him in the *Echo*. Anyway—Ms. Merrygill will be having an afternoon snack soon and then we will be playing bridge. So you're lucky, Eliza, to have arrived when you did."

"Thank you," Shona said. "I won't take long. How is she?"

Ms. Cox looked at her hands for a moment. "I think it is fair to say the news will take a while to sink in. You've come a long way, and perhaps at the right time—before it does sink in." She stood. "Do you mind me asking—how did you come by that walking aid? Is it temporary?"

"I had a mountain climbing accident," Shona said. "When I was a kid."

"I'm sorry to hear that."

"We all have our crosses to bear," Shona said.

"Just like Daniel did," Ms. Cox said. "You know, I think he probably wasn't the same since his dad disappeared. He was just a bairn then. Ms. Merrygill won't talk about that, of course."

"Where did his father go?"

"Away travelling. Not sure if they ever got divorced. But it wasn't a happy home. So, Dan took his mother's name."

"Oh—what was the married name?"

"I can't remember," Ms. Cox said briskly and, not looking at Shona, bustled out of the room. "Come this way," she added, huskily.

They came to a door in a row of doors. Ms. Cox stopped and knocked gently before opening the door slowly and looking around its edge.

She turned back to Shona and nodded, and then pointed to a large digital watch on her wrist. "Ten minutes," she said. "No longer."

Shona nodded.

"Ten minutes," Ms. Cox said to a passing nurse.

With Ms. Cox behind her, Shona entered the small room. There was a loud clicking noise as the door shut, and a sense of clutter, and of shadows crouched around old furniture. There were dark bookcases, a writing desk with flowers in a pot, framed pictures, and a large metal bed slung with a light blue blanket.

Near the bed, in a large chair with wooden arms, sat a silent, unmoving elderly woman. She was wearing a dark blue tracksuit, and had a blanket over her lap. She was pale, and had pale blue eyes. She was looking out of the netted windows to Ullathorne, blurred and indistinct outside.

"Hello, Martha," Ms. Cox bellowed. The woman looked

up, her face deeply lined. "This is Eliza, a friend of your Daniel. She's popped by to have a word."

"Hello," the woman said, slowly, her voice as fragile as crepe paper. "Come and sit by me."

"Ten minutes," Ms. Cox repeated, and left the room. The door shut with an airless clunk.

Shona saw a low wooden stool, like a milking stool, by the bookcase. She put her stick to one side and crouched down on the stool. She turned the Dictaphone app on her mobile phone on, and let it record. Then she darkened the screen again.

"I am so sorry to hear about your son, Martha," Shona said.

Martha's hands were gently crossed on her lap. She had two rings on her ring finger, one with a small diamond. The skin around her eyes was as grey as a dove.

"He is gone now," she said, nodding, her tight white hair unmoving. "But he said, you know, that he had always been there."

Martha spoke clearly but slowly. She moved a hand upward; in it was a crumpled tissue. She wiped away water from her eyes.

"John was too hard on him," she said. "Far too hard, I always said. Spare the rod and spoil the boy, he said. But he was too hard on the lad. And me an old mother. I'm sorry, I am being rude, can I get you tea and a biscuit?"

"No, thank you," Shona said.

Martha turned her head, and looked at Shona. "I don't know you."

"I'm a friend from Dan's work."

"I don't know you," Martha said again, and looked to the window, and the inaccessible world beyond. "I knew what he was doing. And now he's gone."

"What was he doing?"

"When he were a lad, he used to cry a lot, he was a shy boy. Afraid of his own shadow," she said. "He wet his bed. Piles of sheets in the mornings."

She turned her head a little, but did not move. Dust drifted through the light. The books sat stacked on their unread shelves like blank gravestones.

"He was quiet," Martha said. "Such a bonny baby. Then his father left and he was never the same. Never the same. He missed his daddy."

"When did you last see him?"

"He was a sickly child. He had whooping cough, the mumps, suffered terribly with the measles," Martha said. She blinked slowly.

"When did you see him last?" Shona said, persisting.

"He used to go into that room of his," Martha said.

Shona's phone buzzed: a text from Ranald, her editor. She ignored it.

"There was always something going on in that room of his," Martha said. She turned to Shona again, and looked past her. "His room was full of letters."

"Did he write a lot? Of letters?"

"He would lock himself away," Martha said, shaking her head.

Shona rubbed her face. Her time was running out, and she needed more. "Did you know he was sad?"

"He came and saw me on the eve of Epiphany," Martha said, her eyes unseeing. "He held my hand and said I would be taken care of. He'd sold his house, he said, was moving into a caravan. He would be happier there, he said. He said he was nearer to the stones, to the rocks."

"A caravan."

Martha smiled. "It is lovely. Have you seen it? He showed me a lovely picture."

"No."

"He's growing vegetables. He's saving up, he said. You wouldn't know Ullathorne. Not with that accent. Ullathorne gets very dark. Winter is like a cold hearth. I think people from outwith Ully do not understand it. How cold it is, how hard it gets."

"He was telling me about something terrible that happened when he was young, about his friend Andrew," Shona said.

Martha turned her face the other way. "Poor bairn," she said, softly. "Poor wee bairn."

"Terrible business," Shona said.

"Police came around. Blue lights in the kitchen. John upstairs, writing. Police came—Harmire—to speak to Danny but of course he knew nowt. How could he. He left with his friends. He was scared, I was scared. But then . . ."

"But then . . . ?"

"It all went away. It all went away, didn't it?" Martha smiled. "The inspector never came around again."

Shona sensed a body by the door outside. Someone was going to open it. A shadow fell.

Martha's eyes began to glitter.

"Did Daniel leave Andrew with his friends, that night?" Shona prompted.

"He came home. Left his chips by the front door. I remember: the police saw them. Chips and gravy."

The door opened, and a nurse in brown appeared. She said, "Time now, Martha," and nodded to Shona.

Shona stood up. "I am so sorry about your son."

Martha put her hand out, and Shona held it. It was weightless.

"Will you come again?" she said, with a half-smile.

"I live in Scotland, but I'll try," Shona said, and her

stomach turned over. Everything was too awful. She wanted, suddenly, to be at home with her father.

"I'd love a visit," Martha said.

"Now, now," the nurse said.

"I'd like another visit."

"I will visit," Shona lied, smiling.

Martha was crying without moving. A tear slowly rolled down her smooth cheek. She gently pulled at Shona's hand, and she moved closer, almost crouching.

"'*I'm talking to myself, Mam,*' he would say," she said, quickly, quietly. "He said he was talking to himself—in his room. That he could speak to himself. That he was already dead. That's what he said. He told me one night. After Jack left me. Off to write his books, and never came back."

Shona felt a deep shiver run through her. Her shoulders shook. Martha's eyes had become hardened and fixed. She felt the woman's breath on her face.

"Come on, Martha," the nurse said, bustling into the room. "Let's not start all that silly business again."

Shona withdrew her hand, like taking her fingers from a soft pocket.

"That's no way to talk to me, is it, nurse?" Martha said, annoyed, looking up, turning her head to watch Shona leaving the room.

"That's no way to talk, is it?" she said again, and Shona left the room.

Martha's voice, wordless, could be heard down the hall, fading softly as Shona walked away.

The hard light rolled over Shona in waves of destruction.

20.

Alison was leaning on her kitchen island, her face in her hands. Margaret Gildersleve had emailed her. Alison could not shake Peg's words from her mind.

Her children were outside slumped on beach chairs in the long garden, watching images roll and flash on their devices. Airplanes moved heavily across the blue London sky, slowly knitting a cat's cradle of jet trails.

Nigel was back from his alleged business trip. He said he had something to tell her.

She looked about her unlovely house. It was tall and narrow, and in central London: it would sell for a lot of money. They would sell this place, and she and the children would live somewhere else. Away from the city and its incessant demand. From the noise.

They would move into a place of greater quiet, where a deep river ran, and old trees overhung. Where rock and stone stood, and the hills embraced a valley, and time slowed, and there was time to think, and do, and be. The children would not miss their overpriced, demanding, average school. They would not much miss their empty, hectoring father.

Nigel walked into the kitchen, his flip-flops slapping. He was tanned and tall and was still damp and pink from the shower, his heavy head of hair gleaming.

"So," he said, curtly, as if addressing a meeting.

She stared into the stone spirals on her kitchen countertop.

We have found something in the woods, Peg had written.

"Well," he said, clapping his hands together. He lowered his head, and his eyes grew wide. His voice became his version of low, and soothing.

"I think it is time we have a little chat."

"You know at some point you need to move out," she said.

He blinked heavily. "Can we talk first?" he said. "We need to. I think now is the time. *The* conversation."

She knew what it was. She felt it in her body. There was dread in her, but there was no sorrow. She had searched for it, but there was none. Alison had felt deep and angry sorrow before, and this feeling was not the same. This was another place, another feeling—closer to an extended irritation. The heat and itch of a slowly emerging spot.

She turned and looked through the windows at the children. Their tawny heads. All she needed was them. Their frail hands held back the darkness.

"Let's go somewhere else," she said.

"To the pub?" he said.

She looked at his wide face. It struck her, as it had before, as less a face of a grown man, with all the lines of loss and painfully salvaged joy that might feasibly mean, than a moveable screen built for melodrama. She felt a passing twinge of sorrow for him. She had learned, over the years, that instead of deep convictions, or real emotions, he had only a thinly felt series of poses.

"No, not the pub. Somewhere out of sight—away from the children," she said.

She slipped off her high chair and walked past him, checking her phone. Nothing new. No more news. She had texted and received no reply.

In Deepdale, Peg had said. *We have found something.*

She padded past the newly carpeted stairs, the large, framed portraits of the family taken in a white studio, a stand of tennis rackets, lacrosse sticks, and golf bags. All the future landfill of their comfortable, unsustainable lives.

She went into the front room. He did not seem to have followed her. The room had no television and was rarely used. She had once thought that adult guests could gather there and talk seriously about the world. It never happened. Instead, three large cream settees sulked around an elaborate fireplace, under a chandelier, and threatened a low table with heavy books glossily advertising things she did not really care about: architecture, international travel, business, the Himalayas.

A paperback book about self-improvement was on the sofa, something Nigel had been reading since he told her their marriage was over. Alison took the book and threw it across the room. It landed behind a chair.

She looked at the rest of the books—she would burn them all. She sat down and crossed her legs and Nigel loomed in the doorway.

He mouthed almost silently—"Are the kids okay?"

"They're fine. Fed and watered."

"What was that noise?"

"Nothing. A car."

Nigel was now barefoot. "How's your mother?"

Alison blinked. Her mother was fine, a widow living in a bungalow in Cornwall, as far away from Tyrdale as she could manage. She went to church twice weekly and was involved in committees. She refused the policeman's pension, and lived frugally.

"Mum is fine. Still a big fan of Jesus. Why?"

He sat down, and began to wring his hands, his long hairy fingers. He was blinking rapidly.

Alison knew, or nearly knew, that Nigel had met someone else. Finally, someone else to inflict himself upon.

There had been a period when they met, when he had been long-haired and handsome, and his scattergun red-trousered enthusiasms had seemed the kaleidoscopic interests of a man in love with life and all it could offer. And after the religious silence of her mother, the lies and corruptions of her father, his world seemed something to marvel at: something vast and multicoloured. But the endless swirling confetti clouds of his interests, she realised were just that, a swirl of weightless colours. A two-dimensional whirl of nothingness.

"Alison," he said.

"Nigel Osbourne," she said.

To think, she remembered, she had been unsure about marrying him, this erratic, rackety man. Until the board had told her: *Say Yes to No*. And so she had said yes to N.O. The letters still speaking to her, long after the glass had stopped moving.

Gary Watson had always taken its messages so seriously, all those years ago. She wished she had not.

"You look so tired," Nigel purred.

"Nigel, let's get this over with," she said. "For both our sakes."

He turned his head slightly, as if reluctantly accepting a bad offer, and carried on. "Ultimately, Alison, I see this as good news. This is in fact wonderful news." He patted his hands on his knees. "For both of us. But there is no easy way to say this . . ."

Alison suddenly felt violently impatient. She stood up.

"I have met the most wonderful person, the most wonderful woman," Nigel said, with a tremulous voice.

She felt herself begin to shake. She looked to the fireplace.

There were hard black fire irons there, that could easily shatter his fragile skull. Despite his height, he was as weak as a gosling. She was stronger than him. She could break open his face, drag the body to the ornamental pond, sink him in the water, and drive away. It would be a long time before he was found.

He was still talking. He had clearly practised this speech, as he was now gaining confidence, and his voice was clear and unruffled.

". . . we understand each other, ultimately, in a way which really speaks to me at this time in my life. And, to be frank, we have fallen in love! Which is a wonderful thing, isn't it?"

He shook his head, as if in wonder. His hands splayed out, touching at the thumbs. "Do you not want to know who she is?" he asked, as if surprised.

"No," she said, staring into the fireplace. "I do not give a fuck."

He looked momentarily stunned, then carried on. "We should now move on to the next phase: make our arrangements, disinvest, de-couple, disentangle, re-combine. We can talk to Derek. We can talk about our assets, about the house, the children . . ."

She nodded. Then, she began to speak—about the children, about their house—and was pleased with how calm and focused she was. She was making sense. She was not expressing anger, or disappointment. Her tone was even and unemotional. She agreed they could speak to their financial advisor, and talk about the house, the assets, the money.

As she spoke, she was aware that another, cool, eyeless part of Alison was looking at the table, and the shape and solidity of its surface. Then she realised she had said her piece, and there was nothing more to say. She had detached, and reattached. And Nigel was talking on again. His words, his deep voice, rolled on.

". . . maybe we can consider boarding them, so that . . ."

She thought of the pale face of Daniel, dead on the pages of the newspapers. The face from memory, from a time now lost and gone. Unless time did not run to the future and back to the past. Unless there was no time, and he was still alive, and she was dead. Her children were both alive and dead. And Nigel, this stranger, was both alive and dead, both from the past and the future, as well as the instant and the present, which was now already gone.

She was sitting on an expensive sofa in her temporarily intact house, which was also a house of ashes, a house sunk in mud by the swollen river, a house of stone, a house rendered by fire, a house of weeds and ivy. She briefly saw a white body in water, a detached arm spiralling in foamy eddies.

". . . slightly more than half of the house, given my investment in it over the years," he went on.

In Deepdale. We've found something.

The heavy face of her dead father, the police inspector, the man who had led the search for, and not found, Andrew all those years ago, rose to her eyes.

Her father, who had not interviewed her, and not interviewed Gary Watson, and not interviewed the friends all together, who had closed the case while Andrew's flesh was still on his bones.

Her father, dead now. Dead in his disgrace.

"Don't you worry, our Alison, this will all blow over," he had said.

Now Nigel would blow out of her life, too, and she had to return to the source of her discomfort. The place she had left and rejected but still called to her in dreams and daydreams. Tyrdale, the North, was still with her now, in the south, in London. The folded land, within her. It was always there with her. She had to make it real again, and return. She had to leave the life into which she had escaped.

Nigel burbled on.

". . . and seeing their daddy in love—really in love, for the first time—can only be good for them, to be around my own personal joy . . ."

She needed to go back there, now. Andy had been gone for years. Now Daniel was gone. Who remained? Who else was there? All the faces of the past were rising from the mud of time.

We need to talk, the message had said.

Alison stood up.

"Okay, thanks. I think I need to go," she said. "I'll be away for a couple of days. Can you cope with the kids?"

He held a hand to her. "Darling," he said, his eyes brimming.

It says Jet.

"Fuck off, Nigel," she said. She left the room and walked slowly up the stairs, to pack.

She threw clothes in a bag.

The past was suddenly here again. It was as if it had been pulled, crashing through the serried fading coulisse of intervening years by a sudden yank on its ropes. And now it was fully present, in all its blurred, degraded and half-forgotten reality. Shaky on its temporal strings, but there, in front of her, as real as a stone, or a moor, or a tree. As real as her collapsed clothing in her dark brown bags.

She half ran down the stairs, and flung her belongings in her car.

She drove north through the day, and the evening, moving relentlessly forward down a lightless tunnel, as if she was speeding down the course of a vein.

21.

Bax had moved too far, and too fast. He was unsure of the path he was following. But the only way was forward.

He parked his black car a mile from the house, in a mossy dark lane near a stream, hidden by a barn and overhanging trees. He walked in the deepening twilight towards the distant village. He climbed over walls and crossed fields, avoiding the roads, to reach the house at the end of the row. As he drew closer, he could see someone moving inside.

Bax wore black gloves, and his sleek body was wrapped in black cotton and leather. He crouched and ran like a cat.

He had left Watson at Scar Top. The glass had been moving. Their friend had been speaking. And the MP, as was his way, had drawn comfort. Thinking of it, Bax shook his head.

Bax halted by the back wall of the garden, as still as a bone. He waited. A dim light glowed within the house. The garden was darkening, the trees and outbuildings becoming silhouettes, the light moving from the outside to the inside. Natural light withdrew and electric light advanced.

He flexed his fingers within his black gloves. He drew the knife and moved it from palm to palm. It weighed little. Lighter than a gun, and, unlike a firearm, untraceable.

Bax peered up, and observed the stars scattered above in their array, like the cocaine crumbs scattered across Watson's obsidian table.

He moved again, a shadow within shadow, through the garden. He reached for the back door handle, and, as he knew it would be, it was open. He turned it slowly and crept into the kitchen, blade in hand.

He waited a while and listened. There was movement above—someone was running a bath. Water was filling a tub, with a slow and constant rumble. Music was playing somewhere. A man's voice was humming against guitar and pattering drums.

Bax leant against the fridge for a moment. On the fridge door, attached by magnets, were photos of a couple in various years and states: on holiday, at a beach, with some old relatives. There was one of a young girl, the same woman as in the other photos, but in a school uniform, her face pale and anxious.

He moved slowly to a door. He smelled cannabis, and the folk music was louder now. Upstairs, the running water had stopped.

The music was now a woman, singing sadly over minor chords. He could not pick out the words. There was golden, shaking light moving around the edges of the door.

Bax gently pushed and then moved around the door, his knife drawn and held high, ready to strike. The music was glowing from a large set of speakers. Candles were glimmering. Shadows hung tremulous around the room.

He turned quickly, sensing something large and moving. But it was too late.

A large, bearded man with an axe brought the blade down with force, and it caught Bax full in the face. His face collapsed. His skull cracked and splintered into itself, imploding from the weight of iron and muscle. There was a gasp, and a crack, a popping noise, and his released blood fell in a sheet.

His body crashed to the wooden floor. Bax's face was now a sudden open envelope of bone and blood, cartilage, tongue, gum, and teeth. The nose was destroyed and the opened mouth was agape. The long knife in his hand gently dropped onto the wooden floor.

He had fallen into a small occasional table. Candles had fallen. Some had been snuffed out by his warm blood. Wicks hissed. Others still flashed and flamed on the wooden floor. Their light shook on Bax's remaining eye. Candle wax dripped on his unfeeling skin, and hardened to a new coating.

Karl, astonished, dropped the axe with a loud clunk. Blood dripped from his beard. A tooth rolled to a stop in the doorway. Sloppy liquid fell from the ceiling.

"Fuck me," he said to himself. Something wet and thick was gathering on his forearm.

He stepped heavily over what remained of Bax, and yelled up the stairs, "Bev!"

"What? I'm in the bath."

"I think you need to come down."

"What was that noise? Have you broken something?" she shouted from the warm water. "I'm in my bath, yer daft apeth! What is it?"

Karl ran a bloody red hand through his thick bloody hair. "I've killed some fella with the ornamental axe!"

22.

"So where are we then?" Ranald said. His voice thick as liquorice down a clear line from the north of the north.

Shona was sitting on her bed at the bed and breakfast, laptop beside her, her stick on the floor.

"Well, where the fuck are we, indeed," she said. She ran through, in brief, her travels, discussions, and discoveries.

"So, let's recap: we have this guy who killed himself, from this school in the north of England, and this tragic class of which he was part," Ranald said. Somewhere in the background of his voice, dogs were barking.

Shona flung herself back on her bed. "Yeah. Dan, our suicide, was part of this tiny group of sixth-form students. Early 1990s."

"Who else was there?"

"Andrew, Viv's older brother. He went missing ages ago, and is still missing. He is dead, of course. But no body found. The police basically gave up. Viv spoke about him at the wedding that never was."

"Does she know you are there?"

"No chance."

"Is she likely to find out?"

Shona rubbed a hand over her face. "I haven't really thought about it properly yet," she lied.

"Okay, who else—anyone interesting?"

"There is Beverley, part of that class. I interviewed her. She told me about the Ouija sessions. She lives in a village near Ullathorne. Council worker, folk singer, partner, no kids. Not sure I believe everything she says."

"Good copy?"

"Yeah, nice material, but all background."

"Fine, all right," Ranald murmured.

"Then there was this other lad, Robert Stang—Bobby. Big guy. He joined the army, is also back in town, works at a factory."

"Have you spoken to him?"

"No, not yet. I've only just got here."

"Okay . . . maybe you should."

"I will. Then there is this other lass, Alison, who was the star of the class, and moved to London. Made herself a successful career in finance."

"Goody Two-shoes."

"Exactly. Head girl. Her dad was a police inspector in the town."

"Oh, aye? What was his name?"

"Harmire."

"Name rings a bell, but not sure why."

"And then there is something quite interesting. The local MP was in the class, Gary Watson."

"What, 'sink the boats' Watson?" Ranald said. He seemed to whistle, away from the phone.

"The very same," Shona said. "I don't know how close he was with Daniel, but he was there. In that class."

Ranald seemed to think for a while. "This makes it all much stronger already: it shouldn't be too hard to try and get a comment from him, that's a story in itself. We can do a full backgrounder for you. I'll get one of the fellas to do a cuttings file and ping it across while you are there."

"Thanks—anything about his childhood in particular," Shona said.

"He's one of the coming stars, isn't he? He's been on 'top ten MPs to watch' lists for a while. His voting and speaking record speaks for itself. It's as you would expect. He's good on the telly. Good speaker. Can you meet him? Has he commented on our suicide?"

"No. No one's made the connection, I don't think. Why would they?"

Down the line, Shona could hear him tapping a pen against something.

"Oh, and I have words from the mother," she said, quietly.

"The suicide's mum? Fabulous! Any help?"

"I don't know," she said. "I'm not sure we can use them."

"Right, okay," he said, uncertainly.

There was a silence.

"How's Shetland?" she said, after a time.

"It's braw today," he said. "What's it like there?"

"I'm a city girl. All this space and silence makes me itchy. It's pretty, but rural, repressed and hard."

"I had a girlfriend like that once," Ranald said.

"Funny."

"How you getting on with Terry?"

"She swears too fucking much," Shona said.

Ranald laughed. Then recovered: "Look, I think you need to speak to Watson. And this Daniel, you said his caravan was burned out?"

"Immolated. Oh, we . . . came across some of his stuff."

"How?"

"I won't incriminate you by association. It was in the shack I mentioned. There's a camera—a disposable one, it needs developed."

"Wow, well that could be something?" Ranald said, unconcerned about where or how it had been found. "You definitely need to get that developed. Look, Shona, there's something going on here. I mean, I think you have almost enough for a colourful feature as it is, what with the death, the tattoos, the house sale, the caravan, the shack with the tramp, the Ouija board sessions, the school link and so on, but . . ."

"I need more on Watson," she said, nodding. Outside, the town's lights were slowly coming on. A string of white lamps lit the main road beyond the trees. It was a cloudless night. The sky was dark, but sprayed with an arc of stars, more than she had ever seen in Glasgow or Edinburgh.

"Can you stay a couple more days? Get Watson if you can. Surely he's doing some kind of election stuff. Oh—wait . . ."

"What?"

"Here on the old interweb—your man Watson is doing his campaign launch at a hotel in Tyrdale. Near a waterfall? It's on his website. Some place called the Fosse and Rainbow? Near the Great Fosse—is that . . ."

"Yeah, that's a massive fuck-off waterfall around here. When is that?"

"Friday—two days."

"Fine—I'll try to pin Watson down there?"

"It's a plan. Make sure Terry is with you. And until then, dig as much as you can, and get a load of colour, too. School friends, relatives—all that palaver."

"Thanks, Ranald."

"How's your old man?"

"Och, Dad's on the mend," Shona said, tightly. "He has a fucking nun looking after him."

"How do you mean? What—a real nun?"

"Yeah, she used to be a nun. Now she harasses my old man. I'll tell you more another time."

"Okay, it's late and I need to walk the dogs. What you doing next?"

Shona could hear keys being jingled. She had not visited Shetland for many years. She imagined Ranald in a self-built house on cliff edge, staring out at the immense steely sea, the massive sky.

"I think I need either to go on a long walk or get a long drink," she said. "Or both."

"Sounds like a plan. Look, thanks for all this, Shona. We're getting somewhere. You're good," Ranald said.

"Well, I knew that already," she said, smiling, and signed off.

She looked out onto the darkening world. She wanted to get some air. She felt the dead breath of the care home still in her mouth, settling in her lungs. She realised three things: she missed her father, she needed a walk and she was hungry.

The street outside was dark and wide. She walked hesitantly at first, wondering whether to follow the main road into the marketplace, or take another route into town and find another path. She remembered a chip shop on the main street, so she headed that way. A car passed slowly.

She walked on, the only noise her feet and the occasional tap of her stick. She walked on and reached the marketplace, and the wide main street. The stone buildings were dark now. A man was smoking outside the Lion. A couple of youths leaned on the wall outside another pub, the Green Man, chatting and drinking from bottles.

A wave of loneliness suddenly filled her. She thought of Viv and felt a sudden nauseating wave of terrible dread. She stopped walking and leaned against the closed door of the butcher's. She felt a sob building within her, like a sudden wave. She held her face with her hand for a while, and gripped the stick as hard as she could.

"Fuck off," she said. "Fuck off, fuck off, fuck off. Idiot."

She opened her eyes, and wiped her face and looked out, beyond the town. In the city, Shona was often lonely. In the countryside, she felt alone. She felt tiny in this place. Walking in a world on a greater scale than she could fill, or within which she could have a sense of meaning. Beyond these old stone houses was the ancient silent dark. The silence sunk into everything—the air, the light, the stone, the surrounding trees. Even the river was silent now, running darkly somewhere out of sight. Edinburgh, her home, was quiet, thrawn, introverted, interior—but not like this. Glasgow, where she had grown up, was never quiet. Everything was noise, there. She missed it. But she was also hungry. And she had half a story.

And so she wiped her eyes, and walked on. The chip shop's glow was exaggerated in the darkening evening—a puddle of golden and rich light. She clattered up the short steps. There was another customer standing, short and bulky. He was wearing a long grey winter coat with its collars up, a suit, and shiny black shoes. He looked out of place. Behind the glass of the fish and chip display, a small pink-faced man was shovelling chips like a stoker feeding an engine. He had a small white cap on his head. He was sweating, his arms a blur.

"Two fish," he suddenly barked.

The suited man nodded and said, "Aye."

Shona waited by the door. He turned and looked at her. He had a boxer's face: pummelled and smooth. A nose broken years ago. Small white burn scars in array around his ear.

"How's Mr. Watson?" the chip man said, swaddling the food in brown paper. He flipped the package around in his fingers.

"Ready to go again," the hulking man said. He flicked another glance at Shona. She opened her phone and pretended to look at it.

"He'll walk it," the chip shop man said. "He's a good solid Ully lad and speaks plain sense. I knew his old man, you know. Fine man."

He handed over the food and the man paid with a fifty-pound note. Shona moved out of his way as he barrelled past her, trailing the smell of expensive cologne.

The chip shop man looked up from behind the blasting heat of his work. "What yer havin," he said, his face impassive.

Within a few minutes, Shona was jamming slimy hot fish into her mouth and her pocket was lumbered with a can of cold Coke. Her mouth blanched at the tang of vinegar and salt, the crackle of hot batter. She walked slowly to the park beside the ruined castle. It was on a height, crowned by trees—the edge of the woods.

Her phone suddenly buzzed. She swore and sat on a park bench, and put the fish and chips and stick to one side. She wiped her hand on her jacket and picked out her phone. Distant lights glittered on a far road in the darkness.

It was Viv. The phone buzzed on. Shona did not want to answer. But she answered.

"So, Shona," Viv said. Her voice was hard and high.

"Hi, Viv . . . I—"

"You're selling my fucking story to the papers?"

Shona took the phone from her face for a moment, and gulped a dry gulp. Then she returned.

"Out with it," Viv snapped.

"No, I'm not."

"Aye, you are. Shona. Jesus fucking Christ."

"I am trying to—"

"Write me up. Write my family up. Sell it to the papers, Shona! Jesus." Viv choked and seemed to gulp a cry.

"Viv, I'm not. Listen to me. Listen," Shona found herself pleading.

"Can't believe it, to be honest. Cannot fucking believe it."

Shona stood up. Alone in the dark.

"And to think you were going to read my poem!" Viv said, spitting.

Shona closed her eyes tightly. She balled up her strength and purpose. "Viv, listen—I'm not writing a single word about you. Nothing. I'm trying to find out about Dan. I was commissioned. Someone asked me to. So, I'm looking into—"

"I'm not a fucking idiot, Shona. I'm not as clever as you. But I'm no fool. A pal of mine has seen you in the town. She said you were looking into what happened to Andrew. What happened to our Andrew! And you're going to write it all up again, and hook it on Dan's death. Drag it all up again. What's the peg, Shona—what's the fucking peg? My fucking wedding! That never was. My wedding. That's the peg. Or, as we both fucking know, without Dan topping himself like a twat, there's no story. Because we both know my poor brother's vanishing act is not news now. Not interesting. But Dan fucking offs himself and suddenly Andrew is there again for you to rake up. I know he's gone. I know it. But there you are—in Ullathorne, my hometown—scraping around for a story. Fuck's sake, Shona. I can't believe it."

There was a silence for a while. Shona opened her mouth.

"Writing about my family. The worst thing that's happened to me. To my mam and dad. And you're there, asking questions. Dragging it up."

"Viv . . ."

"And if you dare speak to Mam I will find you and—"

"Viv, I am not going to do that—look—"

"No, Shona!" Viv shouted. "I don't want to hear it. I can't fucking stop you. I know that, God help me. I could try but I couldn't stop you. I've seen what you do, and how you do it. There's no stopping you. Even if the bodies start fucking piling up."

"Viv . . . look . . . Maybe you can help . . ."

"Shona! Get to fuck, seriously. No. I don't want to speak to you again. Never a-fucking-gain."

"Viv . . ."

"You going to write about the money as well?" Viv suddenly shouted.

"What money? No . . ."

"What money? You know fine well what fucking money. You make me sick, Shona. Make me sick."

The call ended with a sudden, sharp click.

Shona sat down and was quiet and motionless for a while. She took her stick and kicked it. It skittered on the tarmac of the path, and then fell softly on wet grass.

She dumped the rest of the fish and chips into a bin in the cold dark, as the brown river ran in the night. The castle ruins glimmered. The moon, yellow as a scab, appeared behind ragged, sick clouds.

Shona stood up, and walked slowly alone back to the warm emptiness of her bed and breakfast, along the silent streets of the town, in a senseless fog as if drunk, as if she was concussed.

23.

But she did not get there. A car drew up alongside her as she walked across the main road.

Terry wound down her window, and stuck her head out. "Howdy, stranger." She grinned. "Fancy a drink?"

Shona stood still. Her hands were greasy, and she smelled of vinegar. She realised she was shaking. Or she felt that she was shaking.

"You all right?" Terry said. Her car was humming, and warm. Lights were gold on the dashboard.

"Yeah, fine," Shona said. "Drink where?"

"I know a place?"

"A pub?"

"A place. I have some booze in the car. It's been a long day, let's have a drink."

Shona's stick rapped on the car door as she got in. The car was warm and the seat soft beneath her. She felt tiredness soak her body.

She sat quietly as Terry drove into the darkness. They moved down the Bank, the broken mill sombre in the darkness, and out along the river. Listening to the radio burbling, but not really listening, they crossed the pounding Tyr and moved through black fields and trees in parallel to its wide slow course. The town drifted like an illuminated ship in the dark behind them. They eventually pulled up alongside a large gate to a field. The dark field sloped down to a silhouetted copse, and the river.

"Here we are," Terry said, "hop out."

They left the car, its lights clicking off, plunging the gate and the wall, the field, back into the waiting natural dark. The stray bugs and darting dust that had swarmed temporarily in the car's light blinked back into their hidden minute lives.

Terry climbed over the gate, with a clanking tote bag of tins and other, undefinable, items. Shona stood, stick in hand, satchel over her shoulder in front of the gate. She felt for a moment, afraid, here in the rural vastness, and with an obstacle before her. A long way from home, and from her father.

"Ah, sorry," Terry said, and fiddled with the gate's fastening for a moment, and it swung open.

"I can climb you know," Shona said.

"Well . . ." Terry began to say something, and shrugged. She looked away, and pointed down to the river. "There's a beach down there."

"I think I prefer an old boozer," Shona said, peering down the field, plum-purple in the dim light.

"I am an old boozer," Terry said, laughing, and, swinging the tote, started tramping down the field to the river. Halfway down the meadow she reached into her bag and pulled out a squat camping light. She clicked it on, and like an archaic cleric led the way, by light, to the water.

Shona looked up. There were no clouds, and the moon was encircled by a dim silver aura. The stars were arrayed in chaos and constellation, and a faint arc of the Milky Way could be seen.

She followed Terry, followed the swinging light. When it suddenly dropped out of sight, Shona picked up her pace, her calves damp from the grass, until she could see the light again, stationary on the riverbank. There was a short drop to the beach, but a smooth route had been gouged from earth and sand and grass, and she followed it down to the shingle beach.

Terry was already sitting cross-legged, leaning over a circle of blackened stones. "I think we might borrow this old fire," she said. From her bag she pulled some kindling and fire lighters.

"I hate barbeques," Shona said.

"Why's that?" Terry said, smiling, her face suddenly lit by a cigarette lighter. Her cheeks orange, her eyes flashing yellow.

"If I wanted explosive food poisoning, I could just go lick a door handle," Shona said.

"Fine. But I'm just lighting a fire for us to sit beside. To keep us warm. I'm not going to rustle up a tea."

Shona nodded. Terry asked her to help look for dry sticks, and in the near dark they gathered twigs and river driftwood.

Shona moved slowly. Her eyes adjusted to the light, and she saw curved pale twigs, dropped from the trees above. They were jointed and smooth, like parts of a dismantled tiny skeleton. She gathered them one by one, moving hesitantly, her stick resting by the fire, which Terry was lighting with gusts of breath and handfuls of kindling. She could smell the river, its swirling soil and deep brown water and carried life.

The fire began to bloom, and it licked light onto the beach, and flickered gold and scarlet on their faces. They opened green cans of premixed gin and tonic and watched the river pass by in near silence, the flames now crackling on blackened spindles of twig and stick, rose-orange at its heart where the fire lighters burned hard, gusts of sour smoke rising on the windless air.

"So, a big day," Terry said.

"Average," Shona said, after a long pause. "Did you get general views of the town, of the mill?"

"Yes, boss." Terry nodded. "How's your dad?"

"Fine."

"Can he save his allotment?"

"I have to. I'm not sure what he will do if I can't. It's his world. I will need to get back to Edinburgh and sort it. But instead I'm stuck here, sitting in the middle of the sticks where no fucker lives."

Terry chuckled and threw a handful of snapped twigs onto the flames.

"What?" Shona said.

"You have a way with words."

"If I didn't, I'd be fucked. That's all I have."

"Come on now."

"No, seriously. You must know journalists."

"I do indeed."

Shona drank a gulp of gin. "You'll know, then. We're refugees from society. Some are desperately trying to be important: trying to get *in*. Showbiz for ugly people, as someone said. Some are trying to escape, to get *out* of normal life. To view it all from a safe distance. Others, they just cannot do anything else. Clever misfits, the disenchanted, smart-arse oddballs, and misshapes—like me."

"Like you," Terry said, nodding. She tipped back her gin and tonic and opened another one with a hissing clink.

"Wait a minute, you're driving, aren't you?"

"Ach, yes. But we'll be fine."

"How far is it to walk from here? Ullathorne."

"Half an hour?"

"I think I'll walk back, then, if it's all the same."

The flames popped and spat. Terry leaned over and blew into it. They were on an island of fire and light in the watchful dark. Nearby, the broad river ran silently over rock and stone. She turned to Shona.

"What's your story, then, Shona Sandison?"

"What's *your* story, Theresa Green?" Shona said.

Terry's eyes were very clear. Her hair swept back from her

ears, away from her temple. She looked sleek, like a water creature.

"Nowt to tell," Terry said, shrugging. "Grew up in Richmond—the original Richmond, down the road, not the one in London. Edinburgh art school: it was fun. Did some travelling, did some newspaper work . . ."

"Where?"

"The *Mirror, Daily Record* for a bit, and then some right daft bugger convinced me to live with him in Newcastle—so the *Chronicle, Northern Echo, Teesdale Mercury,* the Tyrdale paper. *Yorkshire Post. Guardian*—northern edition."

"Nice. Good work."

"Has its moments."

Shona looked out over the river. It was glossy and black now, rolling like a dark plastic. A smooth rock at its centre stood out, and the water turned white as it flowed around it, and gently slopped over it, grinning suddenly like a smile, and then disappearing into the black again.

"The daft bugger saw through me in the end, though," Terry said, now poking the warm fire with a stick. "So, I'm freelance in more ways than one." She stared hard into the fire. Her eyes became tigerish with flame. "The North. It's beautiful, it's bleak. It's a bit broken down. It can be lonely. It can be lovely. I moved around. Lived in Durham. Spent quite a lot of time in and around Hawes."

Shona burst out with laughter. "I beg your frickin' pardon?"

"It's a wee town in Yorkshire!" Terry said. "*Hawes*, not whores."

"Maybe I should visit Hawes," Shona said.

"You should. You'd love it. There's a cheese factory. Anyway, what about you?"

"Nothing much to tell," Shona replied, and pulled her legs

up to her body. She drained her can, and opened another. She looked up. The stars were resplendent. The river ran. The trees, whispering, listened. Nothing moved apart from the high branches, and the flames, the water, the two huddled humans by the ancient fire.

Shona breathed out.

"Glasgow born, bred, schooled. Southsider. History at Glasgow. Mam died. Journalism at Strathclyde and Caledonian. Got a job at the *Mercury*—it went bust. Got injured. Had a time-out. Moved with my dad to Edinburgh—got a job at the *Post*. Made redundant by their bastard editor. Won the bloody Reporter of the Year nonsense. Freelance. Signed up with Ranald and his mob. Live with Dad, still. Getting old."

"Tell me about the injury, then," Terry said. "I think I heard about it. You were doing a story about some weird shit, weren't you?"

Shona sighed and winced. The fire was red at its centre, the twigs entwined in their slow destruction, and an arch had been formed within, a gateway to the heart of the fire, a holloway to the furnace. The heat bloomed on both their faces.

"Yeah. I was on a job," Shona said, wearily.

"And?"

"It was complicated. There was this . . . I had been tipped off that there was this fella in Glasgow with all the signs of the stigmata. The wounds in the hands, the feet. The wounds in the side. The crown of thorns on his face."

"The wounds of Christ?"

"No, of Tintin. Yes, of Christ." Shona drank more gin and tonic. She crushed the can, and dropped it on the shingle.

Terry handed her another, its green and silver glinting in the firelight. "Go on."

"He was an old priest, before he had become this mystic,

this prophet. And anyway . . . to cut a long story short, I found him. He was hard to find."

"Where? Was he being hidden?"

"Only by himself. Up a high-rise. A condemned high-rise, that was about to be blown up."

"Oh, wow."

"Wow indeed. Most of the high-rises are coming down. So, it was a weird situation."

"I bet."

"It's hard to imagine a high-rise just now. Just looking around here . . . this darkness. The countryside. The trees, the open land, the river. The idea of a high-rise, the idea of boxes of concrete stacked on top of each other for people to be contained in, to live in . . . it seems absurd, doesn't it? When you're here. It seems fucking horrific. All the emptiness here. All that crushed humanity, there.

"Anyways. I found him, just hours before the demolition guys were ready to press the button. Pull the trigger. Plunge the plunger. Whatever. And when I found him . . ."

"What was he like?"

"He was wrapped in a stinking blanket. Skinny as a rail. Covered in dried blood. Starving, stinking. He had written this big mad book. A third Testament. There was no glass on the windows of his . . . where he was. An old apartment. So, birds had flown in. Birds everywhere. He was sleeping on this old clapped-out sofa, in his own blood. Dried blood, covered in sheets. I interviewed him, got it on tape for the paper. Then I called an ambulance to get him out of this bloody ticking time bomb. There were literally charges all set up in the tower. This tower in the north of the city, looking down over Glasgow. But then he attacked me. He just flipped."

"Bloody hell. Mad!"

"Yeah, he had gone mad. He attacked me, I was there on my own. No snapper. So, he went for me. And got me."

Shona threw her empty can as far as she could. It clinked into the darkness.

"I'm sorry," Terry said.

"Aye. So, he stabbed me with something—with a long nail. It went into my side. Second stab missed my spine by yay-much. Third one into my hip, did some sore damage. I passed out. I was a goner."

"Fuck me, what a bastard," Terry said.

"I woke up . . . I woke up bleeding outside a burning house in the Southside. Don't know how I got there, don't know if I ever will. The man was inside the burning house. His body was found there. I was taken to the hospital. I was fucked. But I got the story. I filed it all by phone to the news desk from the bloody A&E ward. That was that."

"Jesus," Terry said. "I think I remember some of that now."

"Well, it was some story." Shona nodded.

Terry became quiet, contained, and slowly fed the fire with twigs and grass.

"I came out of the hospital with a limp and a stick," Shona said, quietly, almost to herself. "And a massive fucking desire to leave Glasgow. My dad fell ill, too. Maybe the shock of it all. We needed a change, I was offered a job at a paper in Edinburgh, so we both moved there. That was that."

"The attack, though . . ."

"I tried to carry on as if it hadn't happened. I tried to forget it. I've been led to believe that's not healthy."

"I couldn't move home again like that," Terry said. "I like to know my home, know the place where I live. I'm a bit of a homebody. I like my wee place in Newsham. I like sleeping to the silence. Don't mind the trips to Newcastle and Carlisle and whatever for the papers. But then I need to be back in my cave, my home. Newsham is tiny. It probably hasn't changed for a thousand years. It has a blacksmith, for God's sake."

"Is that why you like getting hammered?" Shona said.

"Nice."

"Look, Edinburgh's fine. It's quiet, it's orderly. That's fine. I like the beach at Portobello. My dad has his bloody allotment. Shame my paper made me redundant. Fucking twats. I probably deserved it."

She threw a pebble into the fire.

Terry looked at Shona sideways. Her eyes pale fire in the light of the flames. "You have anyone else, apart from your dad?"

"In what way? I have a cat."

Terry sighed and rolled her eyes. She took some dry bark scraps and threw them into the fire. They flared and crinkled at the edges, and tiny flares of steam rose from their scabby backs.

Shona spoke quietly. "My friends are mainly hacks. I know how their minds work. This place, though, Ullathorne? I can't get under the skin of it. I've got half a story, and . . . I suspect that's it."

"You didn't answer my question," Terry said. She had her phone out, and was staring through its camera screen. Looking into the fire. "Caverns of light, cathedrals of flame," she said, taking images with quick dabs of her thumb.

"Surely the contrast with the night . . . You'll not get a picture."

"Leave it to the professional."

Shona felt drunk. The black trees shook, the river tipped and settled. She rolled up her coat, and put it down, and lay back on the shingle. Tiny touches of cold stone on her neck. She opened her mouth to speak, and then didn't. Then she felt an urge to speak, to answer. She spoke quietly and quickly.

"To answer your question, no: no relationships. No relay-shun-shups. God," she began to suddenly shout, as if released, "I hate that fucking word anyway."

Terry reached into her bag and pulled out another can, and opened it with a crack. "Look at that moon," she said, looking up. "Looks like genuine cheese. So yellow tonight. You can see every crater."

"You're genuine cheese," Shona said. "You're also a nosey parker."

Terry grinned. Shona felt an urge to leave. But she remained lying back on the stones.

"No, no. I just like all the gen. I like to know who I am working with," Terry said. "But I think I knew the answer anyway."

"I think I need to be getting back," Shona said. She sat up straight.

Terry looked to her, and held up her hands.

"Sorry. I'm sorry. I'm a little drunk and I've enjoyed working on this story today. We can talk about what else we need in the morning. I've been through some of the pictures, but we can review more tomorrow."

"Ach, it's all right," Shona said. She was feeling off-kilter, and she would probably not see Terry again after the weekend. She wondered if she minded. She began to speak again, with that feeling of release, of a lightening.

"There was someone, once. But it didn't work out. Five years of it. Bad timing. On their part, on my part. It was a bit sad and agonised by the end. I still haven't made amends, really. Anyway, they're married now, got a kid. What-the-fuck-ever. There's an email I still have, apologising. Saying sorry. I should have sent it. But I never did. The days slide by. Suddenly you're older, and tired. Everyone's older. Every-one's tired."

She was looking into the fire. The golden edges, the heart of throbbing silver and red. Her eyes blurred. The heat glowed on her face.

She stood up, the world swaying a little. "Enough of this chat," she announced. "Now I must go. Thanks for the booze."

She bent down and picked up her stick.

"You can't bloody walk back," Terry said, her face half in darkness, half golden.

"Well, I'm not being driven by a pissed snapper, that's for certain."

"You don't know the way. You're in the middle of nowhere."

"I'll follow the road, genius," Shona said. "Or maybe just follow the river. Just like in the old days."

"In the old days, a single girl wandering in the dark wouldn't have got far," Terry said, standing up.

But Shona had already stepped away from the circle of light and warmth, and turned, waving, and was making her way to the bank. She needed to move, move from the river's edge and this conversation, and the darkness. She had a sudden yearning for a warm bed, a ceiling and walls.

She scrambled up the bank in the darkness and was across the field as the night closed in around her, as Terry called after her.

Soon she had stepped past the cold parked car and turned left on the country road, heading back to Ullathorne.

Shona walked as quickly as she could as the hedges grew high on either side and the road rose and fell. She expected Terry to follow in her car, but she did not. There was silence, apart from the fall of her feet and her stick. The moon glowed in the vast sky. The trees were still and black, cracks in the starfield.

She stopped: something small and quick darted in the hedgerow. Then it was gone.

She stood still on the road. Tiny reflections of the moon shimmered in minuscule puddles on the old tarmac. They looked like stars. Up ahead, there was a dim glow above a low rise in the road.

At its height, she saw a figure standing. A large man, alone. She could not sense him looking towards her, or anywhere. He stood, for a moment, black against the faint glow, and then descended the hill, out of sight.

She walked up the rise, and, glowing in orange and white, the lights of Ullathorne glittered ahead. A clutch of electric eyes gathered in the darkness.

There was no man on the road.

She passed a sign which said DEEPDALE, pointing to a lane into the trees. She heard an engine, as loud as a shout, and stepped woozily onto a narrow kerb as a motorcycle buzzed past, its lights glinting on a road sign, its beam sharply illuminating the path.

Shona found herself at the river, and then on a heavy stone bridge. Skeins of light flickered on the river's flow. In the shadows of the banks, it was deepest night. Under the bridge it flowed slowly and intently, where the river was deepest, following its surest path to the sea.

Shona was cold now, and the drink in her seemed to have settled somewhere. She did not feel drunk. She looked down into the river.

What had happened here in this town? All those years ago.

She thought it through. Bored of the silence and the emptiness, the limits of the town and the limits of its life, a small group of teenage friends had toyed with Ouija boards. And one of them went missing, and had been lost. Who had been there, and what had happened to them? Alison, who ran off to London. Bobby, who trudged off to war. Beverley, who came back, but with the company of Karl, the giant.

Gary Watson: now a politician, the MP for this town and this dale. And Dan, who lived a pale, bloodless life, until he emptied what was left of himself onto the stones of a hotel in Scotland.

What had the Ouija board said to them? Was it the phrases on that note in the suit?

Shona shook her head. Words on a paper, words conjured by hands on a board. She just did not feel the connection.

What had been moving the glass? They had been, of course. The teenagers in the common room, the bored sixth formers behind the curtain of the assembly hall. Their fingers on the glass, pushing and pulling. Nothing more.

She thought of her own youth, of studying physics, biology, chemistry—had she ever really felt that this world, or this existence, contained more? She did not, could not. She looked into the river again, and passed a hand across her face. Why did she think in this way? Maybe it was her father. Hugh Sandison, the warm old socialist, had instilled in her a respect for the material of life, for hard surfaces, for science—for classifications and distinctions, for facts and theories, for observable truth and measurable volumes, for class, and the distributions of power, for privilege, and the absence of privilege. Maybe there were enough demons and angels in those calculations without the need for spirits from another world.

Staring into the dark rushing river, she thought: Did she even believe in the soul? A conscious flame set in some way in the midst of all this soft and breakable flesh? Did she believe in her own? Her mind moved away from it. She was not ready to answer, even to herself.

Instead, her mind moved to her mother. Dead now for more than twenty years. Had she contacted her daughter from the beyond? Come to her in dreams? No. Nothing. Not even as Shona lay, her side rent, incapable, dropped past her senses, in the Southern General. There had been no visitations. There had been no comforting meetings in the passing softness of a shifting dreamworld. No long tunnel of light, with loved ones waiting at its end. And if her own mother could not or would not contact her from beyond the wall of death . . . who else would feel the need to? No. After death, there was nothing, the same as the nothing before birth: just the obliteration of time.

The river ran beneath her, roiled under the bridge, and then passed on its way. She walked on, along the main road, and up the Bank, no cars passing, no one on the street. She stopped outside the church. It was lit by floodlights set in the grassy graveyard spread about it. Its square tower lurched unnaturally bright into the night sky. Its blue clock, detailed in gold, told her it was nearly three in the morning.

Shona tapped her pocket to check she still had the room key. She didn't. She looked in her other coat pocket— no. She swung her bag from her shoulder and, under a streetlamp, looked into it. No, no key. She must have mislaid it: at Bev's, at the old folk's home, or, more likely, on the beach. Terry might have it, but Shona did not want to speak to her right now. Even if Terry hadn't drunkenly driven into a ditch.

She walked the final yards to the Gildersleve Bed and Breakfast, but it seemed to be alive. A light was on in the breakfast room, and figures were moving within. A large black car was parked on the gravel of the drive. She stood at the shoulder of the car, and looked into the lit room.

A tall woman with neat, cropped hair was talking to Peg, who was wrapped in a night robe. The tall woman was wearing gym clothes: a grey hoodie, matching leggings, expensive trainers. She had a car key in her hand and was gesticulating. Peg was standing with her face pale and drawn, her arms crossed.

Shona neared the window. She could not hear what they were saying. A door opened and Ashley wandered into the room, her eyes fuggy—just up from sleep in a large purple T-shirt. She raised an arm, and said something snappy.

On the breakfast table, half in and half out of a black plastic bin bag, was the stained Newcastle United shirt, turned on its face. JET was written on its back.

The tall woman was pointing to it. Her face changed, and her eyes crumpled, her face suddenly drew in, as if pulled by strings, and her shoulders began to shake. She bent over, her face in her hands. Peg moved to her, swiftly, and put an arm around her. Ashley retreated to the doorway. Shona moved to the front door, and pressed the bell, and waited to be let in.

24.

They had discussed it most of the night, but by three A.M. they had decided to bury the body in the garden.

Bev was determined. She seemed to know what she was doing. Karl was surprised by her businesslike manner. Her lack of fear. It was like she had done it before.

So, they would not be calling the police. They would never do that. Karl would be charged with manslaughter, at least. She could not bear to part with him, she said. She had explained, at length, that she did not think he would get through the process of interrogation, of arrest, of confinement, of the legalities, even if eventually he was freed. She could not bear to see that big, bearded head shake with weeping and fear.

They could not transport the body somewhere remote and unfindable—it would inevitably leave a sea of inexpungable DNA in their house, in their car, on their bodies, and on their clothes.

The man had little on him to identify who he was or where he came from. Holding a tea towel to her mouth, and after having covered his smashed head with a bin bag, Bev had searched his pockets. There was nothing, apart from a slim black mobile phone, which she decided to destroy with the meat tenderiser. She knew the phone was trackable. But here, in the dale, perhaps not precisely. She slipped it into the pocket of her flowery nightgown. Bev knew there had to be a car nearby, and with Karl still crying and beside himself, she would have to go and find it.

The man was all in black: black jeans flecked with mud, black socks, black boots—still glinting wet from walking across fields. A black zip-up, a black waterproof jacket. A kind of neck roll, tight and light, that could be pulled up over the face like a mask. Now, there was no face to cover.

The body had to be hidden. A body that would rot, she knew, could not be hidden in the house. But they had a large garden. Nothing overlooked it, apart from the empty moor. Two paths, the left and the right, snaked through it. There were two sheds, a greenhouse, a compost heap, rows of vegetable patches, some fallow, some prepared for the spring. The sun would be rising in a few hours.

So, there was no time. They would have to dig a hole and tip him in.

Karl was now in the kitchen, staring out of the window. Bev held him again. He was washed, but he still smelled of sweat and tears. She asked him to dig a hole in the garden, in the scrap of ground next to the right path, which led between the sheds. They could put the body in that—with the axe—and then cover it up again with earth, and then all the detritus of the garden: the old mower, the bags of mulch, the roller. Karl could dig a hole in a couple of hours. And it would focus his mind.

"All right, love," he said, eventually, wiping his eyes with the back of his hairy big hand. "All right."

"I'll get a smoke," she said. She found one, pre-rolled, in the snack drawer under the microwave. She lit it with a match and the tip crinkled and curled and sweet smoke coiled to the ceiling. They smoked it in silence, passing it back and forth, looking out to the dark garden and the eyeless hills beyond.

"*In the deep dale/ there are many wild creatures*," she said.

Karl nodded. He knew the old Saxon poem.

"Who the fuck was he?" Karl said, eventually.

"We'll never know. A burglar?" she said.

"He was an assassin," he said. "What the absolute fuck."

"Assassin no more."

"Come to kill us."

"Maybe he came to the wrong place. You got him first. We'll never know. The most important thing is to hide it all away. Cover it over. And forget."

"'Say yes to no,' and what-have-yer," he said.

"Exactly," she said.

Karl put the kettle on, and as the water began to bubble, he pulled on his waterproof trousers, his wellies, his waterproof jacket, gloves and a baseball cap.

"Just leave the kitchen light on," he said. "That's all I need. To dig a massive fuck-off hole."

"A massive fuck-off hole is what we need, love. Thank the Lord we got rid of the carpet in the front room," Bev said.

"We'll get bin bags under his head, let's worry about that after," he said. He kissed Bev gently on the head, and headed to the garden. He looked to their only neighbour: it was old Mrs. Flintergill, and she slept late most days. That's why, in Bev's reckonings, which he did not disagree with, he was safe digging a massive hole in his garden in the early hours of the morning.

He stepped out into the night, the light from the kitchen watery on the earth and plants, the small apple tree, the sheds.

Karl set to work, his large body relieved to be working again. As he moved the detritus from between the two sheds, his shoulder twinged. He had hit the man with all his force. The sharp judder of the blade meeting the face and skull had been harsh and sudden. He felt his shoulder for a while, his breath snaking around his face, and then began to dig with his best shovel. The earth gave way easily, as if it was eager to eat the body.

Inside, Bev looked down at the man again. The blood had pooled hours ago, and was now congealing. She noticed the knife, as if for the first time. It had flown across the room and now lay on top of a small pile of LPs, its blade across the faces of King Crimson.

She went to the kitchen and pulled on a pink rubber glove, returned and picked up the weapon. It was surprisingly light.

She realised she did not know what to do with it. She looked down at the calm, intent faces of King Crimson. She looked outside, into the starless night. Karl was out there, his back bent, digging the grave.

She moved to the corner of the room, where a large concrete Buddha sat. His face fat and happy. It was a hollow statue. She put the sword down on the shelf, and tipped the Buddha a little, moving it from its place. Little crumbs of concrete fell onto the hardwood floor. She manoeuvred it away from its place, put the sword down and then tipped the Buddha on its lip, and, after a moment or two of wriggle, lifting and adjustment, slipped the knife inside the statue. A weapon of murder hidden inside the avatar of peace and enlightenment, she thought, and smiled.

She sat on the sofa and pulled the man's phone from her nightgown. There was only one bar of service in this part of the dale. Plenty of shadows and blind spots.

She did not know the access code to the phone. It did not matter. As soon as she tipped it, the screen flared up. The background pattern was rows and rows of helmeted heads at a military rally in the 1930s. She decided to turn it off and keep it, just in case. Then Bev stood up, and with Karl digging furiously in the garden, she went to the kitchen again to find some black bin bags.

25.

Shona was woken by her phone buzzing. It took a moment for her mind to surface. Light was low in her bedroom. She had fallen asleep in her clothes, her muddy trainers by the door.

The phone was on the side table, beside her laptop, which was open. She could not remember writing late at night, but maybe she had been.

The phone buzzed again, and she reached for it. It was Ranald.

"Yep," she said, foggily.

"Wakey wakey!" Ranald said, cheerily. "A warm welcome from Fladdabister. I have some news for you. How is my ace reporter?"

She made an incoherent noise.

"Did I wake you up?"

"No, Ranald, I'm just back from my morning run."

"Do you run?"

"Of course I don't fucking run, you dick," she said, happy to be swearing so early in the morning.

"Ah, right. Sorry, yes. Anyway, I looked a bit more into the disappearance of Andrew Banks. There was some national press, not much, mind. National Library of Scotland had some paper cuts."

"How did you get them when you are in Ultima Thule?"

"Shetland mafia, Shona. Its sinister tentacles range far and wide. Even as far as Edinburgh. Anyway, PDFs were emailed to me last night. The main article is from the *Mirror*. It has quotes from a lead officer of the Ullathorne Police. Harmire. It says here his daughter attended the same school. Is that your Alison?"

"Harmire?"

"Yes," he said, and spelled it out.

"The very same," she said, and yawned.

"Anyway, what else is cracking? Have you spoken to the local?"

"The local what? There's a lot of local around here."

"The local paper—what is it?"

"*Tyrdale Times*. I went to their archive thing. I didn't speak to the reporters: wasn't sure I wanted them to know I was in town, to be honest."

"Might be worth it, though—speak to the editor, mention Merrygill's death? He's bound to know about it. If nothing else, we can quote him or her in the piece and give an extra lick of local colour."

"You want me to lick people now?" she said.

Ranald laughed. He seemed to be in an uncommonly good mood.

"Fine, I'll speak to the paper," she said, propping herself up in the bed. "An old pal of mine worked on it, long ago, strangely enough."

"Yeah? Well, drop her into the conversation."

"He. John Fallon. He was my boss at the *Glasgow Mercury* before it went bust. He taught me a lot."

"Oh, aye, the name rings a bell—where's he now?"

"In the ground. Died a while back."

"Ach, joined the majority. Well—see if dropping his name helps grease the wheels a bit."

Ranald ended the call.

Shona undressed and showered. She remembered she quite liked staying in hotels, bed and breakfasts; they came with bathrooms that she didn't have to clean herself. Fresh towels.

New shampoo. Sometimes even bathrobes. She pulled the white robe on, and looked into the mirror in the small, neat shower room. She wiped her hand across it.

When she had been young, not long after her mother died, she had taken to staring into mirrors. Until her eyes blurred, and her face disappeared. The background and the foreground become one. Her face would merge with shadow and blur and smeared vision. The reflection became a hole, an aperture into nothingness. Then her eyes would hurt and she'd have to close them, wrinkle them up and shake her head. And then, always, she would check in the mirror that she was still there, and understand that nothing in reality had changed. It never had. Her face was her face. Her eyes looked back at themselves, reversed. Nothing else. Her mother never walked into the frame of the mirror.

Shona heard voices in the breakfast room downstairs, and her phone rang again, buzzing and bleating.

"Fuck off," she said, and left the shower room to pick up the call.

It was Bernie.

"Is Dad okay?" Shona said immediately.

"Hello, love, yes, he is. But he isn't," Bernie said.

"Which?"

"Well, my love, we had another rather horrible letter from the allotment people today."

"Right?"

"It says they are going to terminate his tenancy. And charge him for a contractor to clear it up after he loses it. It's a terrible letter."

Shona swore under her breath. "Okay—well. There's not much I can do from here. I'm busy, I'll be back at the weekend."

"But we don't have much time to sort it out, Shona. I went down there last night and it really is a state. I mean . . . those wooden pallets holding the compost, they've all collapsed. Those bushes are out of control. And I am absolutely convinced there are rats in the shed. It's a fine mess. And you know he has his enemies on that allotment. There's been nothing done for months, and with you away . . ."

"He's been in hospital after a heart attack! Of course it's a mess. Maybe I can call them. Is there a number?"

"Not a heart attack—angina. That's different."

"What-the-fuck-ever," Shona muttered.

"No number," Bernie carried on. "It's an official letter. I don't think you realise, Shona. If Hugh loses the allotment"— and her voice suddenly became a hard whisper—"it will be awful for him. He lives for that place. And you, of course. He won't have a reason to leave the house."

"I know. Well, he can leave the house to see you."

"That's nice of you to say. But he needs that patch of earth."

There was a silence. Bernie wanted Shona to do something.

"Look—I'll see if I can find a gardener or something who can get to work on tidying it up. Before the allotment gestapo arrive next week."

"Can you come back now?"

"No, I'm working. I have a job to do."

"But your father—"

"I understand. I'll see what I can do. I'll be back in a day or two. Okay?"

"There is no time, Shona," Bernie said.

"I know that."

"Well, all right." Bernie sighed. "I might see if any of the other allotment people can help, but I doubt it. I mean, we're all mainly pretty old and decrepit, and your father with his heart and me with my hips, and no one really has enough energy even for our own patches, although there's a young family over by the alders who have . . ."

"Okay, Bernie," Shona cut in. "I get it. How is Dad?"

"He's just up, and watching the cricket."

"Cricket? Jeezo, he must still be sick," Shona said.

There was some mumbling in the background of Bernie's line—and the sound of Shona's father, saying something. Shona asked what he'd said.

"He said it is still an English preoccupation and he wants to understand it more," Bernie said.

"Look, I will sort something—must go—bye!" Shona said, who was beyond an acceptable limit of irritation.

She dressed swiftly and left the room.

Through the doors that opened onto a small garden overlooking an open field, Shona could see the tall woman from last night. She was deep into a heated conversation—her head nodding, her eyes screwed up.

Ashley appeared, smiling, and asked Shona what she wanted for breakfast. Shona was looking at the tall woman, still, and Ashley lowered her voice.

"One of Mam's old friends, turned up last night out of the blue. Lucky we had a room free," she said.

"Oh, aye?" Shona moved closer to Ashley to appear appropriately conspiratorial. She could smell Ashley's shampoo and perfume.

"Yeah," Ashley said, her eyebrows rising, "there was a right carry on."

"About what?"

"I found that old shirt in the woods—well, that Jess found. I brought it back, wish I hadn't. Mam has been fretting over it and Alison there went plain mental when she saw it. I poked me neb in last night, but they were hard at it, so I went to bed. Bloody hell."

Shona asked for a couple of bacon rolls and a coffee, sat down and looked out the open doors to Alison, still rowing on her phone. She heard the name "Nigel." Something about children, about money. Alison was a handsome woman, with sleek hair. Her clothes were simple and expensive.

While waiting for her breakfast, Shona looked at her phone. Ranald's email had arrived. It was a massive file, with ten attachments. She opened one, and slowly the PDF unfurled.

It was a picture of a cutting from the *Mirror* from 1992. There was splodgy typeface and a black-and-white photograph. It was page thirty-four. An even page, at the back of the book. The headline read: MYSTERY AS BOY 18 VANISHES.

The article outlined the story, in simple, effective and direct tabloid writing, of Andrew Banks. How he had been out with friends, out drinking in the "small northern market town" and then gone missing. Police had searched parked cars and gardens, and dragged the river where they could. Posters had been put up. Tracker dogs in the woods. A helicopter from Cumbria had swept the moorland. Nothing found. A short quote from the Banks family solicitor. No mention of Viv, or her parents.

A policeman, Harmire, was quoted. He said: "We appeal to Andy to come home. His family are beside themselves. He may have gone to visit friends and stayed over—if so, please get in touch. No one will think less of you if you turn up now."

As she read on, Ashley arrived with Shona's breakfast. There was a small square picture of Harmire in uniform, fuzzy and indistinct. A long face, and intense eyes. He was smiling. The caption said: *Cops: No Sign of Teen.*

Shona expanded the photo with her fingers, and looked over at Alison, who was now facing the doors of the breakfast room. The same long face, the same penetrating eyes.

As Shona ate, distracted, she was suddenly struck with what she once described to Stricken, who recognised it well, as "news panic." It was the desperation to get the crucial interview for a story—the overwhelming, consuming need for it. Her skin began to tingle around her eyes. There was tension in her shoulders. She needed to speak to Alison. Alison was outside, and as far as Shona could see, the only way into the building from the garden was through the French windows of the breakfast room. So, she waited.

A small brown dog with tight curly hair and a face of joy suddenly trotted into the room. Its paws clipped on the stone floor. Ashley followed behind, wearing an anorak. She had a dog lead wrapped around her weaker hand.

"This your last day here, then?" Ashley said.

"Think so—one more night," Shona said, "but maybe two."

"You been busy?" Ashley asked, pushing the dog—who had suddenly stood up on two legs—down.

"Busy enough," Shona said.

"You'll be glad to be out of here and back to the city."

"Maybe."

Ashley looked at Shona and blinked slowly, as a cat might do. "Well, I'm off to walk Jess here. Hopefully she doesn't find any more relics this time."

Jess was beside herself now, running around in a circle, hopping up and down.

"Will your mum take the shirt to the police?" Shona asked.

"Oh, you know, I don't think so," Ashley said, suddenly distracted. "Ta-ra, then." And, along with the prancing, bouncing dog, she left. The front door slammed and, after, the dog barked from somewhere outside.

Shona looked to the garden again, but Alison was gone.

"Fuck's sake," Shona said, rising from her seat, grabbing her things, and moving to the open doors. She saw that in the far corner of the backyard a small gate led to the fields. A track wound its way across a field and down to the tree line and the river.

Shona followed Alison. The air was sharp. The wet grass tickled the skin between her socks and her jeans. The air was chill, and sharp.

The path, although not paved or gravelled or mown, beat a clear way across the large field down to the river. As the field dipped even steeper, she saw a large drystone wall, with a gate set in it. Beyond, there was another field—but overgrown and abandoned. It was full of clumps of tall thistles, and small sinkholes of mud and sand. Somnambulant sheep, shaggy and dyed, were rooting in the grass.

Alison was staring into the river. A dog-walking couple moved past her in matching red waterproofs. The man may have nodded to her, but she was unmoved.

Shona approached her, squelching on the lumpy ground, her shoes wet. The only sound was her feet and the river's numb roar.

Alison did not turn as Shona approached. Shona had long learned to if not ignore, then just roughly ride over nerves when speaking to strangers. She found volume helped.

"Hi," she said, on reaching Alison.

Alison turned to her. She had been crying. Her eyes were watery and red, and the edges of her nostrils were inflamed.

"Hi," she said, and turned back to the river.

White bubbles floated steadily on its brown surface. A large, detached branch was rotating steadily on its way downstream. In the eaves of the far side, several ducks bobbed.

"So: you're the news reporter," Alison said.

"I'm the news reporter," Shona said. "Guilty as charged."

"Peg told me you're in town."

"I was at the wedding."

"Where Dan died."

"Yes. I found his body," she half-lied.

Alison turned, her face unreadable. "What do you want from me?" she said. Her voice still had the flatness of the north in it. But it had been stretched and remoulded by decades of life in London.

"A chat."

"Yeah, I'm not one for chatting," Alison said. She turned back to the river, glancing again at her watch.

"What are you waiting for?" Shona said.

Alison shook her head. "Can you leave me alone, please?"

"I want to speak to you about Dan," Shona said.

"I don't want to talk about poor Daniel."

"I am trying to find out why he did what he did."

Alison looked at Shona, her eyes unmoving. "Good luck with that," she said, and finally she turned away. Her phone bleeped, and she took it from her pocket and began to speak into it. "Yes, Derek?" she said, and moved away, following the path downstream.

Shona thrust her hands in her pockets and watched Alison move away, down the riverside path overhung with old trees.

Shona pulled out her phone. She opened a map application and looked at where she was. For a moment the blue marker pulsed and flared, the GPS not knowing where she was, or how the signal could be tracked onto the large empty land. But soon it found its coordinates, and beside a blue stretch of water—RIVER TYR—she found herself represented by a small blue dot on a yellow path. Closer than they felt, the town's brown buildings spread out behind her, flat and featureless, a grey diagram.

Alison was walking down a path marked on the map. Shona zoomed in on it with her fingers. The path went past the town's sewage works and over more fields, until it came to a large bridge which carried a two-lane road over the river. Over the bridge, about a mile from where she stood, hidden in trees was the ruin of an abbey. Angleton Abbey, the map said.

Alison had now disappeared into the tree line. Shona wondered if she was heading for the abbey. She began to follow her, and the river, downstream. The thistles here seemed abnormally high, their thorns as long as steel needles. The riverbank was high above the water and ragged: here and there, sand and mud collapsed into the brown river.

She picked up her pace. The river had become shallower—shoals of stones were showing above its waters. She glimpsed Alison ahead of her, walking steadily, talking into her phone, following the path, which became darker ahead as trees clustered and thickened.

As Shona walked on, peering ahead, the river became white—it ran steeply down, now, over rocks and rapids. It made a deep growl as it battered, suddenly furious, over the rocks, the steps of stone. And through the thickening trees, as if to match the violent waters, a black stone bridge rose threateningly through the trees. She could see Alison climbing the path, to the bridge. Her hands thrust into her pockets, her head down.

Shona watched Alison walk to the bridge. If she crossed the bridge, she would follow her to the other side, and to the ruined abbey. If she did not, she would turn, and see her back at the bed and breakfast.

Watching the small figure rising to the bridge, hearing the rush of the water, and the darkness of the woods, Shona felt a sudden pang of fear. A cold grip in her chest, in her heart.

Her phone rang. She swore, and fished it from her pocket. It was Terry.

"How do," Terry said, jauntily, albeit with a voice slightly thickened by a hangover.

"So, you made it home alive," Shona said.

"Where are you? You sound like you're in a tunnel."

"By the fucking river again. I'm . . . working."

"Don't believe it. Yeah, made it home. No alarms and no surprises."

"Fuck's sake, Theresa, that's not right. Drunk driving. You'll kill someone."

"Och, I'm fine—anyway, it seems this town will be in the news again soon."

"Why's that?"

"I think it's you, you might bring death and destruction wherever you go. First the lovely Scottish wedding which turns dark, then you come to this sleepy town and everything goes pear-shaped. They've found a body in the woods."

"What woods?"

"Woods over the other side from the town—Deepdale. Somebody was walking their dog this morning and found a dead body in the stream. Just heard it on the local radio."

"Fuck," Shona said. "I was going to go and have a look at that place. Any more details? Who is it?"

"Nope, just that the cops have declared it a suspicious incident, and are investigating. The main path to Deepdale is taped off. I could get in from the western end, park up the high fell . . ."

"Maybe it's just some poor old sod had a heart attack. Dropped dead in the woods. I don't think it's worth spending the effort trying to get near. It isn't really why we are here."

"Maybe so. Deepdale is old trees, primeval woodland.

You can get lost there. Anyway, this MP thing tomorrow, the campaign launch, you want me to come and get pictures?"

"Yeah, for sure. We'll need snaps of Watson on the stump, doing a speech, whatever. And a full formal portrait. It's near the waterfall, isn't it?"

"Yep, dramatic. I think I have a number for his election agent—some fella called Knott, if I remember from last time. I could ring ahead, get some time squared off for us? And you need a lift, I take it?"

They arranged a time to meet, and the call ended. Shona watched Alison's head bobbing along the battlement parapet of the bridge as she crossed over to the other side.

Shona followed. The path was steep now, and her stick slipped on wet soil and caught in undergrowth. There was tiredness in her breath. The river roared below.

She crossed the river. Emerging through trees, on the south bank of the Tyr, the shattered Angleton Abbey stood, resplendent in its ruin. There were large sheet walls, and empty windows. Its nave still stood, huge but broken and roofless. Its chapterhouse was long collapsed, its stones taken in days long past for farms and outbuildings. Henry VIII had destroyed this abbey in his fury, and its White Canons were dust and bone. At its centre were the remnants of its quad, and beside it, the only intact space—a small chapel.

Alison Harmire was there.

26.

Shona struggled up the hill to the abbey. Her side was sore, and her gin hangover was now hanging heavy on her tired limbs. Her stick was clarty with mud. She had walked slowly around the towering ruins. They were stark and sad, with no sign that humans had ever lived there, slept there, ate there and worshipped there.

But it was not all rack and ruin. The central chapel stood as if new. She pushed through the door, and stood at the back of the nave. Instead of a stone altar, there was a bare wooden table. On it was a brass crucifix on a stand, and two simple candles. A bible was resting on a folded pale cassock, which glittered with gold stitching.

There was a large modern stained glass window in the wall above it, which had captured the sun. It was a vertical slide of enraptured light. It had a splaying pattern of diamonds, of leaf-shapes, of spear heads, arrow heads and light flares. Purple and blue, diamond and emerald.

Alison, still, tall, was sitting in a pew.

As Shona walked slowly down the aisle, her stick tapped on the flagstones.

"So, you followed me," Alison said, unmoving, facing away from Shona.

"Yes, of course," Shona said. "I'd like to speak to you. And it was a pretty walk."

"Bonny, as you Scots might say. Do you think you'll go it alone, then? An independent Scotland? That's what I hear."

Shona shrugged. "I didn't think we'd be talking politics."

"I didn't think we'd be talking, full stop," Alison said.

"To answer your question: I think so. Eventually. We'll be a normal country, like everyone else."

"What's normal?" Alison said, as she turned around. She had been crying again. Her eyes were red, and liquid. Her nose had been blown and was pink. A tiny smear of mascara was black on her cheek.

"You all right?" Shona said. She sat on the opposite side of the aisle, a row back. Her feet were wet and ached. She looked up—the roof was high and clean, waterproof, wind-proof. The chapel walls were old, but the roof was new, its heavy gleaming doors likewise, with steel locks. An old place had been renewed.

"Hardly. No—not in any way," Alison said. She wiped her eyes with the heels of her hands.

"I'm sorry," Shona said.

"No, you're not," Alison said. She turned around, her arm resting on the back of the pew. "I know your type. You want a story. I'm not sure what story you want, but that's what you are here for. So, no, you're not sorry. Don't bother with that."

"Fair enough," Shona said. "But I'm sorry you're upset about something."

Alison looked at her for a moment. Shona could feel her assessing her appearance, her demeanour. What it meant to her. Whether she had to give anything, or if anything was due to come to her.

"Glasgow or Edinburgh?" Alison said, at last. She pulled a scrunch of tissue paper from her sleeve and blew her nose. It echoed around the chapel.

"Both," Shona said, smiling.

Alison nodded, unsmiling. "My mum has a stick now," she said. "She had a fall. She mainly uses it to swipe at the dog."

Alison looked up at the window. Light moved across her face in a dim pattern. Her eyes glistened.

"It's beautiful, isn't it," she said.

Shona agreed.

"They put it in in 2000, for the millennium. And the new roof. Everyone thought things were going to change, didn't they? Get better. But they didn't. They got worse. Worse and worse. Do you remember the millennium bug?"

"No."

"You were probably too young," Alison said. "Everyone was worried about it. A complete collapse of worldwide computer systems. My bank at the time, where I was working, spent a pretty penny preparing for the apocalypse. It never happened. Life just carried on. It was just a number on the calendar. It was here, and then it was gone. The company I worked for spent a fortune guarding against it. A fortune. Nothing happened. No apocalypse. Just the usual steady series of disasters. Most of them forgotten now. No one remembers. No one needs to."

"Did you come to this abbey when you were a kid?" Shona asked.

Alison stared at her, as if blank. As if Shona had said something idiotic. "Yes, of course. We used to come here with the dogs. My dad would make us walk here. It's a round-trip walk from Ully and back again. We'd hate it in the winter of course. It would be miserable, cold, wet. But the river is beautiful. And abbey, too, in its way."

"There's a lot of beauty around here." Shona stood up, and moved to the front row of seats, so she was directly opposite Alison. "I am here because of Daniel, because of what he did," she said, quietly.

"You said," Alison said. "What did he do, then?"

"You know—he killed himself at Viv Banks's wedding. He threw himself off the roof of the hotel. I was there."

"I know," Alison said. "I read the papers. Was that you, writing that? Was that your doing?"

"No, Viv is my friend. I wouldn't write about it."

Alison made a chuckling sound, and folded her arms. "A friend? Not for much longer if you're snooping around here."

Shona looked to the stained-glass window. Her eyes frazzled with its incandescence. She wanted to leap into it. "Did he ever talk about suicide?"

"God's sake. I'm not talking about Dan. None of your business. No." Alison shook her head. "Fancy doing that to yourself at a party full of journalists. It's not like no one is not going to try and write about it. He should have got drunk and walked into the hills. Go into the hills, settle for the night with a bottle of whisky, and wait for the weather to do its worst. In the Cairngorms. Or here on the Pennines, up at the top there. It's bad in winter. Can freeze your blood. It's like hell."

"Like an empty hearth," Shona said.

Alison peered at her. "Who else have you spoken to?"

"I haven't spoken to Robert Stang. I am going to speak to Gary Watson. But I've got enough for a story."

"Bobby won't speak to you—he's too sensible to go blabbing to a reporter. He's army: not liable to go shooting his mouth off."

"And Gary Watson?"

"He won't want to talk about the past, that's for sure," Alison said, looking into the light.

"You went to school with him. Was he political then? He's the darling of his party now, isn't he? Tipped for the cabinet."

"I guess so. They weigh his votes around here, rather than count them. He'll win easily. No, he wasn't political back then. I think his dad was. I don't know where this country is going, mind, if someone like Gary Watson is close to the levers of power. God help us all."

"I don't think God gives a flying fuck."

Alison let out a short laugh and shook her head. "I saw some graffiti in New York. It said: 'No God, Only Satan.' What a thing to write on a wall. No God, only Satan. Mind you, it would make sense."

"Was it a description or a warning, do you think?"

"Both. So, you're definitely going to interview Gary?"

Shona smiled, and leaned over. "Why are you in Ullathorne, Alison?"

"None of your business," Alison said, sharply.

"The thing is: I want to talk to you about Andrew Banks, too, as well as Dan. And about your little group. Back then, in 1992."

Alison was still for a moment. Her hands clenched. "What do you mean?"

"Back then," Shona said. "I need to know about it."

Alison stood up. She rubbed her hands on her face. "No," she said, shaking her head. She strode down the nave, her feet heavy on the floor, opened the door, and slammed it behind her. The sound did not echo. It exploded in the air and disappeared.

Shona was alone in the chapel. Something moved across the sun, and the room darkened. The light dimmed in the stained glass, and the crucifix on the table threw the shape of its cross across the stone floor.

She thought of following Alison, but the moment had passed. And her head was aching now, and so were her legs and side. So, she sat in the silent chapel, and after a while, it began to rain.

27.

"Is that Colin Mickle?"

Shona was sitting on a green wooden bench overlooking the river. She had tramped slowly back to the town, along the south bank of the Tyr and past a quiet caravan site, and now sat overlooking the old mill. There were high fallen walls, and signs warning of danger. A large board had been attached to its walls facing the path: a developer had bought the site, and was boasting of new flats and apartments.

At the ground level, there were semicircular windows, barred off. There was darkness beyond the bars as deep as space. In there, the glass had moved across the board. In there, the friends had had their last meeting.

Her legs ached and her trainers were drenched. The bottom of her jeans were splattered with mud and whipped by weeds and the tall grass of the meadows.

"Mickle? Aye, that's me, love," a jaunty Northern voice said.

"Great."

"Many a mickle makes a muckle!" he yelled.

"Sorry?"

"Nothing, pet, never mind. Carry on."

"I was wondering if I might ask for your help, professionally," Shona said.

"Oh, now then—that sounds terribly serious," Mickle said. "Go on."

Shona gathered her thoughts as she spoke. She was hesitant, at first, and Mickle asked questions. But eventually she laid it out—she was in town as a freelance reporter following the death of Dan Merrygill, trying to find out more about his background. She outlined—vaguely—that she had learned of the tight-knit group of teenagers back in the early 1990s. That one of his friends, Andrew Banks, had disappeared. All those years ago.

"So, I was wondering if you could help in any way. If we run anything, you could have a bit of it as an exclusive for your paper," she said. "I could talk to Ranald, my boss, about that."

"It's all before my time, to be honest," Mickle said, quietly. "And I'm not from Ully, so don't remember it. I'm from the other side, Westmoreland. Have you looked in our archive?"

"Not yet, thought I'd call you first," she lied.

"Ah, right, well, there might be stuff in there. It goes back to the 1990s. Why don't you come in? We can have a natter. Paper's gone to bed for the week, so I've got a moment or two."

"Thanks, Colin—I'll come around later."

She shut down the call. Shona then checked a text that Terry had sent her: the details of whom to call to arrange an interview with Gary Watson. It belonged to someone called Knott.

She tapped in the number, and it rang and rang, and then a prerecorded message by someone with a dead grey voice said to leave a message or call another number.

Shona dialled the new number. Again, the number rang out.

She left a message—she said she was a freelance journalist and was interested in interviewing the talented and interesting Gary Watson for a piece to run in a UK national broadsheet newspaper. She left her name and number, and a suggestion that she have twenty minutes, a face-to-face interview, with Watson after his campaign launch, the next day.

She hung up and breathed deeply. The sun cleared some

clouds and a warmth fell on her shoulders. There was a chopping noise, a hollow whop-thok in the air. A helicopter thrummed over the town, and headed up the dale. An ambulance siren briefly sounded, and then was gone, lost in the stone and the trees.

Shona called her father, but there was no response, and she didn't leave a voicemail. She wondered how he was, all those miles away. She thought of his tender head, his messy allotment, his wounded heart. She hoped Bernie was looking after him but at the same time, knew she was. The blessed nun, she thought, was probably blessed in some way. At the very least, her father would be safe, until she got back.

She rose with an involuntarily moan from the bench and walked down the hill to the river and a green metal bridge. The morning, and the chasing of Alison, had been frustrating. Shona wondered if she really did have enough material now for a story. She thought back over the previous days. Yes, she had enough. For a news feature of a few thousand words or so? More than enough. If some outlet wanted a clean, short, follow-up news story, she could probably provide one as well. Add in her own experiences from the wedding and it could stretch further, if desired. After all, no one else had been there when Daniel fell. That was an exclusive, she knew.

But she knew, too, with a sense of vacancy, an ache, that the heart of her story was still empty—the disappearance of Andrew Banks, the Ouija sessions, the group of friends and what they had done. There was a central darkness—an obscurity.

She was not a detective: she could not succeed where the police had failed. She could not find Andrew. He was still gone. Daniel was dead. Alison was hostile. Bobby—she had not tried to speak to him yet. She had not grilled Peg. Bev was the only friendly contact she had made. And she had the words she had found in Daniel's jacket—whatever they meant. She swallowed hard. Viv would see, eventually, that she did not want to stir up the deep soil of old pain. That she wanted to shed light, not inflict further wounds. Viv was angry now. But she was smart, and reasonable. She knew how newspapers worked. She would come round. Shona told herself that. She had to.

She jumped suddenly. Her phone was buzzing in her pocket.

It was Terry.

"What is it," she said.

"Hello to you too. That body in the woods," Terry said. There was music playing, and she was driving. Somewhere on a road, barrelling between high hedges and watchful trees.

"What about it?"

"PR man at the cops has told me something."

"A friend of yours?"

"Kind of. They're going to publicly identify him this afternoon, in time for the news on *Look North*. It's Robert Stang."

"What the actual fuck?"

"Bobby. From the same group of friends as your suicide."

Shona's heart leapt. "Any cause of death?"

"Not that I'm being told. But all the forensics folk are in the woods. It's not a suicide. Where does this leave us?"

Shona looked to her feet. Through gaps in the bridge's frame, she could see the river running below her in unending streams of light and dark. Tiny shreds of forest flotsam spun over and over on their circumference.

"Well," Shona said at last. "Even if he's been done in, it's not necessarily part of my story. On the other hand, I'll need the detail of what's happened to him, to add to the article, because he and the others are all linked by the same past. Ranald will be on about it. No doubt about that. I'd want to have answers to the questions, before they are asked."

"There'll be a cop news release, but it's not like you can get anywhere near the body," Terry said. "Neither can I. We could try for a 'collect.' He has an estranged partner, and a lass. But if the wee girl is with her mother . . ."

"Yeah, no chance of getting a photo from the mantelpiece," Shona said. "Unless the cops release one from the family."

"Aye. I'll ask the press officer. Man. It's dark," Terry said. "Isn't it? This group of people. They have a bloody hex on them."

Shona nodded. Something like a hex. "He was a veteran, wasn't he?"

"Yeah. Army. As far as I've heard, he was a solid citizen. He's not mixed up in anything dodgy. Worked at the bottle factory, he was foreman. Big lad."

"Poor fella," Shona said, her mind moving on. "Look, this interview tomorrow—with Gary Watson: you still okay to pick me up? I need to get to Darlington station after."

"You definitely heading home, then?"

"Yep. Time for me to return to reality. This place isn't it. Or it has its own reality. But it's not mine."

"Of course," Terry said, after a pause. "Well, I will be once again happy to be your personal chauffeur service."

"See you tomorrow. Buzz me on approach."

"If I get any more on this Stang thing . . ."

"Yeah, send it over. Speak in a bit."

Shona walked slowly back to the bed and breakfast. Her legs were tired, and her mind was fogged. She did not hear her phone ring or buzz, but as she got to the door of the Gildersleve, there was a text from Bernie from her father's phone.

*I have prayed on it, and I have had an idea about
how to make things better, which I want to share*

*with you. In the meantime, I will have to act. Not
only prayers, but deeds, Shona. We both hope to see
you soon. B X*

Shona kicked off her muddy shoes in the hallway and
slumped up the stairs to her room. She lay down on the bed,
and threw her stick onto the floor.

She looked around the room, as if for the first time. The
wallpaper was a tangle of tiny green and pale pink flowers
entwined in a repeating pattern. Tiny stems, linking and
unlinking across the pale wall, like a forest, like an alien
world consisting only of vine and flower, of root and branch,
repeating to an obscured horizon.

She had an idea.

She opened her laptop, and emailed Ranald.

*Ranald,
I need a cuts check. Can you check the public com-
ments, speeches, statements, quotes or otherwise, of
Gary Watson MP? I want to see how many times
he has said these phrases: Take the Right Path, Say
Yes to No, and There Is No Time. See also if he has
said anything about Andrew Banks.
Need it by the earliest A.M.
Ta—*

Shona

She closed the laptop.

A heaviness fell over her like a weighted quilt. She had
to sleep. Shona turned on her good side, and too tired to
move, left the curtains open. The sun would dim in time.

She turned on her side and put one arm under the pillow.
She soon fell into a thick deep sleep.

Her mind played monochrome shreds of halting, severed dreams—

A shot glass, held in pale hands, moving over a tattooed alphabet.

A boy on an island, staring at the setting sun from a lonely beach, the sand glowing with light.

A distorted man on fire, twisting like an acrobat in a flaring flower of agony.

A fire on an empty moor, the smoke rising to a blank paper sky.

The face of a grey king in a white shirt, his eyes replaced by coins, carried on a stream of hands into the spiking gloom of a darkening forest.

A body in a suit underwater, swimming towards her, three black eyes in his face.

Her father, in hospital, his mottled shoulders bare, staring out of a window with watery eyes. His hands as black as charcoal, his mouth full of crushed glass. His eyes, turning to her, as white and clear as peeled eggs—

She woke with a start.

It was dark. There was a loud, repetitive noise.

Someone or something was knocking on her door.

28.

Her door trembled slightly as the knocking went on.

"Hello?" Shona said, foggily.

"It's me," a voice said.

Shona, tendrils of her mind still drifting in her dream-heavy sleep, her body leaden, swung her feet from the bed. She looked to the window—it was dark outside, and streetlamps were buzzing on the silent road.

"Who is *me*?" Shona whispered.

"Ashley," the voice said.

Shona moved to the door and opened it, and on the dim landing was Ashley, clad in baggy clothes, pale-faced.

"What's up?"

"Can I come in?"

"Sure—but why?" Shona said, opening the door.

Ashley snuck past her, her sock feet silent as a cat on the thick carpet, and sat on the bed. Her hair was mussed and tangled. "See that thing I found in the woods?"

Shona closed the door and leant against it. She was vaguely aware she had now blocked Ashley's exit.

"Sorry—the thing you found in the woods? The shirt," Shona said. There was a mild irritation in her mind.

"Yeah, the football shirt. I wanted to tell you something about it. Mam has it now. She's out away with it, with her friend."

"Why are you telling me this?"

"I saw you, walking across the fields, following that Alison. You're a journalist, you must be after something."

"I am, and you're right. I'm always after something." Shona smiled and ran a hand through her hair.

"Are you hungover?" Ashley asked with a sudden grin.

"Not anymore." Shona sat down on the chair by the dresser. "Tell me about the shirt, then?"

Ashley looked down at her hands. She held one with the other. "It was a strange thing to find in Deepdale right enough."

"Yeah—and your mother has it?"

"She's kept it. I think she was going to take it to the police, but she didn't. I saw it in the kitchen cupboard. Now she's gone out with Alison, taken it with her."

"Right—so why are you telling me this?"

"Because of that name—*Jet.*"

Shona leaned forward. "Right?"

"Well, thing is, last night, when she and that Alison were talking—when you came back late—they said how they used to go into Deepdale with their pals. About how they would go there to drink cider or whatever."

"Yeah?"

"Alison said the shirt belonged to their friend, that one who went missing. She said it was definitely his. Because of the name on the back. Jet was Andrew's dog. Then they had a row over what to do. Now they've gone off with it."

Shona's heart was pounding now. She felt suddenly hot, almost feverish. "What has your mother told you about Andrew?"

"They were pals," Alison said. "I don't know. Mam did have other friends. She spent a lot of time with my dad, really. By sixth form, Dad was in Darlo, at the college, so she spent a lot of time there. He was studying accountancy. But yes, she knew Andrew Banks, she's mentioned it before how she was part of that group. And how sad it was when he disappeared."

"Has she ever mentioned what they got up to, that group?"

Ashley smiled and faintly blushed. "What do you mean?"

"I mean, what they did together?"

"What, having it off and that? Gross. No."

"No—has she ever mentioned them doing weird stuff?"

"What, drugs?"

Shona stood up, and walked to the dresser. In the mirror she could see them both, reversed. Both dishevelled, in their own ways. Her stick on the floor by the bedside table. Her bag thrown in the corner.

"No, I don't think so," Ashley said quietly. "Although."

"Although?"

"There was this old story she used to wheel out now and then when *Songs of Praise* was on the telly, or some religious thing on the news. Actually, we were watching *The Exorcist* and she mentioned it."

"And?"

"Oh, just, when they were all in sixth form. One of the lasses, one of Mam's friends from church. She came into the sixth form common room and threw holy water on that Gary Watson."

"She what?"

"Yeah, she was evangelical. Can't remember her name now, Mam would tell you. Anyway, she steamed into the common room. Watson was asleep, apparently. She marched in and threw the water on him. Mam says she was half-expecting Watson to melt away on the spot."

"Holy water?"

Ashley shrugged. "That's how the story goes."

"Now why would anyone do that?"

"Maybe because that Watson is a total prick? I dunno."

There was a sudden, deep silence. They both sat, and the night deepened.

"Did you see what he said about . . . disabled people?" Ashley said quietly.

"I didn't. What did he say?"

"He's denied it since, mind."

"I'm sure he has. What was it?"

"There was a thing in the *Mirror*—he was at some posh lunch in London, and he said disabled people should think about whether they actually contribute enough to society. He asked whether we were actually just 'ballast.' Mam went tonto."

"What did he mean by it, do you think?"

"I think he thinks we're worthless," Ashley said. "A drain on society. A burden."

"Well, if he thinks that, he's a fucking cunt," Shona said.

Ashley burst out with a sudden shocked laugh. "You Scottish people don't mess about."

Shona smiled and dipped her head. "We can't afford to. And anyway, where did your mother go? With Alison?"

"They might have gone to the pub. Bev's band are playing again, I think? Maybe they went to see them. Are you going to ask Mam about the shirt? Can you please not say you heard about it from me?"

"I knew about it already."

"How?" Ashley's eyes were wide.

"I have my sources." Shona tapped her nose.

Ashley turned to Shona with pleading eyes. Her lips were wet. She had become pale. "How, though?"

"I saw it, in the kitchen. When you were discussing with your mother."

"Oh, okay. So, you can say that."

"Yes, I can say that. But I did not know Jet was the name of Andrew's dog."

Ashley looked hard at Shona. "Well, you do now. But you didn't hear it from me, right?"

"I can say his sister told me, I am a . . . friend of hers."

Ashley stood up and moved to the door, but paused, her

hand on the plain white doorknob. She was looking down at her feet. As if remembering.

Shona sensed there was something else Ashley wanted to say. "Was there anything else your mother and her friend said last night?"

"There was," Ashley said, nodding, speaking quietly, almost to herself.

Shona waited.

"Mam said they had to do the right thing. No, to take the right path," Ashley said. "And Alison said they had no time to waste, or something. Then she said something a bit weird."

"And what was that?"

"She said they had to do what some other fella said. They had to speak to him. Some guy called Sorley. Mam kind of shivered all over, and then you came back, and it all ended."

"Sorley?" Shona said. Her heart seemed to suddenly turn in on itself, like the snap of a blown sheet in a sudden gale.

"Dunno who Sorley is, like. Must be another friend from school."

"Maybe," Shona said, to say something.

Ashley righted herself, and looked at Shona, and turned the door handle.

"Well see ya then, ta-ra," she said, and suddenly left. Her feet pattered in the hall.

Shona washed her face, and moved downstairs, to the quiet hall, and got ready to go back out into the night. Before she left the lodge, she texted her father:

> Dad—Hope you are OK. Is Bernie looking after you? I am coming home soon. Love you—S

The night was cold, winter lingering in the darkness. Where would they be? Peg and Alison were here somewhere. They might be in a pub, but the town had several. She might have to try them all. She decided to start at the Lion, where Bev's band played.

She realised, as she crossed the cobbles to the pub, that she should have called the *Tyrdale Times*, but had slept through the afternoon and early evening. Tomorrow, she told herself.

There was music playing in the pub, but it wasn't a band. She could hear from the street that a single acoustic guitar was chiming its way through a carousel of minor scales.

She pushed at the door of the pub, and entered a bowl of light. On a low stage, a large man with a beard was sitting, bowed over an acoustic guitar. With one hand he was tightening a string, his eyes low to the frets. At the bar, a man was drying glasses, looking up at a TV, which was showing the evening news with subtitles. The prime minister, pushing back his lank hair, was making a speech outside Number 10 about the general election, which would be held in six weeks. His wife—glassy, immaculate, impermeable—stood beside him, surveying the gathered press corps. The barman was shaking his head.

There were a couple of old men by the bar, damp and antiquated in tweed, muttering to each other over short drinks. One had no hair, the other had too much, squeezed under a green bunnet. Near the slot machine in the corner, which madly flashed in Technicolor, a middle-aged couple were playing dominos. By the stage, some young people in black were sombrely reading their mobile phones. The carpet was loud and old and light bent and splintered from bar brass and optics.

The guitarist looked up as he prepared to sing his next song. Shona recognised him. It was Karl, Bev's partner. He stared at her for a while, and then said, breathily into the microphone, "This is an old one and a true one—'Rufford Park Poachers.'"

He played a skeletal riff on the guitar, his large fingers moving spryly over the strings. He plucked a lonesome arpeggio. As he sung, the beautiful melody rose and fell, and the guitar chimes held and supported the melody for a time, drifted underneath, and then let go. Karl was a solid and hairy man, maybe six foot five, and he sang with a clear tenor that rang true.

Everyone was watching and listening, even the old men at the bar, and Shona realised she was standing in the middle of the taproom by herself. She moved to the bar and ordered a Jack Daniel's and Coke.

Her phone vibrated in her pocket. The glinting dark brown drink arrived and she paid, and by the time she had, the phone had stopped moving. She picked it out of her pocket and looked at it. She had missed a call from a private number. But then it buzzed again: a voicemail.

She half suspected it to be a work call. But Ranald always called from his home line or his mobile. It could be from Hector Stricken, but he usually texted. It was likely a call back from Gary Watson's PR operation. She pressed the button to listen and put the phone to her ear, just as Karl's song came to an end and the sparse crowd clapped.

The message began. There was the sound of rushing, of air moving in a stream over obstacles and around barriers. A keening—a whine of gale moving over the moor.

Then, a voice—deep, uneven, rolled over the howl and tunnelling roil.

"Sandison. I am fine now. I can talk. He left me a lot of money. He left the banks a lot of money. It was a settling of debts. He was ready for his final journey. To go beyond, so he could come back."

There was a pause.

"I am here if you want to know more. He has seen what will happen. He's seen it already. He is in the stones. In the rocks and stones. Goodbye, Sandison."

The voice ended, and the wind returned. Just the flow of air through rock and heather, over lichen and stone. For minute after minute the rolling wind continued, and then, with a clunk, it was gone.

Shona stared at her phone.

"What the actual," she said, quietly. She could not call back, as the number had been withheld.

A large frame was in front of her. It was Karl.

"So," he said.

"Nice tunes," Shona said. "Can I buy you a drink?"

She noticed his hairy right hand was shaking. His eyes were pink and tired.

"I guess you're looking for Bev, and what-have-yer." He leaned on the bar; he looked ready to collapse.

"I am," Shona said.

He pointed to a bottle on a shelf and the barman nodded.

"You all right, Karl?" she asked.

He stared ahead. "Aye, right enough," he said, flatly. "Get a bit nervous when performing, like."

"Fair enough. Was that an old folk song, or one of yours?"

He poured the bottle of amber drink into a straight glass and had a sip. "No, it's an old folk song. About the rich fucking the ordinary folk. Nowt's changed."

Shona nodded. She thought of her father. He would love this chat. And Karl and Beverley clearly thought alike. They were a close couple. They thought and acted alike.

"I thought Bev would be on tonight," Shona said.

"The band were meant to be on"—he nodded—"but it's just me. Bev has something to do. She said it couldn't wait."

"She's meeting Alison and Peg," Shona said, looking at him directly.

He stared at his drink. He said nothing, and drank.

"Is that right? A reunion?"

"I dunno," he said, low, his hand shaking.

"Karl, back on in ten?" the barman said, tapping his watch.

"Aye, sure," Karl said.

"Karl, I just want to catch up with them all together, for my article . . ."

"About that poor Daniel, I know," he said, mumbled.

"Do you know where they're meeting?"

He looked at her. He leaned towards her, his massive head creating a shadow, his hairy face haloed with harsh pub light.

"I'm not gonna say it twice," he said, "so listen on, and reckon."

"Okay, Karl," she said, gently.

"There's something weird going on in the dale. Something dark. Since you've been here. Or since Dan topped himself. There's been . . . incidents. I can't say more. Bev and them are down at the mill. Fuck knows why. I just want everything to go back to the away it was. Quiet. You know they've found a body?"

"Where?" she asked. There cannot be another body, she thought.

"In the woods. Deepdale. Bobby Stang," he said.

"Ah, right," she said. "Yes, I heard." Her mind withdrew from a small panic. A part of her suddenly wished she had spoken to Robert Stang first. But now he was gone.

"Did you hear he was stabbed? Stabbed to death. There was . . . there is someone going around killing people, Shona. That's a bigger story than poor Dan. Isn't it? Bodies everywhere, and a murderer. Not poor Danny—that's not a story."

"I know what a story is. What do you mean, bodies everywhere?"

He looked at her, his eyes wide. His face flushed. There was a tang of sweat.

The barman said Karl's name again, and his shoulders sank.

"I'm off," he said, and sloped back to the stage. Some people clapped, and he wiped his brow and raised a hand.

Shona looked outside. It was dark, with loneliness in every shadow.

Karl picked up his guitar again. He strummed his way through three more songs: all sad, all forlorn, all in the minor keys. One of them, "John Ball's Blues," was very long, building to a heavily strummed climax.

"*When Adam delved and Eve span/ who was then the gentleman?*" he sang, over and over.

Karl was upset, even as he sang. There was something clenched in his tone, something nervous in his body. At the house he had seemed full of bonhomie, a largeness and capacity. Here he looked diminished and scared.

She sat at the bar for the twenty minutes of the set, drinking whiskey and Coke. Karl sang well. Shona was on the verge of texting Terry about nothing in particular—she could not think of a subject matter—when there was a pattering of pub-applause as Karl's slow, sad music came to an end.

"Nice one, Karl," someone hollered from a dark corner.

Karl put his guitar in a soft grey case and looked over at the bar. He saw Shona and wiped the back of his hand over his mouth. He nodded at the barman, who poured a pint instantly.

Karl lumbered over as piped rock hits filtered through the pub's PA.

"Still here, then," he said.

"Looks like it," she said. "I just want to chat a bit more."

"What for?"

"Well, I think you have something to tell me."

"Oh, aye?"

"You're talking to me now aren't you?" She smiled.

He looked around the bar. His massive neck was red from sweat. Neck hair plastered on it.

"Where is Bev?" she asked again.

"There's a place out back," he said, as if not to Shona, but into his pint. He trudged to a door near the dark jukebox. Shona followed. It looked like a fire exit. The door opened into the cool air and silence of the night.

She was in a lane between the pub and the next building, and at the end was a sliver of electric light, where Karl was standing now. She followed him.

There was a backyard, filled with empty beer barrels, some pallets and boxes, recycling bins, bounded by a low wall. Past the low wall was a sheer cliff face, heavy with trees, and the river. On the other side of the Tyr, the streetlamps glowed orange and the streets were silent. A single lamp glimmered on the wall.

"You never heard it from me," he said, at last. Karl was smoking a joint, and the sweet smoke was blown from the river back to Shona and the lane behind. Shona leant against the green wall and waited.

"Okay," she said, softly.

"It were called Sorley. Funny right?"

Shona's heart bumped again, but she did not show any emotion. The smoke dragoned from Karl's joint. It drifted across her vision of the land below the cliff, as if the town's lights were gleaming in a cloud.

"The thing they were talking to," Karl said. "Bev said he, or it could have been a 'she,' I guess, was called Sorley. That's who they were talking to, on them Ouija board sessions and what-have-yer. Back in the day.

"She told me about it at Glastonbury. She was a bit freaked out by something we took. Magic mushrooms. Bad acid. She told me all about it. Said it had all given her years of bad luck. Until she met me."

"This Sorley . . ."

"When you showed up the other day, asking questions about back then, well, it made me think of what they were up to. Maybe it's brought me bad luck an' all."

He shook his head and took a long draft of his joint. He shot out smoke from his large nostrils.

"In what way?"

"Ach, something that's settled now."

She didn't know what he was talking about. "So, this Sorley?"

"Backstage at their school. That Alison, Bev, that poor Dan fella, the boy who went missing, Big Bobby, that other prick. They met once a week. Regular, like. I'm not sure if they were friends as such. Maybe Bev and Peg and Alison. Andy and that Dan were meant to be close. That's why he was at the wedding."

He shrugged and sat down on a beer barrel. His massive frame breathing hard.

"Bev won't thank me for this. I think they were addicted to it. They got in right trouble for doing it at the school, so then they started meeting in the basement of the old Ullathorne mill. The ruined one down by the river there."

"Why are you telling me this?"

"Because I heard your question to Bev. About those messages—the lines you were saying."

"'There is no time.' 'Take the right path.' 'Say yes to no.'"

He blew out a jet of smoke. He rubbed his eye with a palm. He nodded.

"Bev said their sessions eventually got a bit boring," he said, quietly. So quietly, Shona moved forward. "This Sorley, repeating the same messages. Those lines. The glass would move so quickly. Sometimes their hands would come off it. Sometimes it seemed to be floating off the table. Bev said that sometimes, the glass would only spell out fragments, bits, of those sentences. Bit like a parrot who only remembers some of what it's been taught."

"Have you and Bev ever done a session?"

He looked at her, his eyes tawny in the electric light and the flare of his joint. "Not a fucking chance. That stuff scares me, to be honest. I don't want to talk to the dead, with spirits, or what-have-yer. Do you believe in all that? The afterlife?"

"I don't think so. Do you?"

He shivered suddenly. He picked a mote of Rizla paper from his mouth. "I believe Bev. She doesn't lie to me. Plenty of people have, but she hasn't. But I think them messages are cursed. They're bad. Like hexes. They shouldn't have seen them and they shouldn't have said them. But they were young and fucking idiots. For dabbling in that stuff. For dipping their fingers into that.

"I shouldn't be telling you this," he mumbled. "But, you know. I love Bev. She's turned my life around. I would be dead in a ditch by now if not for her. Life is hard. I just know she is in the mill right now, with them lasses, and I am worried it all might kick off again. Dan has topped himself, hasn't he? There's a body in the woods. There's . . . bad shit going on. Andrew Banks was never found. You're here, kicking around the bones and the dust. It doesn't feel right to me."

Shona nodded.

"And," he added, "I just didn't like Bev lying to you about them messages."

He rubbed his hands, and moved to the low wall. He stared down through the dark trees to the murmuring river. A moving shadow upon the shadow.

"You should probably go now," he said, quietly.

"What are you going to do?" she said softly, as she looked at the great bulk of Karl, staring down into the darkness.

"I'm going to get my guitar and drink myself stupid, and wait here for Bev to join me."

"I am going to go to the mill."

"Well, you know now."

"I do, and thank you."

He reached into his back pocket and fished out another long, slim joint. "I don't want to sound over-dramatic and what-have-yer, but this never happened."

"What happened?" she said, smiling.

He turned around and made a soft sound, like a short laugh. Shona turned on her heel, and made for the lights of the town. Karl stood still, smoking, dark against further darkness.

29.

The stars glittered through the ruins of the old mill, which stood, shattered, on the dark banks of the river Tyr.

Shona stood before the boarded-up ruin. She could not see a way into the site, or hear or see anything moving within. Her stick slapping on the flagstones, she walked down to the edge of the building where it bordered the river. But there was not a clear way in—just a sheer wall with no roof, and dark boarded windows like thumbprints in the stone.

But there: down by the river, there was a thin ribbon of light, flickering on the passing water, cast from a low barred window. She looked up. The moon stared back, a scarred bowl of silver, but it was not casting that shiver of colour.

How to get to the window, Shona thought. There was no path down from the bridge. Cross to the other side and wade across the river, she thought madly. But no, no chance of that. The water was deep and driven. She would be taken away and drown.

She figured she could walk to that field, and trace a difficult clambering route along the river's edge, back to the window of the mill. She set off, back up the Bank for a few yards, and then down a short, cobbled street, the bulk of the broken mill to her right.

Stomping past a parked car and its hidden driver, Shona was shortly in the field, under the moon and the frazzle of the town's lights, her stick in mud and thin grass. She walked slowly down to the river's edge. There was a short drop to the rocky beach. The river ran wide here, slow and deep. Lights glittered on the far bank. The night was silent.

She looked over the edge of the short drop. She sat on her haunches, put her stick down, turned around, and let herself drop down to the river's edge. Her trainers hit the scree and scrabble of rock.

The world seemed suddenly changed. The tawny smell of the river was about her, and the world of men was obscured.

The path along the riverbank was dark, pitch black in the eaves. With a curse, she realised she had no torch. But she had her phone. She switched on its light, and it cast a dim blush on pebbles and rock. If she shone it down at her feet, and her stick, at least, she could see immediate obstacles.

She made her way, suddenly nervous and slow, along the stony bank, her stick prodding into the darkness. If she fell, she would fall on unseen rocks. Or she would tip into the river, and be lost. She stopped for a moment to catch her breath. The river ran beside her, thick and dark and relentless.

Above the flow of the water, she heard voices. She walked further on, almost to the bridge, which now loomed near.

There was a semicircular, glassless window close, at the height of her shoulders. She crunched along a shore, and reached it. Inside was an intact basement room, all brick and dust, and there was light: a sharp white fuzz from a camping lamp set on a trestle table. Three figures were around it. They were talking. On the table was a white plastic bag with something soft inside it.

With the river behind her and the ruin in front, Shona looked in to listen. In the lamplight she could see the faces of Bev, Alison and Peg. They were murmuring. Shona took out her phone and switched on the Dictaphone. She set it to record, and dropped it in her pocket.

Peg turned to the window and saw Shona. She lifted her hand to the others, and walked over.

"I figured it might be you," she said, quietly. She stepped up on something in front of the window, and held out a hand. "Come in, then," she said.

Shona passed through her stick, which Peg took gently. Peg then grasped her hand, and then Shona carefully but awkwardly climbed through the empty window frame. Brick scraped her knee, and tore at her thighs.

"Fucking hell," she said, as she landed on the damp basement floor. "That's the most exercise I've had for years."

"Hello, again," Bev said, something dark around her eyes.

"Good evening," Alison said.

Peg handed Shona her stick. "I've got a bit of drink," she said. "Warm you up." She moved to the trestle, and rummaged inside the plastic bag. She took out a flask, which she unscrewed and passed to Shona, who, nodding at the others, took a swig. It momentarily crossed her mind that the drink could be poison. But it stung her tongue and sent a fire up her nose—it was whisky. She handed it back to Peg.

Alison had a small glass in her hand. She put it in her pocket.

"So," Shona said.

"Hi," Peg said.

"So?" Shona said.

"So, what the fuck is going on? Is that what you mean?" Bev said.

"She knows what the fuck is going on," Alison said.

Shona moved forward and leant her stick against the table. "I'm a bit disappointed. I thought you all might be having a wee Ouija board session," she said.

They all stared at her. Bev looked exhausted. Alison was watchful and severe. Peg looked ready to cry.

"You know, for old times' sake—a wee game of spin the

glass," Shona said, the raw whisky spiking alarmingly in her blood.

Alison drummed her fingers on the table. "Okay, we haven't got all night."

"Well, we have," Bev said, looking out to the darkness and the river.

"Tell us what you know," Alison said.

The camping light shone harshly on their faces. They stood, all in heavy coats in the flickering basement. The floor was uneven concrete, with dank pools of water here and there. It was an empty room, its ceiling a rough cast, from which hung strands of muck and cobweb. There was a dark door in the corner, stairs leading to further darkness. The river ran outside, murmuring and listening. In the leafless trees a mumbling breeze was picking up, rattling branches.

Shona took a deep breath, and then ran through, in brief, with some details missing, the past days. She concluded by saying she was going to ask Gary Watson some questions at his campaign launch in the morning.

Alison crossed her arms, and stared at the floor. Bev stared out of the window. Peg leaned on the table's edge, fiddling with the rustling plastic bag.

Shona pointed to the bag. "So that—that's Andy's shirt, isn't it?"

Alison nodded. "Yeah. He was wearing it the last time."

"Some things should stay in the ground," Bev said. Her voice carried out of the half-moon window, and into the water.

"Ashley said the dog found it in some building in the woods," Shona said.

"Yeah," Alison said. "I think I know that building."

Peg looked at her in surprise.

"Gary took me there once. It's a fake ruin—it's not a real building."

"What you on about?" Bev said.

"Gary's dad—he was in the Territorial Army," Alison said, still looking at the floor. "Awful man. They built it as a pretend ruin, to defend or capture, or whatever the fuck they do."

"I've never seen it," Peg said.

"Didn't know owt was there," Bev said.

"You can find it if you look for it," Alison said.

"Gary took you?" Peg said. "When?"

Alison shook her head.

"What are you going to do with the shirt?" Shona said.

"Bury it again," Bev said.

"I think we should take it to the police," Peg said.

"I want to show it to Watson," Alison said.

"Why?" Shona asked.

Alison's face hardened. Her eyes flashed. "What does wee Viv think of you being here? Does she even know you are here?"

Shona bit her lower lip. She pressed on. "Look, the shirt has been found. I know about the Ouija board stuff. I know a little bit more about Daniel. So, I am going to write about all of this anyway."

Silence fell. Bev leant on the edge of the window, and looked out at the river.

"I know you will," Alison said eventually.

"Why," Shona said, "do you think Dan did what he did? It makes no sense to me. He led a quiet life in Darlington. Saw his mother in the home. Was at his friend's wedding . . ."

Alison took something out of her inside pocket. It flashed in the lamplight. It was a packet of cigarettes. She fished out a pink plastic lighter and lit up in a sudden blaze of fire. New shadows shook around the stone and brick, and were then gone again.

"And he was clearly obsessed with the Ouija board. It

consumed him, didn't it? He had one tattooed on his chest," Shona said.

"No, he never," Peg said, aghast.

"I saw it," Shona said. "I saw his tattoo. I saw the mess in his hotel room. The messages he spelled out in stones. I saw all the words he'd written. It was like he wanted them to be found. Like he wanted someone—someone like me—to follow the trail back, back to here. Back to Ullathorne. 'Say Yes to No.' 'Take the Right Path,' 'There Is No Time.'"

"You're deluded," Alison said. "He was sad. He was sick. That's it."

"You're lying to yourself," Shona said.

Bev was nodding at something—a thought, or Shona. Her earrings glittering in the dark. "'Say Yes to No,' 'Take the Right Path,' 'There Is No Time,'" Bev said quietly, nodding. "That's what he always said. That's what they always said."

"Dan killed himself because he was in despair," Shona said. "He had reasons, all of his own. They died with him. We will never know all of them. But when he did, he wanted to say something, too. He picked a public event—the wedding of his friend's sister. He stripped off to show the world his tattoo. He left these messages in his coat for someone, to find. Accidentally or deliberately. He knew Viv worked in the papers. He knew there might be journalists there. He was pointing to something. He was pointing to Ullathorne."

"How can you say that?" Peg said, shaking her head.

"I am here, aren't I?"

Peg shrugged.

"It was the wedding of Andrew Banks's sister," Shona said. "He didn't do it on the spur of the moment. He didn't throw himself under a train. He didn't take an overdose. He didn't slash his wrists in his caravan. He went to the wedding, stripped off, jumped from the roof, left messages.

And I am going to write about it. I'm going to write about it all. I'm going to write about this thing—this thing you might call Sorley. I don't quite know why he was pointing here. But I have my ideas."

"Sorley, eh?" Bev said. She chewed a fingernail.

"I'm going to say it," Alison said, to Bev.

"You'll sound bloody mad," Bev said.

"It is mad," Peg said.

"Dan is Sorley," said Alison.

"What?" Shona said.

"Sorley is Dan, in the other world, in the afterlife. Whatever you want to call it," Bev said.

"Another plane," Alison said.

"Pardon?" Shona said.

"This is what we think," Peg said.

"This is what is happening," Alison said.

"Sorley—your pal from the Ouija board?" Shona said. Bev flicked her a hard look. It was sharp, and lean, but it passed quickly. "How can Dan be this Sorley . . . thing? He was with you when you contacted it. Or it spoke to you."

"There is no time," Alison said.

"That means—you see, it means," Peg said, stumbling over her words, "that time as we know it, here—in Ully, in Durham, in our lives: it seems to go forward. From the past to the present to the future."

"Like the river, from a trickle on the moor to the beck to the sea," Bev said.

"But when you are dead, you are outside time," Alison said. "You can be in the past, in this present, in the future. Dan is Sorley. Dan is outside the river now. He is on the banks. Or in the beck. Or on the beach. Or in the clouds. He has pulled himself from the flow. Out of the current."

Shona immediately thought of old Martha, in the drab

netherworld of her care home. Talking about her son talking to himself—to his dead self.

The shadows deepened. The lights seemed to recede. The world seemed to briefly re-focus, as if a lens had been added or subtracted from her inner apprehension of the reality about her.

She shivered. "His mother said he was always talking to himself in his room."

"His mum has always been a fucking pain," Alison said. "No wonder his old man scarpered."

"His mother is sick, Ali. Yes, Shona. We think he was talking to himself," Peg said. "He was talking to his dead self. He was talking to Sorley."

"So . . ." Shona said. "Have you been speaking to Sorley? Have you been . . . ?"

They all nodded.

"When?"

"None of your business," Alison said. The lit end of her cigarette glowed like a single red eye.

"Sorley is just saying the same things, over and over," Bev said, strongly, clearly. "The same things as ever he did, thirty years ago. Those three messages . . . That's it."

"You told me the messages said nothing," Shona said to Bev.

"I lied," Bev said.

"Lots of lies going around," Peg said quietly.

"Look. We all got obsessed. We thought it meant something," Alison said. "We figured they were orders. Advice. Guidance."

"So how seriously did you all take the messages?" Shona said.

They shrugged. They winced.

"Some more than others," Bev said, eventually.

"Not all of us. I hated it," Peg said, with vehemence. "I

hate it. And I never thought they were instructions. Never thought they were orders."

"You weren't one of Abdarg, were you, Peg?" Shona said to her.

Peg shook her head, as if she did not hear.

"Andrew, Bev, Dan, Alison, Robert, Gary—ABDARG," Shona said.

"I don't know what you're on about," Alison said. "We never called ourselves that."

"But we did take it all too much, all too seriously," Bev said. "We read into it what we wanted to read into it. Gary too, I reckon."

"I made some bad decisions," Alison said, and reached for the flask.

The three women looked to each other, as if trying to divine each other's intentions.

"Do you know what Odeadaheado means?" Shona said.

"What? No," Alison said.

"Never heard of it," Bev said.

Shona suddenly felt very cold. She also reached for the flask, and took more whisky. But she carried on. "So, let's try and take a wee moment here. What you, the Abdarg crew, are saying is: Dan killed himself, so he could die, and become Sorley."

"Yes," said Alison and Peg at the same time.

"Is this not mad? Is this not a bit insane?" Shona said.

"None of us are mad," Alison said. "I'm finally getting divorced. That proves I'm not mad."

Bev seemed to chuckle into her hand.

"We saw it then, we see it now," Peg said, slowly. "All this. I knew there would be consequences. I knew it would come to bad. I never wanted Dan to be the one. Never wanted that. Poor man."

"He never had much of a life," Bev said. "He knew he wanted to say something in his death. And if you think you're already dead, it doesn't take much to get there."

"He couldn't become Sorley unless he died," Alison said. She blew out a jet of smoke. The cigarette bobbing like a firefly in the underdark.

The river rushed outside. The gathering breeze blew the scent of drift and jetsam from the flowing water.

"We need to talk about Andrew Banks, and that shirt," Shona said, sharply, her head beginning to ring with the drink.

"Maybe we do," Bev said.

"It's evidence, that shirt," Peg said. "I didn't think so at first. But I am glad Ashley found it."

"Not sure about that," Alison said. "Why's it been found now?"

"The earth has given it up, Ali," Bev said. "It has laid it up from its grave."

"We should absolutely take it to the cops," Peg said.

"You know what will happen," Alison said, harder of voice. "They will say thanks, and it will be forgotten—it will get filed away. In a box, in a locker, in a room with no windows, locked away. Forgotten. It is useless anyway: after so many years, there won't be anything on it—no DNA, nothing useful. How many winters has it been underground? Soaked by rain. Frozen. It's only because it's made from polyester that it's survived this long. Nothing will happen, Andrew won't be found, and nothing will change. And maybe that's fine."

Shona was becoming more anxious. She rapped her stick against the wall unintentionally. But it got their attention. "Did your dad think it was all fine? Did your dad do fuck-all about it, because you were involved, Alison? You were one of the last to see Andrew."

"Fuck off," Alison said. "Fuck right off."

"Leave her father be, Shona," Peg said. "Leave him be. He had his troubles."

Alison looked at the floor. Her eyes glistened. "He brought it on himself."

"I think we should hand it in," Peg said.

"We can't ignore it," Bev said.

Shona opened her hands. "Ladies, I will write about the shirt—either way," she said, trying to sound reasonable. She let a moment of time pass.

The other women looked to their hands, or their shoes. Bev bit her fingernail.

Then Shona said, "What really happened that night? The night Andrew went missing. I am guessing you have not talked about it since 1992."

"I'm going to say it," Alison said. "It seems to fall to me again."

"Go on," Shona said.

"I think Gary Watson did something to Andy," Alison said.

Bev put her head in her hands. Peg looked away. The river murmured.

"*Did* something?"

Alison nodded.

"How so?" Shona said, quietly. She was suddenly aware of her mobile phone in her pocket, the green light of the Dictaphone app, still running.

"I was with Gary, last. I was with him on the old bridge," Alison said. "After we left here."

"Snogging," Bev said, with disgust.

"Not a crime," Peg said, quietly.

"Snogging, yeah," Alison said. "Down by the river. Then Dan and Andy turn up. They had followed us. Everyone had a laugh, mainly at my expense. No one knew me and Gary . . ."

"I had a fucking good idea," Bev said.

". . . were having a carry-on," Alison said.

"And?" Shona said.

Alison rocked a little, her head began to shake.

"It's all right," Peg said, and moved forward, putting a hand on her shoulder. "It's all right."

"It's fucking *not* all right," Bev said, fierce.

Shona waited. Alison's shoulders were shaking. She grasped her body with her arms. "Fucking Gary, and Andy," she said. "Gary had a bag of pills. Andy was delighted. He wanted to get mashed. So, they went off, across the river, into Deepdale. I saw them cross the road, and go into the woods. Me and Dan, we watched them. Then we just walked home. Dan saw me home. He said ta-ra. I liked Dan. He was so gentle, wasn't he? He waved to me and said he was off to get chips and gravy, that he was going to talk to Sorley, on his own. Sorley spoke to him, he always said."

"And the next day, Andy was missing."

"The next day, he was gone." Alison nodded.

"And we just all fucked off, didn't we? As if it never happened. We took the right path. For us," Bev said.

"I was in the search parties," Peg said, "beating the woods."

"I take it you and Alison were not," Shona said to Bev.

Bev shook her head.

"I never said a thing," Alison said, barely. "I was scared. I told my dad I never saw anything. And he said not to worry. 'Don't you fret, our Ali, this will all blow over,' he said. I somehow knew he would make it blow over."

"Bloody hell," Peg said. "I can't even remember speaking to the police. Not sure I did."

Shona moved. She slipped off the table. She walked to the window, to where Bev stood, her head leaning against the stone. Bev had been crying in the dark.

"We need to tell someone," Bev said, her voice low and gravelly.

"I am seeing Watson tomorrow," Shona said.

"You show him this," Peg said, suddenly behind Shona. She handed over the plastic bag. "You show him this and see what he bloody says."

Alison made a gasping noise. She downed a whisky, and wiped her eyes. "I should have said, I know that. But I was scared," she said, suddenly gulping with tears. "I was scared. I just wanted to leave this town. I'm sorry."

Peg moved to her, and put a hand on her shoulder. Then she drew her in. Alison collapsed into her, and wept, tears running hard.

"I hated him," she cried, thick through snot and tears. "Hated him. Hated them both. Both of them. I hate them."

Out, in the cold night, the moon was lambent. Leafless trees shook in the breeze. The river flowed.

Shona nodded, and slipped her hand into her pocket, and turned off the recording.

Alison wept in the dark, and shook, but was held by her friend. Beverley eventually moved over, too, and put a hand to Alison's head.

"Come on, lass," she said, deep and kind. "It's all right now. It's all right. Nothing we can do."

Alison turned to Shona. Her eyes flickered white in the darkness. "I want to know what he says," she said. "I want to know what that Gary Watson says."

30.

It was early, but Shona had slept badly, and she wanted to get going.

"Here, Reculver," Shona said, the phone pinned tightly to her head.

She was pulling on her jacket. The early sun stencilled gauzy shadows from the trees across the pale bedroom wall. They fell down the wall like water.

In her phone, a rumbling voice emanated from what sounded like a deep pit. Detective Inspector Reculver's voice echoed and reverberated. "Is that how you greet me these days, Shona—hailing me like a dog?"

"Sorry—I'm in a rush. I need your help with something."

"It's the crack of dawn! Help in return for what?" he said. He sounded like he was outside.

"Where the hell are you?" she said.

"I am in London for the birthday of my sister's son."

"Wait, you have a sister? And a nephew?"

"Shona, why do you sound permanently surprised? It's the Glasgow accent, isn't it? Yes, my beautiful sister, who, rather aptly, has a beautiful son. I am with them. I am sure you are astounded. What do you need?"

She slumped on her bed. She could hear raised voices in the kitchen below. Ashley's voice was loud. There was the crash of a pan on an iron stove. The dog barked, once, short and sharp.

"I am interviewing Gary Watson, the MP, today," she said.

"Wait," he said quietly. She could hear movement, and a door close. "Right, that's better," he said brusquely. "Ah, well, good luck. I hear there is some noise about him, some trembling on the wires. And I hear he has a temper, when pressed. But he is the Coming Man. Nothing but good press about him at the moment, I see."

"A temper?"

"I just said that. Yeah, we hear he has a reputation for it in Westminster. Volcanic. But the Whips keep it all hush-hush, of course. You asking him about the suicide?"

"How do you know these things?"

"Old friends, old colleagues, old ways and byways," he intoned.

"We need to speak about your contacts in more depth one day. Look, have you ever heard of a senior policeman in the north of England called Harmire, John Harmire?"

Reculver laughed. It was a bright contrast to his speaking voice. It tinkled and shimmered, like breaking glass. "Oh, my."

"What?"

"Ah, the fragrant names of John Harmire, Bob Hilton, and Sir Bernard Vane?" he said.

"What are you on about?" she said, irritated now.

"Have you searched for him on the interweb, my favourite award-winning investigative journalist?"

"Not yet," she conceded. "I've been busy. I'd rather ask you—"

"You should. There'll be plenty of information, and I don't have the time right now. He was one of three force colleagues who were all rolled up like dirty carpets in the early 2000s. Big corruption case in North Yorkshire, all kinds of mess and murk. Lots of payoffs between businesses and cops. They got 'got,' though. Not sure we got all of them, but they were the big names. I assume you don't know what I am on about?"

"No. Haven't a clue. Never heard of any of it. Man, I wish I'd known this last night."

"Why so?"

"Ach, never mind . . . Oh, fuck." She realised she didn't have Alison's number. She slapped the bed in irritation. "This Harmire, he was the father of a woman here, Alison, who was connected to a disappearance years ago. He led the investigation, but it went nowhere."

"If he was involved, I would be instantly suspicious, to be honest," he said, sighing a little. "Nothing worse than a dirty copper. And he was filthy. Specially where money was concerned."

"There's plenty of things worse," she said.

Detective Reculver seemed to huff, then whistle. "Look. I can hear you're in a fankle. Let us reconvene next week—the Café Royal? Monday? I can walk you through it all."

"Fine. But not the Café Royal. We're always there, it's beginning to look suspicious. How about the Canny Man's?"

"Fine. And good luck with Watson."

"The bent copper, Harmire," she said. "Is he still around?"

"Oh, no—died in prison. Best place for him: the cleansing flames of purgatory," he said, cheerfully. "Better go! The wee man calls. Toodle-oo!"

He ended the call.

Shona stared at her phone. She rang Terry.

"Ay up," the photographer answered quickly. "I'm on my way, I'll be early. What's up?"

"Remember those old photos of the sixth form class, and the stories about Andrew Banks in the local paper? Can you go in and take some photos of them from the hard copy? I'll need them for the piece. Let me give you the dates."

"What, this morning? Sure. Wait a minute, let me write this down. I'll pull over."

"Do you know this Mickle fellow? The editor."

"A bit, aye," Terry said. "Enough to let me in early. Not

sure the place will be open at this time of the day. Here: I've pulled over. Gimme the details: fire away."

Shona gave her the date of the paper she needed: October, 1991.

"Fine, no problem," Terry said, and the call suddenly ended.

31.

"So, there was nothing there? How? For fuck's sake," Shona said. She rapped her stick against the dashboard.

Trees moved by the window as if on casters. Terry was driving, and Shona was making a call. They were driving to the Great Fosse. The launch of Gary Watson's electoral campaign was at 11 A.M. at the hotel near the falls, and they were finally on their way. The clear sun cut sharp shadows on the road and fields. Light and dark had been divided. Terry was dressed all in green—a multi-pocketed heavy green jacket, a green T-shirt with a glittering moon on it, and green pocketed trousers. She looked like she was about to leap into combat.

Terry had just told Shona some inconvenient news: when she got to the *Tyrdale Times* office, the copy they wanted was not there. It was "no longer in the archive." It had been removed.

"Did you ask—"

"Yes. I asked that dim bulb, Angela, to look for it for me, but she said there was no record of it. Then she said, 'There were a wee woman here the 'tother day asking for the same paper, and it wasn't there, either.' And it's not on their digitised record. That only goes to—"

Shona looked fiercely at Terry. "To 1999, I know. And that 'wee woman' was me, and I did see it! Fuck's sake. It had the picture of the sixth form class. She said she would photocopy it for me. Fuck."

"Did you take a—"

"No, I never took a picture with my phone," Shona snapped. "Because I'm a numpty."

"Well," Terry said, after blowing out a hard breath, "that's as shady as all fuck. Mickle is up to something, I reckon."

"Was he there?"

"Nah. I asked—he was heading up to the Great Fosse for the launch."

"I bet he is. Shady as all fuck." Shona nodded, slowly relenting from her anger. They drove in silence for a time. Deeper into the valley, leaving Ullathorne behind in trees and the shoulders of the passing hills.

"Look. I do have something for you," Terry said, in a softer voice, glancing at her passenger.

Shona grunted.

"I've found out something quite interesting," Terry said.

Shona wasn't listening. She was phoning Watson's election agent. The phone rang for a while and went to the answering service—again. She swore.

"I said, I've found something out," Terry said.

"Congrats—put it in an email," Shona said, and tried to call Knott again.

They passed the sign to the Coine Tree. Shona's eyes flicked to it as the car barrelled up the dale. Between her feet her stick lay akimbo.

"You're really quite obnoxious," Terry said, shaking her head, as she drove on.

Shona angrily slapped the phone down on her thigh.

"Why are you like this?" Terry said, half-smiling. "Have you ever considered therapy?"

"I don't need to be fucking audited like a spreadsheet, no. Tell me, then: what is this thing you have found out?" she said. She glanced at Terry, who was gripping the steering wheel tightly for a change.

"Right! Well. That old guy—that shack on the moor," Terry said.

"That freakazoid place . . . Dan's old smelly friend," Shona said.

"Where we found the camera. Which, like your character, is probably still rather undeveloped."

Shona suddenly smiled. Her irritation softened, and began to drain away. "Nice. Yes, it's in my bag. What about it?"

"That auld fella is Dan's dad. Old John is Dan's father," Terry said, looking across to Shona.

"Pull over," Shona said.

"Ya what?"

"Pull over. I can't think in a moving car."

Terry slowed down, and pulled over onto a grassy verge. They were near a village, which was half hidden in the trees. The square tower of an old church rose from the tangled high branches.

Shona turned to Terry, who looked like she was supressing a grin. "How the fuck do you know that? I thought he was dead."

"Nope, not dead. We maybe assumed that. But he is just mad and old. He left Dan's mother many moons ago—they divorced. John is his dad."

"So that's why Dan took the caravan up there," Shona said. "To be near his father. They weren't friends, they were father and son. How did you find out?"

"Well, I know this guy up the dale," Terry said, looking out the window.

"I'm shocked," Shona said.

"It's a long story," Terry continued. "But I was looking through the pictures of Marton's Farm, and I kind of remembered I had been up there before. It's the back of beyond, you know that. But if you keep going on that road over the fell, you come to some farmed forest—conifers—and there's a mad place, a lonely old pub there.

I know a guy there. I rang him up the other night after our campfire . . ."

"I'm amazed you were capable . . . and that he answered."

". . . and I asked him about the caravan fire, and he said he thought it was an insurance job, and didn't understand why he didn't just move in with Old John because that was his dad. Old John would cycle to the pub, he said, in all weathers. He'd come in with a book and sit by the fire. He would talk about his son. How proud he was of him. Said he was coming to live with him soon, in a spare room. My pal didn't think anything of it. He thought Old John was a bit cracked."

"Shit!"

"What's up?"

The voice on the phone. The message she received, in the pub the night before: it had been Daniel's father. Haling her through the whistling of the moor.

"Old John left a message for me on my phone," Shona said. "It must have been him. He said someone had left a lot of money to the banks."

"Maybe he meant Daniel had given money to the Bankses—the family. Andrew Banks."

Shona swore loudly. She banged the car's dashboard again. "I'm a fucking idiot," she said.

"You have your moments."

"Eighty thousand pounds," Shona said. "Eighty grand was put in Viv's bank account. From selling his house."

"Quite a lot of cash."

"A settling of debts, that's what the old man said."

Terry nodded, and shrugged. "Who knows what he was thinking?"

Shona looked into the trees beside the road. It seemed as if they were holding something that she should know. They had seen things that they could not tell.

"So where had John been? Why did people think he was away—or dead?" she said, eventually.

"He'd been a teacher—a master—at the big private school in Ullathorne. But he took early retirement, apparently. Wanted to quit the dale. Did a lot of travelling. Collected books. Then came back six years ago, and bought that tumbledown place on top of the moor."

"Definitely his dad?"

"I checked the electoral roll. John Kinninvie Merrygill, the Grove, Marton's Moor."

"You looked on the roll? Was it a double-barrelled name?"

"I don't think so. Kinninvie, it's a village near Barnard Castle, down the road. But it looks like it's his middle name."

"As John Kinninvie, he's written some weird books about rocks and stones. Occult stuff. Which figures."

"Oh, aye?"

Shona's phone suddenly buzzed. An unknown number. She answered. "Shona Sandison," she answered.

"Knott—you called?" a thick voice said.

"Oh, Mr. Knott, how good of you to call back . . ." Shona put on her friendliest voice.

Terry smirked and lit a menthol cigarette and rolled down the window to blow smoke out into the cold air.

Shona explained she was the North of England stringer for a news agency, and wanted to use the opportunity of Gary Watson's campaign launch to ask a few questions and write a profile. She said she was already in the dale and would only need twenty minutes.

"He's got about ten minutes," Knott said, thickly. "I've not heard of your agency. But our people can check that out. Mr. Watson is being interviewed at length by a local journalist. But maybe we can squeeze you in after. He needs to get away to Bishop Auckland for a party event. You got a snapper?"

"Yes, I'm with a photographer, Terry Green."

"Never heard of him, either. But come to the launch, make yourself known. I'll contact special advisors in London, though—they might have you on our no-fly list."

"Are you his election agent, Mr. Knott?"

"Something like that."

"I'll see you at the Great Fosse hotel," Shona said, and closed the call.

They drove on, further into the hills.

The sun flashed through the trees, and spread bars of light and dark from the serried gate posts and fences onto the tarmac road. There were countless tiny caves in the mossy drystone walls. Shona looked up. A ragged sickle of high birds straggled across the cold sky. They passed Bev's house in Thorsgill and began to climb through emptier fields, knotty with thistle and nettle, the high ground shaking with ferns.

"Not far now," Terry said. The road climbed. The trees about them began to huddle and gather, and a thin wood grew, and thickened, and suddenly they were in forest. Old forest, deciduous and dark, with moss draped and split rocks gaping amidst the towering trunks.

Terry pressed a button and Shona's window slid down. The air was cold as it flooded the car from the woods and dale. The gauzy hum that threaded the air became a churning roar.

Shona could see a cataract—beyond the line of trees, a huge volume of water was tipping in smooth and massive velocity over a sudden ledge of hard rock, into a hidden bowl of crashing white fury below. The old river, severed by the cliff.

"That's the Great Fosse," Terry said, "and this is the venue."

On the side of the road was a large whitewashed stone hotel, its forecourt thick with cars. A broadcast van was outside, its satellite dish pointing to the blue sky. Above an open double door was the sign: THE FOSSE AND RAINBOW HOTEL AND BAR.

They parked. Terry raised her eyebrows at Shona, and they got out. People were gathering. Old dale men in old suits, young men with Gary Watson haircuts in tight-fitting new suits, middle-aged women with bloodred lipstick in black skirts, and farming gentry in tweed were leaving their Range Rovers and 4x4s, chitchatting, smiling, filing into the hotel. Some had flyers in their hands, with WATSON WINS written in black over an image of Gary Watson against the backdrop of a Union Jack.

Terry was laden with her photographic kit: a heavy bag, a camera with a thick, ribbed lens. She smiled briefly at Shona, who was adjusting her satchel and holding her stick tightly.

"Howay then, lass," she said, softly.

"Could be the big one," Shona said, and walked in.

There was a press of bodies in the lobby of the hotel. Men with pink necks in blue suits, young party staffers in shirts and dress shoes, a large woman in pink with a lolling big hat. Posters had been neatly arranged on the wallpaper. Two roll-up banners stood on either side of double doors into a hall or function room, showing a life-size image of Watson, standing with his thumbs up, smiling. There was a murmuring buzz, a fizzing wattage of excitement.

Shona looked around the hotel foyer. By the double doors, a man was checking invitees' names. There were paintings of the Great Fosse on walls and on brochures and leaflets in piles on the reception desk. Music began to play in the room beyond the doors—an orchestral version of "Jerusalem."

Terry was behind her. Shona had a notepad in her hand, a well-bitten plastic pen jammed into its rings, more as a sign of her occupation than as a symbol of intention. Her stick was held firmly in her other hand.

They reached the doorway. Shona she could see a large wood-panelled conference room with high stone windows, and chairs set out in rows in front of a high stage hung with long curtains.

The audience were sitting down, either staring at their phones or leaning over seats talking to each other. Everyone knew each other. There were no strangers. A film camera had been set up at the back of the hall.

At the door, the buzz-haired, besuited man asked for her name. She gave it, with a smile, and waved her notebook gently.

"Oh, aye," he said. "Mr. Knott mentioned. Stand at the back, don't ask any questions during the event—we'll grab you after. There's a room upstairs: you'll get ten minutes."

"Thank you ever so much," she said, smiling.

"And you, flossy," he said to Terry, "no pictures in there. You can get a portrait after, upstairs. None in the room."

"Thanks, mate," Terry said, and followed Shona into the hall.

They leaned against the back wall as the room filled. Shona looked at the audience. They had clean pale faces and an air of anticipation. There were short grins and raised eyebrows. From another door two uniformed policemen entered and stood against the wall near the stage. One of them removed his hat and held it over his chest, as if he was at a ceremony.

The lights flashed and then dimmed, and the audience cooed and writhed like a tickled baby.

"Here we go," Terry whispered.

Martial brass music strode from loudspeakers.

"Give me strength," Shona muttered as a middle-aged man in a blue suit walked onto the stage, whose curtains were now slowly opening, revealing a red podium and a row of Union Jacks. The man—trim, toned—waved and the audience rumbled and cheered. One bald man stood up and began a solo ovation. One of the policemen was clapping.

Gary Watson MP walked not to the podium, but to the side of the stage. He stood there, unmoving. Lights gleamed from his buffed shoes, his slick forehead. The martial music came to a ringing crescendo, and a video began to play on the screen. The bald man sat down as a hush fell over the audience like a sudden hangover.

The video was a dream of green and blue. It showed Tyrdale, beautiful, shimmering under a summer sun. It looked like Eden, luminous trees nodding beside the wide blue river. Walking beside it, in jeans and a gilet, strode Gary Watson, walking a dog, arm in arm with a severe-looking blond woman. The voice of a Northern man, not Watson, was talking about heritage, history, community, enterprise, culture, a profound love of tradition, a love of innovation. Shona was overwhelmed by the colours of it, the volume, the rising orchestral music.

"Values, deep values, forged in centuries and renewed in a new promise and a reforged vow," the voice rolled on. "Heritage, tradition, and the old ways made anew for a cleaner future."

The screen showed the land from high above—the hills, the deep cleft of the valley, the distant blue mountains, the spread of fields, the town with its ruined castle, and the bend in the old river. The camera moved higher until the dale was a crease in the wider land, and then vanished beneath shreds of cloud, which formed a weather system over a gleaming earth—the sun shattering on sea and mountain—and then, the view moved into orbit, and the blue world rotated beneath a rising sun.

"Watson for honour, for history," the voice continued, confident in its resounding depth, its polished grain, its relentless earnest fervour.

"Watson for the right path, for that quiet, confident voice of the Pennines that says a loud and resounding Yes to Now, as much as to Then, and Tomorrow. Watson for Tyrdale— and Britain. Watson Wins!"

The film ended. Watson moved to the podium, his hands in the air, as the audience were on their feet, clapping.

"For fuck's sake," Shona said.

"Is he running for Lord of the Universe?" Terry whispered.

"World King, I think," Shona whispered back. "Was that a wife?"

"I thought he was single." Terry shrugged. "Widowed. Maybe that's just an actress."

Watson began to speak. Compared to the video, he was diminished. His voice was surprisingly flat, unimpressive.

As he spoke—a brief thanks to his staff, to the party, to the prime minister, to the hotel, to the "ceaseless power of the Great Fosse"—Watson recited a series of boilerplate lines from his party's hymnbook of phrases.

Shona began to take notes, squinting to see the notepad in the dim lighting. But after a minute or two of Watson's speech, she stopped. She fished out her phone, looked about her, and turned on the Dictaphone.

As Watson spoke, the audience seemed transfixed— motionless. But Shona sensed a change, somewhere nearby. Terry flicked her head to the entrance. Shona looked over to the double doors. The man with the buzz cut had his back to the room. He was half in the hall and half out. His shoulders were tensed, and he was leaning into something.

There was a shout. People in the audience turned their heads. The shout cut through the air—ending the speech, ripping open the suspension and belief. It was a naked human shout. An old man's yell.

Shona clenched. There was a sudden burst of movement. A pile of clothes fell into the room. There was a loud slap of human flesh on wood. There was gasping. The besuited man was on his side on the floor, his legs in the air, the pile atop him. The pile of clothes re-formed into an old, wild, bearded man, who was yelling. The audience began to shout, and some stood up. The hatless policeman stood on his toes, trying to see over the crowd.

The old man stood up. He had a shock of white hair, and a beard. He was shaking. He stood, staring at the stage. From his tattered overcoat, he pulled out something long and bulky.

"No!" someone yelled.

But it was a roll of cardboard, or paper.

"Now, now," Watson hummed into his podium microphone, flushing. "Who let the in-laws in here, eh?" He ran a hand over his face.

There was some scattered laughter. The besuited man rose to his knees. He seemed to be in pain.

"This is not a hustings, sir! We can debate my policies another time!" Watson said, to more laughter.

The old man unfurled the roll—it was a poster or scroll. On it were phrases, written in large black letters.

"Sorley is here," the old man shouted. "Sorley is here!"

Shona moved. She could see the phrases on the scroll. Her heart moved in her chest, and her throat seemed to dry instantly, and clench.

THERE IS NO TIME
TAKE THE RIGHT PATH
SAY YES TO NO
ODE ADA HEAD O
045 141 8514 0

Suddenly the hatless policeman was upon the old man. They tussled. The room murmured like a sea. The old man was swiftly overwhelmed, and he was dragged to the door. His scroll dropped to the ground and rolled under a chair, snapping back into a tube. The room seemed to be frozen. Shona could hear Watson breathing heavily into the microphone on the stage. There were desperate gasps and strangled coughs from the huckled man. Another besuited man appeared, moving swiftly, grabbing the man's flailing legs, as the policeman gripped a fat arm across Old John's neck.

Terry was taking photographs, on the floor, on one knee. The rapid click of her camera seemed to fill the room.

"You will be in the stones! You are heading to the rocks and stones!" Old John shouted as he was dragged through the doorway and into the darkness of the world outside the hall. "Sorley is here. You are all rocks and stones!"

Shona mumbled an "excuse me" to a prim woman sitting on the seat, who appeared to pretend Shona was not there, and grabbed the scroll.

Watson whistled into the microphone and looked around the room. "Available for birthdays, weddings, christenings up and down the dale: the wizard Merlin!" he said.

The crowd burst into laughter. Watson's sudden grin opened like a slashed sirloin.

Shona took the poster and left the hall, and Terry followed. They were in the reception again, but there was no one around—no one behind the desk. No police, no Old John.

Terry slid past her and stepped outside. "They've gone," she said, on her brief return. "They've probably gone to beat him up somewhere."

"Tip him off the falls," Shona murmured. She was looking at Old John's scroll, opening it on the reception desk. The black words were sliding and smeared—they were written in charcoal or ash. The poster smelled of damp and mildew.

She looked at the numbers, which were linked to ODEADAHEADO by, she could see up close, tiny lines. O was a zero. The other numbers followed the letters' place in the alphabet.

"What does it say?" Terry said.

"Hang on," Shona said. She tapped the numbers into her phone. She rang it. It rang. And went straight to a voicemail, beeping, anonymous. It closed and disconnected. Terry said something but Shona said *shush*, and called Reculver. It went straight to his laconic voicemail. She pressed another number stored on her phone: Hector Stricken. She knew he'd answer.

Inside the meeting hall, Watson's voice was rising and the audience were murmuring, laughing, clapping.

Stricken answered his phone.

Terry had moved to peer into the hall. She glanced back at Shona and tapped her watch—the speech was winding up.

"Shona? What the hell—"

"Shut up—I need your help quick. What's an 0451 number?"

"Phone number? Where are you?"

"Yes, phone number. Do you know? 0451."

"I think it's the number for MPs—I have a few in my book. Let me check."

"I need it now," she said.

"Keep your hair on. Yeah—just looked. Yeah, I was right:

it's the mobile code for the special phones the MPs get when they get into government. Why?"

"Nothing. Thanks, Hector."

"Shona, I need to tell you—"

"Ta—bye." She hung up.

The hall began to empty, and the audience filed out, pink-faced and loud, moving swiftly through the reception to the lounge bar, whose doors were opened by uniformed staff.

Shona's elbow was touched by someone, and she turned around to see a thickset man with pale eyes. He made a hooking shape with a finger at Terry, and she sloped over.

Shona recognised him. She had seen him buying chips in the town.

"I'm Knott," he said. His mouth, a straight line of pink. No lips, like a shell.

"Knott what?" Terry said, with a smile.

"Hilarious. I thought you were a bloke," he said to her, looking her up and down.

"Common mistake," she said.

"Oh, I very much doubt it, love."

He then explained that Mr. Watson had ten minutes in his diary, and that the interview was embargoed until the following week.

"Embargoed?" Shona said.

"Yes—strict embargo. Midnight next Monday: we have announcements planned every day for the next six weeks. This cannot cut across."

Shona nodded, and they moved up the stairs. Terry's camera clunked against her bag, Shona's stick rapped on the wood, before their feet sunk into thick carpet, and the hubbub of the party below receded. Soon, beyond stone walls and down a long silent corridor, they fell into a hush of quiet. Closed hotel doors paced past them.

All this began in a hotel, Shona thought. It will end in one. Transitory. Clean. Liminal.

"Sit here and wait," Knott said, and pointed to two padded chairs in a corridor.

"Bit of a commotion, that, wasn't it?" Terry said to him.

He said nothing and stumped away.

Shona wrote down some questions on her pad. Terry looked at photos on the back of her digital camera.

After some time, Knott came back, asking them to follow him, and they all moved deeper into the hotel.

A small man with red hair came towards them, padding on the carpet like a burglar. He had an ill-matched suit, trainers, and a leather satchel.

"Mr. Mickle, as I live and breathe," Knott said, in an approximation of warmth.

"All done, thanks very much," Colin Mickle said. He glanced at Shona quickly and nodded.

"Thanks, Colin. See you at the do in Bishop," Knott said.

"I'll be there," Mickle said, suddenly noticing Terry and quickening his step. Terry glared at him, her face suddenly as mean as a hawk, but they walked on.

Knott reached a room at the end of the corridor, and knocked lightly. He tilted his head gently, and then opened the door.

"Ladies," he said, and ushered them in.

It was a large hotel suite, filled with light, with large square windows on two sides. Shona put her hand to her eyes. There was a sofa, a low table, and a chair in front of the table. Through the windows there was a spectacle of nature: a tumbling hillside studded with boulders, a thin fringe of tall conifers, and then, beyond the pines, the tumult of the Great Fosse. A white wall of tormented water breaking from the wide river into a haze of mist below. Behind the falls, the moor top, and the bare horizon. Shona looked at the falls, their constant tumult, and stasis. They were silent, beyond the still glass.

It was only with the sound of a clearing throat that she saw, on the sofa, Gary Watson. He had removed his suit jacket and tie, and rolled up his shirtsleeves. He smiled and stood up, clapping his hands. His arms were hairless, as if waxed.

He looked to Knott.

"So, Bax, what do we have here? Another interview? I've given all my best lines to little Colin there."

Knott looked momentarily confused and then went on. "This is Sandy Shonason from a . . . news agency and Terry, her photographer. They have ten minutes with you, Mr. Watson."

Shona said hello. Terry sat in the corner, her camera on her lap. She said she would take a couple of portraits after the interview.

"I'll just be here, Mr. Watson. I'll keep an eye on the time, and just to let you know, Alyce Rutherford is waiting downstairs," Knott said, in a low voice.

Watson turned his head to the square-bodied Knott. "Alyce, downstairs?"

"In the lobby."

"Is Bax around?"

"No."

Watson nodded, and blinked rapidly for a moment.

Shona sat down and put her phone, its Dictaphone application ready, on the table. She felt her stomach turn over. She leaned her stick on the table.

"How do," Watson said, turning to Shona, re-composed. "That was a good show downstairs, wasn't it? Did you enjoy it? Colin Mickle said he'd never seen anything like it."

He looked to Terry, checking her camera, and clapped his hands together.

"Lovely! A threesome, is it?" he said, and laughed a short, dry laugh. "I'll start with the blonde over there. This one looks like hard work."

Terry was impassive. Solid Knott as still as a dolmen.

Shona carried on.

"Nice to meet you, Mr. Watson. Thanks for your time. So, the start of your reelection campaign . . ." She pulled her pen from the rings of the notepad.

"Day one," Watson said. "And onwards to victory."

"Did you know that old man who interrupted you?"

"No." He shook his head and pursed his lips. "But there's always a headbanger or two around. Mentally defective. It didn't really mean anything. I thought it was funny. Hopefully the police have taken care of him. As I said to Mickle—hopefully they've given the silly old coot a quick bath. That's what I would have done."

"He said something about someone called Sorley—do you know who that is?"

Nothing in his eyes moved. Then he smiled. "Sorley? Surely you're mistaken! No, didn't hear what he said. Anyway—fire away, my good man Knott here says we have ten minutes. Don't waste it."

He took a bottle of water from the table and twisted off its cap with a small wince. His suit was blue-grey, well-cut. Bespoke.

He pointed at Shona. "What kind of reporter are you? I'm not familiar with your byline."

"Crime, mainly," Shona said.

"You can't catch many criminals with that bad wheel, eh? Guess you don't chase them very far."

Watson slumped back in the sofa. He took a swig of water.

Shona glanced at the window. The waterfall fell slowly, silently into its constant destruction. "I only write about criminals, Mr. Watson. I leave catching them to others."

"Quite so, quite so," he said, and made a winding motion with his hand. "Let's get on with this, shall we?"

"I'm interested in your election plans," she said. "Do you think you are going to win here in Tyrdale again?"

Watson turned out his hands, his palms facing the pale ceiling. "Well, one should never count the votes before they're cast, of course. That's basic common sense. But we as a team are very confident that we have the right path for this dale, this county—this country. Are you from Glasgow?"

"Yes, the Southside."

"I was up in Scotland recently, you know. I like to visit. Beautiful—it should be called North Britain again, don't you think? Such a resonant phrase. I love both those words: North. Britain. Magnificent. It reeks of ancient splendour."

Shona looked at her notebook. Terry checked her camera. Knott stood by the door, like a bouncer. Shona leaned forward.

"Tell me a little bit about growing up here, Mr. Watson, as you're unusual in being an MP actually from the area you represent."

"It is unusual, Sheena, as you say. I am a rare breed. It's a shame, isn't it: that the root and the blood and the soil of the constituency are not reflected in their MPs anymore? It's like accents. Everyone has the same accents these days, don't they? It's all much of a muchness. On the telly, on the radio. In the streets of the south. It's the influence of America, of hip-hop, of TV comedies. Don't watch them myself. But I'm a proud northerner, I've never hidden my accent. It's authentic, and, forgive my French, I think it's a no-bullshit accent. Anglo-Saxon. But yes, to answer your question in the spirit it was intended: yes, I grew up here—I am Tyrdale born and bred. That's me. Very proud of the area and the stock of the people who live here. It's all about good, hard common sense around here. I was lucky enough to school here, and my father had a bob or two—good for him—so I didn't want for anything and I think that made me really appreciate hard graft, the dignity of the shift, and the value of money. Nowt wrong with that."

"And you went to Ullathorne Comprehensive?"

"I did, that. Grand school—I'm on the board of governors now. Very proud to have guided it towards independent status, and back to being a proper grammar school. The problem with 'comprehensive' education is it was trying to be *too* comprehensive, and that's not actually a meaningful education, is it? Why did I, as a young man, have to learn home economics? Waste of time. But, yes, great school in those days, all that being said."

Shona clicked her pen. She tapped it on her notebook. The phone carried on recording, silently. "In the sixth form, you lived through a bit of a tragic time."

Watson frowned. He drank some more water. "Tragic? I had a lot of fun, and got four As at A-level. What's tragic about that? I don't follow."

"You were in a very small sixth form, and you were friends with Andrew Banks. He went missing. He's never been found. That must have been a tough time."

His face was blank. His voice became reedy and thin, as it had in the meeting hall. "That was many years ago," he said. "And what a shame that was. But you know, Sharon, I didn't really know Andrew. I didn't really go around with that crowd—he was more into books and theatre and poetry and all that. I was more into the sports side of things. Cricket team, the football. But of course, it was a big story at the time and I have nothing but sorrow for his poor family. I do know the police did a thorough job looking for him. Combed the valley. It is a terrible thing. But we all moved on. I didn't lose a friend."

"You didn't know him? There were only a few of you in that sixth form. And you were with him the night he died."

Watson put the cap back on the bottle of water and screwed it. His eyes flicked to Knott, by the door.

Shona looked around briefly. Knott's hands were in his pockets. His pale eyes were fixed on Watson. Terry was standing now, looking out of the window at the waterfall. Spots of rain were gathering on the sheets of glass.

"Andrew was into football, wasn't he? He loved Newcastle United," Shona said.

Watson shrugged, and crossed his legs. His trousers rode up his leg—his skin was smooth, hairless. He spoke quickly. "Aye, maybe so. Well, of course I knew him. But we weren't friends. As I say, a tragic thing. Feel very sorry for his family. And you say the night he died—we don't know he died."

"You were one of the last to see him—Alison told me."

"Alison . . . ?" His eyes were screwed up now. Arms crossed, legs crossed.

"Alison Harmire, your sixth form classmate. Part of your gang back then."

"This is all a long time ago. Ancient history. Before her dad passed. Look—if this is all you're going to ask me about, I am afraid I don't have much to say. I'm here to talk about my campaign and the election. My future. Not the past."

Knott was beside Shona now. He tapped her chair with a thick finger. "Time's up, love," he said. His voice was all edges.

Watson held up a hand. "No, man, no—it's fine. I'm entertained. I want to see where this is going, with this little crippled hotshot reporter. Next question?"

Shona smiled. Knott walked away. He moved to the window, and stood beside Terry, who was looking through her camera at the waterfall.

"Your wife's death in 2007, that must have been hard for you," she said.

"It was, it was. But I've spoken about that before, too. It's all in the public domain. I don't think I have anything more to say on that. Sarah decided to drive on the right side of the road, for some reason. Straight into a truck. But that, Miss Sampson, is all ancient history."

Shona nodded, and made marks in her notebook. She looked up. "Would you say that you are to the right of the party?"

"People say I am. All I know is that I am always right! Little joke there. Look—I think the road we are on, it's taking the right path. I am fully supportive of the prime minister and his mission to bring back civilisation to this country."

"So, you'd say you have taken the right path."

"Oh, yes. And I think the results of this general election will prove it. An empire of opportunity lies ahead of us, if we have the gumption to seize it."

Shona moved on swiftly. "Another one of your other school friends, Robert Stang, was found dead yesterday. Did you know that?"

Watson's face and body momentarily froze, as if he had been paused on a screen by a higher hand. He then un-paused. He carried on. "That's news to me. Oh, that's a shame. I remember Bobby. Great soldier, great veteran—great man. I believe he worked in one of our factories. Shame for him. I think the issue of PTSD really needs to be looked at, in fact if I have any influence in the new parliament—"

"No, he was found stabbed to death, in Deepdale. That's what the police are saying. I have a press release here if you'd like to see it."

He blinked repeatedly. But his face and voice rolled on, smoothly, like a teleprompter. "Well, that is terrible. Youth crime . . . that's another thing, in our cities—"

"And last week, another school friend of yours, Daniel Merrygill, killed himself."

His face a wall of flesh. His mouth agape in it. His voice thin, again.

"I didn't know that. Again, a shame. But that's all I can say. I need to go, I am afraid. That's me done. I have about two minutes."

Knott cut in: "One minute."

Watson reached for his suit jacket, which slithered into his hand.

Shona looked down at her pad. "I was wondering why, Mr. Watson—and my colleagues have looked this up—you keep repeating the same phrases in your interviews, in your opinion pieces for the papers, live and recorded on TV and radio?"

He smiled. His jacket was now on. He pulled a silken snake tie from an inside pocket. "Oh, aye? What scary phrases are they, love? 'Vote for me'? I guess that might scare the likes of you."

She tapped her notebook, as if they were written down. But she knew them by heart. "'Take the Right Path.' 'There Is No Time.' 'Say Yes to No.'"

Not a flicker on his face.

"Just turns of phrase, Sharon. Have you heard this, Knott? Have you heard this nonsense? She's a little bit out of her depth, I think."

"Shona," she said, "my name's Shona."

"Whatever, love."

He stood up, and sat down again, on the arm of the sofa. He was higher than her now, and looked down at her. He shot his cuffs.

"Why do you use those phrases?" she asked, staring up at him. "Over and over?"

"We've strayed off the beaten track here, Shona, have we not? I am content to talk about our independent economy, about the safety of our borders, about—"

"No, Mr. Watson. I want to talk about the Ouija board sessions you and Alison, you and Beverley, you and Bobby and Andrew Banks took part in as teenagers."

He closed his eyes. His put his hands up. "Okay, okay. Game's a bogie! No more of this." He stood and swiftly moved to the door.

Knott looked towards her. Terry, ignored by the men, took photos from waist height, clicking quietly.

"Time for you two to go," Knott said.

Watson brushed out imaginary creases from his shirt and looked at his large silver watch. "Yeah, get the poisoned dwarf and the dolly bird out of here."

Shona gripped her stick. "Mr. Watson. I just want to ask—"

"There's no more time for that, love. You shot your bolt," Watson said.

Knott came closer to Shona, his hands up.

"Don't touch her, you prick," Terry said suddenly, angrily. Knott stopped abruptly, as if shot.

Shona stood up, and moved away from the table, and from Knott. She cleared her throat, and addressed Watson directly: "You were the last person to see Andrew Banks alive, weren't you?"

Watson looked to the door. "This is ridiculous. Just ridiculous." He moved his eyes to Knott, with fury. "Where's Bax? Where is he?"

Shona carried on: "Alison and Beverley. I've interviewed them. I would appreciate a comment, from you."

"You do that, love—you do that. See who gives a fuck," Watson said. He laughed.

The door opened suddenly. A woman stood there, dressed in a dark blue suit. Her face was a mask of sheer planes. Her eyes were dark. Her hair piled atop her head, blond and fixed.

"Alyce?" Watson said, surprised.

"Hello, everyone," the woman said in a deep velvet voice. "Hello, Gary."

"Alyce," Knott said.

Watson smiled at her. His eyes glistened. He turned back to Shona. "You going to write about Daniel?" he spat. "You do that. Haven't seen him in decades. Always a bit weak, he was. A soft lad. If I remember. I had forgotten him, until now."

Alyce nodded at Shona and Knott. "Is this an interview?" she said.

"It's all right, Alyce—it's over," Watson said.

Knott grunted an assent.

"I was at the wedding," Shona carried on.

"What wedding?" Knott said.

"On his body, on Daniel's body, was this number," Shona said, and pressed a saved number on her phone: *Odeadaheado.*

A moment later, a buzz fizzed in Watson's jacket.

Shona nodded towards the sound.

"That's your number, isn't it? Why would Daniel Merrygill have that? Did he get it from the Ouija boards?" she said, doubt in her mind but not her voice. "Somehow?"

"I don't know what the fuck you're going on about." Watson shook his head. "How have you got my phone number? That's a security matter, you know. Knott?"

Shona took out a folded piece of A4 paper from inside her jacket and held it out.

Watson was standing stiffly now. His back against the wall. Alyce peering at him. Knott stood, impassive.

"This is a photo. Of an old Newcastle United shirt found in Deepdale woods," she said. "Just last week."

"Whose is that?" Alyce said.

Watson leaned forward to stare at the picture.

Shona raised her voice. "This is Andrew's shirt, isn't it? He wore it the night he died—the night you were with him, in the woods, taking drugs in the Deepdale? In 1992?"

Knott ripped the picture from her hand. "Fucking give me that, silly bitch."

Shona flinched at his force. Terry jolted forward, her face furious, her jaw clenched, her eyes flashing.

"Terry, it's fine," Shona said to her quickly.

Watson gestured to Alyce, who was languid, leaning against the bland hotel doorframe. "I'm out of this panto-mime," he said. "Alyce? Knott?"

Alyce smiled at Shona and nodded at Terry. Knott grunted and threw the screwed-up picture to the floor. The three moved to the door, and Knott and Alyce left quickly, van-ishing into the corridor beyond.

Shona looked to Terry, who was wide-eyed.

Then suddenly, her eyeline tipped, and a pinching pain stung her. Something hard and forceful had grabbed Shona. It was Watson. He was suddenly there, grasping the scruff of her shirt. She dropped her stick. His lips were moving. She could smell his sweet cologne. It barely covered the seeping sweat of his hairless neck, the clag of his armpits and gaseous guts and something else, something chemical and noxious.

"Write one word about all this, and you'll never write another," he hissed. "I can find you, wherever and whatever you are, witch. I'll fucking fuck you to death."

His fingers were around her throat. Shona shook. Her eyes flared. From somewhere hidden, somewhere deep and hard and lonely, she found the strength to respond.

"Fuck *you*," Shona said, pushing her voice past his hand. "I'll write what I fucking want. You cannot stop me."

Terry took photographs of the two. The flash snapped like lightning. His fingers loosened.

Knott was now at the door, his eyes wide, his mouth open. Watson let Shona go with a sudden violent shrug. She rocked backwards, and fell.

"Right enough," he said. He wiped his face with open hands.

Shona righted herself on the floor, her heart pounding like the waterfall.

"Right enough," Watson repeated, quietly. He turned on his polished heels, and left with quick steps. Knott, eyes closed, shut the door behind him.

Shona slumped onto the soft carpeted floor.

Terry was beside her and put a hand on her shoulder. She knelt and looked into Shona's eyes.

"My God," Terry said. Her eyes were wild and wide. "My God," she said again.

"Don't worry. I'm absolutely fine," Shona said firmly. She reached for her phone, which she had dropped. It had been recording, unnoticed.

"Got it all on tape," she said. "Twat."

"Got what?" Terry said. Her eyes were bright with angry tears.

"Got the fucking story, didn't we?" Shona said.

32.

<*You will resign and withdraw tomorrow. I have informed PM*>

It was dark, but not silent. The waterfall thundered nearby. Behind the trees, behind the wall of night.

That had been the message from Raymond. He'd read it, and it had disappeared.

Watson was alone. Knott had gone—after the interview debrief, he had resigned on the spot, and gone to London. Alyce, shaking her head, not touching him or looking at him, had also resigned. And Bax had not yet come back. No word from him, no sign of him. As if he had never existed.

The campaign event in Bishop Auckland had been cancelled. The diary had been cleared. Knott, before he had left, had told the campaign team to knock off, go home. The phone had not yet rung: the press office in central London had been informed of the incident, but the reporter had not yet called for comment. But she had enough to run a story. He had attacked her. In front of the photographer. That was enough. No need for reactive lines. No need for briefing. No use for balancing quotes. The police had not yet been in touch. But they would be, he knew. His father and Sergeant John Harmire were no longer around to make things go away.

He was still in the hotel room. Bare-chested, wearing only his suit trousers.

"Fuck them," he said out loud, to no one. He held in his hand a heavy square glass. Whisky filled it to the brim.

"Fuck it."

Out, he looked. Into the darkened woods, into the landscape swallowed by the night, except for the nearby line of old trees, lit in strips by the electric hotel light.

He had lain on the bed, the empty glass on his chest. But it had not moved. He had called, and spoken. He had asked, and pleaded. But it had not moved. Sorley had not come. He had taken a break, had a drink—had a few—and tried again. But it had not moved.

He had taken paper, and written it all out, laid it down on the table, waiting, patiently, conventionally, for the glass to move. Nothing. Sorley had not come. Sorley was not there. Sorley, dead, was dead. The dead had died and only the living were left.

How had the reporter gotten his government mobile number? He did not know. Sorley had asked for it once. But it wasn't from Sorley—that reporter wouldn't have known a thing about it. She must have gotten it another way.

The football shirt was another thing entirely.

He looked out to the woods. The Great Fosse thundering, somewhere, beyond. The road outside lit by the hotel light. A string of puddles glinting beside the road, and a path to the great falls. The endless mapless darkness.

He reached inside his suit jacket for the plastic bag of cocaine. A toot of the white stuff. He tipped it out on the table, and scraped it to and fro, with his credit card. He stopped, and looked at the tiny landscape of powder on the tabletop. Crumbs cast thin shadows.

Nothing to fuck tonight—apart from himself, he thought. He snorted it all up, then swallowed some pills.

He looked at his shaking hands. They were dark, wet with his blood. Sliced finely by edges of the penknife. Slippery with strands of cum. His soaked jeans, covered in mud, splattered with blood. His necklace, ripped and broken, a string around his neck, beads scattered like tiny pale eyes in the muddy earth. In the dark woods. In the hot summer night.

No. He shook his head.

No: his hands were fine. His clothes were fine. That was not there. His hands were clean, pink, slightly swollen, dusted with talc. A forty-nine-year-old's hands. Clean, almost. Clean, for years. Nothing on them. Nothing to see. Nothing was ever there.

His head was heavy, swimming. Down by the path, there was a shape. There was a distant figure. Was it Alyce? Tall, pale, elegant. With a white shirt, with—was that a dark skirt, or dark trousers? The figure was on her phone, her face, turned away, partially lit. A ghost light on the edge of the forest. He banged the window. She did not look up. Just stood, in light, at the edge of the trees. He moved to his phone, and called Knott. But there was nothing. He called Bax—again, nothing. He called Alyce—it was engaged.

He pulled on a shirt, buttoned a couple of buttons, and left the hotel room, padding down the corridors. He recoiled from the cold as he left the lobby. His campaign posters were still up. They would be taken down in the morning.

He stepped uneasily across the car park in the frigid air. There, at the roadside, was the glow, which turned, and moved into the woods, along the path to the falls.

He could hear the Great Fosse, thundering beyond the pines. The constant roar of it, grinding and booming. The path was dark, but for the light from the mobile phone, like a blue candle.

He paused to look back at the hotel. He looked up, but the moon was obscured by cloud. The sky was empty; there were no stars. He looked back, once more, and then he plunged into the forest.

The light had gone, but the path was long and winding, doubling back on itself, climbing up and down steps, as it moved towards the Great Fosse. The roar was louder now, as he moved along the path, using his own phone as a light. Its tiny beacon flashed on bark, and board, on fencepost, and into the blackened tangle of the undergrowth. He moved on, peering along the path to where Alyce could be, but he could not see her. It was cold. He pushed back a shiver.

There was a rope-lined bridge over a sudden black crevasse, and he crossed it slowly, and reached the other side. He stopped.

Maybe Alyce had not been there at all. He had been drinking. He was wired and buzzing. He looked at his phone. He called Bax: there was nothing. Just a quick fall of bleeps. No even a voice message. The same for Knott.

"Cunts," he said, and spat.

He stood for a moment in the dark, out of sight of the waterfall, but hearing its thunder. The rocks around were high, and jagged. In the flickering light of his phone, they cast sharp shadows, coiled into odd shapes. He moved the beam about, and a rock became a face—a bearded man with coins on his eyes. He moved it again—a building crowned with battlements, and beside it, a ribbed rock which looked like a field of fingers. He flashed it around him—there was a plane of grinning mouths and blinded eyes, multiplied and magnified in the sharp beam. A tongue, lolling from a fat mouth in a green face full of leaves and vines.

And in the dark beyond the precipice, he saw another shape—the black shadowy resonance of a vast tree. It was monstrous, a giant. It was dark, even against the darkness. It rose to a height above the others, set back in its own glade, an aura of lightless space. Its trunk was more than one body, it was multiform, its branches high and wide, tangled at their tips, and it had a rent in its side, like a tear in a curtain. It stood, vast, and Watson stared into it and saw nothing inside its depth. The light from his phone could not reach it. The light within it was extinguished.

He knew the hollow tree, the great Coine Tree. But it was not here. It was deeper down the dale. It could not be here. Trees don't move. Hollow trees don't walk.

Then, in a blur of movement to the side of his eyes—there was a flicker. He saw, again, in the corner of his sight, a shimmer of light on the trees up ahead. A definite glow. An aura. A tickling radius of light and movement, like someone walking, with an open phone, or a lantern, or a candle.

"Hello?" he called out, although his voice melted into the noise of the falls.

He walked on, his feet slipping now on the wet board, and as he turned a smooth corner, past boulders and huge trees, the volume of the waterfall increased suddenly.

There in the darkness was the Great Fosse, where the Tyr, fresh from the moors and emboldened by tributaries slicing down steep ravines, fell smooth-faced to a constant hammering demolition of foam and cloud.

He could see the viewing platform, some telescopes on metal posts, and a steep stone path down to the edge of the rushing water.

There was no one here. He was alone. There was no Alyce. The spray from the falls settled on his hair and smooth face.

He sat down on a bench, and with water soaking into his suit pants and his back, he stared into the darkness. Until he saw a figure again, below on the narrow stone path. A face, pale, lit by the mobile phone. In amongst the rocks, a billowing shirt. It could be Alyce. But it could be a man.

Something in the bearing of the shoulders. Something in the limbs, the head. It seemed familiar.

"Alyce?" he called into the tumult, into the night. "Bax?"

He moved, as if in a dream now, as if frictionless, in one movement to the steep rock steps. He flashed his phone light again, and its brightness slapped on the descending stair of wet rock. There was a ladder of slanted steps, and at their bottom, the fiercely running water, and the constant cloud of spray. He could hear nothing but the roar of the falls, and the timpani roll of their violent resolution on the jagged rocks, hundreds of feet below.

"Bax? Knott?" he called again. "Alyce?"

Down there, by the riverside, the light glowed. A definite glow. The sub-sea iridescence of a mobile. She was down there.

And if it wasn't her, it was someone. Someone was down there. Did someone call him? Was that a voice? The past, inside the present.

He moved to the tight line of stone steps and began his quick descent. It began to rain. Water on his shaven skin.

As he stumbled down the wet steps, his mind began to detonate with light.

33.

Shona was waiting for the train north.

They had driven from Tyrdale to Darlington quietly. The rise out of the valley and onto the main road had been in faltering sun, and a darkening sky. As they left, Shona had glanced behind, at the valley of the Tyr. She knew she would not see it again. Its silent beauty, its wordless perpetuity, stood, and would always stand, until there were no human eyes left to see it.

Terry had put some jaunty disco music on, and Shona, after a time, had smiled. She didn't like the music, but didn't feel the need to comment anymore. Shona had rung her father several times. But the phone rang out. She left messages. A tightening was drawing together in her chest, and around her heart.

Now they were at the cold echoing space of the Victorian station and suspended in waiting. They sat together in the grimly lit café, their cups empty. Terry was quietly skimming through the images of the events in Watson's hotel room.

Shona checked her phone again. Nothing.

"So," Terry said, at last. "I guess you'll be on your way."

"Yep," Shona said. She looked at Terry briefly, and then up at the monitor high on the oxblood brick wall. A cool wind was blowing through the iron arches of the old station. It was getting dark. An arm of dark clouds was moving slowly across the vast sky. She wondered what the clouds had seen on their journey over the land.

"You all right there?" Terry asked, softly.

"Aye." Shona nodded, but put a hand to her throat. It was sore.

They had considered calling the police. But Shona wanted to hold off, for a time. She wanted the story to herself—and Terry had the pictures. Shona had wondered why Knott had not tried to seize the camera. She had seen that happen before. But Watson's entourage had just disappeared.

"I've had worse," she said.

"Of course you have," Terry said. "But that was rough— are you sure you are all right?"

Shona nodded. She stared at the black square of her phone. She was exhausted.

"Right, well. I am not one for emotional goodbyes," Terry suddenly said, and stood up.

Shona stood, slowly, too. The darkening light cast a dusty drift of gloom over the photographer's fine features.

"Look, we'll talk about your pictures, the images, when I'm back, after I've written all this up," Shona said. "Ranald will want to see them. Package them up. Fuck knows how I'll piece all the words together."

"You've got a hell of a story, you know that?"

"Yes, I have. I know that. I'm not sure how to write it yet."

"Just start at the end. Or the very beginning. "

"That's a very good place to start." Shona nodded and smiled.

"You just need to begin with: Why did Daniel Merrygill kill himself at the Scottish wedding, right?" Terry said.

Shona looked to the station, empty in the early afternoon. The tracks like iron spines.

"I know. And we can only guess," she said, as if pacing out the words she was soon going to type. "But we know, now, he thought he was doing it for a reason. There was a method and a rationale. And it was, definitely, with no doubt, linked to the disappearance of Andrew Banks, all those years ago. He was pointing to it. In a strange and unusual way."

"And his dad was strange."

"His dad is a mad hermit and thinks when we die we go into the stones," Shona agreed. "Maybe Daniel believed him. We'll never know for sure—how could we? But we have enough. And we have enough to fuck Gary Watson, that's for sure."

"Exactly. You've got it," Terry said. "You said you'd need to contact the police down here?"

"I'll have to. I'll go to the Durham police. I don't trust the Ullathorne lot. I have a contact in Police Scotland, who I know will be interested. Ranald will need it legalled. It will be legalled to kingdom come. But I need to write it first."

"Just start typing," Terry said, softly. "It'll come. How many stories have you written? Thousands?"

Shona grinned, her stick loose in her hand. Terry's eyes glittered.

"Thank you, Theresa Green," she said, and moved towards Terry. Terry moved quicker, and they hugged. Terry smelled of light sweat and coffee. A faint perfume, and warmth.

They held each other for a while.

"I'm not quite sure what to say," Shona said, resting her head on the photographer's shoulder.

"What cannot be said, will be wept," Terry said quietly.

Shona gave her a squeeze.

"Right," Terry said, suddenly pulling back. "Have a rest on the train. Don't get into any more fights. Hope your old man is all right—and let's talk next week about pictures."

"That would be good," Shona said, gripping her stick hard.

A train thundered through the station, its lights ablaze. It felt like a mountain was rolling through. Then it was gone. Shona looked closely at Terry's face as light moved across her cheeks and the soft glistening in her pale eyes.

"Do you still have pals in Edinburgh, from art school?" Shona said.

Terry blinked and tilted her head. "Aye, a couple of reprobates. Wait, are you asking me if I ever visit Edinburgh?"

"I didn't, no," Shona said. "I asked . . ."

"You've got my number," Terry said, grinning.

"I've got your number," Shona said, looking down at her bag.

Her train arrived, pulling into the station with noise and movement.

"All right, snapper—see you around," Shona said. Terry nodded.

Shona took up her bag and stick and looked for her carriage. She stepped on board.

It was raining now, outside the station. A sheet of rain fell from the pitched roof. Shona watched as Terry stood, half turned. Then she waved, ran a hand through her hair, seemed to laugh, and then turned away and slumped back to her car for her journey back to the hills.

Shona found a seat and sat heavily. The train moved on, and the grey roofs of Darlington faded away into the brown rain. She rubbed her damp eyes for a moment, and then called her father again. No reply. She looked down at her trainers—they were spattered with mud from Tyrdale. Grains of sand from the riverbank. A tiny green curled leaf, plastered to the side of her shoe.

Her phone buzzed—it was a text from Bernie.

Got your message—can you come straight to the allotment as soon as you get back. Your father needs your help. B x

Shona texted back: *I'll be there—is everything OK? Have you called the doctor? I'm on the train. I'll be there in 2 hours.*

She shook her head. Outside, the passing fields were soaked with rain.

She called Ranald.

"Good afternoon, scoop," he said cheerily. "How is it going?"

"Heading back to Scotland—so, I think I may have something for you. Probably a news feature."

"Marvellous. Can it make three to four thousand words? We can sell that. Should I approach the weekend magazines? Email me a synopsis and we shall go from there."

"Fuck, yeah. Three thousand won't be enough, though. How about thirty thousand?"

"Jeez, Shona, what is this—Watergate?"

"Similar."

"Tell me more?"

The train sped north. The sky looked clear ahead at the border.

"It might be the big one," she said.

34.

By the time Shona arrived in Edinburgh, she had typed out the structure of her story and put it all in a long email to Ranald. She included a rough transcription of her encounter with Watson. She did not know quite how to weave in the new details of Daniel's life: his mother, his deranged father, who believed the souls of the dead vanish into stones and rock. She outlined it in a separate section.

She realised she had ordered the story quite methodically. She had, unusually, used bullet points, bold lettering where it was required. She had hesitated momentarily before emailing it away for Ranald's consideration. Her finger hovered over the send button. Then she pressed it. It whooshed its way to him. The story moved from the entirely secret to the nearly public in one tap.

It was a cloudy day in Edinburgh, but the watchful old city was still resplendent, an opened pop-up book of elegance and shadow, beneath it. Walkers moved like black dots on the head of Arthur's Seat.

She took a deep breath. With a solid dread, with a sinking trepidation, she called Viv from the train. But there was no answer. It rang out, to nothing.

And then, as the train slowed, and moved under the glassy canopies of Waverly Station, her phone buzzed. It was a text from Viv.

> *don't ever contact me. i never want to speak to u again. lose this number.*

The train stopped and she sat as people moved off the carriage and into the blaring station, its glasshouse of anxious noise and movement.

As she unsteadily left the train, Shona felt a heavy wave move over her, and through her. It was too much. She sat on a metal bench on the platform and put her hands to her face. Shona wept. Her shoulders shook. She took deep gasps. Racking sobs. She felt a fine lattice of pain spread across her chest.

"Vivienne," she said, to herself, to her hands. To no one.

The phone began to buzz. It was Ranald.

"Scoop!" he shouted.

She took a deep breath and wiped her eyes.

"Shona?"

"Hi," she said, as firmly as she could.

"You okay?"

"Yeah, fine, what is it?"

"Your amazing story!" he yelled.

"Thanks," she said. She looked around. The platform was empty.

"You must be fucking exhausted. But it's a cracker, an absolute belter," he said. "I think I can sell it to one of the big Sundays—one of the London papers. I'm thinking the *Observer* or maybe even the BBC might take it. Run it online, and—I take it you taped the interview with that prick Watson?"

"Yes," she said. "Of course."

"He fucking *attacked* you?"

"Yes," she said.

"Great! I'll need that recording," he bellowed. "We'll need to move quickly. A sharp intro, a long lead, and let the quotes run. I was thinking maybe do bullet points at the top like you have, get the big lines all spelled out, as it's complex. It's got layers. It's like a puzzle. I'll get someone to do the background stuff on the missing fella, and take in the investigation into the wedding suicide. Do you remember the name of the polis there?"

"Lorimer."

"Fine, fine. I'll get him on it. Now for me, I think we need reaction from the Banks family. This shirt, etc. And what I think the right thing to do is inform the police, and then get reaction from the family."

"Yeah," Shona said, "I'm on it."

"I'll get someone else to do that, don't worry. I know you are close to them, and probably not best for you to do that. Unless you think there's an 'in' there?"

"No, I don't think there is," she said.

"Right, okay, well we can discuss that. Shona, this story will be huge. I've got to say—this could bring it all crashing down. On Watson. And there's so many follow-ups, I mean at this stage we should be thinking . . . and then there's all the occult stuff, which, you know, probably has a story of its own in it, and the weird stuff with Daniel's father . . ."

"Weird stuff," she said.

"I'm thinking here . . . maybe we go to a tabloid first? They can sell it hard, make it the splash . . . and we get a bigger fee. They'll edit your stuff to within an inch of its life, but you will be fine with that, right?"

"Ranald . . ."

"Yeah?"

"I need to go right now. Let's talk tomorrow. I need to see Dad."

"Okay, fine, fine, let's talk tomorrow. And great work, Shona. This is going to take off like a fucking rocket. This is Reporter of the Year stuff."

"Great. Thanks," she said, and closed the call.

She began to shake again.

"For fuck's sake," she said, wiping her eyes with the back of her hand. Blowing out air. Pushing back her hair. Another wave of lonely sorrow suddenly broke, and her head dropped.

A passing train guard stopped beside her. "You all right there, hen?" he said. He looked down with large brown eyes.

"Sure," she said. "Sure I am." Unsteady, she stood up, grabbing her bag and stick, which was spattered with dried mud.

"You need help?" he said.

"Thanks, pal. No. Never do," she said, and moved slowly along the platform and through the ticket barrier.

Her phone buzzed again as walked to the taxi rank on Market Street, where the cabs gleaming like black beetles under the green span of North Bridge.

Shona reached for the phone quickly. The message was from Bernie.

Come as quickly to the allotment as fast as you can thanks Bernie.

Shona swallowed hard and gulped. The train station moved and blared around her. Passengers moved and the tannoy yelled and buzzed. She called Bernie, but again it went to voicemail.

"Fucking hell," she yelled. No one could hear. People with no faces swilled around the space of metal and glass. The whole wretched world moved around her, uncaring and unhearing.

She called Stricken.

"Shona!" he yelled, almost immediately. "Are you coming?"

"Hector." She tipped her shoulder, and her bag slid onto the pavement. The sun suddenly appeared from behind a bank of clouds.

"Where are you?"

"I'm at Waverley—coming where? What the hell . . ."

"With everyone else. To your Dad's—"

"Hector!"

"What?"

"What the fuck are you on about? Come to Dad's what? What the fuck is happening?"

"Everyone's here—to help your dad."

"Where? Why does he—"

"At the allotment. To clear it up. People are here. Bernie's rounded them up."

Shona found a taxi on Market Street. It sped across Princes Street, and rattled its way down Leith Walk to the greener north of the city.

Her father's allotment stood in a field of them, huddled in dappled and pied beauty by an old railway line. Out of the cab in a hurry, Shona, lugging her bag, her stick rattling, picked her way through the neighbouring allotments to her father's patch of land. A group of people were gathering around her father's shed.

The allotment was in a state of disarray. The patch of land was overrun with weeds and grass, and its canes had tumbled and broken. A container for compost, roughly made from wooden pallets, had collapsed, and the compost had slewed out in a landslide of black sludge. Beside the shed, whose roof was tattered and sagged, was a heap of trash—green and blue plastic-cased machinery, bulging and broken green refuse bags, a soggy mound of dead leaves and bric-a-brac. Huge weeds towered.

As she got closer, she could see her father, in a warm coat with a hood, sitting on a foldable chair. Bernie was addressing the men and women as if she was a captain issuing orders. She was wearing waterproof trousers, her hands held in large yellow gardening gloves.

As Shona moved closer, Bernie saw her and gave a quick wave. Her father raised a hand. He looked tired, but his beard was closely cropped, and someone had put a green tartan blanket on his knees.

Shona stopped walking. The sun emerged from behind the shuddering grey clouds, and glimmered on wet wood and soil, on plastic and painted sheds. Exhaustion pulled at her, her shoulders sagged, and she dropped her bag and stick on the duck-board. The directions from Bernie had now been issued, and as Shona reached the allotment, the crowd dispersed with talk and some laughter. Bernie walked to Shona.

"Welcome back, Shona," Bernie said.

"Just in time," someone yelled.

Bernie moved towards her, and Shona wondered what might happen. Bernie hugged her. Shona let her. Bernie was small and solid, bundled in layers of clothes. She smelled of perfume and fresh air. After a moment, she let Shona go.

Then Shona moved to her father, and knelt beside him.

"My love," he said, beaming.

She nodded, only, not knowing what to say, and what it was to see him alive, again, in the garden.

"How lovely you're back with me," he said. "Look at this. Look at what is happening."

He pointed to the people who had begun to work: weeding, ripping up grass and dandelions and straggling nameless greenery and stuffing it into large refuse bags.

"Wonderful of them, isn't it?" he said.

She nodded.

He peered at her. "You've been crying," he said. "What's happened?"

"Allergies," she said.

"You don't have any bloody allergies. What's happened?"

"Nothing you need to know." She stood up to watch the work on the allotment.

"Let me guess, I'll read about it."

"You will."

More people were coming down the path to the allotment. Their wet raincoats gleaming in the new sun, they were carrying hoes and rakes, garden shears, spades and forks. Others were carrying bags and pushing wheelbarrows. They were moving down the slick duckboards, down the simple paths, like pilgrims. Bernie greeted them all with smiles and hugs, with handshakes and laughter.

Shona felt tears on her cheek and brushed them away. She felt lighter, even as her neck began to ache.

Hector Stricken in a bright red anorak emerged from a group of men fixing the compost heap. He stomped over. "What a mess, Hugh," he said, smiling at the old man. "But nothing that cannot be sorted. I think it can be done and dusted in a day or two."

"I cannot thank you enough," Hugh said.

"Shona. You made it," Hector said, wiping his hands on his anorak.

"Looks like it," she said. "Thanks, Hector. For coming."

"Did you get your story?"

"Always do," she said.

He grinned at her—he opened his mouth to ask something. But stopped.

"Thanks again," she said.

"Nae probs," he said, and looked back to the compost heap, where men were dismantling the rotted and sodden wooden walls. "I best get back and help the lads," he said, with some enthusiasm, and stumped off.

Bernie put the kettle on in the shambolic shed, which

was now being emptied and cleared. Out of the shed came rusted shovels and clippers and two large spades. There were plastic pots and tubs ensnared in webs, a broken chair, a strimmer with a frayed lead. There were broken packets of seeds, eaten by mice or rats, and long bamboo canes. Under the roof were slings of cobwebs, bobbled with egg nests, and a woman with a head scarf and determined expression was pulling them away. The whole allotment was moving with people intent on work.

They worked the rest of the short day, and the allotment began to be cleared. Knotty weeds were pulled, and a whole pile of grass, an infestation of marigolds, and a brown, prickly outcropping of teasels was ripped from the ground. Dandelions were dug up and pulled, oozing white blood from their green veins.

Shona helped where she could, ferrying hot drinks and sandwiches for all from a café on Ferry Road, and she held her father, and kissed his bald frail head, and the sun fell, and the garden was clear by the time the shadows of the trees were long and wide over the soil. Shona noticed tiny waxy green buds were growing on nearby branches. They glimmered in the falling light.

The helpers were leaving now, but their work remained. It had saved the garden. As they left, some waved; others held single thumbs aloft. They were exhausted and dirty and happy. The men had nodded to Hugh or shaken his hand. Some women had kissed him on the cheek. Others had worked hard and gone without a word. Hector had hung around for a while, and asked Shona about her story—she had said he would read it soon. He had finally left.

Now Shona stood by the newly tidied shed, exhausted.

"What a wonderful scene. You know, it reminds me of a stained-glass window I saw once," Bernie said, standing beside her, slipping her hand through Shona's arm. Shona had no energy or desire, any more, to shake it off. They admired the tidied allotment, and waved to the last of the helpers, as they slunk off into the twilight.

"Oh, yes? Tell me more. In Edinburgh?" Shona said, looking deeply into the surrounding trees.

"No, love. In a small church, in the north of England. I stayed in this village for a while, after I left the convent. I had no friends. They were all locked away, in my former life. So, I'd go to church."

"And it's in this church."

"Yes. It's a beautiful picture. I used to sit and consider it and pray by it. It shows a garden, and children, and the saints, all in the garden, in the trees, the flowers. There are vines growing, and there is a mother with a baby, and it is all bathed in the most beautiful sunlight. There are gardeners with broad hats, working in the trees, and others are calling in the harvest. There are children, some looking up at the workers, others playing. One child is helping up another who has fallen. The people are working. But living. And loving. It's a beautiful thing. There is a scroll, unfurled, at their feet, with something written across it. Something I think of, often. Especially now, especially since I met your father."

"And what does it say?"

"It says something religious. You wouldn't approve."

Shona looked to Bernie, who was looking out at the allotments, their neatness, their messiness, and humanity.

A light shower began to fall. The leaves shook in the new rain. The dug earth darkened, and tiny pools formed in the folds of the plastic bags of refuse and the new tarpaulin that temporarily covered the tattered roof of the shed.

Shona moved over to her father, sitting in his low chair, staring at his new, tidy garden, and she pulled up his hood.

He was still with her. Still alive with her. She looked across to Bernie, who was standing with hands folded, observing the daughter and her father.

"Tell me then, what did this window say?" Shona said.

"No, you wouldn't see anything in it," Bernie said, softly.

"Try me," Shona said.

"Go on, love," Hugh said to Bernie. "Tell her."

"It says, Shona—my love—*Of Such Work, Is the Kingdom of Heaven.*"

3 5 .

It was a new day. Karl Strutt needed a walk. He wanted to walk to the ends of the earth. He wanted to walk into the sunlight. He wanted to walk through a portal in the trees and step into new light.

Bev had left for work, in a flurry of exhortations and the jangling of keys.

He had been up half the night. She had slept like the dead, while he had spent hours on his computer, on social media, on the internet, searching. But there had been no stories about missing people, or about men in black with knives. There was nothing. No missing men. No swordsmen in the dale. If he didn't have the bruises on his hands, from the solid shock of the axe blade on a very real man's very real skull, he could have dreamed the entire killing.

He walked on. Tramping down the track through his village, and along to the river.

It was early yet. The farmers were up, he knew, but they rose as the sun rose. Spring was coming, the earth was tingling with it, but it had not yet arrived. The buds were closed on the branches, and although some eager daffodils were beginning to shake in the open spaces, and flowering weeds glimmered in the open meadow, the trees were still bare.

He reached the old river. He stopped at the shingle shoreline. The Tyr was wide and quiet here, the water was brown, dark as beer, and deep, flickering with drifting bubbles and lumps of yellow foam on the far side. The trees were tall and ancient, their lower boughs hanging heavy, close to the water that slid by their still branches.

Karl wondered if now, as a murderer, as a slaughterer of men, he could live in this peace. Now, as a murderer, he thought he should run away, leave the hills, hide himself in a city. He could find a cold room above a shabby shop in a backroad drag and live an anonymous life. He could change his name, walk the streets at night, watch his reflection shattered in the oily puddles pockmarking the scars of roads. Live in the stench of it all, his own sinful stink unnoticed.

But here, by this old river, under this old sky, the idea of life in a city seemed unreal. Nothing was as real as what was before him—the moving water, the growing wood, the earth alive.

This was the puzzle, Karl thought. The city does not care for you, and can break you. It constantly changes, but there are comforts to be bought, and attended to. The country does not care for you, and cannot be changed, unless it is destroyed by men. But it can comfort you with its silence, with the beauty, with the peace of the seasons, and the silent nights.

Karl walked on. After a time, he stopped and looked at his phone. Nothing from Beverley. The world turned on with or without his presence. It didn't matter.

The sun was reflected on the slowly surging water and the trees imperceptibly lifted their limbs to the heat. By the river there were small cliffs overhung with hard ferns and thin grass. White roots twisting from exposed slabs of rock. In the low hollows, in the wet mud still, there were hoof marks.

Karl wondered if he should keep walking downstream, away from his village, away from the buried man with the smashed face, into the depth of the valley. He trudged on. Birds were singing their haphazard mad songs. The woods deepened, and pools of shadow lay unmoving in the depths.

He decided to walk to the Coine Tree. It was a mile

downstream, and from there he could walk to a nearby village and catch the bus home.

He trudged the lonely track, until he came to a sign, an old white and black iron sign pointing downstream to ULLA-THORNE, 7 MILES, or west to THE FAMED COINE TREE, ½ MILE.

Karl was about to cut inland. Before he left the river behind, he stopped to look at it again. Something real was invested in its movement. Below him, below an overhanging rock, thick with moss, was a narrow beach. He and Bev had picnicked there many times, lit a fire, smoked and kissed. There were good flat pebbles there, for skimming. On a good day, with a good whip of his arm, he could flip one and reach the other side. A swift white trail of skimming kisses across the water. It was a good beach.

He moved to the edge and looked down at it. Caught up on the flat exposed rocks near the edge of the beach was a white dead body. A slump of flesh, chewed and spat out by waterfall, rapids and river. It had a battered brown pulpy head like a large rotting apple, and an open mouth smashed of its teeth. A single eye, red and open and staring. The body was half naked. Things were amiss: one leg was bent cruelly back, folded against the back, its knee bulbous and distended. One of its arms was missing. Instead, there was the gape of an open shoulder, and dark red and purple sinews were held loosely inside. Karl began to feel sick.

The sunlight shifted, dappling through the river's moving face, bleeding a stream of light across the chest of the man. It illuminated the script inscribed on the twisted body, in a vivid black tattoo: the letters of the alphabet, numbers from 0 to 9, *Yes*, *No*, *Hello*, *Goodbye*, the sun and the moon.

Karl founded himself kneeling. He waited until he was breathing steadily again. Then he reached for his phone, and called the police.

36.

Days later, miles south of the river Tyr, in the never-ending purring hum of London, Alison Harmire lay in bed, pale under the tawny light of the city, her children asleep.

They lay either side of her in their pyjamas, breathing heavily. She gently moved a damp lock of hair from her son's forehead, his closed eyes as smooth as shells. His tears had dried.

The house was empty now; Nigel had packed his cases and finally gone. She gently moved her daughter's head and arm from her chest, and slid out of the bed. She padded across the room. The wardrobe was still open, with Nigel's rails cleared. She slid it shut.

She looked back briefly to her sleeping children as she moved through the dark of the hall to the stairs.

The lights in the white kitchen glowed from copper pans and neatly arranged pots, a bowl of luminous lemons, and the clutched petals of flowers in vases. She moved past them all, into her study. She flicked on a soft standing light, and sat at her desk. The blinds were drawn. The room flashed briefly with the yellow flare of a passing car.

She pulled the scroll of laminated plastic from under her wood and glass desk. Printed neatly on one side were the letters of the alphabet, as well as HELLO, GOODBYE, the sun and the moon, and the numbers 0 to 9.

Alison took the small shot glass. She had stolen it from the Lion, thirty years ago. She placed it carefully in the centre of the board. She waited for it to answer, as it always had, all these years. Advice, confusion, shattered poetry, and a psalter of repeated phrases. Mantras for life from the board of the dead.

But, this night, the glass did not move. It stood dead under her finger. Sorley was gone. From the land of the dead, to nothingness. There would be no more. Alison sat back in her chair, and rubbed her eyes.

She held her head in her hands. She was alone, again.

East of Alison Harmire's house, in the shadow of the House of Commons, Knott was leaning on the stone parapet of a bridge. The Thames flowed thick and strong underneath. It had been a long day. He pulled his collar up to his thick face. The streetlamp's fragile light was lengthened and torn by the moving waters below.

Knott's phone buzzed with a message. He walked along the bridge, and a black car pulled up by the Westminster security gate.

He stepped into the long, low car.

A blond woman sat on the back seat in a grey-green suit, neat as pins. Next to her, a crumpled-face old man in smart country clothes. It was Raymond. Opposite them, Alyce sat, rapt in her phone.

"Mr. Knott, good evening," Raymond said.

"How do." Knott nodded. "Alyce," he added.

Alyce looked up, her violet eyes flashing in the city lights.

The car was moving at pace, gliding through the stuttering London traffic, past Westminster Abbey, wending its way to the airport for a brief journey north.

"You will know Sally," Raymond said, opening a hand towards the woman with blond hair.

The woman nodded to Knott, and smiled.

"Of course," Knott said. "Seen her on the telly."

The woman smiled and looked out of the window to the smear of light and darkness outside. The immensity of it all.

"The new candidate for Tyrdale, Mr. Knott," Raymond said, gently reproving.

"So I've seen," Knott said.

"You will know Alyce, who will be Sally's principal support, and you will, of course, have seen what has been reported about our former colleague," Raymond said, evenly.

Knott shrugged. "Sad," he said.

"Tragedy," Alyce said.

"Very unfortunate," Sally said.

"Indeed," Raymond added, and patted Sally's knee. "Well, he can join his wife at last—which, I think we can agree, is some kind of justice. So, that is the end of that story. But not for us. We remain—and continue."

Karl and Bev had lit the new fire pit in their back garden. Karl had put paving stones and a heavy metal basin over the freshly turned soil. Now, the flames flickered and spat with green wood, dancing in the gathering twilight. Now, Karl was strumming a guitar.

A recent newspaper was beside Bev, gently rippling in the evening air, with a lurid headline about Gary Watson MP, found dead in the river.

She took the front page from the paper and scrunched it into a loose ball, and tossed it gently into the warming fire. She put her head on Karl's shoulder, and he stopped strumming, and put his arm around her, and they watched the flames consume it all.

In the fire, Watson's face blackened and shrivelled, and then collapsed, and crumbled, and was lost in a sudden flaring gout of green flame.

Karl took up his guitar again, and picked out a new tune.

"I'm sorry, love," she said, at last.

"Don't worry. It's nowt," he said, over the chords. "Don't worry."

Bev gently hummed along to his sweet, melancholy strum, and she looked past the dancing fire and out over the garden fence to the old moor and the ancient trees. Her sight rested on the old stones on the high hills. They, at least, would remain.

Until all the days, like even these days, were no more.

It was dark at the Gildersleve Bed and Breakfast in Ullathorne.

Ashley was in her room, her face lit silver by the laptop screen. A cursor pulsed at the end of a sentence. She did not know what would come next.

She was trying to write, her mind drifting in and out of concentration. She wrote as best she could: her left hand fully in control, a single finger ready to type on her closed right hand. She had removed distractions—she had turned her music off, she had switched off the Wi-Fi on the router in the hall. But her mind was flitting and flyting.

Ashley sighed and slapped the laptop shut. Her mother had left her a list of chores, and wanted them done by the time she got back. She was out. Seeing to something that needed done, she said. Off to see the cops, she had said, about the football jersey. Now that Alison had gone back down to London.

Ashley walked into the room where the Glaswegian reporter had stayed. It had not been cleaned. It was unkempt and lank with the sadness of abandonment. She began slowly stripping the bed. There were two used mugs on the sideboard, with cold coffee congealed in small pools. A single black and silver sock lay alone near the television.

There was a small polished pebble on the side by the night-light. Ashley picked it up. It was as smooth as an eye. It had a stripe of paler rock within it. She put it in her pocket.

Then she noticed a note ripped from a reporter's pad which had been dropped under the bed. Its curled edge was in sight. She picked it up. It was scribbled in a mix of shorthand and longhand, in a pen that was low on ink.

Ashley could not understand the shorthand marks, a series of half-letters and swooshes, of dots and contractions. It seemed to be another language entirely. But at the bottom of the note, beside a large asterisk and a doodle of a heart, Shona had written a message to herself.

It said: *Call V.*

Ashley took the note, crumpled it up, threw it in a bin bag, and stood up with a sigh.

She stripped the bed, hoovered the carpet and wiped the surfaces. It now looked tidy and ready for another visitor. It was an empty, barely furnished room, waiting for another person to arrive, and live, and depart.

Shona Sandison had left no mark on it. It was as if she had never been there at all.

The front room in Inspector Benedict Reculver's spacious Edinburgh apartment was filled with light on a quiet Sunday morning.

The clear sunlight fell on the silver frames of the paintings in lancing gleams, and lay warm on the sleek surfaces of his lean furniture. In the bathroom, a man was showering. He was singing a sad Gallic song.

Reculver, in a loose green silk robe, elaborate dragons swimming about his limbs, rubbed his face and smiled. He was sitting on his sofa, reading the Sunday papers, which had been pushed through his letter box early, its many slippery supplements sliding away from the paper in a glossy coiled pile.

He knew Gary Watson MP had been found dead in a river: it had led the BBC news for two days, and his colleagues in the north of England had been in touch.

He imagined journalists from all newspapers now descending on Tyrdale to cover the story, to dig out their own information, to interview the locals, to find new lines and fresh takes. But Shona Sandison had them all—that story was written. She had the whole story, and, it seemed, all the follow-up tales, too. She had not named several sources. Some of Watson's school friends were quoted, but left anonymous. Reculver raised an eyebrow: he wondered why.

One tabloid had given over its front page to her story, as well as several pages inside. Shona's fingers must be several millimetres shorter, Reculver mused. Her boss at the Buried Lede had clearly struck a good deal with the paper, even if all the subtleties and ambiguities of what Shona had discovered had been hacked and mauled into a brutal tabloid style. He read it again:

DEATH MP "MURDER" LINK SHOCK
EXCLUSIVE: MYSTERY OF LOST BOY
AND DROWNED WATSON

GARY Watson, the controversial MP found dead this week, can be linked to the suspected murder of a former school friend thirty years ago, the *Sunday Despatch* can sensationally reveal.

The mutilated body of Watson, 49, found in the river Tyr, County Durham, the day after the launch of his reelection bid, has thrown the general election campaign into chaos.

Today we can reveal a shocking hidden life which would have derailed Watson's career if he had not mysteriously fallen to his death.

An Exclusive Investigation by award-winning reporter SHONA SANDISON can reveal:

- The **sinister links** between Watson and the tragic disappearance of school friend Andrews Banks in 1992.
- **New evidence** linked to vanished Banks has been **handed to cops** after being found in recent weeks.
- How the outspoken **populist MP attacked** our reporter after being confronted at his fiery campaign launch hours before his death.
- The **occult teenage gang** in which Watson was a key member.
- The **mysterious murder** of his ex-Army school friend.
- The **shocking suicide** at a Scottish wedding linked to Watson's bizarre **obsession** with **Ouija boards**.

The story went on, covering the front page, and pages two, three, four and five inside. In the magazine supplement, there was a brief picture-profile of Watson, and a colour piece on Tyrdale, also penned by Sandison.

Reculver looked up. His friend, a white towel tied tight around his limber slick torso, had brought him an espresso in a fine china cup. A small brown wrinkled biscuit had been placed on the neat saucer.

"Merci beaucoup," Reculver said. His visiting French

friend slinked away. Reculver read some of the colour piece, a feature illustrated with luminous photography:

> At the heart of the valley of the river Tyr is an ancient giant. They call it the Coine Tree.
>
> Few people from outside the valley know of it. Tyrdale and its market town of Ullathorne are better known for their natural beauty, with tourists flocking to the pretty town to view its ruined castle and walk in the idyllic glades of woodland beside its famous river. But at the dark green centre of those ancient woods is that tree—said to be the oldest in England. Some say it is the biggest, too. The monstrous tree has been standing deep in the valley's native woodland for three thousand years. It stands as an ancient, silent witness.
>
> What has this wordless giant seen? A long, troubled span of human time. It has seen the people of Tyrdale emerge from the dark green prehistorical world, from the era of clans and tribes and pagan belief, to the Roman Empire, and the coming of Christianity. It has seen the people of the dale overcome the brutalities of Norman invasion and feudal rule, the ravages of plague and cholera, the devastating disruptions of the Industrial Revolution, the loss and sorrow of two world wars, and the social and economic revolutions of the twentieth century.
>
> In all this time, it has gripped the same parcel of soil and stone not far from the ancient river Tyr. It has endured and grown imperceptibly while generations of humans have been born,

lived and died. Both hollow and alive, the tree will stand long after the grim story of Gary Watson and his troubled school friends has been long forgotten.

Looking back on my days investigating this story in Ullathorne, it is tempting to see this deeply impressive, unmoving but living thing as a powerful symbol of all that has been discovered.

Like the branches and trunk and leaves of the ancient tree, parts of the story exist in the world of the visible: the disappearance of Banks in 1992, the rise of Watson to fame and success and then the very public death of Daniel Merrygill.

But this tree also exists in the world of the unseen. Just as the Coine Tree's roots plunge unseen into the rock and soil of the ancient dale, so do the roots of this tragic story. So much is still unclear, and so much is subterranean. Banks's body has never been found. The reasons for his disappearance and likely death remain unknown. And the occult shadows that drove Merrygill to his untimely end, and which clearly engulfed that small group of Tyrdale teenagers in the early 1990s, remain largely unknowable, and may remain lost to the sunken past forever . . .

"Breakfast?" a voice called from Reculver's echoing New Town kitchen.

Reculver bellowed an agreement and stood up, dropping the paper on his coffee table. He reached for his personal mobile phone, which lay on the marble mantelpiece.

He looked down at the paper: it had wrung the story for all it was worth. Above the newspaper title, it boasted: LOST LEADER: WHICH MINISTRY WAS SET ASIDE FOR GARY WATSON? *Page 9 for insight* and another puff said: WHERE NOW FOR PM'S NORTHERN STRATEGY? *Comment section.*

His thumbs moved over the phone's black screen.

Bravo! he texted Shona.

He looked at his screen for a moment, and then put it down. There was no reply, and he suspected there would not be one for several days.

In the kitchen, an egg was cracked onto a sizzling pan, and moved from slick translucent liquid to the firm and the white and the edible.

goodbye

Shona Sandison took a long, slow walk in the gentle sunshine. Spring had finally arrived in Edinburgh, and a field of blaring daffodils, as yellow and vivid as smashed eggs, blazed beside her. She paused and sat on a bench in Victoria Park, an acre of flat green grass and old trees between the burr of Ferry Road and the pretty harbour at Newhaven. She lay her stick beside her.

A small blue coffee van, smooth and neat like a beetle, was serving hot coffee to tired parents and dog walkers. In the playground, children in raincoats clambered over a large colourful climbing frame. In the unlikely warmth, tall boys were throwing around a basketball on the nearby fenced court.

Shona looked to the coffee van and thought about buying a drink.

The BBC had been leading on her story in the Sunday paper, and was running news bulletins on the links between the death of Watson and the human wreckage of Tyrdale.

Ranald had already been asked by Durham police to hand over the audio file of Shona's interview with the late MP.

The prime minister was beginning to be asked questions about how well he knew Watson, what he knew and when he knew it. It was disrupting his election campaign. There was a chance that her story would begin to dominate the news cycle. Ranald told her that a young woman from Spennymoor in the northeast of England had made a five-figure deal with a rival tabloid, claiming to be Watson's lover.

Terry's photographs were everywhere—expertly taken in the heat of the moment, and pin-sharp. One of them showed the MP grasping Shona by her neck. Shona's face was impassive, her eyes wide. Her stick on the floor. Watson's grim shiny face was a tangled root of hatred. It was believed to be the last photo of him alive.

Reculver had texted her, but she was ignoring him, for now. It felt like work. Her phone buzzed again. It was a text from Hector Stricken.

Your stuff is bloody everywhere! Great job. Beautiful job, pal!

It's been emotional, she texted back. The sun flashed on her phone screen. A tiny brown dog with a face like an otter ran up to her feet, snuffled at her stick and sprinted off again.

More to come?

Not from me. I'm done, she printed with her thumb.

Another text zipped to her phone.

What about that poor guy at the funeral?

Despair, shit parents, and guilt, she tapped back. She knew Daniel's death was more complicated than that. More than she could probably ever sensibly explain.

Why do you think Watson ended up in the river? Stricken texted.

Who knows. Only he knows. Cops found enough drugs in his body to stun a horse. But we might never know. Bye for now.

Shona stood up, gripped her stick and headed for the coffee van. There was a small queue.

The sky was vast above her. Her mind felt empty, her body washed out. She looked to the stones in the path, and wondered what they contained. She looked up, to the canopy of reviving trees.

She leaned on her stick and watched a group of children swing back and forth on a large circular swing. Three boys and three girls giggled and laughed in their multicoloured clothes. One boy urged them all to stand up on the swing, to grip the chains. They stood up, and the boy huffed and puffed, his pale hair distraught, and pushed his friends forward. They slowly moved, a pendulum full of young souls, into the air before them, and with yelps of joy, they swung back. The boy pushed again, harder.

Shona smiled. Some adults walked slowly over to the swing, shaking their heads and wagging fingers. The smell of coffee and hot chocolate steamed from the van. The sun glittered on grass and gravel, on stones and the sea of new leaves, the refreshed grass.

She reached into her bag. There was an envelope of photographs, retrieved from the chemists. They were newly developed, but the pictures were old. Analogue, fuzzy, splodged with orange light. Several were darkened with the shadow of a thumb across the lens. Other pictures had been destroyed by time or had never been good in the first place—their images were empty, dim brown, hazy, formless.

The photographs had been taken by Daniel Merrygill, in the summer of 1992. The first few showed teenagers sitting in school fields, squinting into the sun, in the main of light, neat in their last day uniforms.

She moved through them. There was some lad with flossy blond hair giving the photographer the finger. A girl looking shyly from behind a curtain of black hair. Some boys in short sleeves, bending their elbows over a pool table in a dark, wood-lined pub.

She pulled one picture out. She had asked for a copy to be printed in a larger format. It showed all the friends sitting closely together on a grassy incline, smiling. The sky was blue above them, unsullied, framing their faces. They had big hair, brighter eyes, ready smiles. Their last summer together, on the precipice of unforeseen loss and change.

Young Beverley sat in a tie-dyed T-shirt, a garish tear of

colours at odds with the rest of her blue school uniform. Peg was neat, holding a hand to her eyes, smiling into sunlight. Resting his head on Peg's shoulder was a big lad with shaved hair, and shiny new boots—Bobby. Next in line, sitting on a tree stump was Alison, serious, her legs crossed, a small white cigarette unlit in her left hand, a mild smile forming on her lips. Beside her, beaming, was Andrew Banks. He was slim and handsome, with long hair down past his ears. His large, beautiful eyes were wide open, his eyebrows arching, as if he was surprised, as if he was delighted.

And close to him, his arms in the air, celebrating or signalling, knelt the young Gary Watson. His mouth was open, saying something now lost and unrecorded, his eyes squinting, his hair cropped and sharp. He wore white jeans, with a tucked-in white T-shirt. On his belt, there was a small leather sheath which held a folded penknife, and around his open neck, a necklace of white beads. And out of sight, the taker of the photograph—Daniel Merrygill. A young man, already broken.

Shona's phone buzzed again. It was probably Stricken again, or possibly Ranald, excited about some new legal development in the Watson affair. It felt like he had been calling her hourly for days.

She put the phone to her ear without checking who it was. "Aye, what now?"

There was a long silence. Shona looked down at the picture in her hand. Young Andrew, beaming, with only days to live in his life.

"Hello?"

"Hello to you, too," Viv said, at last.

"Vivienne," Shona said.

"Who else would it be?"

Shona felt suspended in the air. Her body felt adrift from her mind.

"I've seen what you did," Viv said. Shona nodded, as if Viv could see her. "And what you have written. The cops called Mam last night. They had a long chat. Nice woman from the Durham cops. There's talk of digging up Deepdale. To see."

"Okay, that's good," Shona said, carefully.

"Mam's been asked to identify something. An item of clothing. The shirt you wrote about."

"That makes sense," Shona said. She said it as softly and as kindly as she could.

"I think it's Andrew's," Viv said. There was a short silence. "I've been busy. Dan's funeral. They've released the body."

"Ah, right."

"It's a quiet one, at the crematorium," Viv said.

"That's good you are doing it," Shona said. "That's kind of you."

"Aye, well," Viv said, "I can invite his old man now, since you've found him. We've been trying to prise his mam out of that care home."

Andrew's printed eyes in Shona's hands were gleaming. Daniel, poor, pale, broken Daniel, was in her hands, too. He had made the pictures, he was the author of these memories. But he was unseen.

"So, can you meet me for a drink?" said Viv, suddenly.

Shona rubbed an eye with her free hand. "All right. But only if you're paying," she said. "Tap into that wee windfall of yours."

There was a deep silence. Shona winced and bit her lip. She looked to the trees again. Birds in formation leapt from the branches and skimmed to the empty sky.

"You've some cheek, Shona fucking Sandison," Viv said, softly.

"But isn't that why you love me?"

Viv seemed to suck her teeth. Then she gave a surprised laugh. "I guess so."

"So, a drink, then?" Shona said.

"Yes. Life's too short, Shona."

"It is," Shona Sandison said. "Far too short."

ACKNOWLEDGMENTS

With much gratitude to my friends, and early readers: Simon Stuart, Allan Donald, Freya Davison, and Callum Smith. With great thanks to Taz Urnov and Alison Rae for their faith and trust, and to Robbie Guillory for his guidance. And with love to Hope: for everything.